D1738751

BEYOND THE RIO GILA

BEYOND THE RIO GILA

SCOTT G. HIBBARD

FIVE STAR
A part of Gale, a Cengage Company

LIBRARY OF CONGRESS CATALOGING-IN-PUBLICATION DATA

Names: Hibbard, Scott G., author.
Title: Beyond the Rio Gila / Scott G. Hibbard.
Description: First edition. | [Waterville, ME] : Five Star, a part of Gale, a Cengage Company, 2021.
Identifiers: LCCN 2019059453 | ISBN 9781432866136 (hardcover)
Subjects: LCSH: Mexican War, 1846-1848—Fiction. | GSAFD: Historical fiction.
Classification: LCC PS3608.I24 B49 2021 | DDC 813/.6—dc23

First Edition. First Printing: April 2021
Find us on Facebook—https://www.facebook.com/FiveStarCengage
Visit our website—http://www.gale.cengage.com/fivestar
Contact Five Star Publishing at FiveStar@cengage.com

Printed in Mexico
Print Number: 01   Print Year: 2021

For Gretchen, whose steadfast support kept the dream alive.

Inquire of the former generations, pay attention to the experiences of their ancestors—as we are but of yesterday, and have no knowledge, because our days on earth are but a shadow.

—Job 8:8-9

What now is has already been; what is to be, already is; and God retrieves what has gone by.

—Ecclesiastes 3:15

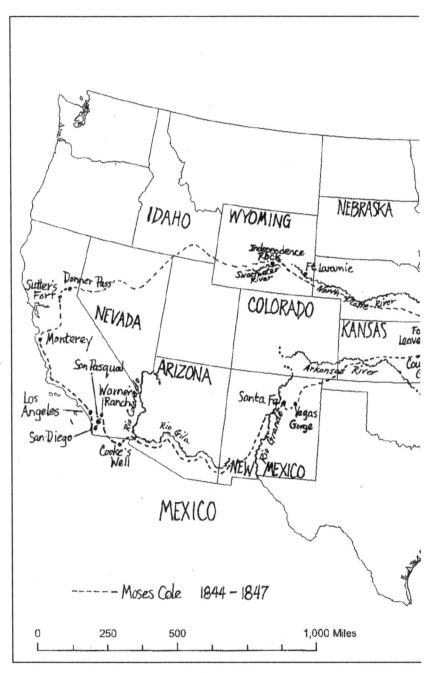

Moses Cole and the First Dragoons, 1844–1847

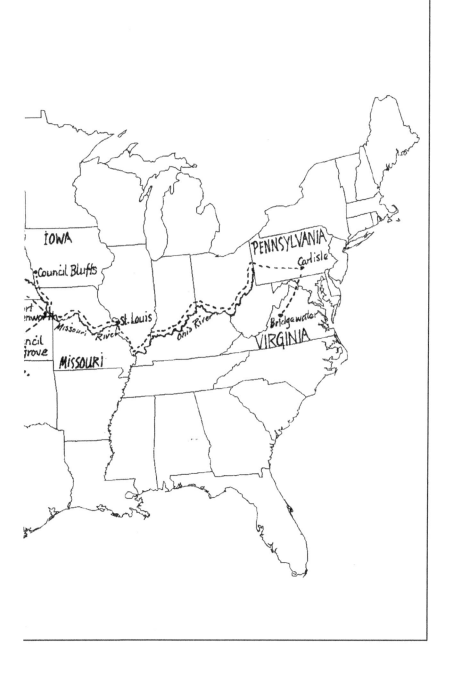

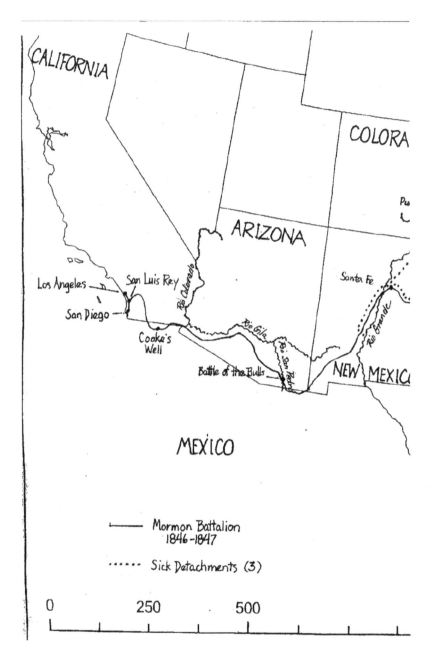

March of the Mormon Battalion, 1846–1847

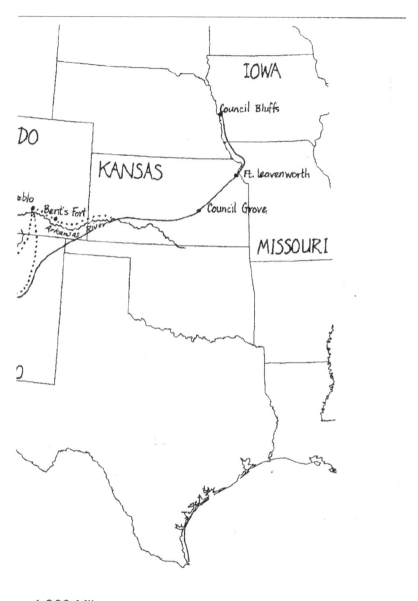

IOWA

Council Bluffs

DO

KANSAS

Ft. Leavenworth

eblo

Bent's Fort

Council Grove

Arkansas River

MISSOURI

O

1,000 Miles

CHAPTER 1

Shenandoah Valley, Virginia, and Carlisle, Pennsylvania,
September 1844

Moses Cole lay on his belly in front of the pig pen, eyeball to eyeball with the hog. Egg yolk bled from the hog's mouth and dripped in the basket he'd dropped when his pa hit him with the number-two shovel. Moses Cole heard more eggs break when the hog lowered its snout in the basket and bit.

George Cole swatted the sow on the side of her neck to turn her from the basket and poked her with the shovel point to prod her back in the sty. He latched the gate behind her and said, "Thank me, boy. Could've waylaid you in the pigpen instead of here on the hardpan. Give you a nose full of the hog slop you're made of."

Moses pushed himself to his hands and knees.

"Should've done it. Soft hearted I guess." George chuckled.

Moses rose to his knees, reached back to feel ribs, and winced. He had the plain face of a yeoman, wide through the nose and cheekbones, slim chin.

"They ain't broke," his pa said. "Not yet anyways."

Moses stood, turned to his pa. George Cole scratched his stubble, black as burnt fur, picked an insect, and flicked it away.

Moses looked him straight on, said, "You won't never hit me again."

"That a fact?" George asked.

"You been on me ever since Ma died."

"I disremembers the event," George said. He leaned closer to Moses. His upper lip lifted to show tobacco-stained teeth. "Bring it home, boy. Tell how it happened."

Moses smelled the still on his pa's words. He looked off.

"You ain't forgot," George said.

The memory never left. Sometimes it startled him, like an animal on his pallet that crept in the bedding. Other times it seized him, hard as a gut punch. His mother's face, wide eyed under the ice, baby-ready pregnant. They broke the river ice, pulled her to the bank. His pa opened her belly with his belt knife, attempted to save the baby that was warm, supple, blue, and breathless. Moses turned away from the innards on the riverbank that spilled like hog offal, saw the chipped fingernails, the scratches clawed in the underside of the ice—that barricade to air, inches away, as distant as the moon.

Moses picked up the basket.

"Pregnant. Eight months plus," George said. "Half the family, right there."

Moses looked at brown and speckled eggshells, fingered through the basket, found none unbroken.

George Cole said, "On account of what you done."

Moses turned and walked to the barn. His pa said after him, "I'm huntin' a hole for memory to fall in, so I can bury it." He snickered. "Stuff it under Massanutten Mountain, and it would still crawl out, like a ghost from a grave, come to cuddle me."

Inside the barn Moses examined the basket his mother had woven from blackberry briars, traced her delicate effort to scrape the thorns away, her finger work that evened the weaving. He wondered how she had seen a basket in a bramble, borne its barbs to crop it with ungloved hands and a paring knife to weave a thing of use and beauty. The handle weighed in his hand, hard as bowed bone. His pa followed him in.

"Don't you never leave a plow broke in the field, walk off,

and not let on."

"Woulda told you if you was here to tell, instead of off and gone wherever you was off and gone to."

"Business," George said.

"Sippin' on your timber liquor."

"What's that, boy? Speak to me, not to them basket eggs smeared with hen crap and hog slobber."

Moses slung the broken eggs out the barn door, wiped out the basket with a gunny sack, and hung the basket on a harness peg. "The blacksmith will hammer out a plowshare and build a coulter while he's at it, replace that wore-off one."

"From the charity of his heart, no doubt." His pa sneered.

"Give my fur money for it. Won't cost you nothin'." Moses pushed the barn door open, stopped, and faced his pa.

"Don't look at me that way, boy."

Moses Cole, one week into seventeen, stood five-foot-ten and broad built. George Cole claimed five eight but had him by thirty pounds, hard from a life of labor, fists big as sledge heads.

"That day won't quit you, but that don't mean I can't," Moses said.

"Don't let that door slam you in the ass, boy."

Moses said, "You won't torment me no more."

"You got till suppertime to fix it." Spittle dripped down George's chin.

"The blacksmith has it," Moses said. He crossed the barnyard and walked to the road.

"Them eggs!" George hollered after him. "Brings the mean out in me."

Moses walked to town. He looked at the dry-goods store when he walked by, saw Miss Isabella's father talking to a customer, and wondered again when Miss Isabella would finish her ciphers and letters in Richmond. He thought of the Sunday picnic where the miller's mule ran over the blanket and the picnic dinner, remembered the sound the china made when the hoof lit in the tea set, likened it to the sound the eggs made when the hog bit in the basket he'd filled from the hens' nests. Even now he heard Isabella's words, how she tendered them, their touch that turned his insides upside down.

Moses kept walking. He walked by farmsteads and passed through towns and talked to travelers who'd quiz this boy on the road alone, weighted with no bag or companion. Moses would say he'd left home to help the grand folks who got on poorly, and he might be there for a time, or that he was off to fetch a mule from an uncle down valley, that he'd be mounted come this time next week. Said he'd lost his grub and getup when he fell in a river up country when he hooked a channel catfish that tugged like an anvil on the end of the fish line he'd baited with a drowned mouse. He'd kept a hand on the fish line, waded further into the current until the river bottom fell out from under him, and there it went, that satchel he'd packed his food and blanket in, sunk in the pool he'd swum from. "That channel cat," he'd say with a smile and a headshake, "big as a weaner pig. Whiskers a woman would use for knittin' needles."

He didn't know he could yarn on like that, tell tales taller than the trees he'd seen. Flat-out lies that blistered the clean place inside, like he'd walked all day in shoes too small.

Folks fed him on occasion, corn and salt pork, beans and biscuits, headed north to wherever it was down valley would take him. He picked up corn cobs dropped at harvest in fields he passed. Stole eggs from a hen house and a chicken from another one. Pulled a brookie from under a creek bank big enough to fill a pan if he had one. Cooked corn on the cob and the trout on hot rocks, cooked the chicken on a stick, and ate the eggs raw.

He thought of the meanness his pa took on when his mother passed, and the guilt chewed him. He allowed that he ran from that, too, the knot that tightened when his mind turned to the way she'd passed. She came to him in a dream, the face as he remembered it when he'd found her—eyes wide below the ice that her belly bumped with her baby in it with the push and pull of the current. In his dream she blinked, and spoke. Her words stuck in bubbles that bobbed against the ice, and her eyes went wide again. His pa appeared, broke the ice with the number-two shovel, and the trapped words bloomed into tulips.

He walked on, pictured Miss Isabella and the light in her eyes, the heart that shone there, wondered what turn she'd take in Richmond with its city ways, wondered if he tugged on her like she tugged on him. The bigger her world grew, he figured, the more his shrank.

He heard the wagon before he saw it with its rattle of tin and metal wares. It rounded the bend ahead pulled by two horses, its load covered with a tarp. The driver reined up the horses and studied Moses. He said, "I'm a drummer, pulling a wagon of wares for dry-goods stores and for anyone with wherewithal, but you bear small resemblance to a customer."

To Moses, his heavy eyelids looked weighted with age.

The drummer lifted the bridle lines, thought again, let them settle. He eyeballed Moses. "My aspiration is for a box wagon that would allow me to carry more goods and dispense with the tarp. Yours, by appearances, is to improve upon the dearth of your circumstances, and I'll tell you where you can do it. Keep on down valley. Bear northeast until you come to Carlisle, Pennsylvania. You'll find an army post there. Dragoons mostly. Look at it as the gateway to the West, where five years of army pay will get you a stake to pay on a farm. You won't get fat, and you won't live extravagant, but my bet says it's better than what you left."

The drummer clucked, and the horses stepped out as if eager for the rhythm of rolling wheels, then stopped when the drummer hauled on the bridle lines to look back at the wayward boy.

"Then again," he said, "might be worse. Depends what befalls you, but sure as I'm sitting a wagon seat and you're walking in worn out shoes, your welfare could stand improvement."

He snapped the lines, and the wagon rolled off. Moses watched the man pitch and right himself when a wheel hit a rock, heard the sale wares bump each other, muffled by the canvas cover. He listened to the Shenandoah River murmur as the wagon rolled away.

Moses walked for eighteen days, many in the rain. When he reached Carlisle, Pennsylvania, he was hungry, cold, wet, and tired with holes worn through his shoes. Horses stood in a pasture with their tails to the rain. He passed a stable, heard a dinner bell ring, saw soldiers file to a mess hall. He shivered, yearned for hot meals, dry clothes, a roof and warm bed. He approached a guard who stood in the rain in a greatcoat, musket at his side. Rain beaded on the guard's polished brogans. Moses asked what it was like in the army.

Skin showed through holes in the hand-me-down shoes Moses wore where mud didn't cover them. Water leaked from his sun-bleached, rain-faded black hat and dripped down his face. The coat and trousers hung on him like empty feed sacks.

The guard asked Moses when he ate last.

Moses thought a moment. "Day before yesterday." He thought some more. His teeth chattered. "Maybe the day before that."

The guard nodded, asked Moses how old he was.

"Old enough."

"Do tell," the guard said. "How old would that be?"

"Seventeen." Moses looked off to the pasture where horses stood in the rain. "Do they pay you to ride them horses?"

"A kingly sum of eight dollars a month to fork manure and brush and curry and polish tack."

"Give hot meals? One of them coats?" Moses said. "Shoes without no holes?"

"Depends if you're Irish," the guard said. He smiled. Rain dotted his spectacles. Gray flecked his moustache. He stooped under the rain-weighted coat. Slender, Moses thought. Easy for a horse to carry.

"Some. American born though." He shivered in the wet clothes.

The guard pointed to a building. "Walk to that building and rap on the door. An orderly will ask your business. Tell him that Private Black recommends you to the lieutenant, who will likely be seated at a desk sipping English tea."

"Thank you, sir," Moses said. He started for the building.

"When he asks your particulars," Private Black said after him, "tell him you're twenty-one with Scots-Irish in the family bloodline."

The lieutenant returned the teacup to the saucer. "Twenty-one, you say."

Moses stood before him. Water puddled below his coat and trousers. He held his hat in his hand. His hair lay flat, parted in the middle as though by water dumped from a bucket.

"I'll say it this way, sir. Someday I'll turn twenty-two, provided starvation don't take me."

"You're a farmer by trade, you say. Scots-Irish."

"Born to it. Done it all my life."

"Let me see your hands."

Moses showed hands with cuts, calluses, a blackened

thumbnail, muscled fingers.

"Education? Do you have any?"

"My numbers. How to write some. Read if I have to."

"Why do you wish to join the mounted service?"

"I like horses, sir. Rode before I could walk. More plowin' than ridin' is the sad part of farmin'."

"You like horses, but you walked here."

"If I owned a horse I'd have rode him."

"Can you shoe and do saddle and tack repair?"

"In a pinch. Enough to get by with."

"I assume you are familiar with firearms?"

"We don't have a rifle, but I do pretty good with a smoothbore flintlock. Time or two I'd hit the branch instead of the possum, have to finish the job with a rock or a stomp. You know them smoothbores."

"And you are twenty-one."

A drop of water plopped from a coat sleeve. "Don't want to lie if I don't have to, sir, to get signed on and all. I want to enlist, cross my heart." Moses crossed his heart. After a bit he said, "I got nothin' else." He clenched his jaw to stop his teeth from chattering.

The lieutenant tapped the desktop. "You ran away from home."

Another water drop fell. "Outgrowed home."

"I see." The lieutenant lifted the teacup, sipped, held it to his lips, looked at Moses over the brim of the cup, sipped again, set it back on the saucer. "And army life? Away from home under harsh living conditions, often without adequate provisions, clothing, or shelter, and long, hard days?"

Moses smiled.

"Have you been exposed to the rougher elements of society?"

"Seen it. Don't take to it."

"Any diseases?"

"Been sick five times my whole life, that I know of anyway. No more than a day or three to a stint."

"Bodily defects?"

"Nothin' busted, if that's what you're after." Moses thought a moment. "What I have was good enough to get me here. Nothin' wrenched out of place." He thought of the shovel to his ribs. "Not no more, anyway."

"Mental infirmities? If you have any, tell me now. It will save you a lot of anguish."

"Not crazy in the head, if that's what you're askin'. No one said otherwise, at least to my face."

The lieutenant tapped the desktop. "A term of enlistment is five years."

Water squished in Moses's shoes when he shifted his weight. "Like I said, sir, I got nothin' else."

The lieutenant pulled a sheet of paper from a desk drawer. "I question your age, but it's clear that the demands of mounted service will not be difficult for you. And your timing is good. Whether that's good luck or bad luck you will know in a year or two. I've had two recruits crippled from horse falls this week, another died from pneumonia, and two others deserted. I need the troopers." He laid a pen on the paper and slid them across the desktop.

"Let's see if you lied about this."

Moses Cole spelled his name.

The lieutenant considered the letters that made the signature. "Very well, Moses Cole. If you are as bold as your letters suggest, we can make a dragoon of you."

"Thank you, sir." Moses smiled.

The lieutenant turned the teacup on the saucer, looked at Moses, turned it back. "One never outgrows home, Private Cole. You will learn that."

CHAPTER 2

First Dragoons, Carlisle Barracks, Pennsylvania,
October and November 1844
The recruits drilled in the mud in the fundamentals of marching. Moses bumped the trooper in front of him when he did not respond to the command to halt.

The sergeant yelled, "Pay attention, Private. Where's your mind?"

His mind was with Miss Isabella in her daddy's dry-goods store, back on that day of the keg of nails and the bag of beans.

"Do you hear me?"

"I sure do, sir."

"That's, 'Yes, Sergeant.' "

"Yes, Sergeant."

The sergeant stepped close to Moses. "Learn to march, or you'll go where that's all you'll do. The army calls it infantry. You'll call it 'hell.' Would you like that, Private?" The sergeant looked down at the boy, eyeball to boot toe, as if to drive him in the ground like a hammer on a picket pin. "Shove your head up a mule's ass. Would you like that, Private?"

"No, Sergeant."

"Then get your head out of yours."

Moses found the new shoes—the square-toed ankle boot with the solitary tie at the top—would take some wear to work into limber and to get used to the heels, higher by a leather layer than what he'd known. Blister with them shoes or bruise without, he figured. Pain either way.

"It's a shoe-boot, my young recruit," Private Abner Black, the guard Moses met when he arrived at Carlisle, told him in the barracks that evening. "Not quite shoe and not quite boot but a blend of the two and, therefore, with the efficiency peculiar to the military, not well suited for either function it's required to perform."

Moses said, "If I wanted to walk in the mud I wouldn't have stopped to talk to the army. I'd have waved maybe, gone on like I had somewhere I needed to get. But no sir. Had to stop and spell my name on a paper."

"Look to the day ahead, not to the night behind," Abner Black said. "You're fed and sheltered here, and freed from the burden of self-direction."

Moses said, " 'School of the Trooper, Dismounted,' is what the sergeant calls it. Join the dragoons and ride shank's mare." Moses scraped mud from the ankle boots with the back of his belt knife. "Never had new shoes before." The shoes showed scuff marks and caked mud. "Hardly wore 'em and can't see the new no more." He wiped and rubbed the ankle boots with a worn-out towel from the pile the sergeant provided. "I thought the dragoons was a horse and saddle outfit."

"You will progress to horseback when the sergeant so deems," Abner said.

"There's another thing I'm wonderin'," Moses said. "Why for is a hand like you marchin' in the mud with dummies like us?"

"Recruits, my young private. Not dummies. To address your question, the simple answer is, to prevent an idle mind from wandering where it should not go, and to assist the sergeant in the rudiments of instruction. It may also have something to do with humility self willed and penance, perhaps, for past misdeeds with a touch of masochism added."

Moses stopped rubbing the ankle boots and looked at Abner.

"A private talkin' like a general. Need a fancy man's college to understand you."

"Ah, my young recruit. Think of the army as a binary beast— part force of arms to serve the national interest, and part asylum for the wayward, which explains my presence as well as yours."

"The lieutenant said there'd be oddballs here, but you don't fit the type he told."

"My associate and confidant John Barleycorn would agree with the lieutenant."

Moses looked back to the ankle boots. "One of them kind," he said. He rubbed the dragoon shoe-boots with the worn-out towel. "Should've walked on by."

They drilled on the battered-grass drill field with the hickory sabers and learned to thrust and guard, to point and cut, to parry against the bayonet and parry against the lance. Private Abner Black assisted the sergeant with instruction and walked among the recruits as they practiced in pairs. He watched Moses and Private Smithwick clack sticks, then said, "If you ever need to use the saber, or any weapon in combat, you had better be serious about it. Do not wave it like you're stirring butter. Use it like you mean it. A life may be forfeited. Do what you must to make it your opponent's. Let me show you."

Abner faced off with Moses and walked him through the moves they'd learned, then jumped to the side and swung the hickory saber hard into the back of Moses's knee, which buckled the leg. Abner knocked Moses on his back with a blow from the hilt to the chest and fell on Moses, knees to the torso, hickory blade across Moses's throat, hand on either side of his neck. He pressed until Moses choked.

He released the pressure and stood up. "A few simple moves and you are dead." He helped Moses stand. Moses felt his throat.

"Nothing from the trooper's handbook, but effective. Remember that. Conserve your strength. If ever you are in combat you will need all of it. Keep it as simple and as quick as possible. The legs are the foundation. Take a leg down, and you have your man. Be ruthless. There is no such thing as fair in a fight."

"Takes mad to do that. For me anyway," Moses said.

"Then get mad. It may save your life." Abner walked off to watch other recruits and sparred with Private Donovan to demonstrate saber moves. Light glinted from a spectacle lens when Abner turned his head to duck a thrust.

Looks like he crawled out of a school book, and he had me in three seconds, Moses thought and massaged the back of his knee. *What hides behind them eyeglasses?*

In the School of the Trooper, Mounted, they learned the proper care of the horse and how to groom with the curry comb and brush. They learned to mount and dismount from both sides of the horse with and without saddle. They rode bareback and then graduated to saddles with stirrups crossed in front of the pommel to learn to sit the seat without stirrups. They began at a walk, advanced to a trot, then to a canter, and on to a gallop.

Moses had grown up riding bareback, so he found the saddle unnatural, a barrier that deadened the feel of the horse, like his shoes did to the feel of the earth when he'd first worn them at school age. Still, he had learned to appreciate shoes and supposed the same would come with the saddle.

They learned the rudiments of horsemanship, how to rein, collect, and control the horse and when to pressure with the leg, spur, and bit. The cropped grass on the drill field turned from green to brown through the weeks of training. Bare spots grew in size and number from the footwork of troops and horse hooves.

They rode on the drill field, and they rode in pastures boxed by stone walls, and they rode over forested hills. In the third week of the School of the Trooper, Mounted, they jumped a snake-rail fence that divided fields. The horse Moses rode sailed over it as smooth as a fish swims, front legs bent at the knee to fold to the girth, hind legs straight as tail fins. When the horse landed it set its hooves. Dirt furrowed from the iron shoes, and it stopped as though it hit a wall, and Moses sailed on, arms out to cushion the impact. The horse ran off, stirrups flopping at his sides.

Abner laughed. "I could have told you that would happen, but it would have spoiled the game." Abner laughed more. "His name is 'Tenderfoot,' but we call him 'Train Brake.' " Abner kept laughing, pulled a handkerchief from a tunic pocket, said between laughs, "It gets me every time." He removed his spectacles and wiped tears from his cheeks. "Now the sergeant will inform you of your prospects with the infantry." Abner chortled, wiped the spectacle lenses. "After which he will instruct me to retrieve your horse." He seated the eyeglasses back in place and returned the handkerchief to his pocket.

"Balance!" the sergeant yelled. He trotted back to Moses. "You're not riding a plow mule, Private Cole. You're mounted on a horse that can stop or turn quicker than you can think."

Moses picked grit from his hands.

"Fall off again, and I'll bust you to the infantry."

Moses brushed dirt from his trousers and tunic.

"Are you fond of the ground, Private?"

"No, sir."

"Maybe you don't hear so good. Are you fond of the ground, Private?"

"No, sir, Sergeant."

"Then stay in the saddle."

The sergeant motioned to Abner and lowered his voice, just

loud enough for Moses to hear. "Catch this foot soldier's horse for him, then have him cross his stirrups so he can think about balance"—he looked at Moses—"unless this recruit prefers the infantry or the cook stove, which I can arrange."

The sergeant rode to the recruits who cantered through the field while Abner retrieved the sorrel named "Tenderfoot" on the company's horse roster.

When Abner returned, Moses crossed the stirrups over the crest of the horse's neck, grabbed a handful of Train Brake's mane, and vaulted into the saddle. He looked at his sleeve. "Grass stain on my soldier coat. That don't look good."

"You are not a soldier, and that is not a coat. You are a dragoon recruit clothed in a tunic."

"Cap stayed on, though, when ole Train Brake tried me for a field plow, so I ain't entirely embarrassed."

"A lad fond of sport. Let's hope you stay that way when Train Brake tries his next trick." Abner chuckled and nudged his horse to a trot.

That evening, between supper and bed call, Abner stretched his legs on his cot, back braced by the barracks' wall, removed the inkwell's lid, dipped his pen, and placed it to stationery. A well-worn edition of *Paradise Lost* served for a lap desk.

My Dear Mrs. Pembroke,

How long it's been since I've written! I apologize, my dear, for my lack of manners in this indiscretion. I rather miss these missives that vent messages wasted on the dullard's ear, more common than naught in soldiery, that disdained vocation of immigrants and others of meager means, or, as you have surmised, those with fondness for Bacchus.

Did I not mention they made a dragoon of me? How little you know of them beyond their repute for vainglory, so I shall endeavor to illuminate as I would from a lectern.

Moses Cole looked up from stitching the tear in his tunic and said, "What you writin' on?"

Abner folded the letter and smiled. "I shall answer your literal as well as your implied question. Stationery, my lad, pilfered from the lieutenant's desk, on which is penned a missive to a former fiancée, now ascending as a matron of high society."

"I would not know about that."

"Nor should you. It is not to be recommended to those grounded in honest earth, although I must admit, there are those of distinction within it, of clear mind if not pure heart."

"Don't know either of them people, them heart or mind kind." He thought of Miss Isabella. "Except one."

"Male or female?"

"A miss."

"Your age?"

"No sir. One year older."

"In your terminology, is she a heart kind or mind kind?"

"Both, near as I can see."

"Does her appearance brighten a man's eye?"

"She's a looker, if that's what you're on to, or comin' on to bein' one anyway."

"Should you return after a five-year enlistment, do you expect her to be available?"

Moses shrugged. "Will or won't. Didn't give up nothin' I had anyway."

"Ah, my young private. But you did." Abner placed the letter between pages of *Paradise Lost*, separate from the others he'd penned and filed there, and returned the book to the trunk.

CHAPTER 3

One Year Later—Carlisle, Pennsylvania, to Fort Leavenworth [Kansas], August 1845 through June 1846

The company of dragoons left Carlisle Barracks in early August, 1845, the year after Moses Cole enlisted. They traveled to Harrisburg, Pennsylvania, by rail, then canal boat to the Alleghenies, where they marched over the mountains like infantry "as though demoted," Abner said, "from the bourgeoisie to the proletariat."

"Talk American," Moses said.

"From aristocrats to plebeians."

"That don't help."

"Imagine a rich man, my young private, who bet his fortune at a table of chance and lost. Dishonored and disowned and cast out from family wealth to discover the drudgery of work."

Moses said, "What would you know about that?"

"More than I'm inclined to tell." Abner looked off. They marched on a wagon road that wended through a deciduous forest lush with spring. After a bit he said, "From soldiers of horse to soldiers of foot."

"Butt sore to foot sore," Moses said. "Shoulda said that first. Would've saved talkin' time."

Abner put a hand to his heart. "You wound me, young private. To choose the dullness of silence over the beauty of the spoken word is to choose tepid tea over cognac. Wiser perhaps, but less enriching."

"Them dressed-up words you talk with would trip and tie my

tongue, but they slide off you like water off a frog. Ornamented, the way you say things. Plain talk shoved in a costume. A body's gotta admire that."

Abner laughed. "Worse yet, before I accepted, shall I say, the call to become a Soldier of Horse, I was accorded a career of some comfort instructing others in the art."

Moses shook his head. "This ole world, the more I see the curiouser she gets."

"We follow the way of Odysseus, my young private."

"Who's he?"

"A man of myth who reaped the reward of hope and perseverance. Like him, we wander, we seek and are tested, and at times indulge our desires. Yet we persevere and journey home in the hope that the love we left pines for us." Abner watched a cloud drift. After a bit he said in little more than a whisper, "And we, as did Odysseus, eliminate her suitors and regain her hand."

They marched on. No dust rose from the road. No sound but footfalls and chirping birds, the sing of cicadas. No equipment to clatter, packed in wagons to follow the troop.

"When I'm done runnin' off and all, I'll get back what I walked off from, like that Odious fella done. You watch and see."

Abner chuckled. "A goal worthy of a young man's whimsy."

"When I left home, I wanted gone. Someplace faraway from Pa and his beatin' on me, that mean his liquor give him. Enlistment done that for me. Follow my feet and my feet's headed west to see a world I ain't never seen, won't mix with him no more. Nice tight package but the bow's gone off it, seein's how she's back there, and I'm out here."

"How wonderful of the army to solve one's problems or, rather, place them in abeyance, by removing one from them. One may, however, find the removal long and arduous as did Odysseus."

"Long arm of Miss Isabella grabbin' me back. Pushed and pulled and tore in half, is what I feel like."

"You suffer a confusion of youth, my young recruit, with a heart inflamed by anger and attraction. However, with reason and intuition, informed by experience and introspection and proper tutelage, you will parse your purpose and clarify your clouded goals, most of which is academic now that you're a pawn in the army."

"How'd we come to partner? You and me's like a fig and pig meat."

"Ah, the culinary delights. More flavors for the layered tongue, one might say, but, to address your question, a teacher needs a pupil."

"Teacherin' on me. Thought I'd skipped off on that but it don't look it." He lowered his voice. "That'll make Mama happy. Never had the schoolin' she wanted me to have, till now looks like."

On the west side of the Alleghenies they took canal boats to Pittsburgh, where they boarded a steamboat on the Ohio River. Moses had never been on a boat, "Not one with an engine, anyway," he told Abner. "Hope it don't buck and roll like Train Brake done." He considered the river's width, how deep it might be, the currents it carried. He wondered if it froze over in the wintertime, and, if it did, whether it would carry footsteps or bait a person from the riverbank, then break to hold the body below it. Moses marveled at the water the river ran, wide and lazy and bigger as they went, like a funnel through forests that gathered the smaller waters.

"Water as clear as an ingénue's conscience," Abner said, "and as smooth as the skin of her breast."

When the steamboat reached the Mississippi, west by southwest from Pittsburgh over the length of five states "counting the states on both banks," Abner said, the easy river turned into a thoroughfare.

Moses wondered, "Where's all that water go? We gonna flood like old man Noah, grow fins and gills before it's done with us, unless that ocean's got a hole in it, or this ole globe ends in a waterfall."

Abner shook his head.

"Say a man ran his boat over it. God knows where he'd end up, fallin' down that waterfall. Fish food probably."

"Probably," Abner said.

"Smashed on the rocks at the bottom of it or, if it's got no bottom, just keep on fallin' 'til you starve or drown. What a waste. Not hardly worth the effort."

"You suffer from a keen mind and are a pupil of humor."

Moses puzzled over Abner's words.

"You've perceived that life is vanity, that our efforts are for naught. A rare insight for one so young."

"That's what I like about you," Moses said. "You're so"—he thought a moment—"peculiar."

"Words written by those wiser than I." Abner read the question in the raised eyebrow. "Ecclesiastes."

"Don't need him," Moses said.

The steamboat turned north at the Mississippi and churned against the current. They passed steamers—stern-wheelers and side-wheelers loaded with lumber and harvested crops, mail and hides and pioneers. They passed a sunken steamboat, stacks at quarter tilt listing in the river like flooded tree trunks where the bank gave way. Loggers cut timber on the banks and ricked it for steamboat boilers.

Perplexed by the numbers of people when they reached St. Louis, Moses pondered how they could fit, all those people gathered to a place like ants to an ant hill. "A whole lotta doin' and not much goin'," he told Abner.

Steamboats docked side by side at the St. Louis levee, like a stable of horses hitched to a rail. Black folk, slaves maybe, loaded and unloaded steamers, drove mule-drawn carts, packed loads on their shoulders, pushed wheelbarrows in and out of warehouses built of brick and cast-iron. A boy rolled a steel wheel to a blacksmith shop. Big, tall buildings, three stories high, with rows of windows with window glass so all those people could see in and see out and tend to each other's business, he figured, or see where the sun was. Smokestacks blew smoke dark as charcoal. Ship whistles split eardrums if you stood too close. A piper played at a gangplank, and a fiddler bowed notes at another one. A ship's captain pushed through a circle of tambourine dancers. Wagon wheels and shod hooves hammered cobblestone. Sales folk with singsongs called, "Apples, cigars, see me for a shoeshine." Moses thought it a wonder to behold but a place unfit to live.

They disembarked, loaded on a smaller side-wheeler, steamed on to the Missouri, and followed it west across the state of the same name "on this ole globe," Moses said, "that don't know 'whoa.' " They'd nap on the deck by the thump of steam-driven pistons and the churning of counter-weighted paddle wheels, stand guard for snags or sandbars covered in water the color of farm fields barren of crops. They watched deer and bear on the riverbanks and white pelicans migrating south, flying in lines like dragoons on a drill field. They'd land in the water, skidding on their feet, to rest and feed from the river. The pelicans hunted their fish, circled their prey, and closed the circle like wolf packs, a Western veteran told him, take buffalo.

After eight days on the Missouri, they saw the flag wave from a flagstaff above the trees on the bluff in the distance. After five more miles of river they disembarked, formed ranks, marched up the hill to Fort Leavenworth—a dozen or so structures built on elevated terrain that overlooked the river. Two red-brick buildings two stories high with verandas and trimmed windows quartered dragoons. Another of similar construction quartered officers. Log stables, a parsonage, hospital, sutler's store, guard house, powder magazine, and assorted houses completed the fort.

"Don't look like a fort to me," Moses said. "Looks like a half breed between a city and a village."

"It suggests a campus, my young private, a shadow, perhaps, of one where I sought my zenith and found my nadir." Abner looked at the pattern of architecture, the walkways and lawns, the bright-white verandas, a porticoed home, and fell silent. After a while he said, "Those polar emotions return."

"What's fell on you sounds," Moses thought a moment, "bent and heavy. Them birds will chirp again once we get 'a horse-back."

They settled in the barracks, drilled on foot for weeks while they waited for remounts, reported for fatigue duty to construct outbuildings and roads, cut cord wood, dig ditches, clean the grounds. Abner Black sipped from a bottle in his trunk when wakened at reveille and before bed call, and when the bottle was gone he'd acquire another. Moses heard the trunk lid lift and close during the night, heard Abner's cot squeak when he lay back down.

Moses said at breakfast, "You're more drunk than sober, nippin' like you been since we lit here."

"Quite right, young private, and I intend to stay that way, which explains my cheerful demeanor."

"You and pa, lips on a bottle like a baby on a mama."

"Right again. Unsurpassed in the love they tender." Abner ate his beef and beans. "A simple emotional equation, if you may. To the left of the equals sign we have a double negative— the daily weight of life in the cantonment with its drudgery of duty multiplied by love lost. To the right of the equals sign we have an elixir to melancholia."

"Me and equations don't partner too good," Moses said.

"Simple math. A negative times a negative equals a positive, which again, my young private, explains my sanguine disposition."

Three weeks passed to a wet November Sunday when Abner took the ferry from Fort Leavenworth to Whisky Point, drank until his money was gone, then sold his greatcoat to drink more. Moses found him four days later, face down in the mud speaking Latin and laughing. Moses redeemed the greatcoat with his soldier's pay, half carried and half dragged Abner to the ferry and back to the barracks where he was remanded to the guard house for his absence without a pass. Abner stayed drunk for two days with nothing but water to drink. On the third day water jittered from his cup. His teeth chattered as if tapping a telegraph key. He grew feverish, talked to shadows only he could see in phrases Moses could not decipher. On the fourth day, he scratched invisible spider bites and woke the jailer with his screams. The surgeon diagnosed bottle ache and prescribed jail rest.

In December, he returned to fatigue duty and the barracks, and Moses told him, "You was a goner to my eye. Pneumonia gone to the brain craze, looked to me like."

"An apt description," Abner said. "Now I shall live clean as a deacon until a disquieted mind drives me to respite."

Moses shook his head. "You and them dictionary words." They sat on their cots. Moses leaned toward Abner, lowered his voice. "You'll stop that bottle huggin'."

Abner smiled, stood, stepped to his trunk, and opened the lid.

"It ain't there," Moses said. "Poured it out on the ground and throwed the bottle in the river." He sat back on the cot. "Stuck a note in it. Spelled it myself. 'Dear Miss Clarissa. Thought of you and drunk it dry.' Wrote your name to it.

Halfway to St. Louis by now."

Abner chuckled. "As they say, there is more where that came from."

"Not for you. Had me a set-to with that sutler when you was in your whisky grip. He looks at the world different now."

"Pray tell, what did you convey to him?"

"Said next bottle I throw in the river, he'd be in it. He come to belief when he seen my axe handle."

"Remember the adage, my young recruit: where there is a will there is a way."

"No more ways out here."

Abner smiled. "Who knows what the future holds, but we agree for the moment. Deacon living, here I am."

"You and me is partnered." Moses leaned close. "You won't do that no more. I'm watchin' on you."

Six months passed with drill and fatigue duty and herding the horses to graze in daylight hours. On a bright morning in mid-June, 1846, Privates Abner Black and Moses Cole were summoned with Privates Donovan and Smithwick to meet with Captain Allen.

"You have been selected," Captain Allen said, "to accompany me on a recruiting expedition to enlist infantry for the Mexican War. A trunk will be provided for your full-dress uniforms and all appropriate accessories, including boot black and brass polish. You will pack your personal effects in your portmanteaus, which you will load in a wagon provided for camp supplies. We may be gone for two to three weeks to recruit among the Mormons, no doubt a peculiar people who may not welcome our appearance or be receptive to our call, which should make our journey all the more engaging. Your charge will be to maintain a military deportment in their presence, and to avoid any comment or gesture that may be construed as derogatory."

Moses furrowed his brow.

"Mind your tongue when among them, Private," Captain Allen said. "Private Black, you will make sure that he does."

Chapter 4

. . . when we are called into the battle field in defence [sic] of our country, and when the sword and sabre shall have been unsheathed . . . they shall not return to their scabbard until the enemy of our country or we sleep with the pale sheeted nations of the dead, or until we obtain deliverance.

—*Jesse C. Little,*
Agent of the Church of Jesus Christ of Latter-day Saints
in the Eastern States,
to President Polk, June 1, 1846

Captain Allen's Squad—East Bank of the Missouri River, Council Bluffs, Iowa Territory, June 30 and July 1, 1846

Five horses stood in the current, the waterline gaskin high. One pawed the water in the rhythm of a barn builder driving spikes. Another bobbed his nose in the Missouri River like he stirred oats in a feed box. The others stood still, as if to listen to the river whisper, feel it knead their forelegs and hocks.

Privates Moses Cole and Abner Black, and Donovan and Smithwick, stood with the five horses. Moses dipped the feedbag, let it fill, and poured water over his horse, brushed him, poured more water, and brushed him again. Smithwick and Donovan did the same and also washed the captain's horse. They'd left their clothes on the river bank and bathed themselves as well.

Abner watched the current flow. He said, "How enticing the

peace of an unturned surface."

"He's getting preachy," Donovan said. "A body oughta head up river, where it's quiet." He dipped his feedbag and poured it where he brushed.

"How alluring its current," Abner said, "so lazy in the humid heat."

Moses thought, then there's winter, and the counterfeit river ice. His father's words surfaced—"Half the family, right there, on account of what you done." He'd said it with a look that told Moses he wished it were Moses under the ice instead of his wife.

"How divine it would be," Abner said, "to lie down and float away, glide off and be gone."

"With the wind you blow you could do it," Smithwick said.

"Not today he can't," Moses said. "Got work yet."

They brushed and rinsed the horses to clean them of mud and dust, led them from the river, and curried them until they shone. They tied the horses to a highline so they would not roll. They cleaned and polished their saddles and tack, shined their ankle boots, burnished their spurs, polished their brass—the double-rowed buttons, ten to a row, and the eight-point helmet plate. They brushed their saddle blankets and their full-dress uniforms and laid them back in the wagon that carried their regalia for this purpose—to meet with Brigham Young, President of the Quorum of Twelve Apostles of the Church of Jesus Christ of Latter-day Saints.

Moses and Abner, and Donovan and Smithwick, gathered sticks from under riverside pine, cooked a supper of beans, side pork and coffee, ate with the captain, and rolled out their bedrolls.

Abner put pen to stationery, tilted *Paradise Lost* to catch firelight.

My Dear Mrs. Pembroke,

We are encamped on the east bank of the Missouri River under a star-lighted sky on the evening preceding the first of July. (Ah, my pedestrian attempts at rhyme! One of my many quirks you grew to disdain!) From here we shall embark upon a mission to recruit among the Mormons, or Latter-day Saints as they title themselves. We seek the young and the hardy and the faintly patriotic for service in the war against Mexico to which we, the First Dragoons of the Army of the West, now march.

Mormons, you ask. But who are they in this age of religious revival with all its facets of fervor? Surely, my dear, you've read of them in the New York Herald *in the comfort of your parlor, these religious pilgrims who fled rumors of troops. Uprooted from their sacred city of Nauvoo on the Illinois bank of the Mississippi River in the cold grip of winter, they fled over ice in the pale gray of day and by lantern light at night. The frozen Mississippi surface popped with their footfalls, infants wrapped in swaddling clothes, clutched by mothers who walked counter to wind drift bit by ice crystals. Surely you've read of them, and of their prophet and author of the* Book of Mormon, *Joseph Smith, murdered by a mob while in the safety of a jail.*

"Who you lettering to?"

Abner said, "One more missive to the missus."

Moses turned under his blanket. "Since when you been married?"

"A figure of speech, young private. A dear friend from a former life, shall I say." Firelight reflected in Abner's glasses. "What intrigue a man's life may hold."

Moses said, "You're like a busted-up pocket watch. Someone who knew what he was doin' could fit them parts together again."

"The assembled pieces," Abner said. "What time would it tell?"

"That's another thing I like about you, that intrigue of givin' puzzle pieces one at a time. Always something to wonder at."

Abner returned to his letter, wrote more, waved it to dry the ink, and folded it.

"You gonna post that letter or stuff it in that book with all them other ones, stuck away like you was a courthouse judge hidin' farm deeds from the widow women?"

"Perhaps I shall burn them, and in that manner restore them to light." Abner folded the letter and placed it behind the others with eight pages of Milton between each letter. "The question, young private, is which would be more instructive to a mind not yet jaded, John Milton's verse or Abner Black's prose?"

"Can't help you there."

"On the contrary. You are the perfect prospect."

"No, sir. I ain't willin'." Moses pulled his hat brim over his eyes and his blanket to his chin. After a while he said, "No one never wrote me a letter, so I never wrote one back."

Abner pulled a sheet of stationery, folded yet blank, from *Paradise Lost* and spoke the words as he penned them.

Dear Isabella,
   I have much to tell.

Moses shot up from his blanket and knocked his hat back. "Put that the hell down."

Abner continued to speak the words that he wrote.

First, I apologize for my abrupt departure, unexpected as it was. To put it mildly, my father and I parted ways after an unpleasant event, which I may relay to you in detail at a later date. Be that as it may, I left home and enlisted in the First Dragoons and am headed west to the war with Mexico.

"I'll burn that letter, so save yourself the effort."

With my penmanship no better than it is I have asked my friend and mentor to transcribe my words, albeit he has taken some poetic license in doing so, but the message behind the words shall be my sentiments.

Moses pulled his blanket up and turned away from Abner. "You're wasting your time," he said. "She's married now anyway, most prob'ly."

Abner said, "Then all the richer the torment shall be."

"For her or for me?"

Abner resumed the letter.

We shall soon return to Fort Leavenworth on the west bank of the Missouri River on the eastern edge of Kansas. From there we shall march to Santa Fe in a northern province of Mexico, commonly called New Mexico. From thence, south to Mexico proper, or perhaps to California. We have not received word of our final destination, but wherever it may be we shall expect to engage forces hostile to the interests of these United States.

Given the dangers involved in a march west, much of it likely under enemy control, and those inherent in armed conflict, I do not know what the future holds for me, but this I do know: to you I shall return, should I survive the perils of war, with outstretched arms and a hopeful heart.

Please remember me.

Yours,

He said to Moses, "Are you going to sign it, or am I?"

"I ain't signin'."

"Would she know your signature?"

"Yours would look too," Moses thought a moment, "polished."

Abner signed "Moses Cole" slowly, deliberately, with his left hand, and below the name he added, in his own hand, "Private,

First Dragoons." He capped the inkwell and placed the letter among the others.

Moses said, "You shouldn't have done that."

In the morning, when the captain excused himself to search for a log for a latrine and Abner watered their horses, Moses charged his pommel pistol with powder and ball, retrieved *Paradise Lost* from Abner's portmanteau in the wagon that carried their regalia, propped the book against a tree, and shot a hole through it, point blank and dead center. The cover caught fire. Flames fed on the gilded pages printed in England. Moses walked away.

Abner ran when he saw what was burning, kicked the book over, and smothered the flames with his saddle blanket. He examined the char, turned the book in his hands, stuck his index finger through the hole, cover to cover through the letters within it.

"Perfect," he said. "A touch of authenticity in the flavor of anger." He laughed and returned the book to his portmanteau.

They donned the full-dress uniforms, saddled their horses, and mounted and rode in formation—Captain Allen and Privates Cole and Black, and Donovan and Smithwick, paired behind him—swallowtail guidon waving overhead.

The dragoons rode to the Mormon encampment that overlooked the Missouri River. Hundreds of shelters quartered several thousand emigrants—tents, covered wagons, willow-woven wigwams, dugouts in bluffs, open wagons with blankets draped from the wagon bed. Across river, the prairie of the Omahas stretched to the west.

The dragoons rode through the encampment. Sweat dripped from Moses's forehead. Wool tunic on a muggy day, collar closed at the jaw line, Private Cole thought. Just like the army. Can't stand comfort.

A boy moved through the onlookers in pace with the horses. He watched the dragoons, saw Moses, and smiled.

Them teeth, Moses thought. Big as horse teeth.

A gust muscled by, flapped the guidon on the lance staff. Moses wrinkled his nose. Them people. No soap since Illinois.

Moses looked up. On both sides of the Missouri, bluffs folded the prairie and shoved it to the river bottom. Pine trees marked the ravines and ridges that fell to the flood plain. His attention turned back to the emigrants. *Look at them. Not a dollar in the camp. The captain will use that.*

The five dragoons rode by a tent, flaps tied back to entice a breeze. In the tent a woman sat on a trunk at the side of her dead child, who lay on a pallet of blankets. The woman wept, waved flies from the child's face with the *Book of Mormon,* waiting for a bishop and the grave diggers.

The boy with the horse-tooth smile tripped on a guy line that held the tent taut and the door flap open. The tent jerked, flies flew from the ceiling, and the woman looked up. "Gabriel Hanks!" The woman snapped the boy's name. Gabriel stopped as if tethered to a picket chain. "Show respect for the dead!" She glared at her neighbor's son, her eyes like fire under ice.

Gabriel removed his hat, stood at the open tent flap, head bowed. "Sorry, ma'am. I was watching the soldiers a little. I didn't see it."

"Watch where you're going." The woman dabbed her eyes with a dish towel and fanned the face of her child.

"Yes, ma'am."

Gabriel jogged ahead of the dragoons, stopped to watch them ride by—blue tunics trimmed in ochre gold at collar and cuff, brass buttons in double rows, stripes of muffled yellow accent to the outside pant leg. The captain's sash, firelight orange and draped to his knee, swayed with his saber. The horses, matching bays with blazes, glistened in the sunlight.

The Mormons gathered as fish to a lure, this splash of splendor like cedar waxwings in a flock of starlings.

Gabriel's mother found him among the onlookers.

"I'm joining," Gabriel told her. He eyed the dragoon hat, the shako with cord and eagle shield, its horsehair plume flowing white.

"You're fifteen," his mother said. "You're too young. I need you here."

"Ma. You heard."

A spur glinted. The fringe from the captain's dress epaulettes jittered in rhythm with the horses.

"Word come two days back that they was comin'. They're recruiting a battalion, to fight the Mexicans. I have to go."

"You have chores to do, for me and the other widows. We can't make this journey without you."

Gabriel's head moved with the aiguillette gilded gold in the sunlight, tags and tassels that dangled at the captain's heart. He ran to catch up.

"Gabriel! Come back here!"

Gabriel matched his pace to the horses, all shod, hoof-falls falling in cadence.

"Gabriel!" his mother shouted.

The guidon danced over the horses. The top half of the banner, red with white letters, read, U.S. with C COMPY. beneath it. The bottom half of the swallow-tail flag showed reciprocal colors, white with red letters that spelled, 1ST DRAGOONS.

A man next to Gabriel's mother laughed. "Boys," he said.

The five rode to the liberty pole, tall as a foremast, at the helm of a large tent. An American flag, one state out of date with twenty-six stars, traced a breeze from the top of the pole. The tent—a canvas mansion relative to the shelters they'd ridden by—sat just back of the flagpole. A stovepipe reached through a tin heat shield in the top of the tent, the canvas blackened by cook-stove smoke. In front of the tent, Brigham Young and the Quorum of the Twelve Apostles stood as if expecting dignitaries—frock coats and hats brushed and shirts laundered. Brigham Young, clean shaven, stepped forward and extended his hand with a smile to warm a pariah. His sandy-red hair covered his ears.

Mister Mormon himself, Moses thought. *Stout enough to tip a wagon and pack an axle away.*

Captain Allen dismounted, shook hands with the Quorum of Twelve, and was welcomed in the tent.

Private Cole led the captain's horse to Mosquito Creek, which ran through the Grand Encampment. He looked to the distance, to the edge of a pine bluff where a village of Potawatomi wigwams sat.

The dragoons dismounted and watered their horses.

Private Donovan said, "My folks was wore down to rawhide, but them people . . ." He shook his head.

Private Smithwick chuckled. "I've seen Indians that look richer."

Abner reminded them of the captain's caution, to say nothing to provoke an incident. They were here to recruit, not to offend.

They led their horses back to the tent and stood to horse, horse to the right shoulder, hitching strap in the right hand, standing in rank side by side facing the place where the leaders met.

Mormons walked by, or stood and looked.

A man in a grease-stained shirt said, "We know why you're here."

"I'll turn Mexican before I'll fight your war," the man in the stained shirt said. "I am Orson Everett, an elder in the Church of Jesus Christ of Latter-day Saints, and I don't like why you are here and what you represent."

"Elder Bear Grease," Moses said. "You could wilt a skunk a mile off, the way you smell. Upwind, downwind, it don't matter."

"Private Cole!" Abner said.

"Private Cole," Orson Everett said. "My comments were not intended as personal slights, unlike yours."

"The United States," a boy with a thin and patchy beard said. "To persecute us Saints, the states are united." His beard resembled a horse tail with mange.

"Freedom of religion," Orson Everett said. He laughed out loud. "That is Phineas Lynch, wise for one his age, unlike you, Private Cole. You know nothing of me or my circumstances, yet you insult me."

"Moses," Abner said. "Not one word."

The dragoons stood to horse, their attention to the distance. Moses clenched his lips.

Another boy stepped forward and studied the shako—the black hat with wide visor and horsehair plume. He smiled.

"Where's your paper, soldier sir? I need to write my name on it. Gabriel Hanks in big letters."

The glory of horses. Like I come to sign on.

"Careful, Gabriel," Orson Everett said. "They're not here to help us." He looked at Private Smithwick.

Them eyebrows are the real deal, Moses thought.

"I want to ride a little," Gabriel said, fixed on the shako—the ornamental gold cords, bands, and tassels. He gaped at the shield on the shako—the eight-point star big as a bear paw, Napoleonic eagle in its center.

Captain's clever, Moses thought. *Uses dragoons to recruit infantry.*

"We are Captain Allen's escort," Private Abner Black said. "The captain is here to recruit infantry for the war with Mexico."

"For what?" Orson Everett said. His eyebrows lifted. "Cannon fodder? To finish what the mobocrats started? To die for a country that expelled us?"

"To the Great Basin we go," Phineas Lynch said. He pointed across the Missouri River. "Away to the west. Territory of Mexico." He looked at Moses. "For us, the United States has no need."

"My son was killed at Haun's Mill, in the year of our Lord eighteen hundred and thirty-eight," Orson Everett said. His eyebrows hooded his eyes. "Shot dead in a blacksmith shop because he was a Latter-day Saint, by Missourians. He was ten years old." He tipped his head slightly and looked away. A dog barked, then yelped when a stick hit its back. He turned to Private Cole. "Where were you peacocks then?"

Gabriel stayed with the shako—corrugated rays stamped in the helmet plate radiated from the eagle.

A breeze moved through. Moses wrinkled his nose. The shako's horsehair plume moved when he turned his head away.

"I saw that," Orson Everett said.

Moses turned his head back, and the plume on the shako waved. Gabriel stepped one step closer. Moses started to say something, then smiled.

"If Brother Brigham wants us to go, all the king's oxen won't hold me back," Gabriel Hanks said.

"Shot like cattle in a pen," Orson Everett said. "My boy and sixteen brethren." His lips tightened. "My wife died soon after. Imagine that." He looked skyward, held his hands wide apart, palms up, as if he carried a catfish one-yard long. "Forgive me, Lord. I wish your curse upon the Missourians, for all they've done, and for all they hoped to do, to us, your Camp of Israel." He looked at Private Cole and lowered his hands. "Surely, Lord, they are Satan's blight on mankind."

Abner said, "May it comfort you to know that neither I, nor

the captain, nor my fellow privates, are sons of Missouri. We are simple dragoons, in service to our country, the one in which you and I now stand."

"Not my country," said Orson Everett, the elder in the greasy shirt. "Not anymore."

The leaders stepped from the tent and shook hands. Captain Allen walked to the edge of the makeshift settlement, followed by the dragoons with the horses, where the people could assemble.

Captain Allen stood in the bed of a freight wagon with a crowd of hundreds gathered to it. His clean-shaven face suggested a New England minister rather than a West Point frontier officer. He looked at the audience gathered before him at the edge of the Grand Encampment—families mostly, plain and weather-worn, with frayed and patched clothing. They stood or sat on the prairie grass or clustered in the shade of solitary red oaks.

Captain Allen removed his shako and placed it on the wagon seat, swept his hair from his forehead, and gestured to the wagon that served as his platform. "Look at this wagon. Its weather-checked sideboards." He leaned over, placed a hand on the top edge of a sideboard.

A party of children played tag. An older boy rolled a wagon rim with a shovel handle. A baby wailed.

"The top edge, rounded from wear. Chipped even." He moved his hand over the sideboard, feeling the weather checks. His tunic darkened where sweat soaked through. "Worn, full of character, like an old face." He straightened, looked at the wagon bed.

Moses and the other privates stood to horse nearby. A breeze played with the guidon and horsehair plumes.

Rode this far to talk to a wagon, Moses thought. *For criminy sake.*

"The bed of this wagon," he moved a boot sole over it, "scarred by freight ferried from New England to your beautiful Nauvoo, your city born of your labors, and now to these Council Bluffs"—Captain Allen scanned the audience—"in the heart of Indian country." He used the wagon as an actor would a stage, three steps one way, three steps back, pacing for dramatic effect. His sash, firelight orange and reaching to his knee, accented his steps with its fluid moves. "Like this wagon, you bear the scars of toil, of endurance, earned in your work to build this land."

Hear him clear to the river, Moses thought.

Captain Allen looked over the audience, stopped, nodded his head. "You've relinquished Nauvoo, your City of Joseph. You've been expelled from your settlements in Missouri. You've been battered by disease. You've pulled and pushed your wagons through miles of mud. Struggled through impossible creek crossings. You've made do with short supplies. You've memorialized your trail with graves."

He paced. The tap of his boot heels punctuated his sentences. His tags and tassels and epaulets glittered in the sunlight.

"Like this wagon, you are essential to building this nation. You are essential"—he paused—"to the Manifest Destiny we share." He stopped pacing, made eye contact with a few of the audience. A mother cuddled a crying baby, then carried it away. He resumed pacing.

"You've suffered persecution. You've seen your homes burned. Family members murdered. Your prophet, Joseph Smith, martyred." He stopped again, stood still. The guidon lay limp where his escort stood to horse, the air heavy as an anvil.

"I cannot excuse those heinous actions of mob rule, but this I can say. These United States"—he timed his words to stabs of his finger—"were founded on the premise of freedom to worship. You need now to defend that right by coming to the aid of your country."

A one-note laugh jabbed from a man in the audience. *The Bear Grease Elder,* Moses thought.

Captain Allen lowered his hand to the hilt of his saber and looked to where the laugh broke. Some stood timber-still, others shifted, most looked at a sideboard or wheel on the wagon, or an object in the audience or in the distance. Captain Allen's voice rose. "If you settle in the Great Basin, in Mexican Territory, and Mexico wins this war, rest assured you will convert to Catholicism or be expelled yet again."

Captain Allen turned his face to the wagon bed, clasped his hands in the small of his back. His chest rose when he inhaled, and he exhaled slowly. He looked up, toward the other side of the river. "I am here to enroll a battalion of Mormons. There are benefits for you in this." He paced, stopped, and faced his listeners. "Your camp rests on Potawatomi land. Your elders, with whom I met this morning, wish to remain here, until next spring, and to quarter another camp across the Missouri River, on Omaha lands. You will need the permission of the government and, if need be, the protection of the army, to do that."

Brigham Young and the Twelve sat at the front of the crowd and nodded at Captain Allen's remarks. The tails of their frock coats cushioned the trunks and boxes that served for seats, carried from tents and wagons for the occasion.

"I am here to represent President Polk, and to offer you this." Captain Allen held a hand up with an extended index finger. He waved his hand, slowly, above his head. "If you answer this call, the government of the United States will give you the right to remain on Indian lands until your move west."

The breeze moved again. A shadow from a solitary cloud slipped on the tallgrass prairie.

Captain Allen took a step, held up another finger. "The army will supply and will lead five hundred of your able-bodied men to California." He paused, nodded his head, looked over the audience. "Five hundred of you, moved to California, at government expense."

Two boys ran toward a mule that crossed the meadow dragging a lead rope.

Captain Allen stepped two paces and held up a third finger, and waved his hand. "Upon discharge in California, those who enlist today will be allowed to retain their government-issued muskets."

Captain Allen pulled his hand down, held the three fingers in his other hand, and paced. The tap of his boot heels carried. "Your migration has severely taxed your financial resources. Due to events you could not control, many of you sold your farms and belongings at a fraction of their value." Captain Allen held his hand back up with only the thumb folded. "You will be paid as soldiers, seven dollars a month, same as any other infantry private in the U.S. Army." He extended all five fingers and slowly waved his hand. "And"—he paced—"you will receive a clothing allowance of forty-two dollars, per recruit, at enlistment." He took two steps, stopped, and pulled his hand down. "You need not purchase uniforms. You may keep that allowance."

Son-of-a-horse-biscuit. Should've been Mormon.

A cow bell sounded at the edge of the meadow. Captain Allen paced.

"With five hundred recruits"—he stopped pacing—"that is a total of twenty-one thousand dollars." He said the number slowly, enunciated each syllable. "You will receive that money when you muster, in two weeks." He smiled, held his hand up again with fingers extended. "That will finance your exodus to the Great Basin."

It would take a yoke of oxen to pull that much money.

Captain Allen resumed pacing, hands behind his back. "I will add one more reason for you to answer this call." He stopped, held both hands up to show six fingers. "Many doubt your loyalty to the United States. The army and President Polk are not among those."

A man could steal that muster money. Buy him a piece of Virginia. Make him a home for pretty little Isabella. Moses felt the familiar pull, then caught himself. *Don't think that thought no more.*

Captain Allen brought his hands down, pounded a fist in a palm as if shaping metal with a hammer. "This is your opportunity to demonstrate patriotism greater than that of your most fervent detractors."

Brigham Young stood up, walked to the wagon where Captain Allen stood. He placed a hand on the wagon box and vaulted onto the wagon bed with his frock coat and stiff-brimmed hat. He extended a hand to Captain Allen and said, "Captain, you shall have your battalion."

Got a voice on him, Moses thought. *Knock a hog back at eight paces.*

Brigham Young motioned to the Twelve seated at the front of the assembly. The apostles stood up. "You shall have your battalion if it has to be made up from our Elders. And if we have not enough men, we shall furnish women."

An army with women. For God's sake.

Brigham Young turned to his people. Men and women with infants shifted or stood still. Toddlers played, watched by children older than they. Boys had wormed in closer to the wagon, Gabriel Hanks among them. President Young stretched his arms as if to embrace the assembly and said, "Come, brethren, let us volunteer."

CHAPTER 5

*Beloved and respected Wife, it is with grief, and disapointment
[sic] although mingled with bright prospects of the future that I
sit down to pen a few lines to you concerning the sudden change
that is about to come across My calculations . . . My faith is
that you wil [sic] not murmur at My volunteering to absent
myself from you for so long inasmuch as I go by council of the
church . . . I believe that the God of Israel will order all things
right for those that act through a pure desire for the welfare of
his Kingdom . . .*

—George Taggart,
Mormon Battalion,
to his wife, Fanny Taggart,
July 8, 1846

Grand Encampment on Mosquito Creek, Council Bluffs,
Iowa Territory, July 1, 1846, Morning

"Must I remind you we've been husband and wife for less than
a month?" Abigail Alcott placed her hands on her hips and
turned her head slightly, as if to sight an eye down a musket
barrel.

Abigail and Mr. Alcott stood under the lean-to at the back of
their wagon among the tents and hovels on Mosquito Creek in
the Grand Encampment.

"Remember the wedding words? Read right from the Bible?"
She turned her head a little further.

"I do," Mr. Alcott said.

"Then what were they?"

"I just said them." He smiled.

"Not that. The rest of it." She eyed him straight on, tapped a foot. "Whither thou goest, I shall go," Abigail said. "Whither thou lodgest, I shall lodge."

"That doesn't apply to the army."

"Why must women always stay behind and worry about their husbands, when we could just as well march beside you?"

"Because you might get shot at."

Abigail waved a hand. "For heaven's sake. As if we Saints haven't been shot at." She cocked her head again. "Mr. Alcott. Really."

"The army's different. They look for a fight, and all of them have guns. You could get killed."

"And you couldn't?" Abigail turned her head back to look him square in the eye. "And if I stay here, the black canker or quick consumption could get me. I could drown in a river crossing for that matter, or get run over by a wagon wheel."

Abigail's attire showed their trials—the gingham dress, worn thin at the elbows with frayed lace at the collar, the darned stockings and mended chemisette, the different fabrics that patched her apron. She stood unadorned—her pierced ears reminders of missing pendants; her neck bare of a necklace; her auburn hair, braided without a barrette; a wedding ring but no bracelet or brooch. All she had she'd traded for simple necessities to supply them in their migration.

"Plain and frugal, faith and love," Mr. Alcott said.

"What?"

"You. How the Lord has blessed me."

"Don't change the subject. Why is it that women don't march with their husbands?"

Mr. Alcott hooked his thumbs in the front of his trousers.

"Lots of reasons. You would not have the company of other women."

"They're taking laundresses, twenty of them. The soldiers will pay them for washing their clothes. They'll earn money, same as the soldiers do. Just not payroll, is all."

"I see," Mr. Alcott said. "It's not more money from the army, it just rearranges who gets it, and it will go the church anyway, so what's the difference?"

"It will help our soldiers, who won't have time for that and would not do it if they did."

"You'd march every day."

"How did I travel from the Mississippi to the Missouri River? In the winter, and in the mud of spring, need I remind you, when the going is particularly tough."

Mr. Alcott rubbed his cheek and chin. "Women have the babies. Soldiers don't have babies."

"I won't be a soldier. I'll be a laundress."

"Same difference. You're still with the army, going where the army goes, living like soldiers live."

"Tell me, Mr. Alcott, just how much different that would be from how we live now?" Abigail extended a hand to indicate their shelter—a wagon with willow arched from sideboard to sideboard with canvas stretched over the willow, high enough to crouch in the wagon bed; a pallet of blankets for a bed on the wagon deck; a lean-to of interlaced branches forming a covered porch at the rear of the wagon; a cabinet and trunk and chest of drawers under the lean-to, placed on sticks so rain would drain under them; a milk pail and stool for seating. His spare pair of trousers, with needle, thimble and thread, lay folded on the stool.

Mr. Alcott turned the pail upside down and sat on it. He picked up the trousers and motioned to the stool. "Please, my darling bride, do have a seat in the drawing room."

Abigail sat down and put the trousers in her lap.

Mr. Alcott lifted his hands and looked to both sides. "You wouldn't have all this." With a hint of a smile, he picked up a stick he'd whittled from an oak branch, drew his sheath knife, and resumed carving a wagon spoke.

"Melissa Brown volunteered to be a laundress, to accompany her husband."

"Well, Melissa would."

"I did the same."

Mr. Alcott stopped carving. "You what?"

"We're going West anyway, but you will go now, with the battalion, and the rest of us will go when—next spring? Next summer? A year from when we were married?"

"But, Abigail! It's army duty! It's not fit for a woman!"

"And how will it be different from what we women do now? It might even be easier, and the soldiers will pay us for doing their laundry."

"You can't do this, Abigail. Women can't join the army."

"Brother Brigham and Captain Allen disagree. You may take it up with them." Abigail put the thimble on an index finger, unfolded the trousers, and stitched a ripped seam with the needle and harness thread.

Mr. Alcott said, "So, what do I call you? Private Alcott?"

"Abigail will do nicely, thank you."

Mr. Alcott resumed carving. "I will say, you have a backbone a blacksmith couldn't bend."

"I took you as my husband, and I intend to be a wife to you." Abigail pulled another stitch in the coil of even, tight stitches.

"I see that."

"Brother Brigham said we could take the wagon."

Mr. Alcott stopped carving. "Have you other surprises for me?"

Abigail smiled.

CHAPTER 6

The prairie was yet what is called rolling; the flat bottoms were covered with the rosin weed or polar plant . . . It is said that the planes of the leaves of this plant are coincident with the plane of the meridian; but those I have noticed must have been influenced by some local attraction that deranged their polarity.

—Lieutenant J. W. Abert,
Corps of Topographical Engineers,
Army of the West, Kansas,
June 29, 1846

Courier Squad, First Dragoons, Fort Leavenworth [Kansas]
to Vegas Gorge [New Mexico], July 25 to August 15, 1846
The dragoons rode west on the Santa Fe Trail, through the gentle, tree-filled hills west of Fort Leavenworth with their hickory and oak, walnut, linden and ash and maple trees, their birch and beech. They rode by hillsides pink with wild rose, white clusters of Jersey tea, the tall stalks of rattlesnake weed. The timbered hills turned to tallgrass prairie with the only green the leaves of cottonwoods that traced the few streams that ran there.

The squad—Privates Black and Cole, Donovan and Smithwick, and a major in place of Captain Allen, who'd remained at Fort Leavenworth to nurse ill health—trotted until their horses heated, walked to cool them down, and trotted on.

Moses Cole said to Abner Black, "This prairie is dull and flat and empty, where nothin' leads to nothin', like the inside of my mind."

"Think of it as the abeyance, my young private, rather than the death of imagination. Herein lies another lesson of soldiery, perseverance through boredom, best borne with the sparkling wit of John Barleycorn, who, to my chagrin, has gone on sojourn."

They rode on, mile after mile on the naked back of Kansa tribe land.

East of Pawnee Rock, Moses stirred from sleep, felt something cool move against his calf, felt it reach to his knee. He lay still in the fold of his blanket, caught between caution and fright. After a time, he eased from the blanket and threw it back to show the prairie rattler as long as his arm. The snake coiled and rattled and stayed on the blanket. Moses retrieved his horse pistol from the pommel holster, loaded it in the soft light of sunrise, cocked it, and shot a hole through his blanket. He reloaded and missed again, yelled the swear words the troopers taught him, and shot the snake with his carbine. The snake writhed with its head maimed from a .54 caliber ball.

Abner had jumped from his bedroll at the first shot and stood and watched.

"What the hell is going on here?" the major said. He and Donovan and Smithwick had sat up in their blankets.

"Shook so bad, thought I'd blow a toe off," Private Cole said.

"Snake, sir," Abner said. "Scared the young private halfway to his maker."

"For God's sake," the major said. He threw his blanket off to get dressed.

Abner stepped closer to Moses. "If you examine your pistol you will find it to harbor a semi-spherical blade at the end of the barrel"—he held up his pistol and pointed to the sight immediately above the muzzle—"about the size of half a penny, commonly referred to as a 'sight.' It was placed there with the expressed intention of aligning the barrel with the eye and the target."

"Well, lookie there. Never seen it before." Moses rolled his eyes.

"Should you desire the ball to strike the target you would do well to employ it for greater economy of powder and ball, not readily replenished in this wilderness."

"Be a whole lot easier if you'd talk plain instead of slingin' them dollar words all at once, like you was a thief spillin' a bag of loot."

"You think I sing a song to a deaf man, yet should I not speak with an educated tongue I would not excite your imagination for language, my young private, and all it reflects upon our perception and interpretation of the situations and places in which we find ourselves."

"That don't mean you gotta shoot everything with a shotgun when a horse pistol will do. Keep it straight and simple, and I'll savvy what you say."

"All right then. You might need those rounds when we catch the Mexican army, or they catch us. Learn to make each one count, especially when under pressure."

"Yes, Master Private," Moses said.

"I will allow, however, you reloaded quickly in spite of less-than-settled nerves."

Abner returned the pistol to the pommel holster, drew a jackknife from the pants that doubled as a pillow, stepped on the snake and cut off the three-inch rattle, held out the rattle, and said, "That's to remind you how close death is. For the Bible saith, 'For what is your life?' " He dropped the rattle into Moses's hand. " 'It is even a vapor, that appeareth for a little time, and then vanisheth away.' " Though dead, the snake contracted under Abner's bare foot.

Moses kindled a fire with buffalo chips. While the coffee boiled, he pulled hairs from his horse's tail, plaited them, and used the braid to tie the rattle to his cap. If nothing else, he figured, the rattle would tell him when he rode untuned to his horse's gait.

The dragoons stopped at Pawnee Rock and saw buffalo fill the prairie to the northwest like a black mass of flowing land. They rode southwest in the Permanent Indian Frontier, rode to the Cimarron Cutoff, and dug for water to water their horses in the dry bottom of the Arkansas. Now and again hordes of mosquitoes and gnats blanketed their horses at all but a trot. They tied their socks to their bridles to flag away horseflies and keep nose flies at bay.

Wind scoured the prairie, drove dust in their eyes and ears, noses, and throats. A dead horse lay by trail side, black with crows. A wolf lifted his head from amongst the crows to watch them ride by.

They rode west on the Santa Fe Trail for nineteen or twenty, maybe twenty-two days, Moses wasn't sure which with one day blurred to another. For the last ride they rode all night, sixty miles to General Kearny's camp to arrive at sunrise. A Santa Fe freighter had told them of the Mexican forces that waited in ambush at the pass near Vegas for the Army of the West. The squad had not ridden this far to miss a battle by a day.

They rode through the valley of the Vegas at day break, passed a field that waved with corn, its rows irrigated with ditches where they watered their horses. A Mexican beckoned at its edge—a woman in stockings, white as bridal lace—and walked up and smiled, shook hands, asked for tobacco in Spanish. The major answered in French and handed her a quid. The squad passed a pueblo that resembled a village of brick kilns and rode to the camp of the Army of the West.

"Look at them boys," a trooper said when the squad rode through camp to General Kearny's tent. "Four privates and a major, wore down and horse weary. The Mexican army has my pity."

Colonel Kearny buckled on his saber at the entrance to his tent and watched the squad approach. He said, "Welcome, Major. This is a pleasant surprise."

"The surprise is mine, sir. I was not sure we'd arrive in time to participate in the battle that rumor on the Santa Fe Trail holds to be imminent."

Colonel Kearny laughed. "Impressive. Trail rumor knows more about this command than the command itself does." He nodded. "Rumor is quite right. We march this morning on Vegas Gorge."

"It is my pleasure to inform you, Colonel, that you will do so as a brigadier general." The major handed the citation of commission, and the stars of rank, to Colonel Kearny.

The major stepped back, saluted, and said, "Congratulations, General."

"I'll be damned," Kearny said. He read the citation and opened the box that held two insignia to be sewn on the shoulders of his tunic, each with a star in silver thread. He closed the box.

"I never seen a general's stars, sir," Moses said. "Could you show us, sir?"

Abner shot a look at Moses.

"I mean, we packed 'em a long way and all."

"Your name, Private?"

"Moses Cole, sir."

General Kearny handed the box to the major. "Pass this among your squad, Major, so that Private Cole may see that the trappings of command are no more than cloth."

"As you wish, sir."

The major's horse stood by his side, rib thin, ganted up, missing two shoes. Dried brine from sweated salts clung to his head and neck.

"You did not need to press your horses to deliver this," General Kearny said. "It will not make a bit of difference in what I do, or how I do it."

"It may give you more sway with the Mexican governor, sir," the major said, "when we reach Santa Fe."

"Let's hope it does."

"We did not wish to miss the engagement, sir, so we pressed on when otherwise we would have rested."

General Kearny nodded.

"We rode sixty miles last night, sir."

"It shows," General Kearny said. "I am impressed. Draw remounts, and rest if you can while I tend to a civic matter in the local pueblo." General Kearny dismissed them.

Abner said to Moses, "Do not ever address a general officer, or a field grade officer for that matter, unless spoken to first, Private Cole. You know that."

"Didn't bother him none."

"It bothered the major, who will likely recommend you for the vanguard when we assault the Mexicans."

Moses said, "That'll give you somethin' to tell Isabella."

"There is a hole in my book, which presents an impediment to a well penned letter when, as is my custom, it serves as a lap desk. Most intrusive to a fluid hand, I should say."

"Skip that word where the paper breaks. Don't need it anyway."

"I'll remember that when it comes to your epitaph," Abner said.

Moses chuckled. Quiet passed. "I deserve that." Moses wiped his nose on a sleeve. "Crime of passion, is what they'd call that shot-through hole." He looked at Abner. "I'm sorry I done it.

That anger run away with me."

"On the contrary. I found humor in it."

"There's another thing. Should've thanked you for pennin' that letter to Miss Isabella. I appreciate what you done for me."

In the village of Las Vegas General Kearny addressed the *alcalde* and the villagers from a rooftop that overlooked the plaza where the villagers had gathered. A mile away at the dragoon camp Moses saddled his remount, a black gelding with white forelegs, knee to hoof, that would place him in the vanguard with the first squadron. He charged the flash pan of his horse pistol and capped his carbine, buckled on his saber, and looked toward Las Vegas for the general and his staff to ride back, saw the sun lift, and waited for the bugles. He felt tighter than a banjo string, too nervous for weariness after the all-night ride.

When the general descended the ladder, the villagers knew they were under control of the United States and were no longer subjects of Mexico. They did not know whether to smile or frown over these words from the man the Indians of the plains knew as Horse Chief of the Long Knives, but they knew force ruled. The village reckoned the dust that lifted east rose from a buffalo herd until a runner told of the white man's army, how it stretched to the sun with its horse soldiers, walks-a-lot musket men, canvas-backed wagons, guns on wheels, horse and mule herd, its cattle massed like migrating buffalo.

The general and his staff trotted into camp, and moments later the bugles sounded "to horse." Troopers mounted and unfurled guidons. Horses perked up, snorted, shed the weariness they'd carried since the Cimarron Cutoff, eager to move as they pushed against their bits. The squadrons of horse assembled by color—first squadron, black horses; second squadron, white horses; third squadron, sorrel horses; about two hundred geldings to a squadron. General Kearny rode to the head of the column, and his bugler sounded "forward—march."

They started at a walk, then trotted toward a gorge in the mountains a few miles off. Mexican regulars were reported to be there, equal in number to the dragoons, barricaded where the canyon narrowed, muskets and artillery pieces trained on the trail, their horses safe at the rear.

Moses drew his saber, felt the stockinged horse lean to the bit, tense as a kettle breaking boil. At a mile from the fortification the bugle blew, and they charged. The black stockinged-horse took the bit, ran through the black horses ahead of him, the stockinged forelegs spinning white. The earth moved with the pound of hooves, rumbled like a flood crushing a village when they entered the gorge. Moses wondered if the canyon would stand.

Moses checked the reins, and the horse responded like a boulder rolling on a fall-away grade.

Moses tasted salt when he placed the reins in his teeth to sheathe the saber at a gallop while the horse closed to musket distance. With the blade in the scabbard and both hands free he jerked and seesawed the bit but could not slow his horse. He expected a cannon to cut him in half or sever the stockinged legs and vault him beneath hooves that thundered.

Abner's words returned: Fear is the province of imagination. Fear has no hold when you live in the moment.

Moses yelled, gave the horse its head, encouraged him with his spurs, and outran the vanguard. If lead whizzed overhead he could not hear it over the charging horse hooves. He saw no smoke from gun muzzles, pictured Mexican regulars hunched behind their barricade with bayoneted muskets waiting with the patience of snakes for their prey to approach. His horse ran on, and Moses thought he would collide with the log wall. At a length away his runaway jumped, cleared the wall, and galloped when it landed.

Moses was the first one over. He saw no soldiers, no muskets or cannon or caissons. His horse ran, and the hooves that pounded behind him softened. His winded horse sounded like a locomotive with a flutter in its smokestack. The stockinged horse answered the bit and slowed. His sweat-wet neck, shoulders, head, and barrel lathered and dripped. Moses felt the runaway's energy drain, wondered if he'd taken a ball in the chest. He leaned and saw no sweat running red, saw no froth from lung blood. He slowed to a trot, then a walk, turned, and rode to the others who'd jumped the barricade. His horse's ribs heaved as if he still stampeded.

The breastwork stood abandoned. The dragoons milled, stopped, or walked their horses to let them cool. A company took the abatis apart.

Private Donovan said, "You're a crazy son of a bitch."

"Not me." Moses nodded to the stockinged horse. "Him."

"Takes one to ride one," Donovan said.

Private Smithwick said, "I'll ride behind you anytime."

Donovan emptied his flash pan. "Them Mexicans love to run." He holstered the horse pistol. "Full of bluff and thunder."

"All bib and tucker," Smithwick said. He sheathed his saber. "All parade and get-up, flags, and epaulets." He uncapped his carbine.

"Terrible far to come to not shoot no one," Donovan said.

Abner wove through winded horses and hailed his messmates. "Ah, the tender embrace of Lady Fortune!" He pulled up his horse when he joined the recruits he'd schooled. "*Compadres* in arms, unscathed on a stage set for carnage." He looked at Moses. "Exemplary horsemanship, Private Cole, given the circumstances, dismayed as I was that you had no weapon ready."

"Ole Smokestack here was gun enough." Moses petted the

horse's neck, then wiped his hand on a pant leg to dry it. "Plumb deadly if he had a handle on him."

"Deadly to you, no doubt. You offered an enticing target."

"That or fall off, and I did not want stomped on."

"Either way," Abner said, "had the Mexicans been here we would not have found enough of you to bury."

Donovan waved as if to brush a fly away. "No grit or grind to the Mexican army. Shit and git like a goosed gander."

Abner said, "So refreshing, the buoyant talk of bravado." He noted the geography, its funnel to the Mexican breastwork.

Donovan said, "Backbone limber as willow."

Abner looked at him. "May they remain so."

A scout reported that the Mexicans had left for Apache Canyon, the gateway to Santa Fe on the Santa Fe Trail, no wider than a wagon boxed in by walls of rock. "Way worse than this," the scout said. "Next to Apache Pass we have a valley here. There, we're fish in a ditch for kids to kill with clubs." He shook his head. "The Mexicans didn't run. They refortified."

A bugle blew, and Vegas Gorge resounded the call. The dragoons furled their guidons. Moses tightened his cinch, remounted, and nudged the stockinged horse, but the horse didn't move. Moses said, "Where'd them wings go? Shucked or stuffed somewhere, feels to me."

"Pegasus molted," Abner said.

Moses nudged him again, and the stockinged horse stepped as if he moved through mud. Moses said, "From wind weight to heavy as a bank safe. Wore out from his runaway." Moses turned his spurs to the horse's belly, and the stockinged horse stepped out to fall in with the other black geldings.

They rode up the gorge and into cedar and piñon and long-leafed pine, a cut-away country with crevices and crags, rifts riven from water runoff, outcropped rock, and boulders cast from a furious earth. Like a shot-up body, Moses thought. Fear snuck up, squeezed out the exhilaration of the charge. That could have been it. No more heartache. No chance to set things right.

Abner said, "Mind, my lads. A whaleman would say we resemble a whaler heaved on a heavy sea, uncertain if we are the hunter or the hunted on the unseen deep." His eyes moved through the fractured land.

They rode on in the habit of endurance, step by step like a hand travels a clock.

Miles passed.

Abner said, "We seek Eden."

"Hear that?" Moses said to Donovan who rode ahead of him. "He's off and gone again, runnin' a trail a bloodhound can't track."

Donovan turned and said, "Disturbin' the peace is what he's doin'."

"California, gentlemen. Reputed to be the envy of Eden. Perchance a veritable Eden itself."

"Throwin' them words to pupil us," Moses said.

"Hand me the cotton," Donovan said. "Don't need to hear it."

"It was Socrates I endeavored to emulate and turned to John Barleycorn for tutelage, which . . ."

To Moses Cole, it looked like Abner Black drifted with the dust that moved with the dragoons marching to Apache Canyon.

"Gets my attention and leaves me to dangle," Donovan said.

"Which what?" Moses said.

"Which led to a change in occupation."

A mile passed. The dust hovered.

Abner said, "The day came when I reconnoitered my situation and found it lacking. John Barleycorn knows the heart as the gateway to the soul, and he had conquered my heart."

"Seen that," Moses said.

"I'd become forlorn and broken and well versed in my shortcomings, resigned to a lack of hope or useful enterprise, which led to a stint with religion, which I relinquished as a refuge of the defeated."

"Done that right," Moses said.

"Which restored me to John Barleycorn, yet I retained sense enough to join the army before sobriety reclaimed its tenuous grip. Once enlisted, I discovered the army becomes me, wherein I am judged by my ability to do as others command, for which I am eminently qualified."

A gust of wind shoved the dust away from the mile-long column of dragoons.

"John Barleycorn," Moses said. "Him and pa was business partners."

"Which explains your father's inconstant temperament."

"Partly." After his mother died his pa took in anger and nurtured it like he would the runt of the litter. He'd simmer it until it boiled over, like water to scald hogs fueled with too much wood. Moses figured. His brother would have been ten years old. Big enough to pick the chicken eggs, clean the coop, ring the necks of stewing hens. They would have been a family, at home in the harmony of farm life. His neglect had changed that. Drowned his mother. Denied life to the brother who never drew breath. Turned his father mean. All from a lapse at a gate latch. He lost what he loved then, family and farm and, later on, the mending Miss Isabella brought to stitch his split heart. Something in him crumbled from events born of his own hand. He pictured paper torn from the Virginia *Herald*, soiled and dropped in the privy pit. He thought leaving home, and the luck of the wayfaring runaway—joining the Dragoons and their march to the war with Mexico—would settle his unquiet mind, but it merely muffled it. If the Mexican regulars had manned their works, they'd have sent him to Hell. That might pay his bail, so to say, but it would not make things right.

"You've escaped your father's darkness, my young private. And now it's Eden we seek, and the prospects that California holds to be its home."

Moses thought, *I run and hid. I ain't escaped.* He said, "If Eve's there with her fig leaves, we'll know it sure." A ball at the barricade would have given him that escape. *Deader than catfish strung from an oak branch,* he thought. *How would that be, Lily Liver? Another phase of your runaway. Face it, Mama would say. Claim what's yours. Fix it or lose it. The farm, your pa, Miss Isabella—all gone if you don't go back. Seal the pieces one to another, and stand your ground, she'd preach.*

"Should we find a maiden in fig leaves, let us hope she holds an apple in hand."

"You are a curious fit for a dragoon," Moses said. *Me and him makes two. Both of us, here to patch over problems. I got an end in sight. Get growed up. Go home and stake my place. But Abner? There's something to puzzle over.*

"En route to California we shall pass through Santa Fe, whose reputation travels with the freighters. I portend that a lesson awaits you there, my young private."

"If it's lessons I wanted I'd have found me a school."

"The school found you. Here's the lesson of the moment— the easiest fruit to pick is that which has fallen."

Moses shook his head, tipped his cap to shield his eyes from the wind-driven grit.

Three days lay between them and Santa Fe with the gateway at Apache Pass.

Two days later the *alcalde* of a local village, fat as a slaughter hog, told them the Mexican troops had gone to hell, and Apache Canyon was clear. The mule sagged under the *alcalde*'s weight and the lope from the village to deliver the news. The messenger's belly moved when he laughed in telling of the vacated canyon.

General Kearny muttered, "Captain Cooke was successful."

"Sir?"

"A word with you, Major." They moved away from the dragoons. "While you rode with your escort to meet us here, I sent Captain Cooke and James Magoffin under a flag of truce to meet with Governor Armijo in Santa Fe."

"Magoffin, sir?"

"A well-known and charismatic merchant based in Bent's Fort, whom the New Mexicans affectionately call Don Santiago. They like and trust him."

"A secret envoy," the major said.

"To negotiate a sensible resolution and, if need be, a draft on the U.S. Treasury to sweeten the deal."

"Of course," the major said. "The diplomatic purse."

General Kearny smiled. "Magoffin's wife is a cousin to Governor Armijo. They would have been well received."

"Evidently with good result," the major said.

"The men must not know they were out-maneuvered by a governor's greed," Kearny said. "They're too green to appreciate what that saved them."

Back in the ranks Abner said to Moses, "Remember, my young private, what I told you, some time ago, about the hole in your body of knowledge?"

CHAPTER 7

*. . . the damndest Pilate in the world could not help saying I
find no fault in this people. On the contrary, to see them as I
have seen them, honest and pure hearted, guiltless seemingly of
evil thoughts . . . to think that any as innocent, should . . . be
beaten, robbed, ravished and murdered, and driven from post to
pillar and pillar to post, till the solicitudes of the wilderness
where famine howls like the prairie wolves round their miserable
shelters, seem to them a blessed refuge.*

—Thomas Kane,
non-Mormon who espoused the Mormon cause,
July, 1846

Mormon Battalion, Mound City, Missouri, late July 1846
"I hoped, nay prayed, to never see Missouri again," Orson
Everett said. He lifted an eyebrow, thick as a barber's moustache.
"But sure enough, as the Lord willed it, for some inscrutable
purpose, here I am." Orson Everett walked with Phineas Lynch
and Gabriel Hanks in the newly recruited Mormon Battalion.
They'd left Council Bluffs some days ago and now marched
through the northwest edge of Missouri. He lifted the other
eyebrow. "Inaccessible to the mind of man, is the way of the
Lord." The eyebrows settled back down.

"It's simpler than that," Gabriel said. "Missouri is on the way
to Fort Leavenworth, and Fort Leavenworth is where the guns
are."

"Rest time, boys," Orson said. They stepped away and sat

down. Orson pulled his shoes off, massaged his feet, watched the brethren pass. No rank and file marched in formation. No uniforms or weapons. Five hundred volunteer soldiers, age fourteen to sixty-eight. Most carried their baggage in haversacks, or bundled with a rope and slung over a shoulder, or tied in a bag that swung from a stick. Some had none at all. Some had enough to pack in wagons.

"If we don't go to Fort Leavenworth," Gabriel said, "we don't get muskets. And if we don't get muskets, we don't be soldier men."

The march included thirty women or so, enough children for two or three school rooms, and assorted camp followers. A few rode horses or mules, some saddled and others barebacked. A smattering of wagons carried families and those blessed with better fortune. Barefoot boys drove cattle on the outskirts of the marchers. All told, maybe six hundred people. More the migration of a lost tribe of Zion, Orson thought, than a march of an army.

The Missouri River lay to their right, bended near the foot of the bluffs, unhidden by trees or distance. Across the Missouri, a party of Omahas watched the wagons and livestock and mass of people pass. Orson looked left where the tallgrass prairie—its big bluestem and Indian grass, coneflowers, and prairie rosinweed—bent and stood again as wind pushed through it. Wooded ravines marked where water courses lay.

Orson said, "It's Missourians I can't stand. Bad memories bring bad habits back." Haun's Mill held the weight boulders hold in his remembering, the son and wife he lost there, the breakage it brought. He snickered. Missouri courtesy, murder by militia.

"A man your age should know better," Gabriel said. He brushed mosquitoes away.

"Your bad habits you have passed away," Phineas said. "The

gift of healing you have to minister unto us."

"Told how to behave by boys," Orson said. He was an elder of the Latter-day Saints and needed to lead like one. He put on a painless face. "How did I go so wrong?"

"Phineas Lynch, you ain't old enough for whiskers, so I don't know what that mess on your face means to be," Gabriel said. He reached out and touched Phineas's thin beard, then wiped his hand on his pants. "Looks like a tree shed of its leaves, took and drug through a busted gut."

"Not once have I shaved since the whiskers started. To die an old man with my first whiskers I intend," Phineas said.

"When old enough a woman to mate, a change your mind will take," Gabriel said. "How many times do I have to tell you, Phineas? Straighten your language. You're not an immigrant."

"Easy now. Don't waste your energy," Orson said. He wondered how his son would have bantered with these boys.

"This air's so heavy and wet," Gabriel Hanks said, "a man could lean agin' it and nap a little, not tip over."

"Get your mind off of it," Orson said. He sucked a breath when the image gripped—the well at Haun's Mill with the pitched-in dead.

"Brother Orson, pale you turned," Phineas said.

Orson shoved the memory away. "It won't help to talk about it."

"Might suffocate or drown midstride. Have a gander here," Gabriel said. He pulled his shirt away from his belly. "Wet as a dish rag. Don't know if the wet's from within me or from without me."

"Don't matter. It ends up the same," Phineas said.

"That's it," Gabriel said. "Nice and straight."

The battalion marched through farm country with farmsteads and fields of corn and oats.

Gabriel reached over and touched Orson Everett's shirt.

"Nothin' gets through that shirt, not wet nor wind nor weather itself." He wiped his finger on his pants, then looked at what he'd done. "Why'd I do that? Now I have grease on my britches." He laughed when Orson shoved him.

The battalion stopped late afternoon to camp for the night. They broke into messes, small groups to build campfires and to cook. Those with riding stock or draught animals took them to water in a nearby creek.

Orson set the pot in the fire and stirred beans in the water. Ashes lifted with the heat, settled in the soup, and simmered there.

Gabriel watched the coals glow. Voices drifted from mess mates gathered at other fires. A cow called from a distant field. A smell of burned biscuits drifted by. He said, "Elder Everett, say again why you joined this marchin' army? You'd have ruther turned Baptist than sign on as Uncle Sam's man, the way you talked to them sign-up soldiers."

Orson said, "Service to the church. Without a family, it is what I have." He shifted the pot. *Get your mind off it,* he thought. "As Brother Brigham commands, so I do, in spite of my personal preference."

Gabriel looked back to the embers, watched a boil break surface. "You, Phineas? What about your turnabout?"

"To the West we go anyway. Money and a gun I get with the army, the church for to help. Said Brother Brigham also."

Orson looked at the meager bean soup and the thin boys. He stirred in three spoonsful of flour.

"Your why-for you tell, Brother Gabriel," Phineas said.

"Them fancy-dance horses. Them uniforms." Gabriel shook his head. "My heart hitched on the second it seen it."

"The wisdom of fifteen," Orson said. "Oh, to be a boy again."

"I want a shined-up horse and a hat with a badge. Can't help it. God made me that way."

"You are an incurable romantic," Orson said. He stirred the beans. They had no salt or sugar. "We could stand more nourishment than this." He stood and handed the stir stick to Phineas. "Missourians owe us that."

Orson walked to a farm a few fields away and found a brindle milch cow untended, grazing in a pasture while the farmer was at supper. He drove her back to the battalion and his mess mates, using a staff broken from a tree branch to direct her with a poke or prod or a lift of it. He borrowed a rope and water bucket from a teamster, fashioned a halter, and tied her to a wagon wheel. He milked her, stripping the milk from the teats by squeezing his fingers in sequence, top to bottom, relieving the pressure from the cow's udder, feeling the udder relax as the milk drained. He skimmed the cream and gave it to his messmates, then walked among the nearby campfires pouring milk in cups. When he poured the last of it he led the cow to a stream for her to drink, washed the bucket, tethered the cow to graze for the night, and returned the bucket to the teamster. He did this for the next six days on the march through Missouri to Fort Leavenworth. She traveled with the beef cattle the drovers herded for a food supply. He retrieved her each morning and evening, milked her, and gave the milk away, starting with his mess mates.

They ferried across the Missouri River and marched to Fort Leavenworth. Wall tents in rows marked the edge of a drill field. Herds of horses and mules grazed the nearby fields, watched by mounted soldiers. The fort, an unbarricaded campus of brick and canvas, served as post to U.S. Regulars. Four hundred Missourians, volunteer cavalry recruited to fight in Mexico, bivouacked there. The Missourians gathered to watch the Mormon Battalion march by.

A Missouri volunteer stepped toward them, jug in one hand and hatchet in another. He spoke loudly, as if to carry over noise in a boisterous tavern.

"Your prophet, that Joe Smith fella, would be with your wives if they hadn't 'a shot him." The Missourian laughed and lifted the jug. "If they hadn't 'a shot him we'd 'a hung him, soon as he set foot in Missouri." He staggered a step and sipped from the jug. "You ought to thank us for keepin' your women pure." He laughed again and waved the hatchet.

Gabriel Hanks turned from the battalion to walk to the man with the hatchet, and Orson grabbed him and pulled him back.

"Ignore them," Orson said. *They have guns,* he thought. *We don't. Not yet.*

"Ignore them always," Phineas said. "In your mind and your heart keep the words of Brigham Young. Christian virtue you will live, he told us. The card playing and swearing you will not do, he told us. Words with Missourians you will not have, he told us also. Our purpose you must remember."

The battalion bunched closer as they marched by the Missouri bivouac.

"That don't sound like Brigham to me," Gabriel said. "That sounds like you, takin' plain talk and tippin' it backward. Why can't you say it straight?"

"My mother the English she barely spoke," Phineas said. "Prussian she was. Married an Irish miner, who died when a baby I was. We lived away on the farm, and speaking I learned from her."

A Missourian shouted. "If it ain't the tribe of Israel! You all make sheepherders look rich!"

"Ignore it," Orson said. Leave vengeance to the Lord. He wondered if he himself were man enough to do that.

"In case you haven't figured it out," Gabriel said, "your ma got the front to the back and the back to the front, so whenever you think to say somethin', turn it inside out and then say it. Maybe it'll come out a little better."

"I see the words in my mind, but out they come different."

"No, no. Start over," Gabriel said. "Repeat after me. 'They come out different.' Go on. Say it."

"They come out different."

"Very good. Keep it up."

"That's enough, Gabriel," Orson said. "Say any more and I'll mention your teeth."

"Say my piano keys, I'll say that grease rag you live in. Next to you, skunk guts smell tasty."

Orson grabbed Gabriel by the front of his shirt and jerked him close, face to face. "Take a deep whiff, so you don't forget how bad it can get." He held Gabriel in front of him, marching with the battalion without missing a step, Gabriel's shirt gripped in his fist. Gabriel scrambled backward to keep from falling, feet pedaling, torso stable in Orson's hand. "Respect your elders. Control your tongue."

"Sorry, Brother Mr. Everett. When I'm bothered, I say what wants out, and Missourians bother me a little."

"They bother all of us. Get a hold of it, or it will get a hold of you." Orson released him.

"Get a hold of it you must," Phineas said.

Gabriel looked at Phineas.

"You—must—get—a hold of it," Phineas said.

With tents not yet issued to them, the battalion camped in the open air, divided in messes of six men who cooked and ate together. While Orson's mess cooked, Orson sorted the milch cow from the beef cattle as he had each evening since freeing her from the bondage of a Missourian, he'd say, to allow her to serve the Lord. Only this time, instead of driving her to the wagon to hitch her and use the teamster's bucket for a milk pail, he drove her to the stable at Fort Leavenworth a mile away. He borrowed a water bucket at the stable, milked the cow, sold the milk, and sold her, then bought a side of bacon and two gallons of whisky from a sutler. He stuck the bacon in the band of his pants, under his shirt, and carried a jug in each hand, nipping first from one and then the other as if to compare the two while he walked, then wandered, toward the Mormon Battalion. Pretty soon he started to yell. It turned dark, and he navigated to the firelight.

When he woke, the sun was up. He lay at a mess site with the bacon slab for a pillow. An English convert knelt at his side and pushed him awake. The jugs were gone.

"Rise up, chap," the man said. "You must find your mess. We will be issued muskets today."

Orson's eyes glowed like coals in a cook fire.

"You were rather loud last night. Shouting, I should say, about Missourians."

Orson rolled over and lifted himself to his hands and knees.

"You wanted to kill them, sir. We had to restrain you from wandering to their camp, not that you'd have found it."

Orson threw up until he retched dry heaves.

The Englishman stood and stepped back. "You were rather drunk."

Orson spit, wiped his mouth on his shirtsleeve, put his hand back on the ground, and closed his eyes to his vomit. When his stomach stopped twisting he sat back on his calves, then sat on the ground, pulled his knees up, and clasped a wrist with a hand in front of his shins.

"You were quite vocal about spilt blood."

Orson blew his nose on his shirttail.

"A bit much, I would say, with cries to kill them, to redeem them of their sins against us Saints."

"I apologize."

"A tad enthusiastic, perhaps to avenge with blood the dead of Haun's Mill."

"I have bad memories of Missouri."

The Englishman looked away, saw the messes gathered in their camps, some at wagons, some with canvas shelters, most on open ground with a few blankets scattered about. Cattle and mules moved in the distance guided by herders, searching for feed in the grazed-off prairie. He looked back at Orson. "You informed us last night. I am most sorry."

"I have my challenges," Orson said. "On occasion, I have resorted to whisky to solve them, but it never has. I had not done so in a very long time."

"Remember the word, as spoken through the prophet Joseph Smith. Act in faith, and you will not be forsaken."

"My head feels split by an axe."

The Englishman left and returned with a water bucket and ladle. Orson dipped the ladle and drank, refilled it and drank again. He picked up his slab of bacon, turned it in his hands, felt the grease in his hair and on his face. He unsheathed a knife, scraped dirt and hair from the bacon, cut off a quarter, and gave it to the Englishman. "I apologize for the trouble I caused you. I'd give you the whole slab, but my mess mates will be wondering where their milk is."

"Pardon, sir?"

Orson waved a hand and stood up. "I feel inside out."

The Englishman brought Orson's jugs from a nearby wagon. Each was a quarter empty. He lifted them to Orson. "Your libations."

Orson filled the ladle, half water and half whisky, gulped it down and filled it half and half again.

"As a brother I must tell you," the Englishman said, "be the person God means you to be."

Orson drank off the ladle, replaced it in the water bucket, handed the jugs to the Englishman, and said, "I won't need these anymore."

"Mind yourself, good fellow. And for goodness sake, get cleaned up. You are a better man than your appearance would indicate." The Englishman shook his head. "That shirt." He shook his head a bit longer. "I'd use it to wrap fish, my good fellow, and then I'd throw the fish away."

Orson nodded and left to join his mess mates.

Orson picked up the pan the boys had used that morning to fry mush and placed the bacon in it. Gabriel eyeballed him. "One thing worse than a Missourian, ma taught, is a drunked-up Latter-day Saint."

Orson swayed, tipped the pan. The bacon fell in the cook fire. Phineas grabbed it, took the pan from Orson, and dropped the bacon in it. He shook his hand, blew on his fingers, looked Orson over. "The red of your eyes. The smell of a gin mill." Phineas placed the pan on the cook fire, drew his sheath knife, sliced the bacon in the pan.

"You look like shit from an ox," Gabriel said. "Smell worse."

Orson sat down, butt on the ground, wrapped his arms around his knees. After a while he said, "You are among God's chosen, among whom I do not number myself." He looked at Gabriel. "Don't swear like a gentile."

"The gift of the Lord you have, Brother Mr. Everett, for healing the brethren. Use the gift you must."

"Phineas," Gabriel said.

Phineas moved his lips, turned the bacon. "You—must—use the gift."

"You boys are younger than my son would have been." Orson Everett watched the bacon sizzle and brown. "I traded the cow for whisky and bacon. She did well to make it this far."

"Weren't much to her. Bones mostly," Gabriel said. "Surprised they give that much."

"The bacon is for you. The whisky was for me."

81

Phineas stuck a slice with his knife and held it to Orson, who waved it away.

"I could not be there for my son, so I swore I'd be there for you." He looked them in the eye, each in turn. "I failed my pledge when I gave in to temptation. I ask your forgiveness."

"Brother Orson Everett," Phineas said. "Forgiveness we give you. Respect you must earn."

CHAPTER 8

*. . . our horse was sick last night but they laid hands on him
and he is beter [sic] to day [sic] . . .*

—*Patty Bartlett Sessions,*
Mormon emigrant, 1846

*For the Church to . . . send 500 of her members, to bear priva-
tions, and encounter danger, in the service of this government,
is, I acknowledge, beyond my comprehension . . . you tell me
that your Battalion is the army of Israel, and I trust it is and
also that you are the Servants of God. Well is it not strange to
see an army of Christians sent out Voluntarily with muskets and
bayonets . . .*

—*Margrett L. Scott*
to her brother, J. Allen Scott,
August 30, 1846

*Mormon Battalion, Santa Fe Trail, West of Fort Leavenworth
[Kansas], August 1846*
Captain Allen, who had recruited the Saints and had been
promoted to be their lieutenant colonel, proved true to his word.
The Mormons received their clothing allowance, were placed
on the payroll, and left Fort Leavenworth with muskets but
without Lieutenant Colonel Allen, who remained at Fort Leavenworth confined to a sick bed. Until he returned, Captain
Jefferson Hunt, a Mormon volunteer, would serve as acting

commander.

The battalion marched with nine-and-a-half-pound smooth-bore flintlocks, each as heavy as a baby. "Stand back, boys," Lieutenant Colonel Allen had advised when the men had pressed in to receive their arms. "Don't be in a hurry to get your muskets. You will want to throw the damned things away before you get to California."

A few carried the Mississippi rifle, the newer caplock Yager. They wore the infantry baldrics—the shoulder belts, diagonal shoulder to hip, white and wide, crossed at center chest and held in place by a medallion stamped with an eagle.

"Don't you look like a soldier man, crossed up shiny-like," Gabriel said. "Phineas Lynch, Uncle Sam's private, eye popper to the women folk. You watch, they'll drop their laundry to watch you walk."

"Bright as your teeth, the leather is," Phineas said.

"See that there?" Gabriel tapped the eagle shield at the center of Phineas's chest. "You know what they call that? A target." He laughed.

The cross belts carried a cartridge box and bayonet—the cartridge box with thirty-two paper cartridges for two pounds of lead; the bayonet and scabbard added another pound. A belt, buckled with a U.S. oval, matched the baldrics and held them close to the body.

"White-leather men and bay-o-nets. Dogs will stop and bark. Make sure everyone sees us."

Orson chuckled. "Who will see us, Gabriel? Buffalo and buzzards maybe."

"Half parade man and half tramp. This army can't decide what we are," Gabriel said.

Each carried a knapsack and blanket, haversack, and three-pint canteen. Most had no change of clothing. All told, the musket and accoutrements and personal effects gave each man forty pounds, more or less, to carry to the Pacific Ocean.

"Like packin' a half sack of spuds," Gabriel said when he lifted his pack, "with Mama's cast-iron pan throw'd on top."

Wagons took mess kits and tents, food and more ammunition, baggage and other supplies. They also carried the women and children and men too ill to walk.

The battalion traveled the Santa Fe Trail to the Cimarron Cutoff through grasslands as big as sky, grazed to the dirt from emigrant and trader trains and picked clean of wood, marching to the horizon that steadily stretched away. They cooked with buffalo chips, a fuel that proved true to its nature when burned, its smell the pinch of ruminant manure that gave its puckered flavor to the meat and dough they'd roast on sticks.

When it rained, the battalion marched in gumbo, pushed and pulled wagons through it, slipped and fell with muskets, jammed locks and muzzles in mud. When the battalion camped in the rain, water ran under the tents and dripped through the canvas. They spent nights in wet blankets and days in wet clothes. When the wind blew, it ripped up tents and tore off wagon covers. When it raged, it tipped a wagon over, pushed a buckboard away with a woman in it, and ran off their animals.

When it turned hot, the plains hardened and baked.

"Elder Orson, remind me why we hike along to the country of California," Gabriel said. "What's there that's not here?"

"A Mexican garrison, with enemy troops and no counter force of United States infantry. From what I've heard, anyway."

They'd stopped in the heat of the day, to "noon a little," Gabriel said. Phineas fried strips of deer liver on an iron tire while the team searched for grass nearby. Gabriel propped his musket in the wagon spokes and said, "Touch that barrel, you'll brand yourself a little. Hot as old man sun hisself." He crawled under a wagon to nap in its shade. "Like a kid at a candy counter and a nickel to his name, this country can't make up its mind." He tossed a buffalo chip from under the wagon. "One day we need Noah's boat. The next day, a camel caravan." He tossed out another buffalo chip, pulled his hat over his eyes, and folded his hands on his stomach. "A man's gotta be half frog, half jack rabbit, just to navigate this country." His hand shot out to wave a bee from an ear.

The water they found lay in holes miles apart, fouled from bands of buffalo that stopped to stand in them and swish flies with their tails. The water, stagnant catch basins for rain, carried the stench of pond-bottom mud stirred by buffalo hooves and suspended as sediment, mixed with manure and urine. The men drank from these ponds, strained water through their teeth, and came to be grateful for it.

With the weather and the work, the wet and cold and hot and dry and the water they drank, stomach cramps and diarrhea became commonplace, coughs and nausea and fevers and chills. Some complained of guts seized-up yet accepted no medicine due to religious principles, believed instead in healing through the laying on of hands.

"Religion be damned," the army physician said. "Do you expect to get well if you do nothing?" He fed his medicine with a rusty spoon. They buried one of the doctor's patients, not long after the doctor fed him the medicine that he'd crawled off in the sagebrush to avoid. They buried him by torchlight, on the bank of the Arkansas River, in a grave that seeped river water.

Lieutenant A. J. Smith, a graduate of the academy at West Point and an officer of the First Dragoons, had recently arrived from Fort Leavenworth with word of Lieutenant Colonel Allen's death. He would assume command of the Mormon Battalion, but he was aware that the issue had been contested.

The volunteer officers had parleyed in the shade of elm trees after Smith joined the battalion at Council Grove. Jefferson

Hunt, appointed captain by Brigham Young when they enlisted, said, "We need supplies, and a West Point officer packs more say-so than we do as volunteers. He's been school-room taught in tactics and such and knows how to train-up troops."

"Walk and shoot," Captain Alcott said, also so appointed by Brigham Young. "Don't need an Academy man for that."

Captain Hunt went on, "Do we want to get paid? Do we want to send money to the church? Isn't that why we enlisted, or one of the reasons we did?"

Some of the officers nodded.

"He's our man, then. When it comes to getting the payroll paid, they'll listen to him before they'll listen to a volunteer who's a Latter-day Saint."

The elms stood still in the windless heat.

"Besides, he's traveled the Santa Fe Trail, which none of us have."

"Hang on there," Captain Alcott said. "We need to shepherd our own flock. As soldiers, we serve the government back there in Washington City," he jerked a thumb over his shoulder, "but as Saints we answer to our church. Besides, Colonel Allen promised Brother Brigham that if he couldn't command the battalion for one reason or some other, then Jefferson Hunt would. Now that Colonel Allen died on us, Brother Jefferson's the commanding officer. Said and done. Talk time's over." He stood up.

Captain Hunt's shirt stuck to his torso in the heavy heat. He said. "We serve a nation that has put its trust in God—"

"So they say," Captain Alcott said. "We haven't seen it."

Captain Hunt continued, "We're not commissioned officers, so if the matter is pressed, the ground we stand on is going to give." He pulled the shirt away from his skin when a breeze wove through the elm leaves. "I don't like it, but the prudent thing to do is to accept Lieutenant Smith as our commander."

"Prudent does not mean right," Captain Alcott said.

They parleyed on, and the majority voted to accept Lieutenant Smith as acting commander until they heard from higher authority.

Captain Alcott said, "The rank and file won't like this."

The sick man sat against a wagon wheel. Orson felt the man's forehead with the back of his hand, placed a damp cloth around the sick man's neck, and said, "This will help to cool you." Orson helped him stand and guided him into the back of a wagon that offered the shade of a hooded wagon bed. Orson helped to seat him on the wagon bed, supported by a sideboard with a blanket for a cushion. Half a dozen others sat in the wagon also, their legs to the center, backs to the sideboards, heads and shoulders braced by the wagon cover. Some moaned. All sweated. The open ends of the covered wagon would admit a breeze if one were about.

Orson stepped to the water keg next to the bullwhip that hung on the outside of the wagon box. He lifted the keg from its hanger, set it on the ground, and pulled the lid—a slice from an oak tree, chiseled and whittled to fit inside the rim—and half filled a water bucket. He replaced the lid and the water keg and carried the bucket into the back of the wagon. He dampened a cloth and sponged the sick man's forehead, prayed to the Lord to bless them with wellness and for the doctor to stay away with his bitters of bayberry bark. He moved to the next patient and sponged his head and neck and asked the Lord to heal these people.

He heard, "Get those men the hell out of there."

Orson looked to the back of the wagon and to Lieutenant Smith, First Dragoons, who stood there.

Lieutenant Smith said, "We cannot tax these draught animals with cargo that can walk. Remove those men."

The battalion had stopped to rest the draught animals, but the mules remained hitched.

"Lieutenant Smith," Orson said. "Welcome to the Mormon Battalion, sir." He dipped the cloth in the bucket, squeezed excess water from it, and continued to sponge the man's face. He wetted another, squeezed it, and placed it on top of the man's head.

"You will follow my order, soldier. Now."

"On my way, sir," Orson said. He worked his way out of the wagon from among the sick men propped against the sideboards. He stepped to the ground and stood between the lieutenant and the back of the wagon.

"Lieutenant Smith," Orson said. "I am Private Orson Everett, Mormon Battalion."

"Your station is clear. Your name I'll remember," Lieutenant Smith said. In this battalion of five hundred, only the First Dragoons, of which there were two—First Lieutenant Smith and Second Lieutenant Stoneman—wore uniforms. The Saints, including their appointed lieutenants and captains, and corporals and sergeants, wore their everyday clothing, discernible as soldiers only by muskets and accoutrements, not by tunics, regulation trousers, and forage caps.

Orson said, "My charge is to tend to the sick and the lame. These men, sir, have been placed in the wagon because they are too ill to walk. You will see other wagons loaded with the same."

"No one rides without my permission." Lieutenant Smith glared at Orson. He rested a hand on the hilt of his saber. "Empty the wagon."

"This is a personal wagon pulled by personal mules. This is not army property, and therefore, sir, not subject to your orders."

"The men are subject to my orders. Pull them out."

"Sir, they are too sick to walk."

"You dare defy me?"

"Leave them alone, Lieutenant."

Lieutenant Smith drew his saber. "Remove these people, or I'll cut you into pieces crows can carry."

"One moment, sir." Orson stepped to the side of the wagon, pulled the bullwhip from its hanger, and gripped it on the whip end of the handle, which, with its heft and weight, would serve as a cudgel. He returned to stand an arm's length from the lieutenant.

"They stay where they are, for their health, sir, and the strength of the battalion."

A man groaned in the wagon.

"If you pull these men out, sir, you may just as well have them shot."

"Are you aware that I can have *you* shot, Private, for insubordination?"

"Sir, I am commanded by my religion to care for my brethren. If these men do not get well, they will be of no use to you. We do not believe in your calomel and arsenic. We believe in faith healing, and we will heal these men. I will not leave a man sick on the ground, so long as I can help him."

A. J. Smith, a West Point lieutenant, glared at Private Orson Everett, Mormon volunteer.

Under his eyebrows, Orson's eyes held firm, cool as shaded granite.

Lieutenant Smith said, "We'll finish this at another time." He sheathed his saber and walked away.

Orson hung the bullwhip back on its hanger, climbed into the wagon, and said, as if to settle startled sheep, "Never mind him." He sponged their foreheads and necks, mindful to moisten but not wet the skin. "He's a young lieutenant and new to command and does not yet know how to lead."

"He's no Lieutenant Colonel Allen," one of the sick said, his voice faint.

Another rocked his head back and forth and groaned. Orson laid his hands on the man's head as if to steady it, closed his eyes, bowed his head and prayed, then dabbed his forehead and neck again.

When he'd tended to each he left for another wagon, stopped and returned, took the bullwhip, and went about his ministering.

Captains Hunt and Alcott told Orson Everett to make it right with Lieutenant Smith and gave him a bottle of whisky for the purpose. Orson studied it, held it at arm's length, felt a tremble begin. He hoped it didn't show. He moved to mask it, lowered his arm, bottle to his side, turned his head, feigned nonchalance, and willed a wall between him and the bottle he held.

That evening, Orson met with Lieutenant Smith and the officers, army and Mormon alike, in front of the lieutenant's tent. Orson Everett poured a dram in each of the cups that Captain Hunt brought for the purpose.

"To your health, Lieutenant," Orson Everett said and wanted to add, "To the health of the men" but thought it prudent not to do so.

He lifted his cup to Lieutenant Smith and the lieutenant lifted his, the officers lifted theirs, and they drank. Orson felt the familiar burn, a kindled craving for the wave of euphoria, a reborn yearning, as a lost lover seen on a street. He fought the rush to embrace it, the impulse to knock it back, repeated until the bottle was gone. When he drank, he prayed he would not taste the sugar of Satan. He needed someone's hand to cork the bottle and leave his cup empty. He asked the Lord to send that hand, to drink no more than the moment demanded.

"Thank you, gentlemen," Lieutenant Smith said. "Good evening."

They were dismissed with nothing said about the wagon and the whip. Orson handed the bottle back to Captain Hunt when they left the lieutenant's tent. He made himself push it away, commanded his muscles to extend his arm, overruled their impulse to pull and hug the bottle to his heart. He felt as if he had given a son away.

Busy myself, he thought, *or I'll tip over the edge.*

He returned to the sick and prayed when he laid on hands.

"Make these men well, Lord, so they may do the work of the Church. Heal them, so they may quell their desires, and forsake their sins and do as you command. Help us, your Camp of Israel, Lord, to right our ships and keep them righted. Lead us away from the sinner's way and sustain our faith. Amen."

He sponged faces and prayed and retired to his blanket in a fragment of moonlight. This is not a one-time challenge, he thought. Like drink to a drunk, one is never enough. He looked at the splinter of moon and the stars beyond it, considered the hint of order constellations implied, the points of reckoning stars suggested. *One good work, one flex of will is only one. One link does not a chain make. I am in this for the length of it.*

Chapter 9

. . . little did he know of the game of sighs and signs carried on between the young fellows and the fair inmates of his house. We had our gayest array of young men out to-day, and the women seemed to me to drop their usual subdued look and timid wave of the eyelash for good hearty twinkles and signs of unaffected and cordial welcome—signs supplying the place of conversation, as neither party could speak the language of the other. The little exchange of the artillery of eyes was amusing enough . . .

—Lieutenant William Emory,
Corps of Topographical Engineers, Army of the West,
New Mexico, September, 1846

Moses Cole, Santa Fe [New Mexico], mid-September 1846
Moses recollected the day he met Abner Black. He'd wandered into Carlisle Barracks—hungry, cold, rained on clean through, no direction but away from home. A soldier stood guard in the rain as if there were something to guard against. Moses wondered about the sight he presented, a skinny runaway, fitted in hand-me-downs his pa had worn out.

The guard he came to know was Private Abner Black, the first uniformed soldier Moses met.

"Long ago I took in a dog that had lost its way, not uncommon among those of us who incline to a sentimental heart," Abner told him later. "I nourished him to good fettle, and he bit me, so I employed my carbine for appropriate recourse. He sensed the malintent I directed his way, which I overcame with Kentucky windage and a proper lead. I accepted another lost dog to contend with guilt and found the same outcome. Any benevolence I coveted for strays I soon discarded, but something in your eye, a glint of your inner quest, perhaps, for what is good and true, told me you were the exception to the lesson, so I gave you a soft-hearted nod against judgment gleaned from experience and took you as my pupil."

Moses called him "Master Private" to honor his tenure in the dragoons and his refusal to accept leadership. Abner schooled him in the manual of arms, intricacies of horsemanship, how to endure a long march. He taught him what he needed to know when he needed to know it, and Abner thought it time Moses learned what a man and a woman do when the door is closed.

"What will you do," Abner asked him sometime in those first months at Carlisle Barracks, "on the night of the day you are united in wedlock?"

Moses considered. "Take your bull and your heifer and put 'em in a pen."

"You know what it means, then, to consummate a marriage?"

"Not put that way. Mount and ride, is what you're sayin'."

"Have you had that experience?"

"No, sir. Not with goat or sheep neither."

Abner shook his head. "To spare yourself embarrassment you require refinement, for which we need enjoin the proper teacher, which we won't find in the army."

"Just as well hammer a nail in a rock as pound a lesson in me. It don't go."

"Think of a horse in a field. The more holes in the field the more likely the horse is to step in one. The more he steps in, and the faster his speed, the greater the chance that he will be taken by injury."

"Where'd the weddin' bed go we was talkin' about?"

"You are the horse, my young private, and the field is your body of knowledge."

"Say again?"

"The field is what you know. The more holes you have in what you know, the more likely you are to stumble. Education fills the holes. Different holes require different teachers. This particular hole," Abner smiled, "won't be found in the army, but with vigilance the teacher will appear."

What appeared, two years later in Santa Fe, was Madame La Tules's tavern and brothel, amber lit with small windows of oiled rawhide. They sat on a sofa with straw-filled cushions upholstered in pillow ticking and surveyed the Mexican whores.

"A woman expects a man to know things," Abner said, "which is why the Lord gave us whorehouses." Abner winked at one of the women, who smiled back. "I'll give it to you in language you understand. Think of it as buying a horse. Pick the one you want to ride, and I'll make the purchase. And to celebrate the occasion I'll buy you a glass of that cactus extract they're so fond of, to work up your appetite, so to speak, like you're at a dinner party at the captain's quarters."

"Don't know nothin' about that."

At the back of the tavern a door opened to a hallway, dark lit with a window at the end, doors on both sides.

A fair-skinned redhead with rouge and lipstick and earrings that jingled walked up with the grace of a dancer and a wide smile. She grabbed each by the hand and said, "We are so grateful to have you soldiers here! Thank you for the honor of your visit. Please, tell me about yourselves."

Abner told her about Moses.

"I love it when it's their first time," Madame La Tules said to Abner. She looked at Moses, saw his eyes drop to her bared upper breasts flattered by the fit and cut of her gown, and pulled his head to her bosom, his nose in the skin of her cleavage.

"My dear boy, you are very welcome here." She petted the back of his head while Abner laughed. She let him up and held him at arm's length, a hand on each shoulder. "Look at you, red as a ripe tomato! My precious young man, I have just the hostess for you but, first, a drink on the house." She waved to a boy to bring two glasses of mescal, took each of them by the hand, and pulled them to sit with her on the sofa. She motioned for a young woman in an evening gown to sit by Moses. As the girl approached, Madame La Tules turned to Moses and said, quietly in his ear, "Don't be nervous. She knows what to do."

They talked, and, when his glass was empty, Abner stood and walked to where the women sat, took one by the hand, and they went down the hall and through a door.

Madam La Tules joined another customer. She told the bar boy to deliver drinks, draw well water, deliver a customer's horse to the livery. With the Army of the West in town business was brisk.

Moses stared at the liquid in his glass, spring-water clear with a burn like lighted lamp oil in spite of its watermelon and cantaloupe slices. The girl rubbed his inner thigh and talked in Spanish.

A scream came from a room down the hall, a sharp, quick cry from a woman, as if surprised by a knife in her side. Moses cringed, turned a shade pale, felt as if a cold hand had grabbed his heart.

Abner came out with the *senorita* he'd bedded, and they joined Moses on the sofa.

"You look like a dog with a belly rub," Moses said.

"Imagine that," Abner said. He smiled and ordered a round but Moses waved "no more" for him.

"Well?" Abner said.

Moses took the last sip of his drink and winced again at the burn. "Was gettin' my nerve up, that beddin' girl rubbin' on me real personal."

"The commencement begins," Abner said.

"Sir?"

"She commenced to abscond with your virginity."

"What?"

"Never mind. You're coming to it. Keep going."

"Rubbin' on me like that she had my attention, then here come a scream with hurt shot through it, and there that went. Took what appetite I'd built, like a squashed possum throwed on the supper table."

"What did the Madame do?"

"Never spooked, but I did."

Abner's hostess gripped her glass and recited three of her six words of English—"Handsome man, hello." She tipped the glass to her lips and set it down empty.

"Then what?" Abner said.

"Bought her a drink and sent her away. Made like I was gonna heave my dinner on her evenin' dress."

"Succumbed to a failure of nerve, I see."

Moses pushed his empty glass away. "All the good my mama taught me, or tried to anyway." Moses shook his head. "There I set, ready to trade it for a penny on the dollar."

"The lesson takes an unexpected twist," Abner said. "Go on."

"Like rollin' over a fox dead enough to stink. All fluff and fur on the up side, and bugs and worms on the under of it." Moses shuddered. "Give me the skin creeps."

"Commendable, my young private. Tempted, yet you retained your bearings, with, perhaps, the intercession of fate." Abner smiled. "You have a guardian angel who upset—or I should say, corrected—my design."

"That scream," Moses said. "Froze that heat she'd built in me."

"The world is full of whispers and screams, my young private, the sweet song of the meadowlark and thunder pounding the empty plains. Live long enough, travel far enough, and you will hear it all."

"No wonder you partnered with ole man Barleycorn. Couldn't figure your own riddles."

"You sorted the virtuous from the dissolute, which was not the intended lesson but one, perhaps, of more import."

"Life was laid out straight, then here you come to fix it." Moses looked at the light at the end of the hall, turned to Abner. "That's somethin' else you're good at. You give a look to life I didn't know it had. Educational, would be a way to say it."

"Clarissa Pembroke taught me well."

"Sir?"

"Never mind."

Abner motioned for the bar boy. "The world is a complicated place, my young private. Given our impending departure, bear this in mind—we're on a campaign, in a war, with a long way to go. We will both be lucky if things don't happen that we will wish had never happened. Worse yet, that we have a hand in making them happen, as men are wont to do."

"There you are again. When I see clouds, you see sunshine. You're so—What's that word you told me?" Moses searched his memory. "Sanguine."

"The budding cynic," Abner said, "Clarissa Pembroke would commend you."

The prostitute stared at her empty glass, said her other three words of English—"Much good, goodbye."

Moses said, "What happened back there, that scream down the whore hall?"

"Perhaps a patron succumbed to a carnal query, a crass

impulse of some sort, or possibly a girl new to the trade."

"Don't tell no more. Don't want to know it."

The bar boy refilled Abner's and the woman's glasses and left the jug on the table.

"No plow mule stuffed you in a furrow and buried you there. You seen the world, the pretty and the ugly of it. Might have give a hand to both, so there's another reason you're a good teacher."

"Perceptive. I chose my pupil well." Abner lifted his glass, tipped it to Moses and took a sip, set it on the table. "If you have a curiosity, address it. Remember the rattle, my young private. Never is death far away."

CHAPTER 10

. . . you stated that you had sent me twenty five dollars in money but as yet I have not received any for the day that I got your letter there was one came from B. Young from the other side of the river stating that their council was to keep the whole of the money that came from the Soldiers . . .

> —Eliza Hunsaker,
> in Council Bluffs,
> to her husband, Abraham Hunsaker,
> in the Mormon Battalion,
> August 24, 1846

This [Arkansas] River is a curiosity in creation. It appears to be a river of sand with now and then a drizzling of water breaking out and then loosing [sic] itself again immediately. Dig in the sand and find fish. Sometimes deep holes of water with large fish. I killed some with my sword. Some men killed very large ones, perhaps four or five pounds.

> —Levi Hancock,
> September 11, 1846

Mormon Battalion, Mid-September 1846, Cimarron Cutoff of the Santa Fe Trail [Kansas]

The poor boy, Abigail Alcott thought. Thin as a willow, and the officers eat. It's not fair, and they don't care. What would Zemira's mother say? The woebegone woman, too sick to make the trip so she entrusted him to me, her one and only, and I can't do better than this?

Abigail baked bread at the battalion's camp on the Arkansas River. It had been some time since she had enough firewood to build a cook fire adequate for the task. She had beans and ox meat and sometimes flour to feed her mess of six officers, but never enough of any of it.

The boy had to be hungry, she knew, though he would never admit it. She watched Lieutenant Smith, seated in her grandmother's Windsor rocker, relish the oven-fresh bread. Smith rocked in the Windsor. His saber, sheathed and buckled to his belt, rested on the edge of the chair. He leaned back, savored a bite, and the hilt of his saber settled between spindles that formed the rocker's back. The saber rubbed when the officer rocked and chewed his bread.

Abigail cocked her head at her husband.

"Lieutenant Smith," Captain Alcott said. He nodded to Lieutenant Smith's saber. "You're saber's rubbing the woodwork. That chair belonged to my wife's grandmother."

"Of course," Lieutenant Smith said. "I was so engrossed in this wonderful bread I took no notice of it. Please forgive me, madam."

Lieutenant Smith carefully repositioned his saber onto his lap. "My apologies, Mrs. Alcott. I'm so used to the old wristbreaker that I forget it's there."

"I should think that if you were so used to it, you would think of these things," Abigail said. She walked away from the mess of officers and returned to her laundry.

When the men had left, Abigail examined the marks the saber had left. The saber's pommel of cast brass had rubbed black paint from a spindle. Between spindles, where the hilt had wedged, impressions from the edges of the guard pressed paint into the wood. On the edge of the seat the iron scabbard had etched a wider mark.

Abigail lifted her hands to her face. Tears seeped between her fingers, rolled down the backs of her hands.

The chair carried a collection of nicks and marks, acquired over generations and ship and wagon trips. Captain Alcott felt the scratches, noted the color of the wood where paint had scraped away.

"And now we have those marks," Abigail said, "so we will always carry that horrid man."

Captain Alcott put his arm around her.

Abigail stepped away, her face flushed.

"How can you lick your fingers when served by a hungry child? Can't you see the boy in the orderly? Have you no sense of what a father must feel? For shame!"

Melissa Brown walked by with a basket of dishes to scour with sand in the Arkansas River. Captain Alcott waited for her to pass.

"Zemira is an orderly to Lieutenant Smith. You know that. Like it or not there are unwritten rules we have to follow to get along. One is to treat an officer's orderly no better than he does, at least when you're with the both of them. It's like petting another man's dog. The dog likes it better than the man does."

"Zemira is not a dog!"

A clatter of tin and a sharp word came from Melissa when she stumbled on a rock that her basket hid from view.

"Rules or not, written or unwritten, it's not right. He's a growing boy. How can you serve the Lord when you ignore his hunger?"

"Zemira's mother begged us to take him," Captain Alcott said. "Zemira begged us, too, so we brought him. An orderly to the acting commander is pretty good duty. Zemira will tell you that. Ask him if he wishes he would have stayed home. I know what he'll say."

"Even so, it's not right."

"We don't have much flour anyway. The bread won't last long."

"In that case, it should all go to Zemira."

"You're the cook, but the rations are army property. Be careful."

Twelve days later sunrise sounded like all the others with trumpets and drums and voices rousing livestock. The sounds of the animals marked their progress—the lowing of oxen and beef cattle, bleating of sheep, a neigh from a horse or bray from a mule, bells from milch cows and lead sheep, voices rising in pitch when animals turned contrary to the wishes of drovers.

Captain Alcott struck their tent, packed it in their wagon, sipped bean broth, and hitched the team. Orson Everett, Gabriel Hanks, and Phineas Lynch rolled their bedrolls, packed their knapsacks, retrieved their muskets from a stack of arms. They answered roll call, formed ranks, and began the march in cadence. Captain and Abigail Alcott followed in what Abigail called "the wagon parade."

They marched eighteen miles across a plain and through small hills and camped by mid-afternoon, close to Cold Springs with its water, trees, and firewood. Orson and the boys stacked arms, gathered wood, unrolled bedrolls. Captain Alcott unhitched his team, pitched the tent, fetched water.

Abigail kindled a cook fire with spruce and cottonwood, and when the flames grew she added cedar. She used as much as she dared and stowed the remainder in the wagon thinking of the prairie ahead. She filled the Dutch oven with the water Captain Alcott brought and hung the oven from a tripod of iron rods by hook and bail. The water heated while the fire chewed through its wood. She poured the water in the washtub and washed her spare dress and undergarments, then rinsed them in a pail of spring water. She made bread dough, kneaded it smooth, and covered it with a dish towel.

When she busied her hands her mind followed, kept it separate from the home she and Mr. Alcott left and its simple pleasures, its farmyard and spring water, sheep and goats, and her craft at the weaving loom. She accepted a mission of servitude when she joined the battalion as a laundress, with cooking and camp chores an unspoken part of it. Things would change when the baby came, more arduous yet full of love and purpose. She yearned for it, and when she was certain, she would tell Mr. Alcott. Soon. She felt it, solid as bone.

When the fire burned down to low glow she poured hot water in the washtub and placed the dough in the number-eight Dutch oven. She spread the coals with a hickory-handled spade, set the heavy kettle in a bed of embers, and chuckled. She shoved some embers up the sides of the pot, mounded the remainder on the lipped lid, and laughed.

"Where's the humor?" Melissa Brown asked. "Won't that be too much heat?"

"Probably."

"Won't you burn the bread?"

"A little." Abigail giggled.

Abigail scrubbed half a dozen pair of trousers on her washboard in her washtub, draped them over wagon wheels, pulled up the Dutch oven, and hung it from the tripod. She swept embers from the lid and lifted it with a nine-gauge wire bent to form a hook and handle. She loosened the loaf with a table knife, pinched it on opposite sides with a fork in each hand, pulled out the loaf, and set it on her cutting board with twigs beneath the bread to allow air flow. She tapped the blackened crust, smiled, and peeled a piece with a fingernail. The burn ran a quarter inch deep on the top and bottom. Only the sides showed a baker's brown.

"For Heaven's sake, I scorched it."

"Are you surprised?" Melissa said.

"Dear me, how could I have done such a thing?" Abigail's smile widened. "I'll have to trim it. It's not fit for officers, now is it?" She covered the loaf with the dish towel and put water, beans, and diced side-pork in the Dutch oven and set it in the dying fire.

While the beans cooked and the bread cooled, Abigail scrubbed four more pair of trousers, draped them over the wagon tongue, and returned to the bread to cut off marks of burning. She trimmed an inch deep to remove the quarter-inch char, collected the trimmings, put them in a dish towel, placed them in the wagon, and summoned her mess to supper. When she served the bread with the beans she apologized for the burn, explained that laundry distracted her, doing what she could while she had hot water. Trimmed up, however, it would be just fine.

When supper was done and the mess dispersed, she called Zemira and served him the scavenged bread. He ate it as he would an apple pie and licked his fingers.

Melissa chuckled and shook her head.

"Funny thing, what a Dutch oven does," Abigail said.

"What will the captain say?"

"Mr. Alcott may be taken up with captain matters, but he is a Saint and a husband before he is a soldier. If he is tested we will see that."

"I hope so," Melissa said.

Abigail shot her a look. "You doubt him?"

Melissa started, as a horse does from movement in a shadow, then said, "No. It's just that I've seen some of our soldiers waver from the faith, but he wouldn't do that. I'm sorry, Abigail. Like my husband says, my tongue fired before my brain cocked."

"Oh, Melissa, I mustn't snipe at you. You are my dearest friend."

"It's a hard life, and it wears on us," Melissa said. "I pray to God He won't quit us."

CHAPTER 11

The women are comely—remarkable for smallness of hands and feet: as usual in such states of society, they seem superior to the man; but nowhere else is chastity less valued or expected . . . The fiddlers accompanied their music at times by verses, sung in a high nasal key. I was surprised, but amused to hear one of our captains join in this—and he could waltz them all blind— but we got him from the navy.

—Captain Philip St. George Cooke,
First Dragoons, Army of the West, Santa Fe, 1846

Moses Cole, Santa Fe [New Mexico], September 23, 1846
Moses sat on a bench against the wall at the fandango and watched the *señorita* dance as if she were weightless, her dress like a ruffled rainbow that lifted and leveled when she spun, and he saw those legs, clear to the knee, and felt the stirring of arousal.

Abner sat next to him and sipped punch that tasted, Abner said, like cactus, tobacco, and melon mixed in a volcano. Abner pointed with his nose. "See those two over there?"

The two *compañeros* stood near the door, its panels of buffalo hide painted to resemble burled wood, and watched them. Clean, dressed in Spanish riding attire, faces one would place on scalp hunters.

"They're not here for their social graces. They're here so her daddy can relax."

The *patrón* joked with Madame La Tules and walked off laughing to join a group of *rancheros*. Guidons and company flags from the Army of the West decorated the walls and hid the chipped and cracked plaster. Bunting of red, white, and blue covered water stains at the tops of the walls.

The *señorita*'s dress wrapped around her legs when she finished the twirl under her partner's arm and settled back to her ankles.

Abner said, "You had your chance at the brothel. You might say it's commerce there and a hanging offence here, only they wouldn't be so merciful as to hang you, not at first, anyway."

The *señorita*'s dress swept the hard dirt floor when she curtsied to her partner. Moses stood when she walked by, chaperoned by an aunt, and she smiled when she saw him. Her skin was almost white, smooth as a calm pond, raven hair bright as a colt's eye.

She stopped and said, "I danced with you near the Vegas."

Five weeks earlier, while the dragoons waited west of the Valley of the Vegas for the artillery and infantry to catch up, a *ranchero* and his daughter rode into camp on caparisoned horses as if on parade, spirited yet collected, silver-plated bits, saddles with silver *conchas*. Father and daughter, Moses thought, rich *rancheros* with a *hacienda* as big as a chunk of Virginia. Two *compañeros* travelled with them with muskets and pistols and quick eyes. Moses caught the fragrance of rose when she rode by. He reckoned the *señorita* was younger than he, sixteen maybe. He tipped his nose to his armpit and wished he would have bathed in the irrigation ditch at Vegas.

They stopped at the general's tent, and the girl lit from her horse with the grace of a nightingale. Her hair danced when she turned her head. Soldiers collected as if summoned by bugle.

"I'll wager the general will allow us to gather and gander,"

Abner said. "For morale." He and Moses joined the circle of dragoons.

A trooper appeared with a fiddle and started to play. The *señorita* beamed, inched up her skirt, and danced. Moses wondered if Isabella danced to another's fiddle, whether she thought of him when she did.

An earring fell when the *señorita* danced by Moses. She continued her movements, circling within the circle of soldiers, who clapped in time to the music and the rhythm of her feet. Moses picked up the earring of silver strings and red gems and closed his hand over it. When the dance was done, he approached the *señorita*, held out the earring, and blushed. She smiled like Isabella, bright and wide and lush with life, returned it to an earlobe, thanked Moses in English, and took his hand to dance when the fiddle started.

Moses didn't know how to dance. The *señorita* laughed and pulled him along. Moses moved his feet and ducked and weaved as if in a boxing match. A jab of those eyelashes and a punch from those eyes, he thought, and she'll knock me to my knees, Isabella or no Isabella. Soldiers clapped with the music and cheered, and Moses found that he moved in a semblance of rhythm. Her eyes darted to the rattle tethered to his cap that jumped with his dance steps. She laughed, and at the end of the fiddler's tune she pointed to the rattle and said in English that was better than his, "I have never seen a rattle that big."

Moses removed his cap and held it to her. She measured the rattle longer than finger length, scissored the horsehair thread with thumb- and fingernail, took the rattle, and wedged it in her hair. She curtsied to Moses and returned to her father.

Abner nodded. "The rattle found its snake."

They watched the *señorita* mount her horse.

"Remember the lesson, my young private. Nothing female comes free."

The *señorita* rode away with her father and the two *compañeros*. She looked back and waved at Moses.

"I'll say it in language you'll understand. You don't want one to strike and latch on, stick her fangs in, and leave them there. That hurts." Abner did not smile when he said it.

"You've bathed since we last met," the *señorita* said.

"Town will do that to a man."

She shook a tail of her *rebozo*, and he heard the rattlesnake. She laughed and showed him the rattle, clasped in the fabric with a hair clip. She told Moses her aunt put it there. "If a man dances with me more than twice she will step in and shake it and look at my dance companion. Then they leave." She giggled.

"The snake lives," Moses said.

Her aunt took the *señorita*'s arm in hers and pulled her away. The *señorita* said over her shoulder, "Perhaps you will dance with me?" To Moses, her skin glistened. "But not more than twice!"

"Mama never taught me, remember?" Moses said.

A few dances later Moses asked her to dance. When the fiddle started, he swayed and moved his feet a half step behind hers. He bumped into an officer, toed her foot once, felt her dress brush his leg when she twirled around him. She took his hand and put her other hand on his shoulder to direct his movements, and, wherever she moved, dancers gave way.

"You leave tomorrow, do you not?"

"Day after."

"Will you be coming this way again?"

"Never thought I'd be here to begin with, so never can tell."

"When you return, I will give the rattle back." Her eyelashes closed and opened.

"I'm wary of snakes," Moses said, "but it give me a lesson."

An officer cut in. "Perhaps we dance again?" the *señorita* said. She smiled at him and curtsied to the officer.

Moses sat down between Abner and Private Smithwick and watched her dance. He felt the eyes of the *compañeros* push him, looked at the floor, and said, "I don't know her name."

"Her name's *Molestia*," Abner said. "That's Spanish for 'Trouble.' She is coming into womanhood, and she plays with its power. Moreover, she is landed aristocracy of Spanish descent, and you are an American country mutt. Let her set her fangs, and they will feed you to a Navajo's dog."

Private Smithwick said, "Poor dog."

"The hardest lessons are those learned as the result of poor judgment, my young private. I annoy you in the hope that you will avoid this one." Abner swirled his mug, smelled it, took two gulps, came up for air, took two more, walked to the punch bowl, and refilled his mug. He lingered, drank, talked with a *comanchero* fresh from months of goading oxen, pulling freight wagons laden with trade goods on the Santa Fe Trail. The *comanchero* refilled Abner's mug with a jug of mescal he carried. A few dances passed. Abner returned to sit with Moses and Private Smithwick and brought the *comanchero* with him.

"Now, with the assistance of the cactus extract," Abner lifted his mug, "one of, shall I say, the more interesting derivatives of Bacchus, my mind ascends to celestial questions and the language of the sublime."

"The mescal's got him," Moses said to Private Smithwick. "Jerk up your cinch, because we're in for a ride."

"What must one do to attain grace? Therein lies the paradox. We are commanded to live righteous lives, yet are instructed that grace is granted, not earned."

Couples filled the dance floor, twirled to sounds from the violin and guitar that passed for dance music.

"What purpose do our worldly endeavors serve? Must one

seek grace? Implore the Almighty for his forgiveness and salvation?"

"All these women in low-cut gowns with their batty eyelashes and he's worried about that," Private Smithwick said. He stood and walked to the punch bowl.

The *comanchero* watched the senorita dance with a light in his eyes. He crossed himself, lowered his mug of mescal, looked at the jug on the bench. "May the saints forgive my impure thoughts for one as beautiful as a stained-glass window."

"I will say that her appearance here is as incongruous as it was on the desert plain, her refinement in this unkempt borough of Santa Fe as intriguing as gems on a peasant."

"You know the *señorita, señor?*"

"Not precisely," Abner said. "Just enough to breathe in beauty lush as a sunset, which moves one to pleasant yet mischievous thoughts."

Moses pictured Isabella, the light her eyes carried. He could desert this night with the distraction of the fandango and knock on her door inside of three or four months. That or march to San Diego, put more life and time between himself and his heart song.

The *comanchero* said, "You and I, *señor,* have been too long on the trail." He laughed and lifted his mug to toast. "To God the artist, who creates such beauty to make life worth living."

They tapped mugs and drank, and the *comanchero* refilled them.

Moses said, "If they caught me they'd hang me."

The *comanchero* studied him and nodded. "Be wary, *mi amigo.* A *señorita* will put thoughts in your head that do no good. God's creation, *señor,* but"—he waved an index finger—"Satan's bait."

Abner tapped mugs with the *comanchero.* "You and I have the wisdom of age, while the young private suffers from the foolishness of youth, as witnessed by his refusal of the local elixir."

Abner nodded to the untouched mug that sat by Moses. "I appear to have failed in the young private's instruction." Abner lifted his mug. "To the angel Mescal, who grants respite, however brief, to remembrances, as my young friend would say, that twist our innards." He tipped the mug and gulped.

"The bench, he wanders a little bit, *señor.*" The comanchero gripped its front edge with both hands, kicked a leg with a boot heel, commanded it to sit still.

Abner said, "What currency flows in the economy of the Almighty? Service to one's fellow man? Faith? Daily office of the prayer book? Good works by the dozen?"

"Master Private, you are two people in one," Moses said. "A saddle-hammered dragoon and pulpit professor, and I never know who it's gonna be or how long he'll be there, which is another one of them things I like about you. You give me wonderment."

"Please explain, so my saturated brain may absorb your thought."

"You keep me wonderin' what's gonna happen next. A man needs that, if he don't want to wither and shrink in this dried-up country they got out here."

"A spark to your inquisitive nature, I should hope. Such is the path of the educator, and, should I provide it, I've served my profession well." Abner picked up the untouched mug that sat by Moses. "We are instructed to do as God commands, but, pray tell, how does one know God's command? No express arrives. No directive spelled on the slate. No rap on the knuckles with the schoolmaster's ruler." He lifted the mug and sipped.

"I don't worry over it," Moses said. "My body goes, and my mind follows, seems like. You're the other way around, and where did it get us? In the same place for the same pay, so I don't see much difference between the two."

"An insight worthy of analytical rigor. As Socrates said at

trial, 'An unexamined life is not worth living.' I have examined mine, and continue to do so, and have yet to determine its worth. You, on the other hand, have a native acumen that seems to know without reflection, a gift of an old soul, perhaps, which I at times envy. But to truly live, one must determine that for which one endeavors to live. A process of discernment, if you will, which, if successful, will chart your life's course to its intended purpose. To do otherwise is to remain aimless."

"I've been thinkin' on that, if I understand you right."

"That's apparent. Be mindful, however, that for some, the more they examine, the less certain they become. Do not fall into that trap, as have I from time to time, which is why I feel"— Abner looked in the mug, swirled it, and looked up— "dislocated, like an arm popped from its socket."

Moses squeezed Abner's shoulder. "Feels all right to me, and I'll tell this, too, you thinkin' you're disjointed and all. You're the savviest man I ever knew, and the funnest to be with. The other thing is," he leaned closer to Abner, "ask the *señorita* to dance. That'll pop it in," he smiled, "but you'll have to stand in line."

Moses stepped outside to relieve himself. He heard a man move behind him, thought it a trooper with the same intent, turned his head in mid-urination to see one of the *compañero* chaperones three steps back, tapping his hand with an ironwood stick the length of a hammer handle.

The *compañero* said, *"Señorita."* He pointed the baton at Moses, shook his head, and said, "No."

Moses said, "I'd rather be a lover than a fighter." He finished relieving himself, buttoned his pants. Abner walked out with a stagger to his steps, bumped the *compañero,* and fell when the *patrón*'s man shoved him away.

Moses helped Abner to his feet and looked at the *compañero,* little more than an arm's length away. "Ease up. He didn't mean nothin'. Just drunk is all."

"Inebriated," Abner said. "Partaking in liberal measure of your fair city's kind hospitality will lead to such. I offer my sincere apology, sir, for my indulgence and its effect on my navigation." He removed his cap and bowed.

The *compañero* pointed the ironwood club at Abner, then at Moses. "*Vas. Vete ahora.*" He pointed the skull-crusher away from the dance hall, added accent with a flick of his head, and said in English, "Go."

Moses saw no light in the man's eyes, dark caves bears could winter in. He moved Abner away from the chaperone and said over his shoulder, "You and him think the same. Tells me to stay the hell off and gone from her."

The chaperone showed no change. His eyes, still cold as frozen stone.

Abner stopped to relieve himself.

The *compañero* tapped the baton.

Moses felt the fire rise, how quickly it burned off fear, the leavening of temper. He turned to face the chaperone. "For Christ sake. He's old enough to be your uncle. He's gotta piss. He's not bothering anyone."

Abner giggled, spewed pee as if shaping letters in the sand-packed alley.

The *patrón*'s man stepped toward them.

"No offense intended, *señor*," Abner said and motioned they'd be on their way quick as he finished. He said quietly, "Easy, Moses. He's a mean one. It's their place, not ours."

"Their place, but our army. He can't push us out."

The *compañero* shoved Moses with the ironwood bar. Moses stumbled on rubble, thought of his pa, the shovel slam to his backside that planted his face in the dirt. He felt for a piece of broken adobe weighted like a hammer head.

The chaperone stepped back when Abner circled.

Light and voice-noise came when the dancehall door opened. The *patrón* walked out, stopped, and looked. The chaperone gripped his baton, shifted from Moses to Abner and back. The *patrón* said, "Manuel, *que pasa?*" He got no answer and said to Moses, "*Por favor, señor, mi hija,* my daughter, one more dance." He held the door open, motioned for Moses. "Her wish, *señor.*"

"How fortuitous," Abner said. "Deus ex machina." He snickered.

The *patrón* stopped Moses as he walked by. His smile faded. "*Solo uno mas.* One more only. *Comprendes?*"

"Yes," Moses said. "*Si, señor.*"

"*Bueno.*" The *patrón* motioned Moses in with a sweep of his hand, smiled at Abner, and said, "Manuel will be watching."

Abner chuckled. "He frightened Saint Bacchus into remission, *señor,* but we had your man in retreat."

"He's ruthless. *Muy bueno,* very good at what he does."

Abner bowed. "So noted. *Gracias.*"

Moses danced with the *señorita.* She pulled him close, leaned to him, and they swayed in rhythm with the fiddle. Moses felt the heat, tried to will it away, wished she were Isabella, and moved when the *señorita* moved.

At the end of the dance the aunt separated them, glared at Moses, and shook the *rebozo.* She took her niece by the hand and led her way. The *señorita* smiled and laughed over her shoulder.

Abner retrieved the mugs they'd left with the *comanchero,* ladled in punch, and held them to the freighter, who added mescal from his jug. He handed one to Moses. "Attend to this rather than the *patrón*'s daughter. It's less dangerous and more entertaining, at least at first." He giggled, tapped mugs with his companions. "To the angels who shield us. May they be with us always."

Moses lifted his mug to Manuel, who stood to the wall and

watched him. Moses winked and sipped and lowered the mug, and the chaperone stayed still, the gesture from Moses like wind on a cliff.

Madam La Tules pulled Moses to the dance floor, showed him some steps with her breasts in his chest, then took him to the girl he'd sat with in the brothel. The madam took the girl's hand, pulled them both to the dance floor, and said, "You have unfinished business." She laughed and hugged them, then danced with Abner.

When the fandango closed, Moses escorted his consort outside. They stepped into the dark, and his partner turned him toward Madame La Tules's tavern. Moses sucked in his breath at the corner of the building from the blow to his belly, heard the girl scream, saw lights in his brain when the ironwood club struck the back of the head. He sagged to his knees, heard a pot break and a thud when Manuel fell.

Abner dropped the potless handle among the pitcher pieces. Manuel groaned, rose to a knee, wavered, and sat down. Abner helped Moses to his feet. "I was a bit tardy in my blow, but it did affect his intended trajectory. Otherwise . . ." He shook his head, picked up the baton, aimed it at Manuel. "Don't point your stick at people like this. It's rude." He flung the ironwood rod onto the roof of the dancehall and helped Moses to his feet. The girl was gone.

Manuel's scalp bled. Abner tossed a kerchief in Manuel's lap and said, "Courtesy of the First Dragoons." Manuel pressed it on the wound to stem the bleeding.

Moses stepped toward Manuel. Abner stopped him with a hand on his chest and one on his back. "Never look for a fair fight, but do not act from meanness."

"He waylaid me in the dark, and he shoved you. I can't have that."

"Vengeance scars the soul. Don't let that happen."

"Had a girl on my arm. Weren't gonna bed her, bought or not. Escort her to the tavern door and leave when it opened, gentleman-like. Something she don't get." Moses turned back toward Manuel. "I'll bust him a good one. He earned it."

Abner grabbed Moses's tunic and stepped in front of him. "Do not act from malice."

"Always have. I'm made that way."

"Not made. Became."

Moses moved. Abner blocked him.

"What would Isabella say?"

Moses stopped. "She's a long way off."

"She's in your heart. How close is that?"

Very close, Moses thought. Don't know how or why, just is. He pictured his mother, remembered her words—our hearts hold our dearest treasure. He put a hand to his head, felt where the club struck. "Got a knot the size of a horse turd, right there for my cap to grab. Don't like that neither."

Abner turned Moses and started toward the camp. " 'Thou shalt break them with a rod of iron; thou shalt dash them in pieces like a potter's vessel.' You each acted to redress some slight of pride. Imagine the hand of the Almighty at work here with a rod and a pot. Granted Manuel's head is harder than pottery, and yours, well . . . a brick for a ricochet, shall I say?" Abner chuckled. "The schoolmaster's rap on the hand. Consider yourself lucky, and accept the instruction."

Moses walked slowly with a hand on Abner's shoulder. He said, "I'd rather be a lover than a fighter. I just don't know how."

CHAPTER 12

. . . as we advanced the roads grew so much worse that both men and teams failed fast, and our only hope of success lay in our faith in God and on pulling at the ropes.

—*Sergeant Daniel Tyler,*
Mormon Battalion

As to me there seemd [sic] scarce grass enough in summer season to keep Sheep alive.

—*John D. Lee, sent to the Mormon Battalion*
by Brigham Young to collect wages for the church,
October 5, 1846, New Mexico

Mormon Battalion, Valley of Tears [New Mexico], October 2, 1846
Moses and Abner rode two days, mostly at a trot, with infrequent stops for water and forage, sparse enough to barely keep their saddle mules nourished, their night stop from midnight to four in the morning. They rode east from Santa Fe on the Cimarron Cutoff to deliver a message—if the Mormon Battalion did not arrive in Santa Fe within eight days they could not be fitted out for California and would be disbanded.

They seldom spoke but rode on, a journey of endurance with urgency to it. Moses had learned indifference to all but food, water, and rest, no talk or thought, as if he'd slipped in a hole and hidden there, prey to a land empty of trees and greenery and the vibrancy of life, a prairie plain as a clock face.

Moses filled the miles with memory, and it always came to the one he relished most, as if to tease him with a hue he'd not noticed. The further he rode from home or the longer his time away, the stronger the pull of that day in April, two years ago.

His pa had sent him to fetch coffee and an awl and there she was, tending customers in her daddy's dry-goods store.

"There you are," she said and walked right up to him. "I have not seen you since you knocked that boy down with a stick."

"Weren't a stick," Moses said. He glanced at her. "Oak-wood axe handle." His eyes moved to the tool rack.

"Do you normally carry an oak axe handle, Moses Cole?"

Moses glanced again. "No, Miss, not normal." His eyes shifted to the clothing shelves. "Just that day is all."

"Why just that day, Moses Cole?"

"Because." His eyes shifted. "Just carved it."

She canted her head.

"Took a twisted wagon rim to the blacksmith. Seen the saplin' on the way home. Hacked it down with my belt knife. Set down and carved an axe handle." He glanced at her. "For the one I broke splittin' stove wood."

The Pennsylvania rifle that hung on the wall passed through his view. Whenever he'd been in the store he would look at the rifle and yearn for it, dream of the day when he might have enough money to buy it. But this time it was just another object to excuse his eyes from Miss Isabella.

"That was last fall," she said. "You were sixteen."

"Seventeen now. Year older than you."

He looked at her and felt a blush rise. His eyes darted to the licorice jar.

She canted her head a little more. "You are half mean, Moses Cole. You did not need to hit him the second time, and you should not have hit him the third time."

"Has he bothered you since?"

"No."

Moses nodded. He looked her straight on, and that's when he felt it, like his soul, or whatever it was that hid where his heart ticked, slid from him to her, quit him for its real home, there in Isabella.

Just then her daddy called her to fetch a bolt of calico. Moses watched her go, then tripped on a keg of nails and fell on a bag of beans, spilling both on the pine-board floor, where they mixed together.

"Shit," he said, and Isabella was there, laughing. Try as he may, as many times as he'd turned that memory, he could not decipher if she had laughed at him or because of him, or both.

Isabella knelt, and he smelled honeysuckle. She helped him sort nails from beans, and all she said was, "I told Daddy to move these nails." All the while Moses felt like he was metal and she a magnet, a lodestone to his soul. It took all he could muster to push off that pull.

Ever since, when he saw her the feeling got stronger, grew bigger sure as a foal grows to a colt. Whether he wanted it that way or another way didn't matter much. Seemed it took on a life of its own. He allowed it lorded over him, that he answered its command. She did, too. That look she give him told him so. Then she gone off to Richmond to live with her aunt, to get "acculturated," her daddy said. To marry right, is what her daddy meant. Hadn't seen her much since then, but when he did that feeling hit him center chest. Like to cave his brisket in, with the power of it. Fair long while gone by now, since he'd seen her last, but that lure in her eyes didn't quit him, lived in him deep like a lunker in a riverbed, bidin' its time.

"Hark!" Abner said. "Yonder lurks the fruit of our quest!"

Moses looked up, saw dust lift in the distance. "Why now? Spoiled my daydream."

"The blow of the lesson, my young private. Spoilage is the destiny of dreams."

Moses looked at Abner. "Hark?"

Abner chuckled and kicked his mule to a trot. When they reached the Mormon Battalion, they slowed their mules to a walk. The battalion resembled a militia—an assembly of farmers, millers, tradesmen, and shopkeepers—gathered to protect families from attack. Moses thought of the Virginia militia his grandfather had talked about during the War of Independence.

They delivered the dispatch, then rode alongside the battalion, head to tail with Abner in the lead. No glistening bays with blazes, no polished brass and black tack bouncing sunlight. No gold cord or epaulettes, cuffs or collar. No shako with plume and eagle shield but the flat cap for field duty. They wore the fatigue uniform, its yellow stripe on the outside pant leg weathered dull. Their mules—gaunt, caked with sweat and dust—held their heads low, ears bobbing as they walked.

A smile caught Moses's eye, and he said to Abner's back, "I'll be go to the Mormons' Lord. Horse Teeth took the bait." They slowed their mules to match the pace of the people on foot. "Said it was infantry," Moses said. "You wouldn't hear it." He kept his eyes ahead, as if he spoke to Abner Black.

"Hello, dragoon sirs!" Gabriel Hanks said. "Seen a little country since Council Bluffs, but I'd ruther seen it a horseback, instead of tuggin' on one of them tuggin' ropes, mule style."

Abner looked at Gabriel Hanks. "My intrepid young fellow. You'd have been better served had you heeded your mother's call."

Moses noticed the eyebrows on the man who walked with Gabriel. "Bear Grease," he said. He sniffed. "That stink slid off and hid somewhere, by God if it didn't." He sniffed again.

122

"Didn't know you without it."

"Didn't know myself, either," Orson Everett said. He lifted an eyebrow.

"What'd you do, burn that shirt or bury it?"

"Boiled it." Orson lifted the other eyebrow. "Soup for the mules."

Abner laughed, dismounted, and walked with Orson, Gabriel, and Phineas.

Moses watched an eyebrow settle followed by the other one, birds' nests bobbing on a tree branch.

"Built a new one from a wagon cover," Gabriel said. "Paid a laundress to do it."

"What else might a man pay a laundress to do?" Abner said.

"Mind yourself," Orson Everett said. "These are religious women, and well protected."

"Heard you say you'd turn Mexican before you'd soldier," Moses said. He looked Orson over. "Don't look Mex to me."

"Brother Brigham couldn't take the smell no more," Gabriel said. His teeth were whiter than his belt and baldrics.

"Different he's been since the sutler's jug," Phineas said.

"Called him a hazard to the health of the chil'ren and exiled him to the country of California. Said an ocean would do him good. Wash him off a little."

"Such impertinence from one so young," Abner said.

Orson said, "School the child, will you? I get nowhere with him."

"Gonna see them sea waves, lappin' and jammin' on the seashore. Might get brave and wade in a little, clean to my kneecaps." Gabriel's teeth flashed.

"Mormons," Moses said. "Walk across the desert to look at water man or mule can't drink."

"My young private," Abner said. "They walked where we

rode and were ill-provisioned in doing so. The feat measures the man."

"The feat of the man speaks to the strength of his God," Orson said.

The order came to halt and rest. Abner led his mule away with Moses riding beside him. They hobbled their mules while the battalion rested. Abner sat down, pointed to a spot in front of him, and said to Moses, "Sit."

Moses sat.

Abner said, "You've jailed yourself within walls of your own creation."

Moses stretched an arm to the distance. "No jail here but the big empty. Sky and land that keep runnin' in front of us. Never get to the end of it." He looked west. "Hit that ocean, board a boat, and keep goin'." He turned back to Abner. "No, sir. No walls out here."

"Ah, yes. The expanse of the possible."

"Sir?"

"You've seen land from Virginia to New Mexico, how varied it is, how interesting it can be. We cross one landscape to find another. Some luxuriant, some desolate. Some you like, some you don't. Each connected to the other. What lies ahead will be different from where we've been. Would you agree?"

"Evident to me, seein's what we seen so far."

"Very good. Now, extend that to life and the differences you've found in people. Personalities, appearances, motivations, to name a few, as varied as the landscapes we've seen. Some you like and some don't. That's true for all of us."

"You're layin' a trail to take me somewhere I can't see."

"The jail in which you've placed yourself is your refusal to see the possible, the expanse of life if you will. It's as if you've locked yourself in one landscape. It may be comfortable, or what you're used to, but it shuts out something different and interesting. It limits your knowledge of the world and, with that, what you know of yourself."

"Keen up my thinkin' without no books, is what you're doin'. Keep on talkin'.'"

"Same with people. You've disliked these Latter-day Saints since we first saw them. Rejected them with no consideration for what they've endured and what their motivations may be. You saw Elder Everett and his repulsion at the very idea of service in the United States Army after the persecutions the Saints suffered. Yet he enlisted. He put aside his personal concerns to contribute to the good of his people, and remade himself in the process. Wisdom, I would venture, inflicted by life."

Moses hung his head. "I see the schoolin' you're doin' on me."

"Young Gabriel is a different story. Horse Teeth, as you crassly call him, although I admit to the humor in the moniker. Brimming with the exuberance of youth. Pulled by an image of glory we were dressed to project. Drawn to the power of the horse, not unlike that which I heard from a wayward runaway on a rainy day in Pennsylvania."

Moses looked at the ground.

"Understand before you venture judgment. Be generous with respect."

"A body's gotta earn that."

"Which they have," Abner said.

Moses looked up. "There he is now."

Orson Everett approached. Abner stood and extended his hand. "Orson Everett, as I recall. I'm Abner Black, and this is my pupil, Moses Cole. Well do I remember you, sir." They shook hands and sat down. "We were just talking about you."

"He's tellin' me you're not bad fellas," Moses said. "Takes me some getting used to, is all."

Orson laughed. "I'm sure I do. Don't know about the others."

"Abner the teacher man, poundin' on me to look in a person instead of stoppin' at the skin or the stink. What do you make of that?"

Orson chuckled. "I'd stop at the stink. That's a reason I gave myself to it, back in the day. Like a wall to keep people away."

"I commend you for the striking change in your appearance and demeanor," Abner said.

"The hands of Jehovah pieced me together and healed me. I learned from the lesson. Sometimes that's the best we can expect from life."

"My compliments, sir. I speak from patterns of habit to say such change requires fortitude, and more so to maintain the change once made. How well you've advanced your attitude." He looked at Moses. "We hope to do as well."

"See what I mean? About that poundin'?" Moses said. "Don't mess with him, though. He studied me up on that."

"It appears that you and I, sir," Abner nodded to Orson, "have been sentenced by the court of life to mentor these youths into the men they can be."

"Sometimes, Private Black, I fail it."

"As do we all," Abner said.

Gabriel Hanks shouted while he walked, "Know what them officer bosses talked?" He came on the double quick as if he carried a pail of lit liquid to pour in a rattlesnake den.

"Here he comes to steal my thunder," Orson said. "His will be more entertaining."

"Officer bosses," Moses said. "True enough."

Gabriel Hanks stopped at their feet. "They're gonna split the battalion. Brother Brigham outlawed the notion of splittin' the battalion, but they're gonna split it anyway. Brother Orson said it was a condition of our sign-up, didn't you, Orson, not splittin' the battalion. It was that letter you brung what done it. What'd it say?"

" 'Send the Horse Tooth Kid to whip the Mexicans. Send everyone else someplace safe,' is what I read," Moses said. "Looks like they'll do it, too, from what you're tellin' us."

"It never neither said that. Our Latter-day Saint officer bosses—that's Captain Hunt and Alcott, too—said we was in an eight-day race to get to Santa Fe or that army general will leave us behind. Flat disband us."

"If I was you," Moses said, "I'd say the sooner the better, and head home to find a sweetheart."

"They split us once already, back on the Arkansas, that crick they call a river out here, back at the start of this Cimarron Cutoff we're marchin' on. Carved off a pile of us, ain't that right, Brother Orson? Sent 'em west to a place called Pueblo. Clear off to the mountains where old man winter lives a little, waitin' for to pounce on the women and the wee ones like wolves on lambs. Sent 'em off on their own. Maybe they make spring, maybe they don't. Uncle Sam's army don't care either which way."

"We've been informed," Abner said. "They had an escort of able-bodied battalion soldiers. They will likely find Pueblo well supplied, and they won't be on their own."

"Thought we was gonna have a rebellion then, but them captains put a crunch on it."

Abner said, "They will arrive well in advance of winter. I surmise they will fare better than you will. Would you agree, Mr. Everett?"

"You might be right, but it's counter to our terms of enlistment."

"And then they done it again," Gabriel said. "Just up and done it. Our fastest half will race to Santa Fe. Start today. The older and slower and sick and such will come along best they can. 'Our weaker elements,' is what that West Pointy officer boss called them, didn't he, Orson? Maybe we hook up again, maybe we don't. Up to that army general."

"General Stephen Watts Kearny," Abner said. "Commander of the Army of the West, which includes the Mormon Battalion."

"And then, if we don't none of us get there to Santa Fe in eight days, we're kicked off the payroll, so we can't never send money to our brethren and sistren wastin' on the prairie, and we give back the guns, and we're left in a land that'll starve a rat. So says Captain Hunt and Captain Alcott. Isn't that so, Brother Orson?"

"That pretty well says it," Orson said.

"Santa Fe in eight days," Moses said. "Afoot." He shook his head. "You're tough ones."

Gabriel looked at Moses. "Got a name on you, or will Mister Dragoon do?"

"He is Moses Cole," Orson said.

"Claims a Bible writer for his namesake," Gabriel said.

"And this man of wisdom is Abner Black, disguised as a private," Orson said.

"Brother Brigham would pull them officers through the hub of a wagon wheel if he knew what they was doin'," Gabriel said, "sendin' our sistren and chil'ren off like that, and walkin' off from the sick and the lame and such. He wouldn't grease it neither. Just pull 'em through. Straighten 'em out a little. Man enough to do it, too."

"If I was you," Moses said, "I'd stop talkin' and start walkin'." He looked southwest, where the mountains lifted in the distance. "You can do it, but you gotta step right out. Not hardly stop to piss on a lizard. We'd help you if we could, but we got a mule apiece, and we gotta git to gittin'." He looked to the country they'd covered from Santa Fe. "Hope you don't get barefoot and baked on the way."

Abner said, "Moses and I discussed a similar issue with a similar message. Do not be hasty to judge the actions of your captains or Lieutenant Smith. I would wager a volume of Shakespeare that you will all fare better for the decisions they've made. Give it time and you will see that."

"Riles me right up, goin' a'gin Brother Brigham," Gabriel said. "Don't seem natural, not to my mind-sight anyway."

"Such is the harsh logic of the army," Abner said. "Callous and circumspect with a focus on the whole. We're pawns on a chessboard, and we're not shown the board"—he turned his attention to the distance—"whether we're in the army or on a grander stage." Abner's attention remained away. He said, "Let's hope the hand that moves us husbands us well."

Later that day Moses reined up his mule, east of Santa Fe, one hundred-fifty miles closer to home than he was a few days ago, if he figured right.

Abner rode a few more steps, turned his head.

"I'm headed wrong, boss. Miss Isabella's the other way."

Abner turned his mule, rode up to Moses. "Finally the voice speaks the mind. It's been there, bold as a sailor's tattoo, a young man parted from his heart."

"What if we about-faced? Skirt them Mormons and keep on goin'?"

"Excellent, my young private, for one who yearns for a thirty-day ride on four days rations on a worn-out mule and a dollar in his pocket, and that's just to Fort Leavenworth, which happens to be an army post, where they would certainly receive you with all appropriate hospitality. Trust me. They'll know you've deserted before they smell you or see you, which might appeal to your sense of adventure, but, as for me, destiny beckons west."

"Seems simple, till you confuse it with particulars."

"Your motives conflict, my young private. One of which is your flight from your father, since replaced with loyalty to your troop, which is deeper than you know."

Moses thought, add the baby that never seen daylight. Mother's innards sliding on the ice.

"The other, the draw your Virginia maiden holds, whose presence has grown in her absence. Unrequited lust, perchance love, you would not yet know which, that simmers in your soul, a flame fanned by the *señorita* that duty won't drench."

Moses thought, add the farm to what tugs on me. Turning trees into lumber and land into fields. He said, "That *señorita* don't mean hair on a boar's ass to me."

Abner started to sing.

> *"All the dames of France are fond and free*
> *And Flemish lips are really willing*
> *Very soft the maids of Italy*
> *And Spanish eyes are so thrilling."*

Moses said, "Didn't know you had a song to sing, or a voice to pack it."

Abner sang another verse.

> *"Still, although I bask beneath their smile,*
> *Their charms will fail to bind me*
> *And my heart falls back to Erin's isle*
> *To the girl I left behind me."*

"Never took you for a troop-a-door. Might need to rethink the Master Private Abner Black."

"Ah, to be young again. How I cherished afflictions of the imagination. How I wallowed in the pathos of the moment."

"Say what you mean."

Abner removed his spectacles and pulled a kerchief from a

tunic pocket. "You suffer a divided mind." He wiped the lenses and examined them. "Remember the epistle of Saint James— 'For he that wavereth is like a wave of the sea driven with the wind and tossed.' " Abner misted a lens with breath and wiped it. " 'A double-minded man is unstable in all his ways.' "

"That don't help much."

"Weigh the merits of each and decide, now and here, and commit to a direction."

"You in a hurry? Miss them officer bosses?"

"Short of that you will give nothing your full attention, which life requires if you are to live it fully and is certainly required if you are to survive a hostile environment." Abner misted and wiped the other lens. "You may see your maiden someday, but this is not the time nor is this the circumstance." Abner folded the kerchief and returned it to his tunic pocket. "I would not risk my life for that which might well prove a fiction."

"Feelin's ain't make believe," Moses said.

"I speak from lessons learned." Abner seated the spectacles and hooked the wire frames around his ears. "Desire fathers poor judgment. Resist the yearning."

"You and them words." Moses lifted his cap, rubbed where the knot faded. "I need that teacherin'. You're good at it." He pulled the cap on, tilted the visor to hide the sun, spurred his mule, and trotted ahead, toward Kearny's command.

"It's 'troubadour'," Abner said after him.

CHAPTER 13

Nothing is heard of the war in Mexico; our position here has been unfortunate, irksome, disheartening—so far from the "sabre clash" of the sunny South! Truly there is a "Fortune of War;" and the pedestal of the goddess is Opportunity!

> —Captain Philip St. George Cooke
> with General Kearny's First Dragoons,
> New Mexico, September 25, 1846

We are haunted by the ghostly shapes of our starving horses . . . they come threading their way by day and by night through the tents; their gaunt shapes upbraid us, their sunken eyes make pathetic appeal.

> —Captain Philip St. George Cooke
> with General Kearny's First Dragoons,
> New Mexico, September 25, 1846

General Kearny's Camp, First Dragoons, Jewel of a Little Bull, Rio Grande del Norte [New Mexico], October 2, 1846
General Kearny and three hundred dragoons rode by a Spanish settlement, its handsome church striking in a hard land, the streets that wended through the adobe village clean as the sun that beat them. They rode by tablelands and dried-up water sinks crusted with salt. They rode over rolling sandhills and a lava seam with holes that hosted nesting hawks. They passed a vast salt flat and camped in the cottonwoods on a bend of the

Rio Grande where some of the trees showed the work of beaver teeth. Ducks with blue wings swam in the river, and the dragoons caught soft-shell turtles and catfish for supper. The aroma of wild sage from close hills carried to the campsite.

Captain Philip St. George Cooke approached General Kearny and saluted. "You summoned me, sir?" Captain Cooke stood six-foot-four, plank straight and door-frame shoulders at thirty-six years old. General Kearny had the slight size a horse likes to carry. Though nearly old enough to be Cooke's father, from a distance, Moses had said General Kearny looked like a boy standing by a man.

General Kearny returned the salute. "Yes, Captain." He motioned to the chairs in front of his common tent. "Please, sit down."

Cooke sat down and folded his hands in his lap. He had high cheekbones and an aquiline nose, square chin, moustache, and side whiskers. When Moses had first seen him, back at Fort Leavenworth, he swore to Abner that Captain Cooke had stepped off a painter's picture.

"You saw the rider," General Kearny said. "Express from Santa Fe." General Kearny leaned forward, forearms on his thighs, hands clasped with fingers intertwined. "Lieutenant Colonel Allen has died."

"Good God," Captain Cooke said. His jaw slackened.

"Congestive fever. Contracted while leading the Mormon Battalion. Which, as you know, he enlisted in July, at the Mormon encampment on the Missouri River. He died on the twenty-third day of August, at Fort Leavenworth, after a two-week decline."

A short way off a trooper cursed when a wagon tongue slipped his grip and fell on his foot.

"He was two years behind me, at West Point," Captain Cooke said. "We drilled together." He turned his head, closed his mouth, looked at the ground. His shoulders sagged. "Why is it always the best ones?" The ground held his attention. "He was a good officer, and a fine gentleman." He caught himself and looked up. "I'm sorry, sir. This is such a surprise."

"Lieutenant A. J. Smith is the acting commander. You know him, I'm sure."

"Somewhat. Another able officer."

"Assuming the Mormon Battalion arrives in Santa Fe in eight days, as they've been so directed, I want you to take charge."

Captain Cooke straightened, riveted to General Kearny.

"I can't have a lieutenant in charge of a battalion."

Cooke turned his head away.

"You are my most seasoned frontier officer, bar none, artillery, infantry, or dragoons. I need you to do this."

Cooke turned back to General Kearny and stammered. Cooke never stammered. He reminded himself of this, tried to breathe more deeply, pondered leading religious volunteers on an arduous military campaign, yet another setback to dim what otherwise might be a stellar career. An unbidden image flashed—a jerk on a bridle rein to a well-trained horse, a stab of a bit in the roof of the mouth, snatching attention from its intended path. Kinship to a finely-tuned, misused Thoroughbred.

"But—but, sir . . ." Cooke spoke to protest but all he could muster was, "This is most unexpected." He wasn't sure what he'd say or how he'd say it, but knew he had to unwind what wound inside.

"I know you requested service in Mexico," General Kearny said. "I've done my best to accommodate that, but we are not masters of our fate. As officers, we are to master our will in service to our country, and to apply ourselves to the task to which we are assigned. I'm asking you to do that now."

"With your permission, sir."

General Kearny nodded.

"The war in Mexico." Cooke motioned southward down the *Rio Grande*. "Any officer worthy of the name wishes to be there. I am honored by your request to command a battalion. I am also disappointed to be further turned from the theater of war."

"Do not mislead yourself, Captain. Hostile forces remain in California."

Cooke paused, worried his clasped hands, leaned a little further forward. "To serve with you, on your staff, General, to march to California with a contingent of picked dragoons to strengthen our garrison there, is one thing. It is quite another to lead an undisciplined militia, which is essentially what the Mormon Battalion is, on an arduous desert march."

"True enough."

"A march in which, if I do engage hostile forces, I do so with ill-trained soldiers."

"That is precisely why I need you to do this. These Mormons will require an effective commander. I think you will find them good, hearty people, who will make good soldiers, but they need leadership to do that. They need an experienced and knowledgeable officer. You are that officer."

"I appreciate your confidence, sir. I would appreciate it more if you would allow me to honor it in Mexico."

"Request denied." General Kearny leaned toward Captain Cooke. "You will assume command of the Mormon Battalion. You will backtrack to Santa Fe, where you will meet it. You will relieve Lieutenant Smith but will retain him on your staff. You will supply the battalion as best you can from any source you can find, army or civilian, and will follow us as soon as practicable."

General Kearny paused to allow the magnitude of the order to settle.

"This is no easy task, Captain, but you are an eminently

capable officer, which is precisely why I have selected you. It will require all of your skill as a leader, disciplinarian, tactician, and soldier to succeed in difficult circumstances, but succeed you must. The conquest of California may well depend upon it."

"I am a soldier and will do as ordered, but I had to be forthright with you, sir."

General Kearny nodded. He continued. "The battalion left Council Bluffs with four hundred ninety-six recruits from the Mormon camps—four hundred seventy-four enlisted men and twenty-two officers." General Kearny paused. "Their leader, Brigham Young, selected the Mormon officers."

Captain Cooke smiled.

"In addition to the men, there are thirty-three women and forty-four children. Most of the women are wives to battalion members, and many of those serve as laundresses."

"Women and children, and officers chosen by a pastor," Cooke said. His smile faded.

"Lieutenant Smith sent some of the women and children, and the sick and older men, to the settlement at Pueblo, a Mexican village on the Arkansas River, west of Bent's Fort. They will remain there for the winter. You may need to do more of the same before marching across the desert."

"Women and children on a military campaign," Cooke said. He shook his head.

"A concession to the Mormons," General Kearny said. "Colonel Allen thought it necessary to complete the recruitment."

Captain Cooke looked at the ground, hands clasped, thumbs turning around each other.

"Do not underestimate the importance of this assignment. In many respects, this will challenge you more than a field command in Mexico."

"I understand, sir."

"You will be given the rank of lieutenant colonel of volunteers, effective immediately." General Kearny smiled, stood, and extended his hand. Cooke stood and shook it.

"Congratulations, Lieutenant Colonel."

"Thank you, sir. This is all so sudden."

"You will leave tomorrow, with a bugler, to join the Mormon Battalion in Santa Fe. I will proceed to San Diego, where I hope to witness the arrival of your battalion in no more than three months."

"I will do my best, sir," Cooke said.

"I know you will, Lieutenant Colonel Cooke." General Kearny smiled, leaned closer to Cooke, and lowered his voice. "Has a nice ring to it, doesn't it?" His smile widened.

"Yes, sir."

General Kearny straightened. "I can assure you, if you conduct this mission successfully, the army will take notice."

Back in his tent, in the thin light of a sun setting toward San Diego, Philip St. George Cooke lit a candle and opened his journal to record his deflected trajectory. He penned a new entry: "I must turn my face to Santa Fe tomorrow. That is turning a very sharp corner indeed; it is very military."

He read an entry close to the front of the journal, made years earlier as a young officer, and thought, so young and naïve then. From the blossom of youth to death by a thousand cuts. Shakespeare had it right, but some cuts cut deeper than others.

He read another entry filled with the exuberance of youth and groaned. He saw life as full of false paths, and paths set upon not of one's choosing, yet here he was, a newly commissioned lieutenant colonel, which he would trade in a heartbeat to be drunk with beauty, young and captured by romance. He felt how distant that had become, as reachable as a dead ancestor.

He closed the journal and thought again he suffered the heart of a poet and the dreams of a romantic, the hope that only the young have. The wonder. The mystery. The sense of adventure. The belief that he was special. One of the youngest graduates of West Point. An officer of horse. A lieutenant of dragoons in the bloom of manhood. Tall. Attractive in the eyes of women. Scion to one of the first families of the Old Dominion. Life seemed so rich and full of promise then.

And now this, a knife to his heart. He exhaled sharply. A shadow moved on the tent wall when the flame swayed.

A horse neighed nearby.

Lieutenant Colonel, he thought. That does have a palliative effect.

He wondered what promise the colonelcy would hold, what the end would be, thought it not the lush wonder of the early entries but, he whispered, "A duller, drier place where dreams are dashed."

A mule brayed, and a mule answered it.

There I go again, he thought, *tending to the poetic when the reality is prosaic.*

He shook his head and put the journal away.

CHAPTER 14

*The Navajoes [sic] may be termed the lords of New Mexico.
Few in number, disdaining the cultivation of the soil, and even
the rearing of cattle, they draw all their supplies from the valley
of the Del Norte . . . They are prudent in their depredations,
never taking so much from one man as to ruin him.*

*—Lieutenant William Emory,
Corps of Topographical Engineers, with
General Kearny, Army of the West,
September 30, 1846*

*About one hundred Indians, well mounted, charged upon the
town and drove off all the horses and cattle of the place . . . The
people of Lamitas . . . seized upon the pass . . . The Indians
seeing their retreat with the cattle and goats cut off, fell to work
like savages as they were, killing as many of these as they could,
and scampered off over the mountains and cliffs with the horses
and mules . . . This same band entered the settlements some
miles above when we were marching on Santa Fe . . . [and]
carried off fifteen or sixteen of the prettiest women.*

*—Lieutenant William Emory,
October 4, 1846*

*Army of the West, Rio Grande del Norte [New Mexico],
early October 1846*

"There is a peculiar sight," Abner said.

139

A Mexican, his horse at full gallop, barefoot and hatless, serape flapping behind him, raced into camp and slid off his horse at the guards and guidons that marked the general's tent.

Abner said, "I've seen a *ranchero* on a fancy-dance stallion. I've seen a villager on a burro smaller than a big dog, turning him with sticks instead of bridle reins. I've seen *vaqueros* with Spanish bits that outweigh a saber, and rowels the size of pie plates, gallop slower than you can walk a mule. But I have never seen that, a Mexican in a race on a steamed-up horse. Surely fright has possessed him."

The Mexican's voice carried over the work of the wheel-wrights and farriers who readied wagons, mules, and horses for the next day's march.

"Hands flyin' like he's battling bees," Moses said. "Talks faster than a snake can rattle."

"Dare say the Navajos raided the village women?"

A bugle summoned C Company to horse. Moses threw down his coffee cup.

"Should not have done that," Abner said. "The more it's dented, the less it holds."

"Ate by a wolf and shit by a bear, is how I feel. Then that bugle. Back in the saddle and go again, for criminy sake."

"Woe to the forlorn soldier," Abner said.

"How far we just ride? Rode like hell to find those Mormons. Santa Fe to damn near Kansas. About face, ride right back only keep on goin', south down the Rio Grande river. Six, eight days maybe, trot right along, that saddle hammerin' on me. Come on the army suppertime yesterday. Settled in just a little bit, then back in the leather on account of an upended Mexican. She-it."

"My, you're delicate today," Abner said. "Must one tread lightly?"

"Livin' like wind, is what it is. Contrary to farmin', where a man sets in to build a place."

"A tale of jaded wanderlust. How did life become so cruel?" Abner chuckled.

Their saddles, draped with their saddle blankets, lay where they'd slept. Moses picked up his blanket. "Rather piss me a pebble than sit that seat. One of them burn-from-the-inside kind you tell about."

"No, you would not," Abner said. "That's another experience I hope you never know."

Moses rubbed the insides of his knees. "My hide's wore through." He rubbed the balls of his hips. "Sit bones tender as hammer-hit fingers."

"I surmise the captain would allow us to remain in camp, but why, pray tell, would we ride this far to miss the call to saddle and saber?"

"Should be broke in by now, but I ain't." Moses felt his saddle blanket. "It's wet with sweat yet."

"Pity the mule that receives that on his back," Abner said, "but he's in the army, same as we."

Moses scratched the matted blanket to knock dirt from the sweat-packed wool. The bugle blew again, louder this time.

"Son of a bitch." Moses looked at Abner. "Something good in swear words. Helps my disposition."

"Ah, the man yields to the beast," Abner said. "Yet again the army does its work."

The troop trotted twelve miles down the west bank of the *Rio Grande del Norte* to the village much like any other they'd passed on the march down river with its mud huts, chickens and goats, geese with clipped wings, stacks of sticks for cook fires. The difference was the scattered cattle and splintered flocks, the absence of horses and mules. A cow stood at the village edge, head hung to half mast, an arrow in her paunch sunk to the fletching. Further on another bawled at a calf that lay on its side with an arrow through its neck, kicking in search of earth underfoot. A few goats lay about, still as stones, the finger-length hair at their throats blood red. A villager knelt at one of the goats and cradled its head in his lap, its tongue limp between its teeth. The track pattern showed the raiders had stolen the horses and mules.

Troopers rode through the dead and dying cattle and goats strewn through the village.

Moses said, "Cruel in the doin' of it." He pictured weasel kills in the chicken hutch, but a weasel ate only its take.

Private Donovan said, "Kill and leave lay. Don't make sense."

"Mean is all," Private Smithwick said.

"There's right killin' and wrong killin', and this ain't right," Moses said.

"Perverse sense of sport," Abner said. "Often they steal the women, just to salt the wounds."

Moses thought of Miss Isabella.

"How would a man harbor that?" Smithwick said. "Have his wife stolen, young and pretty and full of life, to be, to put it kindly, shared among the warriors."

"Humped like a cow in a bull herd," Donovan said.

"There's another reason God gave us brothels," Abner said. "Enjoy the company without the ties that bind."

A cow stood with entrails spilled from her belly. She walked, stepped on an intestine, and lay down.

Moses thought of his mother opened on the riverbank, dead with her blood running, her insides outside of her, too late to save the baby. He hung his head.

Abner pulled up his mule beside him and said, "That's another thing I like about the army. Nothing to hold a man's heart."

Villagers carried a dead man, limp as a half sack of beans,

into a hut. Arrows shot through his serape pinned it to his chest.

The cow with spilled intestines settled her muzzle to the ground.

"Their animals dead or took," Moses said. He flinched when a woman wailed from the hut where the dead man lay. "Some of their men killed. Some stuck with arrows."

A mother hugged an infant and wandered as if searching for something lost.

"We can hunt them people," Moses said. "Make them pay for what they done. Fetch the horses and mules back."

"We are interlopers," Abner said. "We are not here to police or to heal these people."

A crying child ran by.

"Ain't right to leave it go."

"That's not for us privates to decide. You may accept respite in that, or you may seethe if the decision we are given is not of your choosing. Therein lays the blessing and the curse of command. The burden of decisions is not ours to bear, yet we are not absolved of the consequences."

Another villager, an arm around a man at each side, stepped with his good leg and dragged the leg with an arrow through the hamstring.

Moses looked off to the captain, who conferred with the scouts who had checked the trail. "Stand and gab, that captain."

"Catch the heathen thieves, would it be? Wield the hand of vengeance upon those with blood lust?" Abner shook his head. "They have a half-day head start. They're trailing horses and mules, but a chased horse or mule, no saddle or man on its back, will travel faster than you can. Besides, the Navajos know the country, and we do not."

"This ain't right, sit here and look and not do nothin'," Moses said.

Beyond the village, reaching south further than the eye could reach, the valley of the *Rio Grande del Norte* lay as still as a grave.

"Like the Mexican army at Vegas Gorge," Abner said. "All we see is where they've been."

The bugle called, the command mounted, marched a mile south, and dismounted to wait for the Army of the West to resume its march to San Diego.

"They call us an army," Moses said. "All powder and no lead." He unsaddled his mule and spread the blanket in the sun.

Abner unbridled and haltered his mule. "Everything's a mirage, my young private. All is vanity and vexation of spirit." He unsaddled his mule and rubbed its back. "Like those lakes we see in the distance that shimmer and call, then turn into sand and sunlight. We spend our lives chasing ghosts."

"Then I'll take farm life. A man's got something to show at the end of a day."

"Farm life is what these people have. Look what it brought them."

"A farmer builds somethin'." Moses looked down the valley. "It's what Donovan said of the Mexicans. All we do is shit and git. We're no better than the army we come to fight."

"Mind your language. You'll soon be as crude as our fellows."

Abner looked to the distance. Beyond the cottonwoods on the river bottom a tableland stretched rugged with coulee cuts. "A desert awaits, and perhaps a Mexican army." Further off, mountains stark as the desert floor jutted from the tableland. Abner grew quiet, turned a shade pale, came back from the hard mountains.

"You took sick?" Moses asked.

"At times an uncanny hand will grip me with portentous intent. Something sinister, written but not revealed." Abner reached in his tunic pocket, removed the rattlesnake rattle, and gave it to Moses. "The *señorita* insisted that I return this to you."

Moses gave him a look.

"I was drunk but not incapacitated. Odd things happen on the dance floor." He looked in the distance. "If the unfortunate occurs on the march ahead, and circumstances permit, bury me with it."

"What?"

"Why is the question. And the answer? To take the death angel with me."

"You're puttin' the spookery in me. Say what you mean."

"To pull the death angel away from you," Abner said. "Superstitious, I admit. Quite out of sorts with a cultivated mind, but nonetheless real."

Moses looked to the horizon where Abner looked. After a while he said, "You're a mystery to me."

"The uncanny hand does not lie. Something not welcome lurks in our journey."

"Your mind's run off again. I'll water the mules, give it time to circle back."

Moses took their mules to the river to water and watched a bloated goat float by. *Seen meanness,* he thought, *but not this, killin' for the thrill of it. Should've drawed a map, laid out a road to take, found my true north and a compass to hold me to it. Go where I need to get instead of wanderin' along to where I end up. When you're hungry and cold and wet, hat brim to shoe sole, it's plain as day what a body's gotta do. It's when you're free to dream that it gets messy.*

The goat spun around a snag and floated on at the whim of the river.

Seems simple, Moses figured. *Set my bearing to where I want to go, or float along like that goat, dead to the current that moves it. Clear enough, but I never seen the simple in it.*

CHAPTER 15

Camp 68—Two Mexicans deserted from my party last night, frightened by the accounts of the hardships of the trip brought by Carson and his party.

—Lieutenant William Emory,
Topographical Engineer with General Kearny,
Army of the West, October 7, 1846

Kit Carson and the Army of the West, Rio Grande del Norte
[New Mexico], early October 1846
A dust cloud approached from down river, indicating horses or mules at a trot.

"Navajo raiders, I hope," Moses said. He checked his Hall carbine, waited for the command to load.

The dragoons, bivouacked in the adobe ruins of a Spanish village, had marched one hundred-fifty miles down the *Rio Grande del Norte*, south of Santa Fe. They would soon turn west to the Rio Gila, which they would follow to the Rio Colorado. Beyond that the great desert lay and, beyond that, California.

The riders came on, a baker's dozen, Moses figured. They drew closer. Moses put a hand to his forehead to shade his eyes against the sun at the riders' backs. One rode with a blanket over his saddle. Another carried a musket with a feathered fore end. Sun flashed from brass tacks in the gunstock. "Indians, sure enough," Moses said. "Order enough for me." He levered the breech, loaded a cartridge, and eyed the riders. Some wore

146

broad-brimmed hats and U.S. tunics. Some wore buttoned shirts and belted trousers. "White men, too."

"Americans!" Smithwick yelled.

"This God forsaken country has more drama than a Shake-speare play," Abner said. "When can a trooper settle to a nap without such indignant commotion?"

"Americans?" Moses said. "Why are they here?"

"Who else but scalp hunters?" Abner said. "No stronger motive than love or profit, and there is nothing here to love."

The white riders reined up and dismounted. Troopers gathered like wolves to a dead mule. *Trail worn and gaunt, covered in dust, no square meal since the sea side of the mountains,* Moses reckoned. *By the smell of them, no bath water since before that. No clean clothes since wherever it was they come from. No buttons on their tunics. Ankle boots thin as his shoes when he enlisted. Eyes, hollow and dark. Little sleep for weeks. What come on them between here and there?*

The Indians kept a distance. Their moccasins reached to their knees. One wore a red headband knotted at the back. The tails of the fabric, equal in length to his hair, fell to his shoulders.

Moses said, "By the looks of them people, I don't want to go where they been."

The leader of the band stood shorter than the general, and the general was slight. The two of them talked while troopers crowded about.

"It's Kit Carson," Smithwick called back. He stood closer to the riders than Moses did. "Fresh from California."

"Who's Kit Carson?" Moses said.

"Mountain man, Indian fighter, Frémont scout. Turned famous before he turned twenty," Abner said.

Moses judged him at five-five with shoes tied on, late thirties. High forehead and broad across the cheekbones. Legs bowed as from a childhood spent a-straddle a donkey. Hair to his collar and stiff with grease. Buckskins not worn so much as lived in—blood spots from gutted prey, smeared with animal fat, smudged from firebrands, holes where embers landed. He smelled of wood smoke and mules and weeks with no soap.

Smithwick called to Moses and Abner. "We've taken California. War's over out there."

"Shit," someone said.

Donovan said, "At war with Mexico and can't find a Mexican to fight. Should've joined the navy."

Smithwick turned and called again. "Carson's headed to the president. Sixty-day trip. California coast to the Potomac."

"By the looks of that outfit," Moses said, "they won't make Santa Fe in sixty days."

"Saddle bound twenty-eight days, seaside to here," Smithwick called.

Abner said, "That leaves thirty-two days and about two thousand miles." He figured. "That's sixty, sixty-five miles a day, much of it by mule or horseback. My, but they're energetic."

General Kearny took Kit Carson aside. "You've just covered the route we intend to take. I have three hundred dragoons with mules, horses, and wagons. What may we expect?"

Carson said, "The Gila Trail is no trail at all. Up or down. Steep. Hard boned and rocky. Sparse water. Damn little feed. Just enough to starve a goat." A hint of a smile came and left. "Wore out thirty-four mules. Left 'em where they quit."

"You didn't fare much better," General Kearny said. "You could use rest and food."

"I'll get a day in Taos, where my bride lives. Married in forty-three, left in forty-four to scout for Frémont. Two years since I seen her, damn near." A hint of a smile brightened his eye. "She don't know I'm here."

A wind picked up, and they moved to an arroyo for relief from the grit it carried. They sat down, faced each other across the dry and narrow water course.

"Shoulda stood put," Carson said. "Let that wind peel the dust off me." He smiled. "That what my hide's not sucked up. Been so long since I seen clean, won't be white no more."

"From what you've said the journey is more difficult than we expected."

"We pushed harder than you'll have to, but the country, she's a little rough." Carson looked at the supply train—visible even when seated in the shallow arroyo—that carried bedrolls, tents, foodstuffs and cookware, parts for wagon and tack repair, ammunition, clothing, and personal effects. "Them wagons won't make it. Horses neither. Trade them wagons for pack saddles, them horses for mules, if you can get ya any."

"Have you a map, with detailed notes? It would be most helpful, essential I should say, to know where the water and grass is, not to mention the so-called trail. We should know where we can expect to find Indians, which tribe is where and the disposition of each, and where we might find the mules you left. We need to know where the fords are, especially at the Rio Colorado. And once we ford the Colorado and enter the desert, we need to know where water may be found."

Carson tapped his temple.

"I see. On whose orders do you act?"

"Captain Frémont."

"Captain Frémont," General Kearny said. "And the purpose of your journey is to deliver dispatches to President Polk, apprising him of the situation in California?"

"Yes, sir. I give my word to it."

"It does not require a man of your experience to find his way to Washington City from where we stand, but it does require a man of your experience to reach the California coast from here. This is particularly true since your knowledge of the route is current."

"What are you sayin', General?"

"It need not be you who delivers the message to the president. Your skills can be better employed as guide to the First Dragoons."

"I give my word to Frémont, General."

"You are a commissioned lieutenant, are you not?"

"Temporary. Frémont done it. I got my orders."

"Captain Frémont, of the Topographical Corps. I am a brigadier general and commander of the Army of the West." General Kearny paused. "To be crass about it, I outrank him."

"When I give my word, I don't quit it. Like pledgin' my first born, if I ever get a chance to get one." Carson looked north, toward Taos, and did not smile.

"Look," Kearny said. "I'd like you to recognize the merit in my request and agree that you can serve a greater good."

Carson turned his head to the Indians who remained away from the dragoons.

"California may be under American control at the moment, but how long that may last is by no means certain. Rebellious elements remain there, we can be quite sure. Mexican forces may counterattack. My charge is to reinforce our troops in California as part of the war effort with Mexico. That carries more importance than personally delivering missives to the president."

The two men looked each other straight on. Neither smiled.

"I understand the disappointment this brings to you. I expect you were given this assignment in part due to your extraordinary service under Captain Frémont."

"Never seen the East, General."

General Kearny nodded. "Only a select few are given audience with the president. You've been accorded a great privilege and distinguished honor, but a keener purpose demands your attention."

"Last seen my bride two years ago. Gone from her twice as long as I been with her." Carson looked toward Taos. "Four, five days away now."

"The lives of these men are at stake, and possibly the security of the American hold in California. Do you understand the importance of your service to this march?"

"I'll draw a map. Tell you what to write. Talk you through it."

"Not good enough. No map or instruction would be as effective as your on-site leadership. Will you agree to join us?"

"No, sir. I give my word."

"In that case, I order you to hand over your dispatches to another capable courier so you may serve as my personal guide. Your courier will be Tom Fitzpatrick."

Carson lifted an eyebrow.

"Yes, I know of him. His reputation is nearly as eminent as yours. No doubt you will trust him to see that your express is safely delivered."

"Tom and me scouted many trips, not just this one. He's as good as they get."

"You will bring your best guide, next to Fitzpatrick, with you as a second. That would be Robideaux." Kearny showed a slight smile. "His reputation is known." His smile faded. "The rest of your party may continue without interruption."

Carson faced west, toward the Rio Gila and the country that broke down his party. "Wore out and chewed to rawhide, General, then turn back to what done it." He stood there, solid as weather-worn rock. "Bride so close I can feel her breathe."

"You're an officer in the United States Army in wartime. What we want is of no consequence. What we must do determines what we will do. If you refuse this request, I can use force to detain you. If you desert, you will be pursued and treated accordingly."

"It ain't right, General. Plumb contrary."

"I understand that. I empathize with you, sincerely so, but we're in a war."

Carson looked upriver, toward Taos. "Just off yonder there. Touchin' distance." He grew still, as if waiting for prey.

After a bit Kearny said, "The fate of the nation may be at stake."

A flock of sandhill cranes trilled overhead, quartering in a wind that picked up speed. Carson turned to their song—sonorous, as if sung from seasoned oak.

"You are a man of honor and integrity."

Carson watched the cranes, big as small foxes. Their song softened when they winged away. He said from somewhere else, "Come so far. Come so close."

"You see you have to do this."

Carson turned to the general. "You're cheatin' me. You know that."

"It's a matter of necessity, not a question of fairness. I apologize."

Carson looked to the party he'd led from the California coast. "If I know'd then what I know now."

"We need you. I consider it God's providence that you came to our camp, just now, on the cusp of our venture into the unknown."

Carson shook his head.

"Draw rations from the quartermaster. We saddle at daybreak. You and I will inform your party." Kearny started for Carson's group, stopped when Carson didn't follow.

"You wouldn't find me, General, if I put my mind to it."

. . . [the Battalion] was enlisted too much by families; some were too old, some feeble, and some too young; it was embarrassed by many women . . .

—*Lieutenant Colonel Philip St. George Cooke,*
Santa Fe, October 13, 1846

Mormon Battalion, Advance Detachment, Santa Fe [New Mexico], October 9, 1846

When the advance detachment spotted Santa Fe, Gabriel Hanks said, "Those adobes look like flat-bottom boats blowed about a river bay. No pattern to it, not like Nauvoo, but throwed together haphazard like."

Santa Fe sat at the foot of the Sangre de Cristo Mountains with the larger buildings clustered to a plaza. Low adobes spread from there, then dwindled and stopped.

Gabriel gestured to the Santa Fe River that wound in and out of the pueblo. "Ever wonder if God give a bona fide river to this desert country?"

Phineas Lynch allowed he did not trouble with wonder.

"Looks like a mud-fish bog," Gabriel said. "Couldn't drown a kitten in it."

At the edge of Santa Fe, Lieutenant Smith halted the troops to fix bayonets, shoulder muskets, and march in formation to the public square. Soldiers, volunteers for the war in Mexico, stood on rooftops and hollered, waved hats, pulled balls from their paper cartridges, and fired blanks in the air. Bells chimed from the cathedral that marked the front of the plaza. Larger buildings, houses, and stores defined the sides and back of the public square. The battalion halted in the center of it and stood in formation to face an American flag that topped a flagpole.

"Looks like we conquered New Mexico," Gabriel Hanks said.

"Maybe America we never left," Phineas Lynch said.

"We left it. Beat us here is all. General Kearny must've done it."

They faced a tall officer of the First Dragoons. Lieutenant Smith called them to attention, and he and Philip St. George Cooke walked between the ranks to inspect the soldiers. After inspection Lieutenant Smith dismissed them to set up camp in a wheat field behind the cathedral.

"That tall one wanted to plug his nose when he walked amongst us, like we was dog vomit," Gabriel said. "You could tell."

"Vomit you might be," Phineas said. "But dog vomit?" He shook his head. "Worse than that you smell." He smiled.

"Stop that!" Gabriel said. "You're not allowed to smile."

Phineas widened his smile.

Gabriel leaned forward to peer in his mouth. "I'll be dog-gone. They's teeth in there."

Phineas chuckled.

Gabriel jumped back. "What was that?" He looked around. "Heard somethin' I ain't heard but once or twice. Like a wagon smashed a cat."

Phineas laughed.

"Struck a funny bone on Phineas Lynch, like stubbin' a toe on a gold nugget. I'll report on you to Brother Orson Everett, but he'll ask for evidence, for me to prove my allegation, so don't forget how to do what you just done."

"If Brother Orson we see again."

"We'll see him."

"If the Lord keeps the sickness from him from the sick he tends to."

"He won't take sick. He's the Lord's own, so the Lord will put an angel on him."

"Or from here we march before they arrive."

"Wonder may not trouble you but worry do. I hereby proclaim, Phineas Lynch, leave your disquieted mind where you found it for it does no good." Gabriel nodded toward Lieutenant Smith and the tall officer who walked to a building on the edge of the plaza. "Then again, if you're on to consternation, fret on them two. That tall one mostly, business to the bone. Worse than Lieutenant A. J., I'd swear on the Bible to it."

"Need I point out, sir, that we precede the deadline by one day?"

Lieutenant A. J. Smith and Philip St. George Cooke, Lieutenant Colonel of Volunteers, conferred in Cooke's quarters—a room with a dirt floor, plank ceiling, whitewashed walls, single bed, a paneless window with open shutters, table, and chairs where Lieutenant Colonel Cooke and Lieutenant Smith sat.

"Well done, Lieutenant."

"I have demonstrated my ability for command, have I not, sir?"

"Yes, you have. If fact, you've shown exemplary leadership under difficult circumstances. However, it is General Kearny's wish, or more precisely, his order, that I assume command of the Mormon Battalion on its arrival here."

Smith looked at the calico that covered the top half of a wall, tacked there to protect the backs of those who would sit on the bench from rubbing whitewash. He turned back to Lieutenant Colonel Cooke.

"I did not expect this. No reflection on you, sir, but I would be less than honest if I said I were not disappointed."

"You don't know how well I understand that." A wind disturbed a map on the wall. Cooke rose and closed the shutters. He remained standing. "We are all dealt our disappointments, and I often think the military levies those with a heavier hand."

"And the deadline? I was ordered to reach Santa Fe by 10 October or the battalion would be discharged. As I explained, I divided the battalion to do so, and you inspected the hardier half. The rear detachment should follow in a matter of days."

Cooke nodded.

"The leadership I've shown will go unrecognized, in spite of my demonstrated ability for higher command. Is that correct, sir?"

"Until the opportunity arrives. You know how slow promotions can be. You also know that can change quickly when war is engaged."

Smith watched a spider march across the hard-dirt floor.

"You understand that, don't you, Lieutenant?"

Smith straightened. Cooke's look could burn holes through the wall. "Yes, sir."

"Until that time arrives, you will join my staff as a junior officer."

Smith turned to the brighter light, broken by the shuttered window.

"I did not want this command, Lieutenant. I implored General Kearny to post me to Mexico, but you see I'm here. We do as ordered, don't we, Lieutenant?"

Smith nodded.

Cooke walked to the desk, tapped its surface. "Don't we, Lieutenant?"

"Yes, sir. We do, sir."

"Very well." Cooke sat down. "We have a challenging march

ahead of us, to put it in mannered terms. Your battalion must be stabilized accordingly."

"Are half to march and half to be discharged, sir? Consistent with the deadline?"

"I'll put it this way. Urgency for the departure of this battalion remains, but not the deadline."

Smith snickered.

"Yes, Lieutenant?"

"That will please the Mormons, sir."

"Only to be disappointed again."

"Sir?"

"I received word from General Kearny this morning that California is under American control."

"I'll be damned. California taken and we're halfway there. That might disappoint me, but it won't disappoint the Mormons."

Cooke continued. "The general has three hundred dragoons. He will detach two hundred to return here and will continue to California with one hundred. His smaller force will travel faster and will place less demand on the scant water and feed available in the desert."

"I understand," Smith said.

"With his dragoons reduced by two-thirds, our charge, as the general's reserve, becomes more pressing in the event that he encounters hostile forces. As such we do not serve the general well if we are too far behind."

"Our mission remains intact, sir?"

"Yes, with one significant change."

"Sir?"

"With control of California now in American hands, the mission for this battalion has expanded. We are ordered to open a wagon road, for the purpose of commerce, from Santa Fe to San Diego. We will march a southerly route, much of it through a wilderness with no road or trail, unknown to any but natives."

"A southerly route?"

"The general will march a more direct route west, along the Gila River. We will be a good deal south of that. Hardly a march for women and children, or for the old, or for the sick and convalescent."

"The rear detachment, then, will remain as such, sir?"

"Basically, yes. We may add to or subtract from it, but it will be sent to join those you ordered to Pueblo some weeks ago."

"Sixteen September, sir, at the start of the Cimarron Cutoff. You would have thought I sentenced them to die."

"But you set the precedent. This division should prove the less difficult."

"The selection won't be difficult, but its implementation," Smith shook his head. "Expect a mutiny, sir."

"They may resist, but they have no choice."

"They're like sheep, sir. They take comfort in numbers. Many of them refuse to recognize that dividing the whole will benefit the parts."

"That's the lesser of our concerns. Our most pressing problem is supply. There is very little available. We have no money or specie, and few trade goods. The trader who will accept a credit voucher is rare. I've had a hell of a time finding the minimum we need, let alone acquiring it. Mules are impossible to get, with the exception of a few procured by the quartermaster. Rations are not much better. We have damn few tools for opening a road."

"Sounds like a frontier army." Smith smiled.

"Their clothing is nearly worn out, from what I saw today, and we have none to replace it. The men don't look much better, and you tell me this is the stronger half."

"I will add, sir, they have small regard for military discipline, and you will find them to be a rebellious bunch when you butt up against their command structure, which is their clergy, not their elected officers. But they are tough."

"They'll need to be. We have a hard march ahead of us." Cooke stood. "We will depart as soon as practicable, but in no case later than ten days. We have much to accomplish."

CHAPTER 17

. . . the women were moaning and crying about the camp, thinking that they would in a few days be separated from their husbands and left in the care of sick men among savage tribes of Indians but many of our brethren swore in their rath [sic] they would not leave their wives, order or no order!

—William Coray,
Mormon Battalion, Santa Fe,
October, 1846

Mormon Battalion, Santa Fe [New Mexico], October 14, 1846
Captain Alcott and Captain Hunt removed their hats, knocked on the door, and a voice boomed, "Come in." Lieutenant Colonel Cooke, a head taller than they, stood at his table and pored over a map and said, "Too much unmarked space on this map."

He looked up from the map.

"Captains Alcott and Hunt, I believe. Mormon volunteers."

"Yes, sir," Captain Hunt said. "I'm impressed that you know who we are without having met us, sir."

"It is my duty as commander to know the officers in my command. Welcome, gentlemen. What's on your mind?"

"The sick and infirm, sir, with our wives, whom you intend to march to Pueblo," Captain Hunt said.

"I expected as much."

Captain Alcott said, "You would send our wives to Pueblo, sir?"

"I left my wife, didn't I? And you expect me to make an exception for you?"

"Sir," Captain Alcott said, "I suppose you left your wife with family and friends, in the comfort of her home, while we leave ours in a hostile country, guarded by sick men, to march off to a frontier settlement to find what shelter they can, with winter coming on."

Cooke looked at the table, considered the map, located Santa Fe, and traced the route north-northeast that the women and children and the sick and infirm, defended by a few able-bodied guards, would follow—Glorieta Pass, the Pecos and Canadian Rivers, Raton Pass, the Purgatoire River, then Pueblo, four days west by wagon of Bent's Fort, a supply and trading post downriver on the Arkansas. He thought of his family he'd left at Fort Leavenworth, perhaps back in Philadelphia now, his daughters and son and his lovely Rachael, the waist he could nearly wrap his hands around on their wedding day, and the image rose to haunt him again. His color left when he saw her scarring, recalled her patient suffering in the five-year wait for surgery that could only do so much, how she forgave him when he could never forgive himself.

"Are you all right, sir?" Captain Hunt asked.

Cooke wiped his brow with a handkerchief. "Desert water will do that on occasion." He looked to the map. A breeze nudged a shutter at the window.

"Here's what I'll do. There are twenty-two wives with the battalion. The wives of officers and sergeants may accompany the battalion provided you furnish their transportation and rations at your expense. They will, in no manner, lag or impede the battalion. If they accompany the battalion they are committed for the duration of the march, and it will be very difficult, I can assure you. That will be four or five of them. The balance will be detached to Pueblo as planned, but I will permit their husbands to remain with them if they choose."

"Thank you, sir," Captain Hunt said. "That's fair."

"If my wife takes sick before we reach San Diego, what then, sir?" Captain Alcott said.

"The march shall not be impeded. Do I make myself clear?"

Captain Alcott watched Cooke roll up the map.

"Do I make myself clear, Captain Alcott?"

"Yes, sir."

Cooke inserted the map into its leather scabbard and buckled the cap. He looked at the two Latter-day Saints whose clerical leader had named as captains. Worn-out clothing. No insignia, no mark of rank. Hats in hand, limp brims from years of weather. Hair cleaned and combed. "No more goddamn whining. I will remind you that you are in the army, and I am your commanding officer. What I say goes, whether it's contrary to the dictates of Brigham Young or God himself. If you disobey orders I can have you shot. Dismissed."

CHAPTER 18

We are still to look for the glowing pictures drawn of California.
As yet, barrenness and desolation hold their reign.

—Lieutenant William Emory,
Corps of Topographical Engineers, with
General Kearny, Army of the West, 1846

Army of the West, early October to early December [New Mexico to California] 1846

General Kearny sent an express rider to Santa Fe requesting pack saddles. He dispatched two hundred dragoons and the wagons to Santa Fe, but even at that the country west would be hard pressed to sustain one hundred dragoons with their mules. Kearny kept the two mountain howitzers. Carson thought with their narrow frames and large wheels they might make it.

They marched downriver three days, stopped and waited three more until the pack saddles arrived. With them came bags of mail.

Abner received a letter. Smithwick and Donovan as well. Moses went empty handed.

"Should you expect better," Abner said, "when you tell no one the course you've set?" He held up the letter from his former fiancée, Clarissa Pembroke. "Our parting was amicable, an association disjoined but left unsevered. Yours, perhaps, carried a different tenor?"

Moses wondered if Miss Isabella would have written had she

known his whereabouts. He could let up, let Abner write that letter. He wondered what he would say. *Rode through country to dull a quick mind. Charged a Mexican army that run before we got there. Seen a Mexican dead with arrows. Got me a lesson in a Santa Fe whorehouse. Nothin' ahead but dry and drier. I come west, but my heart stayed home along-side of yours.*

If he did write, when would the letter get there? Like Abner said, he could be dead by then. In that case she'd have his last words, but why weight her with those?

He'd left home. He'd leave it at that.

Abner stepped away, sat by a cactus, opened the letter.

Abner my darling,

How glorious to receive your precious letters! How I've missed your clever sentences! I often wonder how you've fared, so imagine my delight to find you still irrepressible and in new pursuit. To the catalogue of your impressive talents I shall add, "ability to land on one's feet," but then, that should not surprise me. You have always been as nimble as a feline, or African cat rather, complete with claws, now that I think of it, so effortlessly extended and retracted, each with its nick of flesh. My precious Abner, how I yearn for our tête-à-tête combats, replete with your charm and your wit. My dear one, what a vacuum you've left in parlor entertainment. Our cherished soirées, and the enchanting aftermath of the afterward dalliance, departed with you.

I dare say your road has taken an exotic turn! Such a wayward course excites the imagination, in part, no doubt, because it falls well below your station. My Abner Black, my loved one, companion to my soul as no other could be, how much you resemble an elm, so grand and majestic, warped by a lightning strike. How you would have graced society, were it not for that most mundane of failings.

Please explain, my bittersweet, the annoying hole through the heart of your prose. How intriguing, as if your words resemble roses floating on a brook only to disappear with the appearance of a footbridge and then appear again, but alas! Not with luscious rose clipped of its thorns, but lily-of-the-valley with its poisonous berries. I liken the hole centered in your stationery to a cavern that harbors your darkest heart. How well I liked to wander there!

Abner my darling, what a match we would have made. Your keen sense of villainy never failed to titillate me. I regret that you abandoned that most beguiling twist in your character—that which fueled your brilliance at the lectern.

May you be well, my dear Abner. I worry for your welfare given the hazards of your situation. If only you could return to me, healed of spirit, perhaps we could begin anew, albeit discreetly with my marriage well placed with the kind and stalwart Mr. Pembroke, with whom I have mastered the art of proper appearances. Concern yourself not for me. I am well-tended.

Yours, with the warmth of my heart,
Clarissa

Abner placed the letter in its envelope, took it to his lips, folded it to fit in his tunic pocket. He removed and wiped his spectacles, put them next to the letter, and lay on his back with his hands on his eyes.

The next day, after a twenty-mile march further south on the *Rio Grande del Norte,* more mail came. A partial bag only, arrived in Santa Fe a day after the soldiers left with pack saddles. The commandant at Santa Fe knew this was the last chance for mail for General Kearny's dragoons this side of California, so he sent it by express rider. A lieutenant called those who received mail. He called for Moses Cole.

Moses groomed his mule, out of earshot. The lieutenant sent

the letter with Abner.

Moses looked at the careful penmanship with rounded letters, addressed to Moses Cole, First Dragoons, War with Mexico. The return address read: Isabella James, Bridgewater, Virginia.

Abner said, "You look like a boy with a Christmas pudding smothered in sweet cream." He smiled. "I mailed the letters from Fort Leavenworth, yours included. They weren't destroyed," he smiled wider, "only ventilated in a curious manner."

Moses started to say something, stopped, and walked away. He went to the river's edge, sat down, held the letter in both hands, listened to the current, watched autumn leaves float by. He opened the envelope with a careful cut with his belt knife.

Dear Moses,

Thank you for sending a letter. No one knew where you had gone, but a drummer passed through and stopped at Daddy's store to sell some wares and in conversation described a boy that looked like you. So we had some notion that you joined the army. Now we know, and I wish you well.

I see your pa when he comes to buy dry goods. He is fine, and we shared the news from the drummer.

Life is pretty much the same here. Richmond is nice with my aunt and she schools me, but I do not fit in the city. I go back to Richmond each year for a time, and when I'm not there I work in the dry-goods store.

Remember the boy that got brassy with me and you knocked him down with the axe handle you carved from an oak branch? He has had a come about and wants to turn preacher. He is nicer than he used to be.

It was very good to receive a letter from you. Your letter made me blush. I hope to see you home before long.

Sincerely yours,
Isabella James

Moses reread the letter and found within it hope and worry. He felt as light as a leaf fallen from a cottonwood and shoved by a breeze, autumn gold, poked with worm holes.

The one hundred dragoons, pack trains, and two mountain howitzers turned west from the *Rio Grande del Norte* to march to the Rio Gila. They trekked through valleys of grama grass and frequent streams, by cedar and long-leaf pine, oak and walnut, bluffs and broken boulders.

Moses wondered at the country, probed what lay beneath Isabella's ink. *Nicer than he used to be, the letter said. Is he courting her? Asking her daddy to call on her Sundays?*

They went on through the valley of the Mimbres, dense with cottonwood and vacant lodges of an unknown tribe, crossed the Rio Mimbres alive with trout.

Him turn preacher? Can't savvy that. That axe handle lit a lantern for him maybe. Circled back to beat on me, if that's what it done him for.

They rode by crumbled adobe homes deserted after Apache attacks, passed abandoned mine shafts lined with iron pyrite. "Fool's gold," Abner whispered so none could hear. "The pot to end my rainbow, its deepest hues—those Clarrisa shone that filled my life with color—now bland as desert sand."

Five days from the *Rio Grande del Norte* they reached the Rio Gila where the mountains squeezed into peaks, twisted into ridges, and split into ravines. Downstream the valley narrowed to a canyon that narrowed to a gorge. The one hundred dragoons, pack train, and mountain howitzers climbed the side of a mountain on the way without a trail that Carson had warned about.

Abner felt Clarissa's cold and hot hold. *My princess, my bewitching Clarissa, how I long for your embrace, your quick brilliance that lighted my nights, your vicious wit that darkened and filled my heart, the beautiful enigma you gave my vacant days.*

Saddles and packs shifted and reshifted in the steep ravines. Mules edged their hooves into the sharp hills, scrambled in scree, bruised their soles on a faint trail knotted with rock, walked to the clack of loose shoes. One fell from a precipice, scattering its pack, and lay at the base of the slope, head folded below his shoulder.

Sores showed under saddles and cinch rings, grew larger, deeper, more numerous.

Moses checked the raw spot on his mule's withers. *Sored deep like me on the inside. Nothin' to salve it with neither. A come about, she called it. Courtin' on her, sure as that mule's broke-neck dead down that mountainside. Can't do nothin' for neither one. Toughen that hide and mount up, trooper.*

The dragoons rode on, through a land of lizards and tarantulas, and even they, Moses said, would quit this country if they had legs that was up to the job. The troop passed escarpments, wended through arroyos and over bluffs, and named the trail the Devil's turnpike. They descended to the Rio Gila, found soil like ashes, a foot deep and soft as cotton.

Abner saw an ash heap of broken hopes.

Moses said right out loud, "Give me the jealousy, is what she done. Didn't think I had it in me."

The canyon pushed them from the river to pick their way through tortured terrain before it opened a return to the water course. The riverbed varied from sand to lava to boulders of quartz, from squared rock to river-rolled stones.

Abner heard the water talk, whisper, and rage, sounding the tumult in his heart.

Moses saw the line she penned, stamped in his memory. Your

letter made me blush. Wrote that down, right there on the paper. Moses petted his mule, told him, "We'll be all right, pardner. Keep them hooves beneath of us, hear me? Give us time, we'll heal up with open country."

They woke with blankets covered with frost and marched in moonlight on black sand. A city on the hills rose in the distance that turned into spires of stone when approached. Sandstone bluffs, red and green and burnished bronze, and to Moses's eye, layered like stacked lumber or bent like blankets folded and rolled. They passed a promontory of pitchstone, crossed over lava beds, touched hieroglyphics—evidence, Abner said, of an ancient race, the end of life but blood on rock.

The dragoons pushed on through knee-deep dust that reddened their eyes, rode by cactus smaller than Miss Isabella's teacup, Moses said, to taller than her daddy's dry-goods store. *Hopes to see me home before long. Wrote that down, too. Teasin' me or meanin' it, might be one, could be the other, depends on the day maybe, or what that preacher boy said in his visit, the look he give her.*

The gap between grasses grew. Leaves changed from green to brittle. Mules weakened, started to die.

Though nimble for carriages with their ten-foot wheels and three-foot axles, the howitzers proved too cumbersome for country this rugged. Broken spokes, cracks to wheel rims, axles, and iron tires required endless repair with rawhide wraps.

Moses shook his head. *Huntin' a trail to track through that letter, and it don't lead nowhere but back to where it started from. Consternating myself with a riddle I can't solve, so stop figurin' it.*

Apaches came to trade but stopped on the crest of a hill, eyes on the big guns. Kit Carson rode forward, parleyed for a time, and returned with Chief Red Sleeve. He and Carson parleyed in sign language and few words.

Carson said, "They're scared of the howitzers. Think they

shoot through mountains."

More sign language passed, interspersed words in Apache and Spanish.

Carson nodded to Red Sleeve and said to General Kearny, "He knows we've taken New Mexico. They'll help us kill Mexicans. They fight for the laws of Montezuma, and for food, not land. Friend to whites. Feed us if we're hungry. Give mule or horse if we're afoot. He wants to trade."

Kearny said, "Tell him we want to trade as well, especially for mules."

Carson signed. Red Sleeve waved for his people to come in.

Carson said to Kearny, "Trust them like you would a scorpion on a baby's belly."

The Apaches brought mules and mescal, lariats and horse whips and braided horsehair tack. The dragoons brought knives, needles and thread, blankets, red shirts and scarves, biscuits, and sugar.

Abner unsaddled his mule to grease his galled withers, then negotiated a trade for a skin of mescal. He offered his knife, but the Apache shook his head, nodded at the book that lay by Abner's saddle. Abner picked up *Paradise Lost* and handed it to the Apache. The Apache examined the charred and gilded pages, gave Abner the skin of mescal, and carried the book to a bush like a waiter with a tray with his finger through the bullet hole. He squatted, defecated, tore pages from the book, and wiped himself.

Abner untied the buckskin thong at the neck of the skin, tilted his head back, and took a long swallow.

A lighter-skinned boy travelled with the Apaches. Nose and cheekbones of aristocratic Spanish. Dressed Indian, Moses thought. Breechcloth and moccasins, red headband. Moses approached him and said, "Where you from?"

The boy smiled. After a moment he said, "Been a long

time"—he paused, moved his lips as if sampling the words he'd said—"since I heard English. It sounds," he paused again, "funny." He laughed.

"Who are your folks?"

"My birth mother was American. She raised me with English. My father, Spanish."

"Why are you here? What happened?"

"I wandered off from the hacienda. I got lost. The Apaches found me. I was eight."

"What are you, twelve years old now?"

The boy laughed. "It's funny to talk English." He figured. "Could be. That was long, long ago." He smiled. "Apache now."

"Don't you miss your kin? Civilized life?"

The boy looked at the Apaches. He looked at the dragoons. He looked at the rough country. He looked at Moses. He said, "My home is here. My Apache father is"—he thought a moment—"kind. Giving. Fierce warrior. Like the spirit of the big-wing bird. My Apache mother, loving. I don't know the whites."

An Apache called him to where he negotiated a trade with Smithwick. The boy picked up the steel bladed knife and examined the handle, the rivets that held it secure, the bevel on the blade. He checked the stitching in the shirt, its buttons and buttonholes. He turned the blanket in his hands, felt the woven wool.

"What do we have here, a stolen child?" Smithwick said.

The boy smiled. "They're family now." He looked at the braided rawhide lariat and horsehair headstall. He said to Smithwick, "Give another shirt."

Another Apache called for the boy to examine the wares offered for trade.

Smithwick watched him walk away. "I'll be damned. A regular Jewish merchant."

General Kearny tried to buy the boy to return him to his

family. The boy's Indian kin refused. Kearny upped the ante with four worn-down mules and their pack saddles. A dragoon added his harmonica to the offer. Another pitched in his straight-edge razor and shaving mirror. General Kearny dropped his pocket knife with its mother-of-pearl handle on the trade blanket, and the Apache dad remained adamant. He signed to Carson that the boy was not for sale, and he walked away.

The boy smiled at General Kearny. "Thank you anyway," he said. "I am happy here."

The army marched on, lost more mules. Half the command used their saddle mounts for pack animals and led instead of rode them. They'd crossed the continental cordillera, and twenty days from when they'd entered the Rio Gila country the twisted hills gave way to a desert plain.

Willows and cottonwood shoots lined the river course. Waves of waterfowl flew overhead. They passed sand buttes and ponds of salt water and abandoned oxbows full of ducks, crossed a land littered with pottery shards and the hollow rock of corn grinders. Their mules grazed on cane and willow and flag grass on the banks of the Rio Gila.

Abner thought, *I've found my wasteland. How Clarissa's missives bring that home. How odd, the glee we found in malicious quips. A battle of wits that cut to the quick. No wonder I searched for solace in drunkenness and sometimes found it there. Yet another false pursuit, one that shunted me here, lost to my bearings, none of the comforts that grew familiar to me, no mental mazes to titillate the intellect, no frisson from lustful touches our eyes implied. But to here, a journey that cuts out life by the pound with nothing at the end of it but the false gold a fool pursues.*

Salt in the soil made it look like they walked on frost. They crossed the trail of a horse herd that resembled a snow rope that spooled to the end of the desert. "Must be where the dead ones go," Moses said. "Looks like a trail made by ghosts of horses."

A trail to the ghost of my soul, Abner thought.

They traded with the Pimas and the Maricopas, rich with irrigated fields, then went on to ford the Rio Colorado and cross a desert of floating sand littered with mussel shells. They dug a well there, found water limited to the cupful. The army marched by a lake that reeked with dead predators, found a spring that bubbled sulphur.

Moses gaped at snow-coated peaks. "Them'll put the fear of the Lord in a man." He looked away, cursed the long-leafed cactus plant that tore at the legs of man and mule.

Abner looked to the vista, felt a thorn cut through a pant leg. *I no longer know the purpose of my yearning. Professor of Rhetoric. A life for the idle, filled with fancy, crafting veneer to brighten rotten walls.*

With six weeks between them and when they'd left the *Rio Grande del Norte,* Kearny's command crossed the divide to the Pacific Ocean to see oak trees and evergreens, valleys waving yellowed grass, streams, and forbs. "There she be," Moses said. "That Eden you told about."

Eden indeed, Abner thought. *How you haunt me, my daunting Clarissa, your voice an echo in my hollow heart.*

Kit Carson pointed out the valley of the Aqua Caliente and said they would find there a *rancheria* owned by an American named Warner, a Connecticut native who took Mexico for his country and changed his name from Jonathan to Juan José. Carson reckoned Warner for a cold host.

General Kearny said, "We can trade for what we need from Mr. Warner, or, if it's to be *Señor* Warner, we can take what we need. It is up to him."

CHAPTER 19

The Battalion followed the flag and I followed the dust.
—Sarah Jane Brown, age twelve,
daughter of Eunice and James Brown,
Mormon Battalion, 1846

Mormon Battalion, Rio Grande del Norte, south of Santa Fe
[New Mexico], November 10, 1846
"Think of the work we do. The laundry. The cooking and nurs-ing, and yet he has the audacity to think we're a bother," Abi-gail Alcott said.

They sat on the bank of the *Rio Grande del Norte* in the shade of cottonwoods, their feet in the water as the battalion nooned and watered the animals, ate, and rested before marching further south, closer to Mexico.

"His concern is his career, not the welfare of those he com-mands." Abigail pursed her lips. "To send the families and the sick away to fend for themselves." She shook her head. "I mean, what a stain on a commander's resumé for women to die under his watch."

Melissa laughed. "I should hope we'd be more than stains on a military career." She took Abigail's hands in hers and examined the cracks in the fingertips and on the sides of joints—tiny, razor cut-like splits that stung like spider bites. These were the hands of a laundress bearing the marks of hours in dish and laundry water, no balm but desert air pulling wetted skin apart.

"Your poor hands," Melissa said. "I must find a salve for them."

"Yours are just as bad."

"Axle grease and lard would help, neither one of which we have," Melissa said.

"In that case, as nurses we shall check for head lice in the men," Abigail said. "Plenty of grease there."

"I've tried that," Melissa said. "It stings."

They giggled with their feet in the river. The *Rio Grande del Norte*, wide, braided and shallow and shaded by cottonwoods, eased on and eddied as if it resisted the call of the salt water Gulf and stalled, waiting for next year's rain.

Melissa massaged her toes and foot soles, then pressed her feet in the mud and asked Abigail for hers, one foot at a time.

Abigail lifted a foot, Melissa dried it with her dress, placed it in her lap, and pressed her thumbs in the sole as if to knead knots away. She touched the big toe. The swelling had eased, but the nail had blackened. "You may lose this nail."

A breeze lingered in the cottonwoods, picked leaves as yellow as sun.

"Do not let a mule step on your toe," Abigail said.

"You are so fortunate that he was not shod."

"Never, ever, trust a mule," Abigail said. "He knew what he was doing. He just pretended he didn't."

The leaves fell, slow as river water, and settled on the river's surface.

Melissa sang a verse of "Old Hundredth"—Praise God from whom all blessings flow—while she worked Abigail's foot. Abigail watched the river run, and Melissa continued to sing—Praise him, all creatures here below. She resumed humming. Abigail watched the shadow of a fish swim counter to current just out from the foot she soaked.

"Please keep singing. You have such a lovely voice. It's like songbirds in a spring meadow, full of wildflowers."

Melissa smiled and resumed the hymn.

"Your beautiful voice pulls my mind away from that awful Lieutenant Colonel Cooke."

"Now Abigail, we must be fair. He is not beyond kindness." Melissa worked her fingers between Abigail's toes.

"When was that man kind?"

"Remember when he offered his big, white mule to me?"

"Oh. That."

"I was so ill that day. Honestly, I didn't know how I could make it, and up rode Lieutenant Colonel Cooke on his big white mule, dismounted, and offered him to me. He even helped me mount the poor thing. How can I forget that?"

Abigail said, "How I miss our sisters and brothers that were sent to Pueblo. We were a community then. Now we're just a part of an army."

Melissa stretched Abigail's toes by easing them back. "Yes, but we have our husbands, and you, my dear Abigail, have your precious baby growing within you. You're almost to the point where it's difficult to conceal." She worked her thumbs in the arch of Abigail's foot.

"Perhaps that is why I miss the women and children so, with the baby coming." Abigail put her hands on her stomach, felt its firm, rounding swell, and wondered if she would carry her baby to term with the exertion of it—five to twenty-five miles per day, day after day, week after week, close to four months now, often with little water and a diet that narrowed to meat. The worse the conditions, the more she walked as the mules weakened. And yet her baby grew. She felt its movement, thought if it survived this march it would survive anything. She wondered if it knew her thirst, suffered her hunger. She felt its spirit, a male, come to guide her. At moments in the weary marches she could swear she drew from its strength, from its wisdom even, to keep going, one step and then another, to rest somewhere ahead. At those times, she told Melissa, her baby carried her more than she carried it.

Melissa finished massaging the foot. "Work your feet into the mud. It feels so good."

Abigail put her foot back in the water and wormed her feet into the mud. "This baby," she said, blinking tears. "So very, very wonderful."

"Angels take mysterious forms," Melissa said.

"And some not so mysterious." Abigail put an arm around Melissa. "You could be my younger sister, but you are so much wiser than I. I thank the Lord for you."

Melissa lay her head on Abigail's shoulder. "Oh, but I thank Him for you. I could not endure this journey without you."

A leaf flowed by, floating a grasshopper. Abigail watched the leaf spin at the speed of the tick-tock hand of the family clock, stowed in the wagon she and Captain Alcott drove. She said, "You must help me when the time comes."

"Of course I will, but that is a long way off." Melissa lifted her head from Abigail's shoulder and took her hand. "You work too hard and eat too little. I pray for your health and for that of your baby."

"If only that martinet valued families as much as he values his army," Abigail said. "Might as well ask an ox to talk."

"You surprise me, Abigail. You know as well as I do the wonders the Lord works. Commander Cooke is simply another prospect for the Lord to give a turn-around to, like he did Saint Paul. Like he did for me."

"I could soak him in my washtub with water at the boil point, and his skin wouldn't wrinkle. He's made from the coldest metal I've ever seen."

"All the more reason to pray for him."

"What will he do when my baby comes? Shoot me like a

horse with a broken leg? He can't have his army slow down, can he? Not for a baby. Not for a mother who can't keep up."

"I will say, Abigail, he's a hard man, but he's honorable. That's as obvious to you as it is to me."

"May the Lord damn him."

"Abigail!"

"Melissa, you're my dearest friend. I can't hide how I feel or what I think. Not from you. Not with a baby on the way. May the Lord forgive me for it, but I can't do otherwise."

"Yes, you can. The Lord helps us rein in our unruly spirits, if we let Him. Pray for guidance for you and for Commander Cooke."

"Someone else can pray for that man. My prayers are for my baby, and for the families he banished."

"Of course they are, and mine are, too. Always for you and your baby. I'll just say, the Lord does not want our prayers to stop with those we love."

"Mine do. For a prayer to take hold you have to mean it in your heart, and my heart is barred to that man."

Melissa lifted her feet, rubbed off the mud, and pulled them from the river. "Enough about that. You need to eat."

Abigail said, "You know what I want right now? Pickles and liver, and I've never liked either one."

CHAPTER 20

One yoke of our oxen got mired in the mud. We took off the yoke when one got out. The other we undertook to pull out with a rope and unfortunately broke his neck . . . This was a dark time, and many were the earnest petitions that went up to our God and Father for Divine aid.

The next morning we found with our oxen a pair of splendid young steers, which was really cheering to us. We looked upon it as one of the providences of our Father in heaven.

—Lieutenant Willis,
Mormon leader of the Willis Detachment,
the last detachment sent from the Mormon Battalion
to Pueblo [Colorado], November 11, 1846

The Mormon Battalion, Janos Road, South of Santa Fe
[New Mexico], November 21–22, 1846

Philip St. George Cooke, lieutenant colonel of volunteers, retrieved his pocket compass and turned it in his hand. A nice little piece, heavy for its size, the domed lid snug to his palm, the brass case as yet undented. He considered the miles he'd carried it on horse- and muleback over the last five years and numbered them close to four thousand. He lifted the brass lid, held it level, and studied the dial.

"Son of a bitch," he said.

He looked up, watched the back of the chief pilot, Ebenezer Green, riding just ahead, left of the column. *Look at the old half-*

breed, he thought, *plodding along, swaying with his mule's gait, his mind empty as desert, following a road to God knows where because it's easy.*

The directional needle floated beneath clean crystal, marked with thirty-two cardinal and inter-cardinal points. He wanted the fleur de lis of the north cardinal point to indicate they headed west, yet the dial remained oblivious to his yearning.

The road reached to the south with no sign of turning, to Janos, Mexico, from the copper mines at Santa Rita, abandoned since the Apache attacks. To the west lay the trackless desert, the mountains in the distance probing the sky, eroded to the bone. San Diego is what, Cooke wondered—a quarter of a continent on the other side of those?

Ebenezer Green slowed his mule, then rode beside Cooke. Green nodded to the compass. "Smart little thing, ain't it, Cap'n? Sand storm, snow storm, fog, or the starless dark. It don't care. Always knows where north is." Green smiled. Creases from his eyes to his ears suggested canyons in a landscape. His tan could pass for Mexican, as if driven in by wind and baked to make it stay there. "I don't intend to argue with the little bastard, but I know somethin' it don't. Water to the south. Dry to the west. One way we live, the other we don't. It's pretty simple."

"It's equally clear to me, Mr. Green. To go west, go west. Don't go south, day after day, and then turn east."

Green laughed. His creases deepened. "Damnedest thing, a compass is. Trade judgment for science." The sparkle in his eyes did not match the miles in his face. "Nature don't think like we do, Cap'n. To survive in this country, you gotta think like an Apache." His smile faded. "Forget that crap they teach in soldier school. Listen to the land. It'll tell you what to do."

Cooke reined in his big, white saddle mule. "Mexico or California?" he said.

Ebenezer Green tilted his hat, dipped his brim toward Cooke as if to deflect the question, and plodded on, eyes to the horizon where the Janos Road went.

As if we need a guide to follow a road, Cooke thought. He threw his hand up. The bugler sounded halt. Cooke stood in his stirrups, used his full height to command the attention of the desert.

"This is not my course!" His voice boomed into the halted column. "I was ordered to California, and I'll god damned if I'll march around the world to get there!" He surveyed his troop of trail-worn Mormons. "Bugler, blow 'to the right.' "

Ebenezer Green trotted back to Cooke. "Ain't nobody been there, Cap'n. No water to that country."

"If no one has been there, how do you know there's no water?"

"Indians and Mexicans been in this country a long time. If water's there, people would live there, and if people lived there, we'd know it."

"Would you rather we march through Chihuahua? Into the lap of the Mexican army?" Cooke's sunburn turned another shade of red. "Leave this road. Turn west, Mr. Green." Cooke faced his mule to the battalion and stood in his stirrups, his voice equal to his stature. "We go to California, or we die in the attempt!" He settled in his saddle. "Bugler, must I repeat my command?"

"Right, sir?" The bugle hesitated at the bugler's chest.

"Right, goddammit! Blow 'to the right!' "

The bugler lifted the bugle and blew the command.

The Mormon volunteers moved forward and hinged right where Cooke and Green sat their mules.

More like an exodus, Cooke thought. *A paupers' army that had staked all on faith and left trail-side graves to mark the way. Bedouins in search of an oasis, worn-out and poorly provisioned, a diaspora of the destitute, the Almighty their only compass.*

"It's a hell of a gamble, Cap'n," Green said.

"Lieutenant colonel," Cooke said. "For five weeks now. You ought to know that." *Into an unknown waterless waste while fame and rank are won in Mexico, while I'm here, commander to ragtag and bobtail church volunteers with a half-ass guide, for Christ's sake.*

"All the same to me, Cap'n. I'm no soldier-man. Just hired on to pilot you folks, and I'm thinkin' the money ain't that good."

Cooke recalled the nautical charts he'd seen at West Point, faded with age, the warning penned in bold letters to mark unknown oceans—*Beyond Here There Be Dragons.*

"More guides than a ship has sails, and not a damn one of you knows which way the wind blows," Cooke said.

"I trapped on the Rio Gila on the other side of that there"—Green lifted his chin to indicate the wasteland they faced—"but I come on it from the round-about north, not straight on with nothin' but sand and sun and lizard hills to the front of us. No man would do that."

"You are free to leave, Mr. Green."

"Broke beats dead, but dead beats Apache bait, which is what I'd be if I left this outfit they call an army."

"God bless you, sir colonel!" Phineas Lynch shouted when he turned toward San Diego. He saluted and waved at the sky when his hand left his forehead.

Look at these people. Pilgrims who'd savor a rat for a meal, and I have them for an army.

Gabriel Hanks shouted, "We prayed last night, and the Lord listened up a little!"

The naiveté of faith. What a blessing.

"We thought you was takin' us to the war in Mexico, but the Lord seen you to change your mind," Gabriel said when he wheeled right, in rank with the battalion marching four abreast, each to his own cadence, muskets shouldered. "You're an angel doin' Brigham's work."

Reverence misspent. So little respect for this oldest of institutions, an army marching to war.

Gabriel turned his head left as he turned right to keep his smile on Lieutenant Colonel Cooke.

That boy could eat an elephant with those teeth. Which is what crossing this desert will be. Eating an elephant. Cooke remembered being told Mormons were peculiar people. *'This people,' as Brigham Young calls his Saints, as if to imbue them with biblical importance. Stiff necked in the Old Testament sense. Stubborn to the point of defiance. Made mules seem eager to please.*

Cooke watched the column wheel right. They had learned some hint of military maneuvers after all, but taught on the plains instead of the drill field.

"Them Digger Indians," Green said. He watched the Mormons march by. "Shot my horses full of arrows once. Thought they'd eat 'em, but I built a big ole fire, cut them horses into pieces I could carry, and burned 'em." Green laughed, rocked back and forth in his saddle. "Had to bust up the wagon and chop mesquite to keep the fire goin'." Green laughed again, rocked more. "Didn't have no horses to pull it anyway, after they quivered 'em all."

Four yoke of oxen swung wide to turn right pulling a wagon loaded with flour and corn.

"Would've give them Indians a hind quarter if they hadn't a stole my traps."

Wagon wheels churned sand turning west.

"I owed 'em that much, after the killin' I done."

Cooke looked at him. "What killing?"

"Ma and pa of the squaw I stole, when the hate come on me."

Cooke remembered the wounded infant, Fox or Sauk tribe,

Black Hawk war of 1832, on the bank of the Mississippi below the mouth of the Bad Axe River, wailing at a breast of its dead mother. The soldier's musket ball had passed through the infant's arm and through its mother's chest while she nursed it. They took the baby away to amputate the arm, and he didn't know if the baby made it. Even now, fourteen years later, he shuddered at the memory.

"Mornin' ma'am," Green said and nodded at Abigail Alcott, who rode on the wagon Captain Alcott drove. Their mules sweated, pulling their wagon through the sand.

Cooke looked at Green. "Ma and pa of the squaw you stole," he said.

"All they got was the gut piles, and I don't mean the hearts and the livers. I burned them, too." Green chuckled.

"You stole a woman and killed her parents and burned your horses?"

"Stole her and sold her to Mexico." Green bobbed his head. "The Indian in me done it. Or maybe the white man. Ain't sure which."

Jesus Christ, Cooke thought. *Into whose hands are we commended?*

"If them were Apaches, they'd have eat my liver in front of my face." Green nodded at a Mormon who smiled. "Cut eyelid from eyeball, just to be sure I seen what they was doin'."

Wagon wheels cut tracks ankle deep. *If this keeps up,* Cooke thought, *we will march double file, in front of the wagons, to tramp down sand for the wagon wheels. If need be, we will rope up the wagons, and the men will help pull them.*

"There's money in them Digger Indians, Cap'n. Fifty dollars a scalp to Mexico. But I wouldn't mess with an Apache."

"Good God," Cooke said. He cued his mule and rode toward the head of the column and pondered their situation. *To venture ahead is to bet on providence. It's a bet on water in marching* distance, a bet to find it before we expire a man at a time. Lose the bet and the desert will do its work until all that remains is metal— locks and barrels, iron tires and keg rims, harness parts and cinch rings, wagon bolts and the like scattered in the sand. Mule shoes with the hooves rotted off, had the mules been shod.

Ebenezer Green trotted to Cooke and rode beside him. "A Digger ain't mean like an Apache is," he said.

Cooke looked ahead as if he'd not seen Green. *I've come to this, a dragoon on a mule charged with the inane and the strange, risking the life of each of these people in the name of commerce. Ebenezer Green, chief pilot.*

"Sheep thievin' bastards, them Apache Indians," Ebenezer Green said.

Turn the battalion back. What has the army made of me? Has it taken my humanity? Or is it the higher purpose, country and distinguished service?

Pots and pans clanked, hung on the sideboard of a wagon, when the wagon rolled through a rut.

How far I've marched from my heart.

Quit it. I'm here. I've chosen my path. I'm committed. Allow doubt and failure follows. If I fail, these men fail. If these men fail, the army fails, and, if the army fails, Mexico retakes California. "For the want of a nail the Kingdom fell." Don't be a loose nail. Keep my resolve and show it. Be a lieutenant colonel.

Ebenezer Green eyed what waited to the west. "Yes, sir, Cap'n. Got a dry one up yonder."

The battalion marched nine miles after Cooke turned it west, camped, and marched twenty miles the next day before they camped for the night. Ebenezer Green unsaddled his mule, looked up, and said, "What in the Sam Hill?"

Jean Baptiste Charbonneau walked into camp with his saddle and saddlebags, bridle, rifle, and pistol slung over his shoulders.

He set his gear down, propped his rifle on the saddle, sat, and pulled a moccasin off to massage a foot.

Green said, "Grizzly eat your mule? Or chew up the bones and spit out the meat?"

In his early forties, Charbonneau was the son of Sacajawea and a French trapper. Born on the expedition with Lewis and Clark and educated in Europe, when old enough to choose his place Charbonneau returned to wanderlust as if destined to chart the West. He proved an uncanny guide who always knew their whereabouts in that faceless wasteland.

"Apache Indian steal him in your sleep?"

"That mule and I were partners, or so he had deceived me," Charbonneau said. "I assumed he understood we needed each other to survive."

Charbonneau removed his other moccasin and massaged the foot.

Green waited.

Charbonneau examined his toes.

"Well?" Green said.

Charbonneau trimmed a toenail with his belt knife.

Green drummed his fingers on the fore-end of his musket.

Charbonneau shaved another toenail. "I dismounted to let him graze, and he kicked me too close to the family jewels. I could not ignore that, but I would have, had he not run off with my saddle and pistol in the pommel holster."

"I hate that," Green said. "Afoot and gun-naked in Apache land."

"Any closer it would have doubled me over. As it was I limped after him through the cactus and yucca and the arroyos and over hills and ridges, but he would not let me near him. The last thing I wanted was Apaches to ride him down and shoot me with my own pistol." Charbonneau whittled another toenail. "That mule thought he'd fare better solo, but he proved a thimble short of clever." With the tip of the knife Charbonneau dug a thorn from his foot and studied it as it lay on his blade.

Green squinted toward the sun. "Gettin' on in the day."

Charbonneau sheathed his knife. "Either he misjudged the range of the Mississippi rifle or he didn't think he'd see the muzzle end of it." He chuckled. "You should have seen the surprise in his eye when I unbridled him. Flat on his side, and I still had a fight. Had to lever him with the rifle to pull the saddle off."

Green looked at the Mississippi rifle propped on the saddle, the best for far-off targets. "She's a crooked shooter now, you tell me?"

"I could have finished him with my pistol"—Charbonneau pulled a moccasin on—"but I left him to watch the buzzards circle. I owed him that much."

Green put a hand to an ear, listened to the distance. "Ever hear a mule laugh? It's there, you listen right." He relaxed the hand. "Fancy France education and fooled by a mule. What them schools will do to a man." Green laughed. "He left you afoot in the desert and not a mule to be had till you buy or steal or trade for one, somewhere between here and that ocean they tell about, which ain't apt to happen."

Charbonneau pulled on the other moccasin. "Oddly enough, walking does not bother me, once I'm used to it, provided I don't have to carry my tack."

"Nothin' to scout anyway," Green said. He surveyed the reach of the miles. "Desert and more desert and empty in between. Best you could do is scout us a burial site."

CHAPTER 21

As for you, my flock, thus says the Lord God: I will judge between one sheep and another, between rams and goats . . . Was it not enough for you to graze on the best pasture, that you had to trample the rest of your pastures with your hooves? Or to drink the clearest water, that you had to pollute the rest with your hooves? Thus my flock had to graze on what your hooves had trampled and drink what your hooves had polluted.

—Ezekiel 34:17-19

Mormon Battalion, Mexico Territory [New Mexico], December 1846
Orson Everett saw the big white mule and those the staff rode, noses to the water, the hawk-nosed Cooke and his lieutenants mounted, watching their animals slurp the dish-thin pool. When he neared the spring, the mules pulled their hooves from the mire, and Lieutenant Colonel Cooke and his officers rode away. Orson and Phineas Lynch fell to their bellies to slurp from hoofprints they'd left.

"Lieutenant Colonel!" Captain Jefferson Hunt, Mormon volunteer, spoke in a voice to cower an attack dog.

Cooke looked over his shoulder. Orson and Phineas looked up from the mud at their lips. Both gaped at their erstwhile commander, who had led the battalion from Fort Leavenworth to Council Grove while Lieutenant Colonel Allen's health declined and before Lieutenant A. J. Smith arrived from Fort Leavenworth.

Captain Hunt approached Cooke and said on the way, "We have men who are close to dead for want of water, and you ride your mules in the spring?"

Cooke reined up his mule. His officers followed suit.

Captain Hunt stopped at the side of the white mule. "We are willing to march, and suffer the privations of the desert, but not if we're treated second to mules."

Of the three lieutenants who rode with Cooke, two were dragoons, the other a Mormon volunteer. Captain Hunt glared at the lieutenant who was a Latter-day Saint.

Cooke said, "We need our mules, Captain. If they fail, we fail. If you do not know that, you should not be a captain." Cooke rode away, followed by his officers.

Captain Hunt returned to the muddied spring.

"I can't believe those people," Captain Hunt said, "and one of them, one of our own."

Orson said, "Thank you for saying what you did. Cooke needed to hear it."

Captain Hunt shook his head and watched the officers ride off to mark a campsite. "Some of the brethren forget they're Saints first and soldiers second." He took off his hat, knelt and leaned on his hands, sipped, and sat back on his haunches. "There's more to drink from a wrung-out dish rag than there is from this spring." He watched water seep into the bottom of a hoofprint. "Not water. Brackish sand."

Phineas slurped, looked up, and said, "On the inside of my hat band, there is more water than this." He tried again, swallowed sand and insects. "Cleaner, it would also be."

"Might taste better, too," Orson said. "But I won't try it to find out."

Phineas looked off to where Cooke and his staff rode. "In the water his mule stepped." He shook his head. "Respect, he squandered."

"Think of it as a lesson from the Lord. He shall provide, whether through Cooke or in spite of him."

Others straggled in, lips like cracked clay. Phineas moved so another could take his place.

Orson Everett retrieved a three-gallon cask from its cradle on the side of a wagon, pulled the spoon from his knapsack, and left his musket propped on his pack, there in the mottled shade of a stunted mesquite tree. He returned to the spring, pulled the spout from the cask and covered the hole with a kerchief, spooned water from the spring, trickled it through the filter, and filled the cask, one skim at a time while the sun climbed. He estimated its water weight at thirty pounds and fashioned a sling, placed a blanket between the rope and his neck, and retraced his way, walking counter to the column that strung out for miles.

Ebenezer Green returned from a scout and shouted behind him. "Water up yonder, Mormonitos! Keep them gullets headin' west!"

To Orson Everett that meant two things. Either water lay in reach true to his words, or he used a ruse to spool out hope. They had seen both from this guide.

Ebenezer's voice caught him again. "No Navajos, neither."

The voice followed him as he walked contrary to the straggled column.

"Unlike the captain's army, Navajos got sense enough not to be here."

Orson wished for the baked plain they'd crossed two days ago, remnant to an ancient lake bed, firm and smooth as a bowling green, where wheels and feet didn't sink. Since then they'd roped up wagons to pull them over sand hills, twenty men to the rope, lugging with draught animals, wheel rims slicing channels in the sand. Orson pictured rowboats in the ocean, oarsmen worn to shells of themselves, the empty plain, whether sea or sand, draining their life away, the battalion itself becoming the mirage.

Green's voice carried. "Not a lot of water, but enough to stall off dyin' for a while."

Orson looked back to see brethren gathered to the guide, like dogs to a soup bone. Ebenezer swayed in his saddle as he spoke.

"He better be right this time," Orson said. He told himself he could not save his son, but he would do all he could to save his brethren to fill the hole in his heart. He wondered if a man died by the trailside waiting for water while the white mule drank, the lieutenant colonel seated in the saddle. Orson recalled that David refused the cup carried from the well at Bethlehem, refused to slake his thirst when his men could not but poured it out to the Lord. There was a commander, one who suffered with his troops to ease their suffering, unlike this one, a stranger to inspiration.

Stragglers sat by the roadside, young men resembling men five times their age, skin like desiccated leather that broke when bent. Orson gave them water as he went and came to Gabriel Hanks, sitting with his head between his knees. His musket lay in the sand at his side. He couldn't talk. His shoulders had blistered and sunburned where his musket had rubbed through his shirt.

Orson unslung the cask, removed the peg from the spout, tipped the cask, and poured the cup half full.

Gabriel smiled, took the cup, and gulped it empty. Orson covered his eyes with an elbow. "The glare off those teeth." He smiled. "And I thought the sand was bright."

Gabriel said something that sounded from the throat of a bullfrog. Orson poured another half cup, and Gabriel gulped it.

"Them eyebrows," Gabriel said. He worked his tongue. "Should've singed off a little, hoggin' the sun like they do."

"You're all right," Orson said. He poured another half cup.

"I believe I've lost my reason," Gabriel said. He gulped the cup down. "Like this land we're lookin' at, tossed upside down and stirred up." He waved an arm toward the horizon. "So much sand, the Mississippi River would disappear." He worked his mouth, attempting to wet his lips.

"I can't give you more water now," Orson said. "We have a lot of stragglers yet." He looked over the terrain they crossed, the rise and dip of sand, ravines carved by water run-off, mesquite as tall as donkeys, mountains cut to their edges channeling the valley to a saddle that marked the head of the valley, teasing the traveler onward to find another just like it—long and broad, empty and dry—a pattern repeated for weeks. He wondered if it would ever end.

"Satan's Hades, by God if it ain't," Gabriel said. "Maybe that's why the ancestors left."

Orson looked at him.

"Remember the figures we seen on them rocks? Lightning and creatures and figures and such, drawn or painted on? What about them holes, big enough to reach in up to your elbow, cut perfect round in that table rock?"

"Indian work, I suppose."

"Maybe the ancients, the Nephites the Book of Mormon tells about. Ancestors to us Saints."

"Could be," Orson said. He plugged the spout of the water cask with the peg whittled for the purpose. "Probably just the sun beating on your brain."

"My tongue feels like a sock of sand," Gabriel said.

Orson moved his fingers over the ground, picked out a pebble, and handed it to Gabriel. "Suck on this. It'll keep your mouth from drying up." He smiled. "Then again, maybe you shouldn't. I've liked the quiet."

Gabriel looked at Orson like an engorged milch cow, late for her milking, looks at a milkmaid. "Satan's here, Brother Orson.

Keep him off me."

Orson removed a small bottle he carried around his neck with a leather lace, took out the stopper, and placed a drop of oil on an index finger. He removed Gabriel's hat and placed his hands upon Gabriel's head, squeezed with gentle fingers until Gabriel bowed, and rubbed the oil on the crown of his head. He spread his hands over Gabriel's hair, bowed, closed his eyes, and prayed to the Lord to wrap his arms around his servant, Gabriel Hanks, to carry him across the desert and fend off Satan with his mighty shield.

"Hosannah and Amen," Gabriel said.

Orson placed the stopper back in the bottle of oil and looped its lace over his neck. "Get up and keep moving. The Lord will look after you."

"Thank you, Brother Orson."

Orson stood and placed the sling over his neck and a shoulder. "Remember. Moses crossed the desert to reach the Promised Land." He adjusted the blanket under the rope to lessen its bite. "We're tested, same as the Israelites. Don't give in." Orson braced the cask with his hands and walked on.

CHAPTER 22

The pools in the old bed of the river were full of ducks, and all night the swan, brant, and geese, were passing, but they were as shy as if they had received their tuition on the Chesapeake bay [sic], where they are continually chased by sportsmen.

—Lieutenant William Emory,
Corps of Topographical Engineers, with
General Kearny, Army of the West, 1846

First Dragoons, San Pasqual, California, December 6, 1846
Like all the other mules, his had saddle sores. The difference between them was a matter of degree, from tender red to wounds that wept. Those that fit the saddle better had raw spots on the withers and loins from the saddle bars. Those with flatter backs and rounded withers, those the saddles did not fit, had spots where the hide had worn away to uncover muscle. The same held true beneath the cinch rings with the constant chafing of skin on metal. Most of the dragoons had adjusted and readjusted their cinches throughout the journey, centered at first, then long on the left, then long on the right, to move the cinch rings to unchafed hide. In this manner severe sores were avoided, or postponed, at the expense of multiple lesser ones.

At Warner's Ranch, Moses coated the sores with kidney fat from a butchered ewe. He washed his saddle blanket in the creek, scraped it with his knife blade to remove sand and dirt caked in the blanket, grit glued to wool by blood and mule sweat.

He felt each rib where it fixed to the spine when they saddled under moonlight, thought it would take three more blankets to cushion the corrugated bone from the rub of the saddle. He thought of his blistered feet, back when he was a boy, lost and wandering, taking the pain and walking on even when infection came. Moses said, "Sorry, pardner. This is gonna hurt, but I can't do nothin' about it but try to go easy-like." His mule flinched when he placed the blanket on his back, flinched again when he set the saddle, reached around to nip him when he drew up the latigo. Moses slapped his muzzle away, slipped a foot in the stirrup, and mounted at two-thirty in the morning.

Scouts had reported a force of lancers camped ahead. *Californios*—the Spanish-speaking ranchers and *vaqueros* native to California, many of Spanish descent—who would fight with the Mexican regulars.

To avoid ambush they rode to the ridge top. The rain of the previous day had stopped. The frost on Moses's uniform made him think of a shield skimming wind away. He flexed his fingers, wiggled his toes to see if they moved, dismounted, and led his mule, reins in one hand while he swung the other one. After a bit, he switched hands. His saber slapped his thigh when he walked. He thought the company of dragoons sounded like blind men jumping coins in cups.

The dragoons stopped within a mile of the enemy campfires after a nine-mile ride. Moses, still wet from yesterday's rain, shivered in the predawn chill. It would help if his belly were full, which it hadn't been since Warner's Ranch, four days before, when he and Abner and Donovan and Smithwick, with the bugler and a corporal, ate a sheep in one sitting.

With the exception of the cottonwoods they found on some of the water courses, at Warner's Ranch they saw the first real trees, big and green and leafy, since they'd left the American states. Warner's Ranch commanded a broad, open, grassy valley with full streams of fresh water. It boasted a horse barn with floors in the stalls, corrals of pine rails, an adobe chapel, and a home with a porch. *Señor* Warner, a caretaker told them, had been jailed in San Diego for his Mexican allegiance, so the house sat vacant.

Chickens pecked and scratched about the buildings. Sheep, cattle, and horses grazed what Moses said were the first honest-to-God pastures he'd seen since the Arkansas River, with grass enough to fill a horse in a twenty-by-twenty square. And there were the trees, the magnificent trees. How he yearned for those in Virginia, the comfort of their canopy, their shade for the summer, the wood they gave to heat his winter, rooted in the soil of his soul.

Moses wanted to stay there, the only place since Santa Fe that would support a white man. To survive this country a man had to be half coyote and half mad, or wise in the ways of nature like the Pimas that fed them on the Rio Gila. He wanted walls and a roof, a fireplace with a Dutch oven baking biscuits and a kettle cooking stew, stirred by Miss Isabella with a ribbon in her hair, smoke curling through a chimney, window glass with the rain and the chill kept to the outside of it.

The farm back home looked better than ever, but he'd never been further from it. He knew he couldn't be there, ever since his mother's death changed how his father saw him—from a loved son of his own get to an unwanted foster child, it felt to him like, cold shouldered by his pa. He was a boy then, inattentive to detail, and left the door to the chicken coop open when he harried a weasel from the hen run and chased him into the trees that January day on the backside of a cold spell that came along, his mother had told him, but once or twice a lifetime. The chickens ran to the river, and his mother tried to herd them from the ice that proved too thin.

Moses looked at his shoes, where a seam meant to hold shoe top to shoe sole had rotted out, allowing his toes to show, scabbed or bloodied on the toe tips. He shivered in the greatcoat, and his teeth chattered. He thought, *cold and wet and hungry, back to where I was the day I signed on with this shoeless-mule outfit.*

When they'd marched into Warner's Ranch four days ago, the Mexican and Indian ranch inhabitants fled. Moses didn't blame them. The U.S. dragoons appeared as if they'd wandered from an island, ship-wrecked and starving, uniforms little more than suggestions of themselves, a band of brigands intent on pillage. That night they proved to be so—a patrol rode fifteen miles to steal a herd of seventy-five horses and mules from another rancher with a Mexican name. Fewer than half proved rideable. Most were wild. Short of time and short of strength to the point of becoming frail, the dragoons turned the rough stock loose. Moses had not been issued one of the few fresh remounts and rode his worn-down mule, numb now to the saddle and cinch sores, within a mile of enemy campfires.

Thirty-nine marines from the garrison at San Diego had reinforced Kearny's dragoons a few days ago in response to a courier Kearny had sent. They brought a howitzer, its carriage in good repair and pulled by a fresh mule, unlike the guns the dragoons had with their carriages spliced with rawhide. Kearny had asked for more marines, but the commodore at San Diego, with his back to the harbor and the *Californios* hostile, thought that many a stretch.

Moses noticed the sky had lightened, saw a mist-filled valley where scouts had spotted the camp of the *Californios*. They stopped. Officers talked. Moses clenched his teeth to stop their chattering, thought the stark hills hostile at heart. No canopy of trees to hold off cold. No roll of green fields, no soil soft with humus, but woodless hills and rock and sand and scattered mesquite. Moses remembered the cactus when they approached the Rio Gila, standing like timeless giants, arms lifted to ward them away.

The officers formed the troop in two columns to descend into the valley and the mist that held back sunlight. The choppy strides his mule took on the downhill ride told Moses the mule's shoulders hurt, stove up from steep ravines of the Rio Gila and the Sonoran Desert trek. Moses thought it a wonder the mule could walk at all.

He saw the mist thin and the figures, dim and indistinct, waiting in the valley. The sky lightened, the dimness lifted, the figures sharpened into *Californios*—ranchers unsurpassed in horsemanship, their primary weapon a nine-foot lance with wood shaft and metal spear point. Their leader rode across their front with the shako and tunic and high-top boots of a Mexican officer.

General Kearny ordered the vanguard forward—twelve dragoons on horses fresh from Warner's Ranch, followed by fifty mounted on mules, Moses and Abner Black among them. They started at a walk, then trotted. At a quarter mile from the *Californios* they charged.

The sun breached the horizon line. Moses saw puffs of gun smoke, heard a musket ball whiz overhead, felt the breath of another brush his cheek, heard the musket reports from the *Californios'* camp. It occurred to him he'd not been shot at before. The twelve on horses charged, yelled and waved sabers, and pulled away from the mules that could do little more than shuffle. Moses saw the gap between the mules and the horses widen to a gulf, and he felt like he was riding a burro in a thoroughbred race. He saw the number of *Californios* grow in the lifting sun and split to pinch off the vanguard.

Moses screamed "No!" and whipped his mule, but the animal

had no more to give, its charge somewhere between a walk and a trot. The *Californios* enveloped the twelve, and he screamed again, "Look what they're doin'!" His comrades parried lance jabs, and Moses yelled, swore, and spurred his mount, who grunted but moved no faster.

When the fifty troopers on shuffling mules reached the vanguard, they found most had been unhorsed. Some lay still and quiet. Some groaned, gripped wounds. Those left standing attempted to deflect spear points with hands and sabers. Moses found a brawl rather than a battle, dust and yells and mounted and riderless horses, movement missing coherence like the gestures of an idiot. Moses sliced with his saber and cut a lance in half. His mule, in spite of the fury about him, moved as if he were walking in ankle-deep sand.

A dragoon staggered. Half a lance jutted from his torso, the other half in the attacker's hand who spun his horse, charged, and jabbed Moses with the broken lance staff as if stabbing hay with a pitchfork. The blow split his upper lip and knocked him from his mule. Moses found himself on all fours. The world spun in horse hooves and dust and frenzied yells. He worked his tongue, pushed an incisor through the split in his lip, watched it plop in the blood that pooled beneath him.

Moses spit blood that bubbled with saliva. He looked up. Abner Black stood still, on foot, empty handed. A *Californio* charged at a gallop, speared Abner through the back, and impaled him with the spearhead out his belly. Abner clutched the lance, mouth open and soundless as if emerging from a plunge in ice-capped river water.

Moses screamed Abner's name. The *Californio* released his grip, and Abner dropped to his knees, tipped backward to the balance of the lance, righted, and fell to his face. The shaft stood as a flagless flagpole that wiggled when he kicked.

The *Californio* worked the spear to pull it free while Abner screamed. Moses jumped up, ran to the lancer and pulled him from his horse, slammed him on the ground and jammed his knees in his belly, gripped his neck, and choked him—that splendid *Californio* horseman who handled his weapon as deftly as he did his bridle horse—until he thought the lancer's eyes would pop. When the *Californio* quit kicking Moses released him, grabbed a rock and crushed his skull, and yelled, "Back-stabbin' bastard!"

Moses saw blood drip from his chin and fall on the face with the stove-in forehead, twisted lips, eyes blank as wafers. Moses dropped the rock, stood up and stepped back, stared at the work of his anger. He picked up a saber, walked to Abner to guard the body, its eyes wide in wonder, mouth open for oratory, still as the horseman's corpse.

The blow knocked his breath out, and Moses found himself on the ground, saw a horse step over him, saw the same lancer who'd knocked his tooth out, the same broken lance shaft. The *Californio* smiled and rode off as if he'd counted coup. Moses couldn't breathe until he gasped at the pain in his shoulder blade. He knelt, clutched his arm to his torso, gasped for air, looked about him. Abner lay there, dead as his mother on the river bank. Moses choked up, looked off, blinked tears away, tried to harden his heart. Horses and mules passed through his vision. He saw one of the howitzers a quarter mile off, back where they had started the charge. The mule pulling the gun balked. Lancers charged the stalled field piece, and the artillery-man slid off the mule to hide under the limber. The *Californios* speared where the gunner scrambled under the gun carriage too small to shelter him. When they'd finished, they shot the mule, cut the traces, lassoed the gun, and towed it away. Moses looked back to Abner, felt his shoulder bite when he locked his sobs in. He dropped his head, spit blood, and felt himself topple.

CHAPTER 23

The sick, by the indefatigable exertions of Dr. Griffin, were do-
ing well, and the general enabled to mount his horse. The order
to march was given, and we moved off to offer the enemy battle,
accompanied by our wounded, and the whole of our packs.

—*Lieutenant William Emory,*
December 7, 1846

First Dragoons, San Pasqual, California, December 7, 1846
He woke to stillness, rolled onto his back, gasped for breath,
heard moans from soldiers nearby. His shoulder stabbed like a
canine had ripped it. His lip—could've been a horse kick, split
like it was. He rose to his knees and looked. Dragoons and a
few *Californios* lay scattered among their dead and dying saddle
mounts. Mules wandered in search of forage or stood still, heads
hung. The one Moses rode from Santa Fe lay nearby, legs
beneath his belly, muzzle on the ground. He groaned, sagged to
his side with a lance broken in his brisket. A hind leg twitched,
then quit.

Moses eased himself to his feet, winced in a grip against
pain. He held his arm in, shuffled to his mule, knelt at his head,
petted his neck and face. Blood bubbled from the nostrils. The
skyward eye blinked, went wide. Moses closed it. "I'm sorry I
whipped you with the reins and gigged you with the spurs. You
done your level best." Moses looked at the dead dragoons.
"They shouldn't have outrun us." He remembered the pincer

movement, his fury when he knew what it would do when he and the others with their worn-down mounts would arrive too late. Even then, their powder was wet from the rain they'd ridden in.

"They was outnumbered. I was tryin' to get in the fight." He petted the mule. "Sorry, ole pardner. You give it your all." He felt his eyes well. "Forgive me. I didn't mean it personal." He leaned to the mule but stopped when the shoulder bit.

Troopers tended the wounded. Private Smithwick came up and said, "You've been slugged with a musket, by the looks of that lip. Knocked a tooth out, too."

"The bastards got Abner," Moses said.

"I see that."

"I got the one who done it. He's layin' right there."

Smithwick looked, gagged, looked away.

"Never been that mad."

Smithwick said, "He's plenty dead."

"Never killed no one before."

"You made sure you did him."

Smithwick whistled through his teeth when he examined Moses's shoulder. "You've been stabbed with a busted stick. Wood in there. Torn up muscle." He looked closer. "Can't tell about bone. We'll see what the surgeon makes of it."

"I seen it. Abner standin' there, no saber, no nothin'. Like he planted there to get run through."

"Hit in the head and lost his whereabouts, maybe," Smithwick said. "They got nineteen of us. Wounded seventeen more, and some of them might die. Got the general too, but he'll be all right. All from lances. Would have got us all if we'd have been strung out more."

Moses sat by his dead mule while Smithwick went for the surgeon. His lip had swollen like a leavened biscuit, and when the surgeon came he scraped the crusted edges with a scalpel, closed it with thread a woman would use to stitch her lover's name in a kerchief, and told Moses to consider a moustache.

Moses sucked up his breath when the surgeon dug in his shoulder with his pincers and pulled a splinter from it. When he recovered, he swore.

The surgeon smiled and said, "I'll take that as a compliment." He tied a bandage in place, told him bits of lance shaft might be imbedded in his muscle, which color and touch would tell in a day or two. If that happened he'd open it with a scalpel and do what he could. "No bone is broken, but I suppose you're right handed."

Moses nodded.

"You'll use your left for a week or two, whether you want to or not."

Moses returned to Abner, face down with the lance standing in his back. Moses sat down. Here lay a man unlike any he'd known. To him, part father, part uncle, part brother, part teacher. The best friend he had ever had. Abner had opened the world to him, one more complex and wondrous, one less clear and certain, than the one he'd left. Moses bowed his head, recalled the prayer his mama said. "Our father which art in heaven," and his throat knotted. His head sagged between his knees, and he cried for the first time since his mother died.

Dragoons moved about to collect the dead, and they left Moses alone.

Moses straightened and wiped his eyes, tried to soften his sobs. He sat by Abner and let his breath settle. *Abner's insides wrapped on a lance shaft. His mother's, spilled on the river bank. Split open, his own guts laid bare, was how it felt. How would he go it alone, his innards ripped from him? His leader, his teacher, his best friend, layin' there dead? Thousands of miles from what was home. Like he'd come to the end of his map to find a cliff to fall off.*

Smithwick returned with Donovan, and they sat with Moses.

Moses said, "Can't figure it. He just stood there. Like he quit, didn't want to live no more." *Somethin' done him wrong somewhere. Might have seen it, if I'd have give him more mind. Helped him maybe, but no. Blind to it, seen only me, instead of them that mean more to me than the air I breathe.*

"The man was a mystery," Smithwick said. "The most interesting person," and his voice tightened. He waved a hand to say he'd talk later.

Donovan said, "Dead as your mule. For what?"

"Dead except for what he teachered us," Moses said, "and he did me more of that than I know." He wiped his eyes. *Stay alive in me, Abner Black. At night or in the mornin' or the middle of the day, whenever your spirit moves on you, speak your piece so I can hear it.*

Smithwick stood up and put his hands on the lance, jerked it, and pulled it loose. Moses stood, held his hand out for the lance, and said, "You two go on for a bit."

"Of course," Smithwick said.

Donovan nodded, and they walked off.

Moses wedged the lance blade in the rocks and broke it off. He rolled the body over with his left arm with the care he'd show an infant. A spectacle lens had cracked on Abner's glasses, but the wire rims remained in place. Moses clenched against the shoulder pain and used both hands to remove the spectacles as if they were priceless china. He tried to close the eyelids, but rigor mortis had them. He took Abner's handkerchief from the tunic pocket under the greatcoat, wiped the blood from the lenses, and replaced the wire rims by hooking them behind the ears as he'd seen Abner do.

Moses used the lance blade to scrape entrails from Abner's clothing and covered them with rocks. He closed the hole in the coat—a cut in the fabric below the buttons of the double-breasted greatcoat square in the middle of the belly. Most of the dragoons had pulled their buttons for trade exchange with the Pimas and Maricopas but not Abner Black. Always the model dragoon. Rather go hungry than cut off a button. The brass buttons featured an eagle with a *D* on the shield on the eagle's chest, all but the button on the upper left, which had the infantry *I,* which was temporary, Abner had said. He'd cut it from a coat a soldier had discarded on the Santa Fe Trail to replace the one he'd lost on a trot through trees close to the Missouri. "I shall requisition a proper button when circumstances permit," Abner had said. "As it is," he'd said, "no one will know the difference barring an inspection from a West Point lieutenant, which is unlikely on a war campaign."

Moses looked at the lancer, saw what he'd done with bare hands and a rock. *Plumb primitive. Animal mad. Didn't know he had it in him, but there it was, brain-smeared hair.*

He stood and rolled the lancer over with a push from a foot so he lay face down.

He imagined what Abner would say, and how he would say it. He could hear Abner's pattern of speech, but he couldn't speak it the way Abner would. *"Uneasy with the meanness that lives within you, brutalized by brutal events and brutal in return. From passion to action with no check between the two. Roll him over to conceal the deed." Somethin' like that, is whut Abner would say. Anymore, I don't know who does my thinkin', Abner or me, the way his teaching crept in my head. Hardly thanked him for it either. I regret that.*

Moses removed his cap, unsheathed his knife, cut the tail hair he pulled from his mule at the *Rio Grande del Norte* to tie the rattle to the inside of his cap. He placed the rattle in Abner's tunic pocket, closed the greatcoat, and buttoned it. The rain had stopped before the battle began, but Abner had not removed his coat, chilled as he was from the prior day's rain. Moses covered Abner's face with the handkerchief.

The dragoons and marines drank from water kegs they'd brought on mules. They spent the night on ground a goat would vacate, lying among the rocks and cactus thirty-nine miles from San Diego. Moses spent the night sitting up with his back against his mule's belly. The men shivered and moaned, and their wounds grew hot.

Those not wounded buried the dead using *Californios'* lances for spades. They pried and piled rocks as if they dug ore rather than graves. A wolf howled, and Moses Cole pictured the ghost of Abner Black wandering in the starlight, lost from his body and his mount, shackled to the death angel. Another howled, and he felt something like breath on his neck. He watched the grave diggers work, listened to tossed rocks find the ground again. He shifted and winced when his shoulder moved.

The dragoons laid nineteen of their fellow troopers in the long grave, covered it, and walked mules over it to pack the grave fill. The bodies of the several *Californios* they'd killed they moved away to lay in a coulee. When wolves came, the lancers would be the first disturbed.

At daybreak, the dragoons and marines fashioned travois to transport the wounded. Cottonwood saplings from the Rio San Bernardo served as shafts. Buffalo robes formed the beds, tied to the rails with strips of hide cut from newly dead mules. The wounded gripped the travois shafts when their lacerations ripped, each rock and dip jarring the sledges they'd mimicked from Indians, the bow of the poles slung over the pommel of the saddle, the stern of the shafts furrowing the rock-studded earth. Hemp lariats tied them to the rail frames and bit their armpits. The buffalo hair of the sledge beds crusted with blood when lance cuts reopened. To Moses Cole the moans of the wounded sounded like the vespers of Hell.

General Kearny's command inched its way west with the injured and the pack mules at their center. The dragoons and marine reinforcements, with a quarter of their number buried or bandaged, ended the day's march on a hilltop with the *Californios* lancers circled below them, guarding the creek bottom where the water flowed. The command's food was gone, and they knew that time would kill them and save the lancers the task.

The *Californios* hovered like vultures, just beyond musket range.

Chapter 24

. . . every vegetable growth is guarded with thorns against all comers that may assail.

—Samuel H. Rogers,
Mormon Battalion,
December 19, 1846

What a loss to my regiment! Ah! Who but loved [Capt.] Johnston—the noble, sterling, valued Johnston! And who had warmer friends than poor [Capt.] Moore! Peace to their ashes! Rest to their souls! May their country honor the memories of its heroic champions, who, serving her, have found their graves in distant and desolate regions!

—Philip St. George Cooke,
after learning of the battle at San Pasqual,
January 11, 1847

First Dragoons, Mule Hill, California, December 8–10, 1846

Kit Carson offered to sneak through to San Diego and impress upon the commodore that, without reinforcements, Kearny's command would end at Mule Hill. Carson left after dark with Chemuctah, a Diegueno Indian guide, and Edward Beale, a young Navy lieutenant. They left their canteens, so the water slosh and clink on hard objects would not betray them. Carson and Beale stuffed their shoes in their belts to muffle their steps. Chemuctah wore moccasins.

They crept off the hill, navigated away from the upright lances silhouetted in the starlight that marked the horsemen. They heard a horse approach and hid among the rocks. A *Californio* sentry rode up, sat his horse, struck a flint, and smoked a *cigarillo*. Its glow flared when he drew in smoke, traced the lift of his hand. The three scouts waited, a few steps from the sentry. Beale's hand moved, and Carson stopped it, nodded to the half-cocked hammer, and shook his head "No." They stilled their breathing while the sentry smoked and his horse lowered its head. When he flicked the last ash and rode away, Beale panted and said he'd feared the guard would hear his heart beat. They waited, then crept on until dawn, found they'd lost their shoes in the passage. They kept to arroyos to hide their profiles, used the skills of the hunter to avoid the huntsmen. They walked in the canyons and on the rock of gully washes, picked their way by the brush, dripped blood on stones and in their sand prints. They walked and crept in terrain where each step threatened a barb, a bruise, or a cut, where each step called for the will of a martyr.

By afternoon, twelve miles from San Diego, they spotted more sentries and split up, hoping one could get through. Alone in an unknown land, beyond exhaustion with no food or water and cactus stabbing his feet, Lieutenant Beale reached delirium yet stumbled on. Carson and Chemuctah, at home as solo scouts, stretched their endurance, but cactus favored no one. That night, scattered from midnight to dawn, they each reached San Diego and the marines and sailors from the warships in the bay. Lieutenant Beale ranted about prickly-pear pathways, feet split into ribbons, ships sailing on sand. Orderlies carried him to the infirmary in the sloop of war *Portsmouth*, where he remained for a month. With a ship's surgeon tending to thorns embedded in their foot soles, Carson and Chemuctah would walk after a week.

★ ★ ★ ★ ★

While the three scouts picked their way through cactus, Kearny's command christened Mule Hill by eating mules. They dug holes and slurped what little water seeped into them. When night fell and the cold came, they burned sage for heat.

A sergeant, married the day before they'd left Fort Leavenworth, succumbed to his lance gashes, and they buried him there. Some of the cuts the men suffered began to knit in the absence of jarring from travois. Others turned color, stank of gangrene that grew in wounds slotted by spear points. Moses's shoulder turned tender and hot to the touch. He took on a fever and chills, saw shadows move in bright daylight, heard Abner's Latin, thought the pain meant a bone break.

When the surgeon opened his scabbing, pus popped out. He instructed Private Smithwick to spread the cut muscle so he could probe with scalpel and pincers. Smithwick watched blood laced with pus spill over his fingers, felt its heat, smelled something rotten, and gagged. Moses clenched the carbine in his lap and moved his mind to green fields in Virginia while the surgeon manipulated the pincers to remove wood bits.

The surgeon said, "Some of the injured developed gangrene. If that happens to you, you're done. I can't amputate a shoulder."

"I'll live then," Moses said, "unless I don't."

"Desperate events call for desperate measures. I haven't done this before, and it might or might not help, but it could be your best chance."

"Dyin's bad enough, but dyin' here is worse. Do what you gotta do."

"Give me a few minutes," the surgeon said.

He returned with Private Donovan, a waist-belt cartridge box, and a tin cup holding a live coal. He told Moses to lay on his stomach and Smithwick to spread the wound open. He tore open a paper cartridge and poured gunpowder on raw flesh, ripped one more and did the same, blew on the coal until it glowed, told Smithwick and Donovan to pin him, tipped the cup, and dropped the coal on the gunpowder.

The flame singed the surgeon's eyelids, and Moses screamed.

"It'll feel better when it stops hurtin'," Donovan said.

From his haversack, the surgeon pulled a canteen with a leather cover laced tightly to it. "I'd flush it with water, but you know how scarce water is, so I'll use this." He pulled the cork, picked up the coal with the pincers, and splashed the burn with whisky. He packed the wound with gauze and told Moses he'd do the same daily until his supplies ran out, which would happen in a day, two at the most. He rigged a sling, tied arm to torso, told Moses he'd done what he could. If gangrene did not settle in, he'd heal in two or three weeks.

The wounded French guide nudged Moses from his half sleep, moved his face closer to Moses's face, and sniffed.

"What?" Moses said. He sat against a boulder with his knees pulled up and a greatcoat and blanket wrapped around him. He held his right arm to his chest and leaned to the Frenchman, who lay by his side, covered with saddle blankets coated with frost. "Gangrene?"

Robideaux sniffed again.

Moses turned his head to his bandaged shoulder and sniffed. "Must be you. All I smell on me is burnt meat." He leaned against the boulder, shifted his covers, and saw the stars as bands of lanterns.

"Can you not smell *le café*?"

Moses sniffed again. "You've lost too much blood for your mind to work right. Be quiet. Heal up."

"*Non.* There is coffee. One cup will save me." The Frenchman shivered in his blanket.

Moses sighed. *Next comes the death rattle. We need a fire, with firewood big as a blacksmith's arm.*

"I beg of you. Bring the cup of coffee."

Moses pulled his greatcoat tighter. "I'm lookin, but I don't see it."

"*Non, non,* Monsieur Mo-zess. *Le nez, oui.*" The Frenchman touched his nose. "*Les yeux*"—the Frenchman pointed to his eyes and waved his index finger—"*non.*"

"I'm lookin' for a New Orleans café, and a mademoiselle with a tray on her fingertips." Moses peered into the dark. "Must be to the other side of them boulders."

"I beg of you, please, Monsieur Mo-zess, bring it to me. *Maintenant, s'il vous plait.*"

"I suppose you want fixins with that." Moses stopped a laugh when he bumped his shoulder on the boulder. After a bit he said, "One cube or two?"

"Please, Monsieur Mo-zess. One cup will save me."

Moses pulled the covers from his legs and shoulders with his left arm. "I'll bring the mademoiselle and a featherbed quilt while I'm at it." *No blood in his brain. Dead by daylight. Humor him to help how I can.*

He rose slowly, put the greatcoat over his shoulders, and spread his blanket over Robideaux. He put a hand to the Frenchman's forehead, felt his chill, peeled off the greatcoat, and laid it on his patient. "One cup of coffee, comin' your way," he said and walked toward a firelight.

At the fire, a scout used rocks for mortar and pestle to grind coffee a bean at a time. He brushed the bean bits into a tin cup of water he'd skimmed from a hole and heated at a fire of wild sage, then repeated the procedure until all fifteen beans had been added. The cup spanned the gap between two brick-sized rocks, an edge perched on each rock. A small fire burned beneath it.

"I'll be go-to-hell," Moses said.

"Touch that cup, Moses, you're a dead man," the scout said. His wizened skin spoke of a life away from walls.

"I swear," Moses said, "Robideaux smelled it before you smashed the first bean."

"Robideaux would. He sniffed his way through Apache country more times than he should have."

"Americans got five senses," Moses said. "Frogs got six."

The coffee heated to a slow roll.

"The way Robideaux talks," Moses said, "if they'd offered coffee to Christ, he'd a' crawled off the cross." Firelight flickered in the scout's eyes. His hair, stiff with grime, didn't flex when he moved his head. He reached in his haversack, retrieved a buckskin pouch sized to silver dollars, untied the drawstring, shook out the last of his sugar granules, and stirred the brew with a twig. He laid the pouch over the cup to hold its heat.

Moses chuckled. "He'll take milk, too."

They sat him up, placed the cup under his nose, and pulled off the makeshift lid. Robideaux's eyes shot open. His face shined like sun found it. He inhaled, blinked, sipped, and groaned. "Never have I had better coffee. *Merci beaucoup, mes amis.*" He took the cup in his hands and breathed its aroma. "*Ça sent bon!*" He sipped again, closed his eyes, held his nose close over the cup. "*Mon nez, c'est mon coeur.*"

"Frogs," Moses said. "If we stuck a perfumed woman under him, he'd jump up and bark."

"I would, too, and so would you," the scout said. "Mexican or Indian, painted or plain. Wouldn't matter."

Moses stared at a boulder. *My God, Isabella. What would that be like? Should've gone to Richmond instead of Pennsylvania. She could be took by now.*

"Quit your dreaming," the scout said. "Find something to burn."

They gathered sage and carried embers from the cook fire to start a fire for Robideaux.

"What else you got in that cook shack?" Moses said, nodding to the cartridge pouch on the scout's belt.

"Cartridges," the scout said. "They don't eat too well."

The scout blew on the embers to ignite the sage. He blew more, added sage, and watched the fire climb. He rocked back on his haunches. "You can eat the paper, use the powder to start a fire and season your mule meat. Boil the ball in your coffee water." Squint lines at the scout's eyes deepened when he smiled. "That's how to stretch a coffee bean."

Robideaux pulled a biscuit from under his covers. "It is my last one. Please, *mes amis,* you take it. A small token of my greatest appreciation."

Moses took it, gave half to the scout, and examined his half in the firelight. It was black from dirt. Worms crawled in it. He ate it, licked his palm where crumbs lay, said, "Little gummy for a biscuit."

At daylight Moses saw the *Californios* at the foot of the hill mounted with lances. *Glorified Mexicans. Treed like a lion by a buncha back-stabbin', chicken-shit lizards.*

The dragoons and marines stacked rocks to fortify their hilltop. In an attempt to frighten the army's mules away, the *Californios* tied dried hides to the tails of horses and drove them at a gallop toward the hilltop, whooping like drunken Texians stampeding cattle. The *Californios* turned their mounts away before they reached musket range, and the horses charged the hill, running wide-eyed, fleeing the things that chased them.

Moses stood, laid his carbine over a boulder. He'd never shot left handed before. He pressed the butt in his left shoulder, sighted with his left eye, and clenched his teeth, expecting the recoil to jab where the bandage was packed.

The marines discharged their field gun, and the blast turned most of the horses aside. The burned powder smelled of rotten eggs, and Moses found his hunger stirred by the hint of food.

He waited and shot a *Californio*'s horse at ten paces. The horse somersaulted, the dried hide flying like a jerked kite. Moses dropped the carbine, panted, held his right arm in, waited for the pain to quit. His tongue worked the gum and the stitched lip through the gap the knocked-out incisor left.

Horses ran by. The tail-tied hides slapped the ground. Their hooves sounded like a steamboat's paddle wheel churning a current. The mules, too spent to be frightened by frenzied horses, stepped aside to let the horses pass by.

Another horse had been shot. They found them good specimens of well-fed horseflesh. They cut the meat in chunks, stuck it on whittled sagebrush sticks, and roasted it, turning it to keep from losing the fat in the fire.

The day passed. The order came to prepare to march off the hill at daybreak.

Moses told Robideaux, "Die here or die down there. Don't much matter." Moses braced his saber in the crook of his right arm and worked its edge with a pocket whetstone. He found it awkward with his left hand, found it required concentration to keep the strokes of the whetstone even. He kept his wrist and fingers still, found a slower but more stable stroke using his arm muscles. "Except up here, we're closer to the buzzards."

Robideaux dozed by the rhythm of the whetstone sweeping steel. Night came, and the cold came with it.

As dawn approached, Robideaux nudged Moses, huddled under blankets with Robideaux to fight off frost. "Do you not hear it?"

"Hear what? A French fiddle?"

"*Non! L'anglais!* There is English spoken at the bottom of the hill!"

Moses cupped a hand to an ear. He heard the tramp of marching soldiers.

"Mexican regiment, most likely."

"Non, non! They speak English! *C'est les Americains!"*

Moses listened, strained to define a word from the marchers.

Standing sentinel, Private Donovan yelled. "Who goes there?"

Moses smelled dust from massed feet climbing Mule Hill.

"Who goes there?" Donovan yelled again, half an octave higher.

Moses stood, laid his carbine over his boulder, capped and cocked it, nestled its butt against his left shoulder.

A voice carried from lower on Mule Hill. "Americans! Hold your fire!"

Someone whooped.

"Carson and them," Moses whispered over the boulder. "How did they do it?"

Another whooped, and they started to cheer. Some danced a jig around a sagebrush cook fire.

Moses removed the percussion cap from the nipple and eased the hammer down. He turned away from Robideaux and wiped his eyes.

Eighty marines and one hundred-twenty sailors marched to the hilltop, slowed, and broke formation when they saw the dragoons in tattered clothing, thin as starving Indians, many in dirty bandages, cheering and slapping them on their shoulders. The marines and sailors shared their clothing, their hardtack and tobacco, and water from their canteens. A musket ball whizzed overhead, and when daylight came the *Californios* had gone.

CHAPTER 25

Many bulls surround me;
fierce bulls of Bashan surround me.
They open wide their mouths against me,
lions that rend and roar.

—Psalm 22, verses 13–14

Their terribly beautiful forms and majestic appearance were
quite impressive.

—Sgt. Daniel Tyler
regarding the bulls at the San Pedro, Mormon Battalion,
1846

The Indians have killed nearly all the cows, & the bulls are as
dareing [sic] & Savage as tigers.

—Henry Boyle,
Mormon Battalion,
December 11, 1846

Mormon Battalion, Battle of the Bulls, Rio San Pedro [Arizona],
December 11, 1846

They'd seen wild bulls for some days now, feral cattle from the ranch Ignacio Perez abandoned when the Apaches came. The Apaches hunted the cows and calves and left the bulls alone with their horns and belligerent dispositions. Bridle horses, horses Ignacio Perez may have ridden with Spanish bits with silver shanks, ran wild as well, wondering, perhaps, where the *patrón* went, what became of the stable and grain, where the endless desert valleys ended.

The battalion marched on, through wind that bit their eyes with sand and clouded their breathing. They marched through wind-driven sleet they thought would freeze them, as if dunked in a winter lake. They marched on, and the bulls grew into herds of hundreds as skittish and tough as buffalo, and as ferocious when hunted for food and wounded. Wild horses appeared and disappeared in the distance when the winter weather left.

They approached the Rio San Pedro to noon there, to drink and fill water kegs and canteens, to cook a meal of beans and feral beef, to water and rest the mules. When the soldiers appeared on the bluffs on each side of the stream, a herd of bulls ran to the creek with its trees and cane grass tall enough to hide wagons. Some ran when the wagons appeared as if the wagons were eying them as prey. Others approached the wagons, as if to challenge these beasts that rumbled. When the bulls came close their horns dominated their bodies. Some had horns as wide as a man is tall; some had horns that curved in; some had horns with one curved up and the other curved down.

The battalion marched to the river, and the bulls came closer. Some bellowed as they will with their nose to the spot where a carcass had leached in the ground. Some fought, pushed horn to horn, and stirred up dust. Others ran and milled. Some trotted to the oxen, and, when they hooked the oxen with their horns, the drovers shot them. A bull smelled the fresh blood and bellowed, and his brothers came running.

One stopped, lifted his head, eyed the white mule Lieutenant Colonel Cooke sat. Cooke admired the horns that curved forward, their tips that glinted when the bull dropped his head and charged from a hundred yards.

Corporal Lafayette Frost stood by, musket cradled in the crook of an elbow, and watched the coal-black bull come at them. To avoid accidental discharge the order stood to march with arms unloaded, and Cooke now ordered Corporal Frost to load his musket. Frost remained still, musket cradled in his elbow, a pace away from the white mule. The bull reached fifty yards.

The white mule lifted its head, eyes on the charging bovine. To Cooke he looked bigger than the mule. "For Christ's sake!" he yelled. "Load your damn gun!"

Frost stood still, as if deaf or dumb with fright. The bull closed to thirty yards.

Cooke yelled, "Run, you idiot!" He felt his mount tense and fidget, head raised high, perked to his predator. The mule lifted a hoof, and Cooke refused his movement, insisted he stand like a soldier in rank.

At twenty yards, Corporal Frost lifted the musket to his shoulder, sighted, waited, and shot the bull in the center of the forehead at six paces. A horn furrowed the sand when his knees buckled, and he slid to a stop a wagon bed shy of the white mule.

Cooke said, "Damn fine shooting for an empty gun."

Corporal Frost smiled and reloaded his musket.

"You're either the bravest or dumbest son of a bitch I've ever seen." Cooke chuckled and thought himself no better to risk himself and his mount only for the sake of appearance. He thanked God that Corporal Frost had disobeyed his order. Cooke's humor drained when he saw the whole herd charge, and the thing take on a life of its own.

A bull caught Ruben Cox halfway to the river, water buckets in hand, gored him in the thigh, and flipped him over his back. Ruben scrambled to his feet and tried to run, limping with a hand on his leg, then hid in the canebrake while bulls ran by.

Gabriel Hanks ran to help Ruben to the wagons, but a bull appeared as if spit from the cane grass and caught Gabriel square on his buttocks at thirty paces from the wagons, a horn to the edge of each hip. The bull pushed him, wedged between his horns, as if he were a log caught in a waterfall. Gabriel dropped his musket at the impact and gripped a horn in each hand to keep from falling underfoot while the bull bobbed him, then tossed him over his shoulder.

The bull stopped and spun, lifted his head, hunting Gabriel hunched in the tall grass, and sagged to his knees when four musket balls slammed him broadside.

Amos Binley reloaded, then ran when he found himself in the path of running bulls. He sprinted, felt weightless as if shoved by a gale, and dove into sagebrush when hoofbeats were almost on him.

Cooke saw one jump instead of gore Amos Binley and run on as if swept by momentum.

Lieutenant Stoneman, one of the three dragoons, blew part of his thumb off when he fired his repeater with two cartridges jammed in the chamber. He noticed the missing part when he retrieved his horse pistol and tried to thumb the hammer back.

Another charged a team of mules that stood in bridles with blinders hitched to a wagon. The bull horned the near mule in the belly and threw him over his teammate. The mule screamed and fell hitched to the whiffletree, his intestines draped over the wagon tongue. Chewed and matted plant bits leaked from the holes the horns punched in his stomach while his teammate pitched and kicked in the traces.

Another slammed a wagon and pushed it sideways. Soldiers shot him, and he chased Phineas Lynch under a wagon before he fell.

Then they left as quickly as they'd come. A blend of dust and musket smoke hung at the wagons and the broken cane grass. Dust lifted where the bulls ran, marking their flight from the Rio San Pedro.

Cooke rode through the carnage. *These men behaved like soldiers. Acted on instinct and self direction with no orders shouted to sort the chaos. What could I have said or done in the pandemonium? Surprising marksmanship, untutored in shooting as they are. No panic but that from a dragoon lieutenant. Shot his own thumb off, for God's sake. Ruined a magazine rifle, which we can't replace. These Mormons have shown their mettle. Maybe there's a battalion here after all.*

The men shot the gored mules and butchered some of the bulls. They dressed the one that chased Phineas under a wagon, and Phineas carried the heart in his hands to Orson Everett. He poked a finger in a hole bored by a musket ball and placed a second finger in a second hole two inches from it.

"Twice shot through the heart, but under a wagon he ran me still." Phineas held the heart up with his fingers in the tunnels the musket balls cut. "In these beasts the devil lives, Brother Orson." Blood from the heart dripped down his hand and muddied the dirt on his shirtsleeve. "Brother Orson, from harm the shield of the Lord kept us."

"The Lord has a big job to do," Orson said.

"Every day and every night a big job," Phineas said.

"So we help him by doing all we can to lighten His load. You did that when you dove under that wagon."

Gabriel walked up with a thumb and index finger an inch apart. "An angel held me just so." He bobbed his hand in and out to call attention to the space his thumb and finger framed, closed his left eye, and sighted his right eye on Orson Everett, peering through the one-inch space. "An angel held me, smack in the middle of them antlers."

"His believers the Lord preserves," Phineas said.

"You seen that one that drew a bead on the colonel?" Gabriel said. "Lafayette stood there, like he was playin' snake on a flat rock, sunnin' hisself and too lazy to move, then pole-axed him like he weren't but a hog in a butcherin' pen with his snout in a slop bucket. Dumped him right there, so he wouldn't have to step but three times to gut him."

"Tired of walking, I guess," Orson Everett said. He laughed.

"Wore out, his shoes must be," Phineas said.

Gabriel winced.

"His shoes must be wore out," Phineas said.

Gabriel nodded. "If he was Moses Cole, he wouldn't have wore-out shoes. A mule would do his footwork for him."

"Slice that heart and fetch the liver," Orson said. "I'll start a fire."

"A gift of the Lord," Gabriel said, "like the manna the Moses people eat in the Bible times."

"This easy I hope the Mexican soldiers will be," Phineas said.

"Won't be no soldier fight, was Brother Brigham's prophesy, if we do right by the Lord," Gabriel said.

Orson said, "So far, events have unfolded as he said they would."

"He never seen the bulls though, takin' us on like they done," Gabriel said. "But this here was combat a little, which leads me to believe some of the brethren are fudgin' on the work of the Lord. Not full blown but cheatin' a little. Brought antlers at us instead of guns."

"What do we do now, Colonel sir?" Gabriel said when Cooke rode by. "Got a lotta meat layin' about. Mule and free beef both."

"Looks like you're fixing dinner. Seems like a good idea to me." Cooke rode on and said to himself, *They're doing just fine.*

CHAPTER 26

I have conversed with the principal chief, Juan Antonio, and he and another have supped with me . . . He said I could see they were poor and naked, but they were content to live here by hard work on the spot which God had given them; and not like others to rob or steal; that they did not fear us, and run like the Apaches, because they made it a rule to injure no one in any way, and therefore never expected any one to injure them.

—Lieutenant Colonel Philip St. George Cooke
regarding the Pima Indians, December, 1846

Mormon Battalion, Rio Gila [Arizona], December 21–22, 1846
The bay mule muzzled grain from the pan where Cooke's mule fed. Cooke stepped from his tent and shooed the bay away. Cooke went back in his tent, and the bay mule returned to the grain that the white mule seemed willing to share. Cooke came back and shoved the bay's neck. The mule turned his head but did not move his hooves. Cooke slapped him on the shoulder and said, "Get your ass out of here!"

The mule walked off, then went back to the grain when Cooke sat with his lap desk.

Cooke rushed out, yelled and pushed the bay away, threw his cap at him, and chased him further. The mule trotted, then stood off, ears, long as bayonets, poised to the angry voice.

Cooke told Ruben Cox to load his musket, went back in the canvas, and pulled the flap closed. Ruben pulled a cartridge from his cartridge box, bit off the ball and put it in his pocket, loaded the powder and paper in the barrel, and rammed it with the ramrod.

The bay came back. Cooke stepped from the tent, grabbed the musket from Ruben, walked close to the broadside animal eating the white mule's grain, cocked the musket, aimed, and fired. The mule jumped and looked at Cooke, then returned to the feed pan.

Cooke threw the gun on the ground.

"Damn you!" he said to Ruben. He stomped into his tent and pulled the door flap down as if to dampen the laughs from nearby soldiers. He felt the boil, the anger that corrupted judgment, his nemesis when dreams drowned. *Ridicule,* he thought. *No one to blame but me.*

He sat on his cot, put his elbows on his knees, and rested his head in his hands. *I do my damnedest to keep mules alive and then I try to shoot one. What is the root of this anger that lays skin deep? What took hold of me? Embarrass myself in front of these men? Am I not equal to this campaign? I lost the battle with emotion and must regain control.*

He rubbed his eyes with the heels of his hands.

The armor breaks. Stop it.

What is the greater lesson? I do not control my destiny. To fight it is to pick a battle I cannot win. Like a draught animal or saddle mule, I'm assigned a burden I must carry. Balk and I get prodded until I do as commanded. Accept it. Adapt and re-plan. I've done so in mind, but not in heart. I'll companion with discontent until I do.

He rocked his head in his hands.

Voices sounded outside, followed by laughs.

He lifted his head and stared at the canvas wall.

A day later they camped on a dry ditch, dug by the Pima Indians to irrigate a field near their village. The Pimas opened the ditch at the Gila to bring water to the camp. The men drank it, washed in it, and cooked with it. Abigail Alcott kindled a campfire, heated water in her Dutch oven, and laundered soldiers' clothes in her washtub.

Pimas wandered through the camp looking at the men and their equipment. Black, luxuriant hair hung down their backs in braids or lay coiled on their heads. Men and women alike wore loincloths or white cotton blankets loosely wound from waist to knee. All were bare-chested. Some soldiers slept, too exhausted to care about the presence of natives. Others fidgeted with Indians among them, bigger and fitter than they. Ebenezer Green laughed at Gabriel Hanks, who loaded his musket while his eyes darted from brave to brave, mounted on enviable horses. Their black hair, accented by the white blankets at their waists, moved as if alive as they trotted by.

"Them Pimas won't hurt you. Them Pimas won't steal a damn thing." Green rocked in his saddle while his mule stood with his head hung as if dozing. Green stopped rocking. "If you was to drop your dented cup," he waved a hand, "say it fell off your pack without you knowin' it and they was to find it, one of them Pimas you're loadin' your musket for would travel a day to give it to you and ask nothin' for it, knowin' all along there weren't no profit in it."

Green watched some bare-breasted women walk by, rocked in his saddle, and looked back at Gabriel. "How many folks do you know, white man or Mexican either one, who would do the same? Not a damn one, you and me and your Mormon Pope throwed in."

Green stood in his stirrups, put a hand to his hat brim, and surveyed the beehive huts thatched with straw and cornstalks that reached beyond sight along the Rio Gila. He looked across the desert valley and its cactus and mesquite. He looked to the raw hills carved to sand and rock.

"I'll be a chewed-on soup bone, damned if I won't. Don't see no church." He studied the Indians walking among the huts to the east and to the west. He dropped his hand and sat back in the saddle. "Don't see no preacher neither, wavin' the Bible in one hand and your Book of Mormon in the other, tellin' the road to the Lord. They just come by it natural." He scratched in his whiskers, pinched an insect, looked at it, and flicked it on the sand. "You'd do you worser than to set down and live with them people, and I'll guarantee to you, it would be a whole lot better for you than it would for them."

Gabriel Hanks said, "Come to think of it, Mister Green, I have never seen you afoot. Do you sleep in that saddle?"

"Only in the daytime."

"Can you walk?"

"Did once and he kicked me, so I kicked him square in the pecker so neither one of us was happy." He laughed and slapped the pommel of his saddle. "Must 'a split his pisser." He laughed longer, then spit something colored. "Set a washtub under him, and he won't hit it, but two coffee cups three feet apart he'll fill 'em both." Green petted the mule's neck. "He's my bettin' mule. Won me a drunk or two. Won me a mornin' on a Mexican whore once."

Green's pats on the mule's rump sounded like soft slaps.

"Coffee cups win every time." He cackled and rocked in the saddle. "Besides that, if I was to walk I might step on a snake or a cactus plant with nothin' but moccasin between me and it." He shook his head, as if to shiver. "Then where would I be?"

Pimas walked by Green, smiled and gestured, and spoke a language he found soothing. He indicated two women with a lift of his chin. Their age difference and resemblance suggested a mother and daughter, each with a baby on a hip, walking arm in arm and smiling.

"Look at them two, titties bared off for all to see, swingin' in the sun like a heifer and a nanny goat and thinkin' nothin' of it." Green tipped his hat and smiled at them. "Parade them titties like Sunday hats." He watched them walk by. "Ain't no devil in their life." He squirmed in the saddle as if to scratch himself. "No devil, no shame. Just live and give, is what they do." He watched the women walk and lifted his eyebrows as if something occurred to him. "Say you peeled back their head bone, had a gander in the Pima mind. You wouldn't find no clutter, no twists or turns or caves like you would in yours or mine. You'd find a clear trail and a warm sun." He watched the women and nodded his head. "The best thing we can do for this earth is to leave them people be."

The Pimas brought cantaloupes and watermelons, corn and wheat and pumpkins and beans in sacks and woven baskets. They brought flour and honey in ceramic jars. They brought water gourds and cotton blankets to trade for buttons and ragged clothes. They gave the soldiers cornmeal cakes, and when those were gone they gave them more.

"Put a Pima in the middle of the desert with a blanket and a stick, and he'll bring back a bushel of corn and a basket of oranges," Green said. He reined and kicked his mule and rode off talking. "Them ain't civilized people, church-up on Sunday and thieve a neighbor on Monday." He tipped his hat to some other women with children in tow. "Ma'ams," he said. He laughed and rode on.

A girl walked between her mother and father, smiling and holding their hands. She released her mother's hand, pointed at Phineas's beard and then at a mule's tail, and laughed. She took her mother's hand again, and they walked among the Saints and their knapsacks, Dutch ovens and tin cups, muskets and harness and makeshift tents rigged from squares of canvas. Cooke admired her complexion, smooth as looking glass, soft as rabbit fur, the color of the fruit of a peach. The girl's smile showed bright teeth. Her eyes shone with the luster of a colt. Cooke thought her age close to Flora's, his daughter whom he had not seen in nearly a year. In another ten days, his precious Flora would turn eleven.

Cooke removed a scarf he'd tied around his neck that morning, one he'd never worn before—silk, festive, and new—and tied the scarf around the girl's head. Her buoyant, black hair shimmered where it cascaded beneath it. She felt the scarf with her clean fingers, giggled, and jumped and hugged Lieutenant Colonel Cooke. Her parents laughed and offered their blankets to Cooke, who smiled and bowed when he refused them.

"She is beauty itself," Cooke said. "Happiness incarnate. I have received more than you know."

Her parents nodded and laughed at the strange language.

A tune from a violin attracted natives like a town crier calling a meeting. Natives crowded close to the fiddler. Some looked with dropped jaw and wide eyes, others smiled and gestured, and others bobbed and danced and laughed.

The girl's parents quickened their step to follow their daughter in the bright scarf who ran to the fiddler. Cooke watched them and thought of Rachael, his wife, and their promenades hand in hand with Flora between them on the parade ground at Jefferson Barracks. He'd heard nothing from Rachael since he'd left St. Louis and had posted his last letter from Santa Fe to notify her of his reassignment from the war in Mexico to the command of the Mormon Battalion. Of course, he'd heard nothing in return. Running ahead of mail carriers was the nature of military campaigns. *Perhaps her letters waited in San Diego*, he thought, *having travelled around Cape Horn via sea vessel.*

He shuddered at the recollection of Rachael's scarred face, pushed it aside, and remembered instead her beauty, her rich complexion before the marring, her quiet, forgiving spirit that calmed him. And Julia, the wee one, born at Fort Leavenworth four years ago. Would he recognize her, barely more than an infant when he saw her last? And their eldest, John, who would turn fourteen, or perhaps fifteen depending on the course of his deployment, before he would see him again. Not long from now, John would be of age to enroll in the academy at West Point. Is that the direction in which he should steer his son? How could he steer John in any direction, absent as he was during his formative years? Oh, the burden of duty! Could he ever escape it?

The encounter with the girl had interrupted Cooke's walk-through inspection of the battalion's camp, and he remained still to watch the festivity. A pack of boys brushed by as they ran to the fiddler.

Julia would never know how beautiful her mother had been before the infliction, and for Flora, soon to turn eleven, the un-scarred face could be her earliest memory if she were to remember it at all. John, of course, saw the thing happen. Could they forgive him? That might explain why he continued a military career instead of the practice of law, where he could have lived, in deed rather than in name only, as husband and father.

Natives walked by on their way to the fiddler until they stood ten or fifteen deep while Cooke stood back to watch.

These peaceful people. Knew they no anguish? Oh, the joy they show in living lives of little choice! The greater the choices one is allowed, the greater the margin for achievement and regret.

Away with these thoughts! With a battalion to command there is no room for doubt.

Cooke walked to the mules to inspect harness sores while soldiers sang to the fiddler's tune, and the girl in the bright silk scarf danced where the Mormons made music.

CHAPTER 27

We reached the mission of San Luis Rey, and found not a human being stirring. The immense pile of building, illuminated by the pale cold rays of the moon, stood out in bold relief on the dim horizon, a monument of the zeal of the indefatigable priests by whom it was built.

—Lieutenant William Emory,
January 1847

Revenge, at first though sweet,
Bitter ere long back on itself recoils.

—John Milton,
Paradise Lost

Army of the West, Expedition to Ciudad de Los Angeles, California, December 29, 1846–January 10, 1847
Sailors and marines marched with artillery pieces from San Diego to take the Ciudad de Los Angeles, again under Mexican control. The force of five-hundred-plus included fifty-seven troopers—those not dead or wounded from San Pasqual, or sick or injured from the trek west.

"Dismounted dragoons," Moses said. "That's army talk for a poor man's cavalry, demoted from four shod hooves to two feet in wore-out shoes."

They marched inland from the sea they beheld from hilltops, through pastures bereft of streams and trees except for the now-

and-then lone live oak, and they walked on ridgeways rife with chaparral.

"First sailor gives out, I'll own his brogans. Easy to dicker with"—Moses turned the words—"once they're prostrate in my pathway."

Private Smithwick looked at him.

"That's Abner talk," Moses said, "for laid out flat, face first, like he'd get when he run with John Barleycorn."

"I see the master private's tracks on you."

"Up one side and down the other. Best officer I ever knew, and he never become one." Moses pictured Abner buried with his fellow dead, his greatcoat buttoned up, one button with the infantry *I*, the lance cut below the button rows that Moses pulled closed, his face covered with the kerchief to keep dirt out of his mouth. Moses pulled his attention back to the shoes to shake the image of worms boring beneath the spectacle lenses.

"Look at them sailors. Limpin' like there's needles in their feet." Moses worked the arithmetic, figured eight or ten from a ship deck for each dragoon. "Join the dragoons to tramp with the navy. Like Abner said, the army has a curious logic, which kept his interest in it."

"You'd limp too if you lugged a muzzleloader," Private Smithwick said. "Like packing a fence rail."

"This carbine's bad enough," Moses said. He heard the surf to the west, saw mountains to the east shine with snow, the sky as blue and enticing as Isabella's eyes. They marched on soil softened with recent rain, and he thought of the rock and the desert where the common grave lay. He looked at the ground, saw green at the base of withered plants. New growth with winter in the hills, life among the dead. *Ain't that a curious twist.*

Moses said, "Don't know how to behave, suckin' in air that's got no dust to it." *Talk on, he thought. Moves my mind off Abner.* "It's throwed me off kilter."

"The navy had your attention," Smithwick said.

Moses indicated the seamen with a lift of his head. "Nothin' but ship deck and saltwater for them sailor shoes, and they grease them for that. Sturdy as the day they were made." *One step, and then another. Keep on walking.*

They marched through the missions at San Luis Rey and San Juan de Capistrano, through San Bernardo and Buena Vista, and, when they came to Santa Ana, the town folk bolted doors at their approach. The makeshift battalion walked on, through the *rancherias* of Alvéar and Saint Marguerita, over treeless and rolling hills and tablelands. They trekked through stream-fed valleys and waterless vales and pastures rich with grasses. They tracked up hard sand on a low-tide beach and walked over open plains, passed vineyards and cornfields. They forded the Soledad and Santa Ana rivers, and, at the Rio San Gabriel, eleven days and a hundred-twenty miles from San Diego, they met the *Californios* lancers and Mexican regulars with muskets and artillery.

The Americans forded the knee-deep San Gabriel, found quicksand in the riverbed. Moses worked to free a foot when a Mexican field gun boomed, and the river spouted like an anvil slammed it.

"Nine-pounder!" Smithwick called.

Another fieldpiece fired, and the water splashed like someone had slung a bucket of hammer heads.

"Grapeshot!" Smithwick called.

"Get across the river!" the captain yelled.

Sailors pulled the guns into battery and fired on the Mexican gunners, which unhinged the enemy's aim. Round shot passed overhead. Water spouted and splashed the soldiers. The Americans labored across the river and kept their powder dry. They reached the riverbank, climbed out, fired on the lancers when they charged, and pushed them to the hilltops.

Quiet came.

The Yankees advanced, camped after nine miles in sight of enemy tents pitched on hills, and awoke in the morning to find the tents gone. They went on, crossed a mesa between the Rio San Gabriel and Rio San Fernando with parties of lancers on their flanks. A day away from the Pueblo de Los Angeles they found the enemy lined on their right. The Americans kept on, and *Californios* horsemen deployed in pincers to envelop them. The invaders countered with a square pen—a "Yankee corral," in sailor speak—with their artillery, supply wagons, and draught animals at the center of the infantry. Lancers charged on two sides.

At a hundred yards, some sailors fired, and officers yelled, "Hold fire!" *Californios* came on with lances lowered, horse hooves pounding like waterfalls falling on rock. Musketry rose to a roar and with the cannons and grapeshot drove the lancers back.

"Ain't that a pretty sight," Moses said. *Californios* galloped off with their wounded, and horses ran with them without their riders. Moses yelled, "Powder's dry this time!" *Shoot every lancer for Abner Black.*

A horse stood and lifted a leg with a shattered knee. The captain said to shoot the poor son of a bitch.

Moses reloaded the Hall breech-loader with a paper cartridge with elongated bullet for the rifled bore, held the carbine snug to his healed-up shoulder, aimed above the horse's head to allow for bullet drop, and squeezed the trigger as if a week of meals depended on it. The palomino's head pitched when the .54 caliber bullet hit, and he collapsed as if severed from his legs.

A lancer sat nearby, held his stomach with his hands, and slumped to his side. His moans carried to the Americans.

Moses levered the breech and reloaded the carbine.

Private Donovan yelled, "Your *compadre* is worse off than you are." He said to his companions, "See that one there?" He pointed to a lancer on his back, still as a fieldstone. "Shot him off in a somersault." He lowered his voice. "I hate them for what they done us at San Pasqual. Got no mercy for a back stabber." He shouted at the wounded *Californio*. "Bayonet him! See how he takes to it."

A sailor said, "You dragoons are animals."

"You'd be one, too, if you fought at San Pasqual," Smithwick said.

Donovan said, "That one I shot, his spurs glinted when he rolled over his horse's croup." He chuckled. "Last light he'll ever shine."

The Americans turned to the Ciudad de Los Angeles, four miles northwest. When they marched away the *Californios* galloped to the fallen horses, stripped them of their saddles and bridles, picked up their dead and the wounded they'd missed, and carried them away on horseback.

A lancer lingered, taunted the Americans from the back of a stallion, yelled in Spanish. They heard *Americano, muerto,* San Pasqual, *estúpido, viva los Californios.* He wore a dragoon's greatcoat with double-breasted buttons.

Moses asked, "Permission to shoot, sir?"

The captain said, "Dump him like a rabid dog."

Moses stepped forward, capped the carbine, lay down, rested its fore-end on a rock, found it low, and added a haversack to the rifle rest. He sighted on the lancer, squirmed his belly and legs into the dirt, judged the range at one hundred-fifty yards, give or take ten. He slid back a bit to raise the barrel, sighted a head higher than the lancer's hat, inched the muzzle to the left to allow for bullet drift in the crosswind, cocked it, and squeezed the trigger.

Moses knew the sound, like a mule kicked a mule, when the

bullet slammed the lancer from the stallion. Dragoons cheered. Moses looked at the lancer on his back, saw his hands go to his chest. The stallion trotted off, head cocked to drag the reins to the side, away from the path his hooves took.

"Permission to fetch the coat, sir?" Moses asked.

"You earned it. If they come back, lie down. We'll open with grapeshot."

Moses reloaded the carbine and walked to the lancer. Smithwick and Donovan went with him.

Moses knew the coat—the twelve buttons in place, the one on the upper left with the infantry *I*, the lance cut below the buttons sewn closed since San Pasqual. How had the man retrieved the coat? Moses buried Abner in it.

The lancer's hands covered the wound at the base of his chest. Blood bubbled between his fingers, colored the corners of his mouth. The lancer looked at Moses, eyelids half open, coughed up blood.

Moses knelt by the lancer. "I know that coat. Belonged to my friend."

The lancer's eyes widened when Moses set the carbine down and drew his sheath knife.

"Closer than a brother."

"Moses," Smithwick said.

"Ought to carve your hair off, tie your scalp to a lance, and run it in your guts."

"You already killed him," Smithwick said. "Give him a minute, and his wick will burn out."

Moses lifted the lancer's hat with the tip of the knife, the back of the brim bent between the ground and the lancer's head. "You got hair enough to wrap a hand around."

Smithwick put a hand on Moses's shoulder. "Careful, Moses, or you'll become more Indian than Christian, like that Apache white boy."

"Let's get the coat and go, before his *compadres* come back," Donovan said.

Abner's voice came to him. A spirit's whisper. *Scalp him and his ghost will own you.*

Moses pulled the lancer's hat back in place and said, "Don't need no more ghosts on me."

The lancer moaned when they rolled him to one side and then to the other to pull the coat off. Moses probed a piece of lung the bullet punched out. He picked it up, held it where the lancer could see it, flicked it away with a fingernail. The lancer's eyes shifted to the knife and back to Moses. He gurgled, moved his hands to cover the wound.

Private Donovan rolled up the greatcoat and started back.

Moses stayed by the lancer. "You dug up my friend and stole his coat."

Smithwick tapped Moses on the shoulder. "We got what we came for."

"Then you left him for the wolves to pull apart. Same as we'll do for you."

"Let's go, Moses."

Moses stood, and Smithwick walked off. Moses knelt back down and said, "You know American like I know Mexican, so you don't savvy a word I say, but you understand me. I don't like what you done." He placed the blade at the lancer's throat, and he heard again what Abner said: *To avoid regret, don't do that which you may come to regret for the stain stays with you.* To that Abner added, *Do as I say, not as I do.*

"Moses!" Smithwick yelled. "Get over here!"

Moses rocked the beveled edge against the lancer's throat until specks of blood rose.

"Now!"

"His name was Abner Black." Moses stood, considered the lancer's calfskin boots, leaned over, and said, "I want no part of you." He sheathed the knife, picked up the carbine, and walked to the dragoons.

CHAPTER 28

*Some went A head with [pick] & Shovel in hand & dug wel[l]s
in low places So that we did not quite parish [sic].*

—Albert Smith, Mormon Battalion,
January 11, 1847

*I had spent the night without water, and thirty miles of desert
were still before me; the men way-worn and exhausted, half fed,
and many shoeless.*

—Philip St. George Cooke,
mid-January, 1847

*Mormon Battalion, Rio Colorado and Cooke's Well, California,
January 9–11, 1847*

Ebenezer Green rode into the Rio Colorado. His mule's hooves
broke ice an inch thick in the slack water on the edge of the
river. California waited on the far side, a half mile straight across
but a mile by river ford angling downstream where the river
split into two channels. The river ran wider than the Missouri
here and proved just as muddy. Green wondered how fish could
live in it.

Green rode in to test the ford, gasped when it reached saddle-
seat deep, gripped the thin mane when the river's bottom fell
away from the mule's hooves. Even at the ford, the river ran
swift enough to drift his mule downstream.

On the California side, Green found mesquite thickets too

dense for wagons to roll through. He kindled a fire and warmed himself, watched steam lift from his wet britches, and thought of his spirit rising and finding fire.

He recrossed the river, plumbed again the depths of the ford with smoke looming behind him. Flames raced away from the California bank, darted and stabbed the cold air, danced in the north wind to music only they could hear. He reported to Lieutenant Colonel Cooke that he'd fired the far side to clear a way for wagons, and they'd by God like that heat once they crawled from winter's water.

The battalion camped on the east bank of what some called the Big Red River. Of the twenty-five wagons they'd wheeled from Santa Fe, nine remained, plus a handful of private wagons. With the cold sharp enough to ice over slack water, the tar on the wagon wheels hardened, which made a harder pull for the mules. Their mobile commissary also clustered there—one hundred-thirty sheep and twenty cattle they'd bought or traded for along the way. After the desert miles, scant feed, and less water, their animals showed the toll a winter on sand would take.

The Mormon soldiers gathered mesquite beans by the bushel, spread a part of their harvest on a sandbar for mule feed, and used part of it themselves. Some roasted the mesquite beans, and some ate them raw. Others ground them in coffee mills, patted the meal into cakes and fried them in frying pans, boiled them for coffee, or stirred them for mush. Others added flour and called it bread dough. Some found it bitter; some found it sweet; they all found it locked their bowels. Accustomed as they were to discomfort they continued on, bearing the day as yet another in the life of a soldier.

Cooke felt the press of time. Mules weakened with no feed east of the Rio Colorado other than mesquite beans and meager leaves of cottonwood boughs, and a hundred-mile desert ahead.

Cooke paced. If they could not arrive in time, whatever that would be, all their sufferings, and the test of this command, would be for naught. The fate of California, and Kearny's dragoons, remained unknown. A simple truth stayed indecision—delay meant less chance to fill their mission, and perhaps, the difference between life and death of the Americans ahead. To dally, to not give full measure, would tip the scale toward failure.

The Saints unwedged wagon boxes from the running gear—the axles and wheels, reaches and tongues—from a handful of wagons. They stuffed clothing and blanket and tent scraps in the decks of the wagon beds and between sideboards, wedging them in with the dull sides of sheath knives to make the boxes river worthy. The Mormons lashed them two by two, end to end to fashion ferry boats, cut dry cottonwoods for pontoons, and lashed the wagon boxes between the trees. They used tent poles or saplings to push their makeshift ferries across the river. In this manner, over the course of a night and half a day, they ferried the men and the baggage and the sheep to California. With the boats crossing to the fired side of the river, flames flaring to light the night sky, it looked, Orson Everett said, like the mythical ferryman who floated souls over the river Styx to the harbor of the dead.

Some of the men who poled the boats worked through the night, having learned the tricks of the river. Others, fatigued, traded with one who'd rested, each coaching his replacement where the snags and currents and sandbars lay. A north wind rippled the river surface and fanned campfires thin men in meager clothing huddled over, waiting their turn to cross while others slept in tents. It took an hour and a half to pole a wagon-box boat across and back.

When day came, they hitched mules to the remaining wagons, and the mules pulled, then swam the wagons in the river. The deeper current shoved the wagons, which pushed the mules to quarter angles, swimming upstream to tack across, as if to mimic ravens caught in a crosswind.

Men rode mules and swam the cattle over. Others rode bareback, unbridled and driven in the *remuda* by those on saddle mules. Some mules quit in the current, submerged their heads as if to graze the river bottom, floundered sideways, ribcage parallel to the river surface like beached fish, and drowned.

A wagon leaked, took on water, sunk to the top of the sideboards, and got stuck in a sandbar. Too weak to pull it the mules stood wither-deep in the current, chilling in the river with icecaps in the slack water. Teamsters worked to free it, diving to wiggle wood under the wheels.

After they'd ferried everything, they re-cleated the wagon boxes to their running gear, greased the wagon hubs, and secured the wheels in place. They hitched the mules and set off to cross California.

The fire Green had set smoldered and burned and raged in places. Teamsters cursed Green, worried the wagons might burn, feared coals would ruin mule hooves. Men without shoes picked their footsteps. The mesquite had not burned cleanly. Main stems remained, trunks with branches burned off, stobs standing like broken lance shafts. Smoke moved with the wind, sometimes lingered, caused coughing and eyes to burn. They pushed through it. Sand softened, opened to the north, stretched like an Arabian desert. Beyond that, at the end of eyesight, mountains stood covered in snow, or white rock, or capped in sand.

Fifteen miles later they arrived at a well. Deeper than the height of a man, sloped like the top of an hourglass, with sides of sand and dry as the desert air. A dead wolf lay in the bottom of it.

Gabriel said, "Burnin' with thirst the last hundred miles, and what do we get? A sand well with a rotten wolf in it. Don't it fit a Mormon soldier?" He chuckled, stepped into the well to pull out the wolf, felt the impact of the smell held in by the well sides, saw maggots move where wolf hair slipped, bent over, and retched.

Lieutenant Colonel Cooke ordered the well dug deeper, while others dug a second well. At eight feet they found enough water to shine shovel blades. At ten feet the damp sand turned to quicksand and sloughed as they dug—for each shovelful shoveled, a shovelful slid in. Someone suggested a washtub would serve to wall the sand back. Another said if they punched holes in the bottom of the tub, water would percolate up.

Cooke told his adjutant to request the washtub from Mrs. Alcott as soon as the Alcott wagon arrived.

Captain and Abigail Alcott drove their own team and wagon and freighted a fragment of home—blankets, pots, pans and plates, utensils, an extra dress, a quilt Abigail's mother had made, the washboard and washtub, a six-penny looking glass, the Dutch oven and clock, coffee mill and lamp, the Bible, and the Book of Mormon. To lessen the weight the mules pulled they'd left the chest of drawers, the bed and the cupboard and the Windsor rocker when they turned to the desert at the *Rio Grande del Norte*. When Captain Alcott summoned help to unload those items Abigail bit her cheeks, refrained from speaking, and walked on, her face to the west. She felt as if she were orphaning family members, abandoning parts of her childhood home to sand and mesquite.

Lieutenant A. J. Smith had ridden by shortly after they had unloaded their furniture, had stopped and looked at the Windsor rocker and noted where his saber had rested when he ate the fresh bread. He rode to the baggage wagon he shared with Lieutenant Stoneman, the other dragoon lieutenant, and ordered his personal chair removed and the Windsor rocker loaded in its place. He rode to Captain Alcott and informed him that he would have his wife's chair delivered to their camp each evening and would take it to San Diego for her. He hoped, he said, this would redeem him of his ungentlemanly conduct for the damage he had done to it.

That was two months ago, and still Abigail wept when she thought of those things, but could smile when reminded each evening what Lieutenant Smith had done that day.

When the adjutant, a Mormon lieutenant, delivered the commander's request for the washtub, Abigail said, "No!" in a tone that would chase a starving dog from a plate of table scraps. She'd brought the tub from Nauvoo, the possession she cherished among all household items—one she refused to leave as their mules weakened, the thing that tied her to civilized life. Her jewelry she'd sold in Illinois, all but the wedding ring, to buy the mules and wagon. At first, she rejected, then accepted, then welcomed the test of faith their surrender implied—trading baubles, those treasures of feminine accent, for things of use in a journey of the Lord. All but the wedding ring. Crafted in England, worn by her husband's grandmother and his mother and now by her, she felt its bond to those strong and disciplined women, and to her husband, in a union graced by the Lord in the limestone Temple at Nauvoo. Its lineage, she was determined, would not stop with her. The Lord, she knew, would forgive her coveting this item of the heart for the honor of the family. The others, the indulgent adornments, she converted to utilitarian goods for the work of the Lord.

The adjutant stammered, then looked at Captain Alcott and said, "I don't know what else to say. We're in the army. The lieutenant colonel wants your tub."

For Abigail, five things made the desert crossing possible—

caring for her husband, her friendship with Melissa Brown, nurturing sick soldiers, her joy in her pregnancy, and the washtub. The tub changed her from being a burden to filling a purpose. It anchored her essence, and it provided income. Without it, and, she admitted, her status as wife to a captain, she'd have been sent to Pueblo.

Now her belly swelled at six months pregnant. She would need the tub to keep the baby clean.

"It's private property," Captain Alcott said. "The colonel has no right to it."

"But the colonel sent me. We need it to keep a well from collapsing."

"It belongs to my wife. She won't part with it, and I don't blame her."

"You don't understand," the adjutant said. "No tub, no water. No water, we die. You and your mules, too."

"The army has no right to our private property. You're a Latter-day Saint. You know that. Tell the colonel to do something else."

Captain Alcott slapped the mules with the reins. When they didn't move, he slapped them again. They leaned into the traces and nudged the wagon ahead. The adjutant left, and Captain Alcott pulled the mules up, stepped from the wagon, unhitched the singletrees, walked the mules away from the wagon tongue, and unharnessed them. Abigail sat on the wagon seat and bit her nails, or tried to bite them. They were worn too short for her teeth to gain purchase.

"What the hell do you mean, they refused the request?"

The men at the well stopped digging and looked at the adjutant fixed before Cooke.

"Sir, they won't part with the tub." The adjutant stood, still as stone.

"They won't part with the goddamn tub," Cooke said. He looked at the men at the well, then back to the adjutant. "Do you mean to tell me they're willing to imperil the lives of this battalion, the lives of their fellow Mormons, so they can keep their clothes clean?" Cooke's sunburned face turned redder. "For Christ's sake."

"I told them our survival depends on it. They don't care. It's their private property."

"And he's a captain," Cooke said. "Volunteers." He shook his head. "Put it in language they'll understand. Take two men and seize the damn thing."

"Yes, sir." The adjutant pointed to two soldiers who sat by the well and motioned for them to accompany him.

Cooke checked the second well, the new one the men took it upon themselves to dig. The diggers found hard clay, which slowed their digging from shovelfuls to slivers, but the walls held firm.

Cooke sent for Green and posed the question: What if we returned to the Rio Colorado and marched south to connect with an old Spanish trail?

"Go downriver," Green said, "you get a muddy river and a Mexican desert. Don't get you nothin' you don't have now."

"And ahead?" Cooke said. "The next water is three days away?"

"Ain't never crossed it, Cap'n. Don't know nothin' more than what I've heard. Two days and a night to the next well, which might have water, and two days and two nights to the well after that, which might have water." Green pushed his hat back and scratched at the hairline. "Either way, I'd lay odds less than even."

"I was afraid you'd say that."

Cooke nodded and walked off as if on a mission of business. He looked to where the sun would set, wondered when the desert would end. *Forge ahead and we have a hope of a wet well after three marches. If they carried water the men might make it, but the mules? Impossible to take water for all, even if the wells yield it.*

Cooke walked to his mule, pulled his journal, pen, and sealed inkwell from his saddle bag, sat on the sand, and thought what he might write. *Had he led these men to their deaths? They could retreat to the river, strain and boil water, but what about food? They would exhaust their rations soon. How many mesquite beans would it take? How many miles would foragers travel to harvest enough? They would eat the mules and sheep and cattle, but then what? To retreat to the river would be to place themselves under siege, the end of their days marked by the last animal. Had Kearny made it to San Diego? Are they dead in the desert ahead? From the lack of water? Food? Engagement with Mexican forces?*

Cooke opened the journal, dipped pen in ink, and wrote: *Beyond the Rio Gila, lifeline to this desert trek that led us west, its end at the Rio Colorado that turns it to the Sea of Cortez. Once again, we enter an uncharted desert.*

He paused, considered what he'd written, dipped the pen and put it to the page: *We cannot retract our choices.*

Cooke stood, returned the journal, pen, and ink to his saddle bag. There was no option. They found water here, or it would be a matter of time before they died, whether at the river's edge or in the desert ahead.

He walked back to the wells. They'd dug the first well to ten feet deep and placed the washtub in the bottom. Water seeped up through the holes they'd punched in, then sunk back in the quicksand.

"Pull it," Cooke said. "Knock the bottom out."

They did so, reset the tub, and water came in faster, quit, and withered.

One well left, dug in an untested place, a cast of chance, Cooke thought. *What a thin veil hope is. Pull it away and bleached bones appear.*

He checked the second well, now deeper than the first with mud in the bottom. He ordered a fresh detail to relieve the clay diggers, walked away, and waited.

Abigail wailed when they punched holes in the bottom of her washtub. When it didn't work, and they pulled the tub and knocked the bottom out, Abigail shrieked as if she'd miscarried.

Captain Alcott restrained her, told her that to defy an order by a lieutenant colonel constituted mutiny. Melissa Brown came to console her, sat by Abigail on the seat of the unhitched wagon, and told her it was only a thing, one that could be replaced someday. Melissa tried humor, jibed about no water to launder with anyway, cooking for messes of men with nothing to cook.

"What will happen at payday, whenever that comes?" Melissa asked. "Hired as a laundress but they took your tub and knocked the bottom out."

Melissa held Abigail's hand, quipped that if nothing else the army owed her a tub, a new one, without a dent in it. Abigail would not be comforted. Melissa sent Captain Alcott away.

"Tears take water," Melissa said. "You have none to spare. Think of your baby."

"I am thinking of my baby. I need the tub."

Melissa squeezed her hand, told her the tub was an object for work, not worship. "It's not right to covet a thing so," Melissa said.

Abigail whimpered, lifted her dress to wipe tears. At twenty-two, Abigail was four years older than Melissa.

"It's a sacrifice for the Lord," Melissa told her. "You give up something you treasure for the good of the many."

Abigail dabbed her eyes.

"If the tub helps the men find water, then it's done a lot

more than wash clothes," Melissa said. "If it doesn't help, and they ruin your tub, at least you did all you could. If only for a little while, you gave them hope."

Abigail quieted, told what the tub meant to her, blamed her behavior on what a woman went through when her body moved to motherhood.

"Dear Abigail," Melissa said and put an arm around her. Melissa looked to make sure no one would hear her. "I have a secret to share." Melissa looked again. The men continued to straggle in, filling an area the size of a church square. They sat or lay down, or gathered at the well and waited for water to appear. Melissa whispered, "I've had the sickness, for two days now. It's awful." She smiled widely.

Abigail threw her arms around her.

"Oh, Melissa!"

A mule lifted an ear.

"My dear Melissa!"

Men turned from their digging to the pitch in Abigail's voice. One shook his head and resumed the shovel work.

"Hush," Melissa said. She blushed.

Abigail hugged her and whispered. "What fun we shall have raising our babies together!"

The mules stood unharnessed, heads lowered, flanks hollowed with shrunken stomachs.

Dusk came. Stars spotted the sky, brightened, became thicker. Cooke paced, sat by his campfire. His adjutant approached with a lilt to his step. Cooke stood.

"Got water enough to dip a camp kettle, sir, and it keeps on coming."

Cooke felt the lift he saw in his adjutant and pumped the adjutant's hand. He smiled until he thought his voice would hold. "Thank you. My compliments to the well diggers for an extraordinary job."

The adjutant beamed, saluted, said "Yes, sir!" and walked back to the well.

Cooke retrieved his journal and sat on the sand. He uncapped the inkwell, dipped a pen, opened the journal to the last entry. He leaned toward the light of the campfire, put the pen to a page, found his hand shook too much to scribe readable script. He set the pen and the journal down, recapped the inkwell, and dropped his face in his hands—then thought better of it, saw the posture as unbecoming to a lieutenant colonel. He stood and walked into the dark as if carried by a great hand. He felt tears rise, his throat tighten. He walked further, stopped and looked at the stars, and thought, *We live by an accident of clay, which formed a bottom for water or channeled a seam from the Rio Colorado. Was it chance to pick that spot? Was it the fortitude of faith to keep digging, or the power of desperate men? The providence of God, or simple, dumb luck?*

Cooke looked around him, saw no one close, and wiped his cheeks. He knelt and folded his hands, then looked up as if to receive a visitor. He considered how he appeared, shifted to kneel on one knee and looked at the ground as if to search for a lost object, and prayed his thanks.

We went to the well and found it dry, went again and it provided. Once more found fullness in the world. He'd found richness in much—the inspired Romantic writers, verdant nature in the eastern states, athletic and sensitive horses, graceful and cultured women. He'd found it in the Pima Indians, those noble savages so full of love and trust, of meager means yet joyous to give all away. He'd found it in the fortitude of the Mormon volunteers—in their belief in their church, and in their confidence in his leadership to deliver them to San Diego. He'd seen enough to know there was more at work than the eye could see, especially, perhaps, in this void of a landscape.

He knew he drew strength from faith, but faith in what? In a shadow behind the veil? In the credo of the officer corps? Or was it faith in discipline, in endless effort, in the providence of practice?

Like the well that derived its supply from a river, he wondered what supplied his well. Was it hope? A promise of hardship relieved? A wish turned real? Was it the God of Episcopal catechism that lit this darkest hour bright as a noonday sun?

Two wells, one of quicksand, one of clay. In which had he dug his? How would he know until he'd dug too deep? Would his well probe a seam to a great river, or will he, at the end of his efforts, find it dry?

He'd gone beyond the Rio Gila. He'd made his choices. He could not take back his steps.

Cooke stood up, rubbed his knee, saw lanterns and men gathered to the well. *Drink deeply,* he thought, *drink very deeply.*

CHAPTER 29

*When our colums [sic] were halted every eye was turned towards
its placid surface, every heart beat with muttered pleasure, evry
[sic] Soul was full of thankfulness, evry [sic] tongue was
silen[ce]d, we all felt too ful [sic] to give Shape to our feeling by
any expression . . .*

*—Henry Boyle, Mormon Battalion,
January 27, 1847*

Mormon Battalion, January 27, 1847, San Luis Rey, California
They passed the mission at San Luis Rey, its walled courtyard
with archways over the gates, date palms and olive trees, cisterns
and wells, and paved pathways where a padre waved. The
compound boasted colonnaded porches, barracks or some such
of adobe brick, tiled roofs, a church white as desert sunlight, its
bell in a cupola. They walked by vineyards, fields with sheep
and goats, milch cows, geese and chickens, orchards and
gardens, padres in robes with ropes for belts.

Indians stood from their hoeing to watch the soldiers—white
men poor as Digger Indians, gaunt as scarecrows with hair on
their faces, ragged as wind-ripped corn stalks, armed with
muskets. The Indians fidgeted, uncertain whether to stand or
hoe, run or hide. They looked to the padres who talked to the
soldier on the white mule and saw them smiling.

The soldiers walked through noon and the reach of the day,
through fields and pastures of flowing grass and oak-dotted

251

hills. Near evening they neared a rise that lifted westward.

"Hear it?" Orson Everett said.

A rumble rose and fell, lay still and rose again. Men stepped away from the file of soldiers to listen to the thump and fall, the pulse of the rumble, pulses slow and set apart.

"Thunder," Gabriel Hanks said.

He stopped and cupped a hand to an ear. Phineas and Orson stopped with him and listened. Gabriel studied the sky.

"No rain cloud nowhere. Don't make no sense."

"Surely the magic of the Lord it is," Phineas Lynch said.

"The Lord's talkin' to someone who's deafer than a wagon plank," Gabriel said, "or he's singin' him a song about the mighty Mormon Battalion."

The Alcott wagon passed by with Abigail and Captain Alcott and their mules' ears intent on the close horizon.

"Could be," Orson said, "but in physical fact, it's waves."

"How do you know?" Gabriel said. He listened closer. "You ain't never seen an ocean. For all you know it's a volcano, which you ain't never seen neither, snortin' and blowin' hellfire, tellin' to go back to where we come from."

Phineas ran his fingers through his whiskers.

"Maybe it's Mexicans launching cannonballs, blow Phineas clean off his bare-skin feet, nothin' but smoke where Phineas Lynch used to be."

"Could be," Orson said.

"Look at them feet," Gabriel said. "Nothin' but callous where the tickle used to be."

Phineas looked at his feet.

"Actually, there's just dirt. Can't tell where the ground stops and the feet start."

Ebenezer Green, chief pilot, shuffled by on his mule and said, "Get to walkin', Mormonitos, afore all your brethren suck up the view up yonder and don't leave nothin' for you to see."

"Whoa-up, Mister Green," Gabriel said. "What's that cloudless thunder we're hearin' a little?"

"That's what the end of land sounds like, and it ain't a pretty sight." Green reined his mule up. "Nothin' but ocean from here to China." Green looked toward the sound, pushed his hat back and scratched, looked at Gabriel. "You think you seen desert?" Green pulled his hat back in place, where it seemed to belong, as if it were an appendage. "Ain't nothin' more God forsaken than the top of an ocean, then you got all them creatures hidin' underneath of it." Green's hat brim bobbed when he nodded his head. "Think of all that land, hidin' under that water. What a waste."

"They got mermaids down there?" Gabriel said.

"One to every rock. Smile and flip that tail. Bat them eyelashes. Reel you in so a wave can smash ya. Women, you know. I'd be careful, I was you." He spurred his mule, then pulled him up after two paces, turned, and looked at Gabriel.

"That's what the cap'n's compass done. Brought us to a bevy of mermaids, not a split tail amongst 'em." Ebenezer Green threw his head back and laughed, rocking in the saddle. He spurred his mule and rode off, hat brim bobbing.

"He's been in the desert too long," Orson said.

"Great God of the sea waves," Gabriel said. He fell to his knees, threw his arms up and held them out, palms up, face to the heavens. "Don't let me fall off the edge of the world! Don't let a mermaid smash on Phineas Lynch with a scaly tail!"

"Left him with the Indians, we should have done," Phineas said. "But that we would not do to the Indians."

Gabriel laughed and threw his hat at Phineas. "First thing I'll do, if I can call up the courage, is take me a bath, get presentable to the Lord and give him thanks for pullin' Satan off me in the sand country."

"You do that," Orson Everett said. "The Lord may not have

heard from you in a while."

"Jump right in, rags and all," Gabriel said. "Wash up the all of me a little."

The three hundred thirty-three soldiers climbed a slight rise. The rumble grew as they approached its edge. Talk stopped. The hard air of the desert softened here, warmed instead of burned, as different as a blanket from a board. The breeze held a hint of moisture.

When they reached the bluff, they spread out and beheld the ocean they'd marched for seven months and nineteen hundred miles to see. For a group that liked to fiddle and sing they were oddly quiet. No one summoned a word to say. They watched waves pound the rocks that marked the end of the continent, and beyond the waves a flat surface bigger than the prairies and deserts they'd crossed. Behind their backs the Sierra Nevada lifted snow to the sky. To their sides hills rolled away, flush with green grass mid-calf high, with mustard and clover and oats waving like a field promising harvest and, below those, valleys fertile with fruit. They looked at the sea, and the sun that settled in it without a ripple, the light that danced there, soft as the breeze the sea sent.

CHAPTER 30

The battalion passed . . . by cross roads over high hills . . . to the mission of San Diego . . . The buildings being dilapidated, and in use by some dirty Indians, I camped the battalion on the flat below . . . The evening of this day of the march, I rode down, by moonlight, and reported to the General in San Diego.
—Lieutenant Colonel Philip St. George Cooke,
January 29, 1847

Thus, general, whilst fortune was conducting you in battles and victories, I was fated to devote my best energies to more humble labors; and all have cause to regret that the real condition of affairs in this territory was so little understood. But it is passed! and I must be content with having done my duty in the task which you assigned to me, if, as I trust, to your satisfaction.
—Lieutenant Colonel Philip St. George Cooke,
February 5, 1847

Mormon Battalion, San Diego, California, January 29, 1847
He rode alone in the moonlight. The village lay four miles west of the mission where the Mormon Battalion camped. Both were named San Diego—one the mission where the battalion stopped, the other the village where General Kearny and the dragoons bivouacked. He looked at his compass, not to check the direction, but to give it the honor of indicating due west where the village of San Diego sat, that point of reckoning

placed before him on the 2nd of October last, east of the great deserts.

To Cooke that seemed an eternity ago. He counted the days to be just short of four months, thought it a bridge of time to a former life.

Something bubbled up, a thing he'd not felt since St. Louis, before his career jumped track with his reassignment from the war in Mexico to the Army of the West. How easy life had seemed, how adventuresome it had been. Then came command, that stern teacher that hardened him with a harsh hand. Was he the better or the worse for it?

And now a new-found joy, like a spring in the desert, or a song finding voice again.

He stopped on a hill that overlooked the village. Beyond it on the moonlit sea, perhaps a twenty-minute pull in a launch with eight oarsmen, a squadron of U.S. warships anchored. The waves played in the moonlight, as if tossing it from wave to wave, or moving through it, like a foot under a blanket. He marveled at how still the ocean lay, so vast and placid and empty of turmoil. The Pacific, true to its name with its peaceful deep. If only his soul could be so.

Just short of the shore, thirty or forty buildings composed the village—a scatter of clapboard and adobe structures. The only avenue that resembled a street marked the front of a three-tiered building and the half-dozen structures aligned with it, side by side with their backs to the sea. The placing of the other homes, barns, and sheds and shops appeared haphazard, as if built where freight wagons broke down and the teamsters quit, each favoring the whim of its builder in the direction and angle it faced. Many of the structures stood no taller than horse-head high. Some boasted verandas, suggesting sun and sea breezes that came in the summertime. Balconies, one to a floor on the three-tiered building, overlooked a plaza with room enough for a six-yoke wagon to circle. Lanterns on all three floors suggested boarders, officers of the First Dragoons, sailors, and travelers on *El Camino Real.*

He wondered at the odd fit—a lieutenant colonel, approaching thirty-seven, worn down with the worry of keeping the battalion alive, yet buoyant with the weight of the campaign lifted. How would the general receive him? Part savior? Part soldier reporting for duty?

With the march accomplished and the leadership he'd shown, he might be granted a command in the war in Mexico. His ship, perhaps, might yet come in. He could almost see it's sails billow, there on the sea in the soft light of the moon. He yearned to feel the romance again, freed of the pedestrian oppressions of a desert march with a religious militia. The things a regular army took for granted, like discipline, proper care of arms and mules, how to march and maneuver by platoon, shoot a musket, and assemble in formation. The Mormon Battalion knew little of that when he had taken command.

He thought about Green, one shoe short of a shod horse, a vacant landscape his place of choice. A carefree soul with simple hopes who lived each day as a day of conquest. But to Cooke, the purpose of the day was to reach the destination, and there it lay, down there with lanterns lit.

How would he contain this ungainly joy, this boyish spirit gushing forth? General Kearny, of course, would know of their arrival with word carried by travelers or unseen eyes, some skittish figure in the distance, some shadow moving in the wind.

He felt the dream that withered a summer ago bloom again. There it was, the heart of the romantic youth that he thought had died in the desert. He might be better served if it had.

Moonlight shone on white adobe, dimmed on roofs of terracotta tile. A dog barked in the village. An ember lifted from a chimney. A shout came that ended in "bitch." Notes floated from an accordion accompanied by a sailor's chantey. When the song ended, a villager's goose ruffled the quiet.

He nudged the white mule forward and rode down the hill.

Moses Cole stood at attention in front of the hotel at order arms—Hall carbine held upright at his right side, butt on the ground at his right foot. The carbine reached midway up his ribcage.

A dog trotted up, stopped, and stood at the edge of the light that reached from the windows. His tail, bushy as a coyote's, did not wag. Moses shifted to shoulder arms, and the dog barked. At quarter-hour intervals, to relax the strain of standing straight and to stay awake, Moses would switch between marching in front of the building and standing at attention before the door. His relief would arrive at midnight.

He thought of home as he often did during the boredom of a march or garrison duty. He wondered again how the farm got on without his help. *Ole pa. Ole George. How'd he take it when I up and left? Not knowin' where I went, whether I'm standin' or planted? Maybe he'd give a nickel to know. Maybe he wouldn't.*

The dog barked when Moses turned an about-face.

How's he farin' without a kid to whip?

Moses marched the length of the veranda, turned an about-face and marched back.

Never imagined I'd miss the farm, have a longin' come on to work the place. Beats poundin' a saddle seat, buildin' a tough butt. Sufferin' through country as foreign as the ocean when I could've stayed put, seen to Miss Isabella, if it weren't for the old man. If it weren't for the weasel and the river ice. If it weren't for bein' a boy.

Moses thought of the picnic the church folks had in the pasture at the parson's house.

Moses played mumblety peg with some other boys. The older

ones sneaked glances toward Miss Isabella to look, he was sure, at how her body curved. Moses watched her set the basket on the blanket, then saw the miller's mule bolt from the trees, chased by chickens that flapped and squawked at its neck and girth, tied by their legs to the mane and rib rope for the fear they'd put into the colt. The mule headed for the blanket as if it were a place of safety. Moses ran to turn him and reached the blanket just as a hoof landed in the linen-lined basket that held the tea set—teapot, cups with handle loops too small to fit a man's finger, saucers, sugar bowl and cream pitcher no bigger than wrens.

When the mule ran over the blanket it scattered the women, Miss Isabella's father said, like quail with a dog on them, and ran into the trees at the edge of the pasture. Miss Isabella's aunt lost her footing and fell. Moses helped her to her feet while Miss Isabella's mother gawked at the fragments that littered the blanket with the basket flipped over. Black tea saturated the blanket, woven in a Richmond woolen mill, which Miss Isabella's aunt saved for special occasions.

Parishioners gathered about to inspect the carnage, tell of pranks the miller's boys pulled, their idle minds the devil's tool shed. A man laughed at the chickens and the terrified colt, and his wife said to hush up, how dare he laugh at the misfortune of animals, the poor thing that was only a colt that would run himself crazy and break the wings of the chickens in the trees pounding them dead with his running.

"He's a mule," the man said. "He'll think on it and stop."

"I will scalp those boys!" Miss Isabella's aunt said. "Always up to their pranks that they think are harmless. Now look what they've done! We could have been crippled from that stampeded beast! We could have been killed! And they find humor in it? How dare they!"

She picked up the basket, sorted through the remnants on

the blanket, found no tea piece whole beyond a saucer and the sugar bowl.

"The miller will answer for this," she said. "He will learn to control those boys, and he will pay the price in the process." She swept the pieces from the blanket back into the basket as if she wiped crumbs from a table and marched toward the mill-house, basket in hand.

Miss Isabella's mother said, "I would not want to be the miller. His mule kicked the queen bee's nest, and she's taken wing to get even, which she will."

They watched Miss Isabella's aunt march off.

"A hurricane is about to run through his world. I would pity that man, if he didn't deserve it." She folded the blanket and carried it away to clean the tea stain.

Parishioners drifted back to their picnic meals, and Moses turned to leave.

Miss Isabella said, "Thank you for trying to help, Moses Cole."

Moses stopped. "I seen it comin'. Not soon enough though. Had to do somethin'."

"With church folks about, yes you did." Isabella smiled. "That's a joke, Moses Cole. You would have helped anyway. It's in your nature."

Moses tipped his head toward the ground to shield his face with his hat brim, wondered how she would know what's in his nature.

"It scared us," Isabella said. "We heard the chickens and the shouts but didn't see that colt until he was on us."

Moses looked up. "You all jumped like frog legs in a stove pan. If I was the mule I'd have spooked, but then he had them chickens to contend with."

A horseshoe clanged on a pin, and people shouted.

"He was distracted," Moses said, "by them chickens poundin' on him the way they was, squawkin' and grabbin' with them chicken toes." He thought, *Stammer on, you dummy.*

"For being distracted, he had good aim," Miss Isabella said.

"He was not gunnin' for the tea basket. It just got in his way."

Miss Isabella pointed to the cakes that lay on the ground. "Better eat one," she said. "Maybe two or more. Be a shame to waste them." She picked two cakes from the grass, both of which fit on one palm. She picked pieces of debris from them with thumb and forefinger, dainty-like, as if picking burrs from birds, and handed one to Moses.

A boy yelled, "Waitin' on you, Moses."

Moses ate the cake in one bite. Isabella gave him two more.

"Like bread with sugar in it, and plenty of butter," he said, "like Mama used to bake." His smile broke at the memory.

Isabella looked away. "So sad," she said.

Moses tipped his hat, said "Miss Isabella," and left to rejoin the boys.

He saw her yet—the smile, the light in her eyes, the glow of her complexion—standing unrattled, as if a hoof in the tea set was nothing to fret about.

The dog barked at each about-face. Moses wanted to shoot him. He saw no window or door open in the hotel, turned to the dog, and snapped, "Git!"

The dog barked and stood still.

Moses turned about-face at the end of the hotel, where the smell of dead fish slid from the shore. The dog barked. Moses wondered how he could remain the rigid sentry, yet get rid of the dog that annoyed the peace of the evening. Moses looked in the windows, saw General Kearny press his face to the glass. Moses marched twenty paces, turned about-face. The window that had shown the general now showed only lantern light.

Moses picked up a rock and threw it at the dog. The dog ran a few steps, stopped, and barked at him.

Moses drew saber and ran at the dog, saber in one hand and carbine in the other. The dog's bushy tail dropped to his hocks, and he ran off. Moses stopped and waved his saber.

"Choke on a fish bone, son of a bitch!" he yelled.

The hotel door opened. General Kearny stepped out.

"Are we under attack, Private?"

"We were, sir, but I run him off."

"Indeed." The general smiled. "A fearsome charge. Exemplary, I'd say. Well done, Private."

"Thank you, sir."

Moses sheathed his saber, placed his carbine at right-shoulder-shift, marched to his position in front of the door, turned to face away from the hotel, placed his carbine at order arms, and stood at attention.

General Kearny walked to the end of the veranda and breathed in the sea air. "Cigars, Private. A man needs a cigar to cover the fish smell."

"That he does, sir."

"I'll take a stable any day." General Kearny clasped his hands in the small of his back and listened to a chantey sung to the sea meander through the plaza. He rocked on his heels, listened to the sailor's tenor braid with an accordion, tapped a toe to the music. One stanza became another, and then another, until the last stanza found its end. Somewhere in the village a goose honked.

"In fact, I miss that smell," General Kearny said. He returned to the front door, pushed it open, and paused. "Pretty quick on your feet, for a dragoon," he said. He chuckled, stepped inside, and closed the door.

Moses watched a rider approach on a tall, white mule. He didn't know the mule. When the rider drew within thirty paces, Moses shifted from order arms to arms port, placing the carbine diagonally across his chest, in position to shove someone.

At twenty paces, moonlight glowed on the white mule, showed the saber hilt, the dragoon cap, and baldrics. The tall mule fit the rider's height. Moses snapped to attention, musket at order arms.

"I'm glad to see you made it, sir."

"We're glad to be here," Cooke said. "I take it this is the general's quarters?"

"It is, sir."

"Will the general receive Lieutenant Colonel Cooke?"

"I'm sure he will, sir."

Cooke dismounted, saw no place to tie his mule.

"Sir, may I ask a question?"

"Go ahead, Private."

"How'd them Mormons do?"

"They did well," Cooke said, "for volunteers." He smiled, handed the reins to Private Cole, and stepped on the veranda. He stopped, held the posture of a West Point cadet, and looked at Moses. "I will say, Private, it's good to see a dragoon." Cooke stepped to the door of the hotel, knocked, and went in.

When the door closed, Moses said to Cooke's mount, "Tall one, ain't he?" Moses examined the animal, gaunt, weary, head hung low. "Takes a tall one to pack a tall one, don't it, soldier?"

He wanted to stroke the forehead, work his fingers under the headstall, rub the white mule's eyes, scratch behind his ears and under his jaw line, but he pulled his hand back. To pet the lieutenant colonel's mount would be a breach of etiquette, and he dared not breach etiquette with Lieutenant Colonel Cooke.

"Long ole trek across the desert, you old dragoon," he said. "Ain't eat much since Santa Fe, have you?"

The mule lowered his head more. Moses leaned close. "After

a month of California, you'll be fat as a brood mare." He led him to a hitching rail at the side of the building, set his hand on the mule's neck, and said, "I'll be a worm-eat biscuit if they didn't make it."

He tied the reins to the rail he called the sailor's hitch—an oar with the blade sawn off, lashed with line from a ship's rigging, posts scavenged from a snapped mast—and wondered if the Horse Tooth Kid fancied soldier life, if Bear Grease reeked or remained clean.

He marched back to the door and stood at attention, stiff as Lieutenant Colonel Cooke, carbine at order arms.

CHAPTER 31

Some of the leading men of the place told us that when they heard that a set of Mormon soldiers were coming to San Diego they had a great notion to pack up and leave the place, for they had been told that the Mormons would steal everything they could lay their hands on. Not only that, but their women would be in danger of being insulted by them.

—*Private Henry Bigler,*
B Company, Mormon Battalion

Mormon Battalion, Mission of San Diego de Alcalá, California, January 30, 1847

"Look at that crawlin' thing. Big enough to eat a chicken."

The shield-backed katydid popped when Gabriel stepped on it. He lifted his foot and pointed at the stain on the brick floor. "Phineas! You spit or blow snot here?"

Phineas looked up from sweeping.

"I thought you was housebroke," Gabriel said. "Should've knowed better."

Four miles east of San Diego, the Mission of San Diego de Alcalá sat on a gentle elevation of tableland near a river that reached to San Diego Bay. Built by the Catholic Church a year before the Revolutionary War and now a Californio rancho, the mission stood like an unloved orphan, abandoned but for a handful of Indians. Rats and insects lived there. Debris gathered there, as if summoned by a mysterious force of its own. The

265

church and mission barracks framed a plaza, a square of weeds not graced with paving stones.

"What lies you tell, Gabriel Hanks."

Fatigue details of Mormon soldiers cleaned the compound of rubbish and piled it beyond an outside wall. Other details swept out rooms in the mission barracks. With no windows, the whitewashed walls kept light alive that reached through doorways.

"Pullin' your leg, Phineas. First one and then the other one to lengthen 'em a little. Easier to step on a horse that way, with that leg length."

Each room had two doorways—one that opened to the plaza, and one that opened to the veranda in front. Few of the doorways had doors. Dust bloomed with each broom stroke, showing years of neglect. The sweepers tied their shirts like bandanas to cut down the dust they breathed. Their woolen underwear, once white but now stained, ragged, and closer to brown, collected stirred-up dust. Phineas and Gabriel worked a small room.

"Horses I hate."

"That's a problem needs tendin' to," Gabriel said. He stooped to step through a short doorway onto the veranda, leaned against the door jamb, and pulled his shirt from his face to breathe cleaner air. Phineas kept sweeping.

A company of dragoons rode through the space between the vineyards.

"Company's comin'. Dragoons on mules," Gabriel said. "Knew they was in the country, haven't seen hoof one. Where they been hidin'?" He rested his hands on the broom handle. "Chasin' Mexicans, my guess says."

He watched them ride four abreast.

"A man's gotta have a purpose in life. Mine's to get horse

flesh between my knees. Not mule, mind you. Bona fide horse hide."

A soft metallic sound carried from the column where saber sheaths, capped in copper, bumped stirrups.

"For the savior a donkey was plenty, but a horse you fancy."

"The savior was a sandal man. Didn't ride but a mile."

Phineas stopped sweeping. "The Lord, he was. Man, he was not."

A guidon at the front of the formation marked them as U.S. Dragoons.

"Had him a horse, how many more folks could he have brung in the fold?"

Phineas resumed sweeping. "A farm and a family and the love of the Lord. For what I want that's the all of it."

Mormon soldiers stepped from rooms to the veranda to watch the dragoons ride by.

"Phineas Lynch, with bona fide horse hide between your feet, instead of ground beneath 'em ever since Ioway, you'd be back to wherever it is the women went. You'd have a boy by now. Go out in the evenin' time with a spotted dog by your side. Count your corn rows."

The dragoons skirted the mission to ride through the archway at the plaza's entrance. Gabriel moved from the veranda to the plaza-side door to watch them. "Give it a look-see, Phineas. No parade no more, not to them boys. Chewed on and spit out, that marchin' and starvin'."

Phineas stood his broom on end to tighten the twine that held wheat straw to the live oak handle. "Six months—no, seven—we have now been gone." Phineas tugged and tied the twine. "Children I would not have."

A bugle blew. The dragoons formed four rows, facing the front of the plaza.

"My point is, you could be there, instead of here. Man to a

wife instead of housemaid to the army. Comes down to transportation."

Phineas turned the broom over and resumed sweeping.

The bugle blew again, and the dragoons dismounted. There were fewer than sixty.

Gabriel watched the dragoons unsaddle their mounts. "Same as us, not good enough to camp amongst the town folk."

"A roof and walls we have here. For that I am thankful."

Gabriel watched the dragoons brush their mules. "Show up when the housework's done. I like their style."

The dragoons placed their tack against a plaza wall. Gabriel smiled. "Look what a mule brung in." He waved to Moses Cole.

After Moses unsaddled and brushed his mule, and the mules were herded out to graze in the mission fields, Moses walked to Gabriel, stopped a few paces short of the door, put his hands on his hips, and studied the boy. Gabriel smiled.

"By God you ain't," Moses said.

" 'By God you ain't,' what?"

"Growed to them teeth. Thought you might've by now."

"Would've, but the army yanked my feed bag." Gabriel stretched his woolen underwear tight across his torso. "Skinny as a whisker in Phineas's beard."

"Rawhide and rib bone. A woman would take you for a washboard," Moses said.

"You put heft on since we last seen you," Gabriel said. "Manned up a little, looks like."

"Weren't the groceries," Moses said.

Gabriel turned his head slightly to the left and looked at Moses's upper lip, then turned his head slightly to the right to study it more. "What'd your lip do, split a little when a mule kicked your tooth out?"

"Yep," Moses said. He stuck his tongue through the gap where the incisor had been. "Feels good to rub in there."

"Mean with a hind hoof, a mule is," Phineas said.

"Bear Grease make it? That Orson Everett?"

Gabriel leaned out from the door and yelled where dust bloomed from doorways. "Brother Orson! It's Moses the Bible writer's namesake, askin' after you!"

Heads popped out from doorways for the reach of the barracks wall, Orson Everett among them. Orson leaned his broom against the wall and walked toward them.

Gabriel said, "Phineas, where are your manners?" He pulled the shirt down that Phineas had tied as a bandana. "This here is Phineas Lynch, the beard boy." After a moment, Gabriel pulled the shirt over Phineas's face. "There. A face rag befits you."

"The recruitment dragoon," Phineas said to Moses. The shirt over his face muffled his words. "Gabriel Hanks you must take."

"Phineas twists his words a little. Can't line 'em up right. Makes you think your ears traded places."

"Could use a stable boy, if we had a stable," Moses said.

Orson walked up. His eyebrows, heavy with dust, resembled *cigarillo* butts. "I'm pleased to see you, Moses." He took Moses's hand and shook it. "I've often thought of you."

"It's you without the bear grease," Moses said.

Orson chuckled.

"You give it up good, looks to me. Same as you were eight days from Santa Fe. Leaner and weather worked, but no stink on you."

"The faith of the Lord done it," Gabriel said. "Cleaned his life up, outside and inside both. Go on, ask him." Gabriel feigned pulling on a watch fob to remove a watch from a waistcoat pocket and looked at the watch the pantomime suggested. "Hope you got time to kill." He feigned placing the watch in its pocket, leaned against the door jamb, and placed his hands on top of the broom handle.

Orson said, "The trials of life, Gabriel. The hand of the

church and the grace of the Lord. May they do as well for you."

"Takes a tough man to walk across the desert," Moses said.

"Takes a thick head and hard feet," Gabriel said. "Us Saints fit the bill."

"That's, 'We Saints,' " Orson said.

"We Saints was right for the job."

Orson shook his head. "Brigham Young prophesied that all of us would make it if we adhered to the faith and mended our ways when we wandered. It required vigilance."

"Brother Orson seen us through it," Gabriel said. "Some of the brethren kept him busy a little, with the playing cards and the swearing words."

"It was the providence of God, and the leadership of Lieutenant Colonel Cooke, that got us here," Orson said.

"The providence of God's a bit stingy, from the rags you're wearin'." Moses gestured toward Gabriel. "Thinner than an army mule. Should have listened to his mother."

"She knew more than she let on," Gabriel said.

Captain Jefferson Hunt walked up and said to Orson, his words tight as though pried out, "We've been ordered to clean these rooms, then vacate this section so this man," he motioned to Moses but did not look at him, "and the rest of the dragoons can move in." A vein rose on Captain Hunt's temple. "We Latter-day Saints will be quartered at the far end and in the wing across the plaza and wherever else we can fit."

He walked on, issuing the order as he went.

"All this work for someone else." Orson shook his head. "Like Missouri or Illinois. Build a place, and the gentiles take it."

"Their order, not mine," Moses said. "I'm a soldier like you, do what I'm told."

"Not soldiers," Gabriel said. "Housemaid to the army if you're a Latter-day Saint."

"Should've listened to mama," Moses said.

Gabriel smiled. Lines of dust marked his teeth. "And not see what we seen? Not see what we'll see yet?" Gabriel looked at the dragoons that moved about the courtyard. "Where's the fella you travel with?"

"I'm wondering the same," Orson said. "Abner Black."

Moses looked through the plaza door, through the room and the veranda and the withered vineyards to the brown hills. When he'd seen the lance through Abner's belly, he'd felt his gut split like Abner's had. *Days since, he'd done his suture work, was how he thought of it. Stitchin' his ripped innards. No preacher words to heal with. No Isabella to soften his loss. Just him, the crude hand of a farm boy with harness thread, was how he would say it, sewing his heart shut, and now he felt the stitches rip.*

Gabriel said, "Eyeglasses. Fancy talk."

Moses worked his tongue through the space the incisor had occupied, felt the heat rise to his eyes. "Dead," he said. *Dug up,* he thought, and walked away before the breakdown came.

. . . in fact he [Cooke] is a miserable creature and often curses and dams the soldiers He is as mean as I ever saw a man . . . he is a small low lived cuss . . . The Devil I believe would hate his oppression towards any body and would let him have no power in his kingdom and would let him no authority over any body . . .

—Private Levi Hancock,
E Company, Mormon Battalion

Had it not been for the cool headedness and sagacity of our stern commander . . . we must have all perished . . . Colonel Cooke was one of the ablest officers then in the Army to undertake such an enterprise with such scanty supplies at his command . . . he appreciated our services to the cause that he was engaged in and which he expressed to the battalion.

—Private John Riser,
C Company, Mormon Battalion

Mormon Battalion, San Diego, California, March/April 1847
Lieutenant Colonel Cooke's annoyance grew. The Mormon soldier showed himself capable of only turning right, regardless of the command.

The battalion drilled on the outskirts of San Diego, beyond the plaza and the hotel boarding house. With minimal instruction on the march and none before it, Cooke drilled the battalion in the fundamentals of soldiering.

In the mornings, Cooke schooled the officers in the manual of arms. In the afternoons, he supervised the sergeants as they drilled the battalion. Days passed in this routine with progress slower than Cooke demanded.

Cooke paced on the edge of the drill field, saw the troop movements disconnect from commands shouted by the sergeants. He'd instructed enough to know he was a better teacher than the confusion on the drill field suggested. When the sergeants barked each gave a different order, or stated the same in divergent words. It was as if Chinese talked to Swedes and Swedes to Greeks, no language common among them.

A soldier turned right regardless of the command, oblivious to what the other soldiers did, as if controlled by an involuntary twitch, like an eyelid gone awry.

Cooke raised a hand and yelled, "Stop! Everyone, stop!" *Not halt,* he thought. *Stop. They ought to understand, "Stop."*

The battalion stood face ahead, looked about, shuffled feet, adjusted muskets, wiped noses, or fixed hats. Phineas Lynch turned right.

"Still!" Cooke yelled. "Everyone! Stand, still!"

The battalion stood at attention.

Cooke walked to Phineas and put his hands on his shoulders and turned him to face ahead to match the stance of the battalion.

"Soldier," he said. "Stand still, face ahead, like everyone else. Do you understand?"

"Yes, sir," Phineas said.

"When I lift my hands from your shoulders, see if you can stand still."

"Yes, sir."

"Are you ready?"

"Yes, sir."

Cooke lifted his hands, stepped back, and Phineas turned right.

"Damned if he can," Cooke said. He walked away, dismissed the battalion, and summoned four of the sergeants.

"Either you don't care, or you are stupid, or defiant, or incapable of learning, or unwilling to do so." He studied the four. "Or, you don't listen to me, none of which is acceptable."

He let the air lay between them.

"March nineteen hundred miles and can't tell right from left or forward from back. You are indeed a peculiar, stiff-necked people." Cooke stood straight as a flagpole, a head taller than the tallest sergeant. "You are relieved of your duty as non-commissioned officers. You will drill in the ranks as privates. Dismissed."

"But, sir," Amos Binley said.

"Dismissed."

The four saluted and walked away.

The battalion dispersed from the drill field. Most went into the village, where they worked for hire in their free time. They built a brick kiln, fired bricks, and built a courthouse and a school. They plastered houses and dug wells, ran a tannery and a blacksmith shop.

The sergeants stopped Orson Everett as he walked from the drill field. The battalion rank and file wanted Orson for an officer, but he refused the request to become one. If he were an officer, his official duties would interfere with his duties to the church. He would minister to the men less. He was clear in his purpose. He did not want conflicting allegiances. Orson carried authority not sanctioned by the army. He was the one with whom they wanted to speak.

"Brother Orson," Amos said. "We don't know the drills, or

the drill commands." He moved his toes in the dirt. "The lieutenant colonel reduced us to the ranks."

"Buzzard Beak canned us," Ruben Cox said. His neck, short and muscled, resembled that of a bull. "Busted to privates." He slapped his hands as if to smash a mosquito. "Just like that."

Ruben walked with a slight limp since the bull gored him on the Rio San Pedro at the Battle of the Bulls. Since then, and with his short neck, the brethren called him Bullneck Ruben.

"Hawk Nose plucked your feathers, did he?" Orson said. He smiled. "Care about the Lord's work, gentlemen, not about the army of the United States government."

Orson set his musket down, butt on the ground, hands at the end of the barrel. "Remember why we're here. We've shown we're not disloyal to the United States. We've earned wages to support the church. We've come to California at government expense. We'll be mustered out in a couple of months, with pay and with our muskets. We will return to Zion to do the work of the Lord."

He studied the four before him.

"That's what bears importance, not the disapproval of an officer in the United States Army."

"Still, we was throwed off a job," Bullneck Ruben said. "That don't suit us too good."

"Of course it doesn't. You have a good work ethic," Orson said. He placed a hand on Bullneck's shoulder. "You served the church well. The leadership you men showed helped get us here. You've done your job. Drilling for the sake of becoming better soldiers might serve us well at some point, but not here, for Uncle Sam, preparing for a war that is none of our concern."

"We'll make less money. Half as much, about," Amos said.

"Someone will make it, and it goes to the church anyway. The whole is not diminished."

"Maybe we liked being sergeants too well," Amos said.

"Not me," Ruben said. "Gets tiresome, doin' the thinkin' for other folks, then bossin' 'em to it."

"Put it behind you," Orson said. "Come help at the school."

Ruben and Amos helped Gabriel, Phineas, and Orson lay bricks for a schoolhouse. A tramp walked by, stopped, and watched them. For a reason Orson couldn't name, he felt troubled by the man.

"Never mind him," Ruben said. He stirred mortar in an oakboard cart. "He's a beggar and a tramp and a scallywag thief. Deserted Frémont's army." He mixed the mortar with a shovel.

"Frémont?" Phineas said.

"Lieutenant Colonel John C. Frémont," Ruben said. "Come to California in '45 with a buncha mapmakers. Throw in hunters and scouts and had him sixty men. By and by the Mexican War come. Gathered up mountain men and settlers and such. Called it the California Volunteer Battalion. Whupped some Mexicans north of Monterey. Declared the Bear Flag Republic. Put a bear on their flag. Looks like a pig, huntin' a baby to eat."

"You haven't seen their flag," Amos said.

"Heard it told." Ruben stirred the mortar. "By and by, here come Commodore Stockton. Anchors at Monterey. Unloads marines and sailors. Tacked on colonel to lieutenant so he had him a lieutenant colonel in John C. Frémont, and him and Frémont put the run on the Mexicans."

"How do you know them things?" Gabriel said.

"He doesn't know them," Amos said. "He invents them."

"Once upon a time I was a sergeant," Ruben said, "and when you're a sergeant you hear officer talk, and that's the talk they talked, them officers."

The beggar stood beyond earshot and watched them.

"Then Commodore Stockton declared Frémont Governor of California, but Stockton, he don't have the authority to do it."

Gabriel set a brick in place and trimmed the mortar in the joints. Phineas stood still, listened to Ruben.

"Keep workin', Phineas," Gabriel said. "We don't get paid for bricks we don't lay."

"By and by Kearny come, month and some ahead of us. Sent to govern California by the president himself." Ruben added water from a well the Saints had dug a month ago and stirred the mortar mix in the oak-board cart. "You see the problem. Kearny an honest to God general with president orders. Frémont a lieutenant colonel and made-up governor."

Gabriel scooped mortar from the cart and plopped it on Phineas's mortar board.

"Pissin' match a-comin'. Frémont thinks he's boss in charge, but he ain't," Bullneck Ruben said. He looked at Amos. "Officers told it. You heard same as me."

Ruben indicated the beggar with a tip of the shovel handle. "That one come with Frémont. Run off when his mind got to him. Hid in the mountains till his body give out. Look at him. Walks bent, like he come out the back end of a horse wreck." Ruben stirred and talked. "Begged eggs off a village lady. Stole a knife off her table when she fetched them eggs."

"More gossip than a spinster's sewing circle," Amos said.

Phineas spread mortar on top of a brick, laid a brick in place, and leveled it with taps from the trowel handle.

"She got on to it but softened in the heart. Took the knife back but let him keep them eggs."

Phineas trimmed mortar from between the courses.

"I'd have kept them eggs and give him the blade, used his ribcage for a knife sheath," Bullneck Ruben said.

The beggar watched the Mormons lay bricks. Orson wondered if he knew the man but could not place him. Orson carried bricks from a wagon and stacked them in piles for the length of the wall. The tramp watched from twenty paces. When

Orson finished, he walked up to him. Deep lines in the beggar's weathered complexion resembled split wood. Dark circles under his eyes spoke of days without sleep. His hands were imbedded with dirt.

"What troubles you?" Orson asked.

The beggar's eyes teared over. "I beg forgiveness of you Latter-day Saints."

"For what?"

Ruben and Amos mixed mortar while Phineas and Gabriel laid bricks, each with an eye toward Orson and the intruder.

"Haun's Mill." The man paused to recover his voice. "We fired on those people in the fields. Two hundred-some of us opened up." His lip trembled. "We would not let them surrender." The man's voice broke. He paused before he could continue. "A bunch of them ran to the blacksmith shop." He choked back another sob. "We shot them between the logs, then walked right up and stuck our muskets through the gaps in the walls, and shot the pile of bodies. Shot them until they quit their moaning and moving."

The man cried outright.

Orson felt the ice inside turn to fire.

The tramp said, "I found a boy hid under the bellows. I still see the flats of his hands, palm side toward me. I hear the boy's voice beg for his life." Between sobs the man said, "I shot him anyway."

Orson buckled to his knees, fell to his hands with his face in the dirt when the images flashed—sunlight beaming through holes shot through the forge cowl, the splintered bellows, a spent ball mashed against the anvil, musket balls bored in the log walls, the ball-pocked millstone, a piece of skull and scalp with neighbor John's fire-red hair.

"One of us hacked up an old man with a corn knife, after he surrendered his musket." The man sobbed again.

Orson had arrived a day later to find his wife bereft of reason, hair as wild as her eyes, gesturing to the blacksmith shop on Shoal Creek. Orson went to the shop, then to the well where the bodies were buried, dragged by the women to dump more than inter them, eyes to the tree line for the Missourians to reappear. He pictured the bodies there—none laid straight, face up, arms folded in repose, but contorted, piled in haste so the living could flee to warn the living. As though Sheol of the Hebrew people yawned and swallowed them near the bank of Shoal Creek. The shaft of a grave, marked by a circle of dirt in a grass field, would bloom with weeds in the spring. A shiver gripped him.

The man continued to cry. "I can't shake that sight."

The others ran up. Ruben grabbed the man and yelled, "What'd you do?" He twisted the beggar's shirt in one hand and held a brick in the other. "I ought to bust your head open!"

Amos asked Orson if the tramp had hit him. Phineas and Gabriel helped Orson stand. Ruben said, "Bust your skull right here!"

"I followed orders, orders that were wrong." The man took a deep breath. His voice evened. "I left Missouri and wandered west. I joined Frémont's topographical corps as a hunter and came out here, but the longer I soldiered the more the memory haunted me. I deserted Frémont and ran from anything military and lived like a hermit for a year, moving from mountain to mountain and valley to valley. I lived with Indians and bummed from Mexicans, but wherever I go that boy goes with me." The man tapped his head. "I cannot get him out of here." A crack in a lip bled. "I've lived with it for nine years. I can't take it anymore."

"What was it you done?" Ruben said.

"Haun's Mill," Orson said. "Give me the brick."

Ruben handed him the brick.

"Release him and step back."

Ruben released him and stepped back. The beggar removed his hat and bowed his head.

"That was my son you murdered. He was ten years old."

The man went to his knees, hugged Orson's lower legs. Orson shoved him away, stepped back, and said, "I'll kill you right here, you son of a bitch."

The man looked up, eyes teared and bloodshot, kneeling in front of Orson. He said, "Forgive me first, I beg of you."

Orson pressed the brick's edges in his fingers, thought if he gripped it harder the brick would break. His son's killer, bowed before him, asking salvation. His own soul, crushed to dust from the loss this man wrought. Lice crawled on the balding head before him. In the tattered coat, layered grime, unkempt beard, and greasy hair, Orson saw the beast that whisky unleashed, knew it lived in him still. His fettered demon that strained against its chains. A blow from the brick would slay them both. He said, " 'To deliver such a one unto Satan for the destruction of the flesh, that the spirit may be saved in the day of the Lord Jesus.' I've lived with that verse for as long as you've lived with your sin, hoping, if not praying, for this day."

The man knelt before him, head bowed. Sobs shook his shoulders.

Orson weighed the brick in his hand. "To save the spirit of the sinner, shed the blood."

The man said between sobs, "I've wanted this day as much as you have."

Orson felt the brick, as sure as the pull of a drink in his hand, wondered if it were Satan's temptation or a tool of the Lord.

The man said, "Would've done it but my nerve failed."

Orson felt the sun's touch in the hard clay, smelled the stench of the unwashed, remembered the sobriquet Moses Cole had given him, Bear Grease.

The beggar said, "Get on with it. I can't take it anymore."

Orson bobbed the brick. "I won't spare you your anguish." He dropped the brick. "Reap what you've sown."

The man looked up, eyes wide, seized in fear. "Please! Forgive me! Kill me!" He started to tremble.

" 'Vengeance is mine; I will repay, saith the Lord.' Leave us."

"I beg of you! End this!" The man wept.

Orson walked back to the wall they built, his back to the tramp. He looked to the peaceful sea, thought of waves breaking as hate breaks on the door of the Lord, no admittance for the bearer of ill will. He wondered if ever he could walk through that door, thought maybe he savored his hatred.

His son would be Gabriel's age.

The man cried behind him.

"Should've thumped him," Ruben said.

The man limped off, stooped as if he were pushing a cart loaded with mortar.

CHAPTER 33

This is a hard way to serve the Lord.

—*Mary Brown, laundress,*
C Company, Mormon Battalion

Abigail Alcott, Mormon Battalion laundress, San Diego, California,
April 1847

The contraction sucked her breath in. She clutched the smock
that served for a pregnancy dress and thought, *finally it comes to*
pass. She had conceived, she was certain of it, the night before
they left Council Bluffs—their last claim to privacy—the sickness that started with the march, nine months to the day. From
the bank of the Missouri River to the Pacific shore a life grew,
then pulsed within her, a tiny bit brighter with every mile
covered, a spark of God glowing among them.

A contraction bit hard and held her belly.

"Juanita!" Abigail called with more edge than she intended.
She told herself to regain her composure, that women had done
this since God made Eve.

What a journey this has been, Abigail thought. *So much weather,*
so many days, so many miles to journey here, a poor man's village
half a continent apart from her family when she needed them most.
At least she had Melissa, and Juanita, the Mexican midwife
with a heart of heaven who had opened her home for the birth
of the baby. Abigail marveled at the providence of the Lord in
her hour of need.

All the cravings of the palate she'd had along the journey she had still, yet was unable to satiate. During the march, she ate what the soldiers ate, too many days of little else but too little meat, too often not enough water. She craved maple syrup, Brussels sprouts, chocolate and beets, liver and vinegar, apricots and cod. It surprised her how little her diet had improved since arriving here, this land that promised more than it gave.

A contraction squeezed. Abigail panted and pushed her mind back to the desert trek.

She walked or rode in the wagon, often with Melissa Brown, and they'd visit and sing as they went. She cooked what little they had to cook and gained no weight while the baby grew. When the team wore down, her husband, her Captain Alcott, no longer permitted Melissa to ride with her, and Abigail rode alone with the tiny life inside her. She walked when she could but rode in the wagon more as she grew with child. She thought of her unborn babe as her desert oasis with its promise of life. She wondered now if the green that shimmered beyond reach to pull her across the desert would prove a mirage.

For a time, Melissa walked beside the wagon seat, but her companionship ebbed with her strength and her own pregnancy that grew. When Melissa had no food or tea to bring she visited less frequently. The singing ended. Days became tests of endurance, pressing forward as their strength dwindled. Still Melissa checked on her as she would the soldiers, chiding them in that pleasant manner of hers when they'd eat several days' rations in one sitting. Improvident men, Melissa told them. No more sense than boys. The ordeal lessened after Warner's Ranch, and then they sang again. Abigail thought she could never express to dear Melissa how her slender shoulders had lifted her over the waterless reaches.

Juanita hurried into the room.

"Dear child, may this be the happy day."

"I am frightened," Abigail said.

"Do not be." Juanita smiled that big, infectious smile of hers. "Women are made for this."

"Please," Abigail said. A contraction stole her breath. Juanita steadied her as she panted, and when her breathing slowed Abigail whispered, "Please, get Melissa."

"Yes. You sit." Juanita helped her settle in the chair, then hurried from the room.

Abigail sat, then stood to relieve pain in the small of her back. She paced and grabbed the chair when a contraction gripped. She prayed. "Heavenly Father, be with me, please, Lord, in my time of need. I ask You to see this baby here. I ask You to see me through my deepest purpose as a woman. Lord, I beseech You, help us both. Amen."

By the time they had reached Fort Leavenworth, she knew she was pregnant. Her husband considered resigning from the battalion for her sake, then reasoned it would be better if he didn't. If they returned to Council Bluffs, they would travel in the spring with a newborn infant. If they stayed with the battalion, they would reach the Pacific before the last two months of her pregnancy. Then, when the baby was old enough, they'd travel to wherever Brigham Young settled the brethren. It would be better for the baby that way, and for Abigail.

That was why he'd been chosen for captain, she reasoned, for his practical mind. He had assured her that Brother Brigham was right, that all would be well if they abided by the faith. They did so, and they reached the end of the march, the worse for wear she would admit, but on the brink of becoming a family. Abigail knew to expect this birthing pain, but she had never before borne a baby. She worried about the baby's health. The march had been too hard, too long, too many days of too little. Too many miles walked or jarred in the wagon to come here, where two babies had died since the battalion arrived. The

Indian baby bit by a rattlesnake, and the Warner baby buried at dusk three weeks past. Abigail wondered if an evil spirit, a killer of infants, stalked this place.

Her time had come. The Lord would strengthen her.

She groaned when a contraction hit and sank to the board floor, gripped a table leg, and squeezed.

She felt as if a cactus was tearing through her. She screamed and squeezed Melissa's hand. Juanita dampened her face with a washcloth. The surgeon from the general's dragoons wormed his hand inside of her. She imagined her baby, scant as a cactus, parts of her insides draped from its spines.

When the baby came, she expected the pain to abate, but she bled, turned feverish, and the pain worsened. The surgeon did what he could. Juanita prepared a poultice, covered her belly with it, nursed the baby with her own infant. Melissa dampened her forehead, teased out the threads of Abigail's delirious conversation, sang the familiar songs, and wept. Captain Alcott kept the waste bucket emptied, washed bloodied bandages, and rewashed them when they stained again. He swept the floor, carried water, washed pots in the kitchen, anything to keep occupied. He named the baby boy Diego, the first born of American parents in San Diego. Orson Everett anointed her with oil, laid his hands on with Captain Alcott, and blessed her.

Her lucid moments grew fewer. In one of those moments when clear thoughts surfaced she asked Orson Everett to pray for her, to ask the Lord to forgive her for the washtub episode.

"It was childish of me. It was a hard time."

Orson patted her forehead with a damp washcloth. "Your tub kept the battalion alive. You did God's work when you brought it from Nauvoo."

The sliding board window that opened to the sea allowed sun in the room. It was in the 80s, with no breeze in the home. Abigail shivered and sweated beneath the blankets.

"How could I have put my selfish interests above the welfare of everyone else?"

"We all wear our hair shirts," Orson said. "Now rest. Let the Lord heal you."

Two days later Phineas Lynch gave a washtub to Abigail that he'd crafted by shaving boards with his sheath knife and banding them with rawhide. It was heavier than the tin tub she had but equally as big, and it did not leak. He had carved her name in it. Abigail wept when he set it by her bed.

"How is she?" Gabriel asked when Phineas came out of Juanita's home. He stood with a group of Mormon soldiers, all of them looking at Phineas, not a word among them.

Phineas shook his head.

Two weeks passed, and then, there in front of her, just beyond arm's length, Abigail saw her favored aunt, dead three years now, beckoning.

CHAPTER 34

. . . Los Angeles, a town which could boast, perhaps, of more lewdness than any other upon the coast. Though stationed for such a length of time in that sink of iniquity, the character of the Battalion for sobriety and virtue was maintained. As a proof that the men did not partake of the immorality of the place, it may be remarked that a hospital surgeon was heard to say that among over seventy soldiers which he treated at Los Angeles for a loathsome disease, only one was a "Mormon."

—Sergeant Daniel Tyler,
Mormon Battalion

In the afternoon the seanry [sic] of drunkenness was lamentable. The screams & yells of drunken Mormons would of disgraced the wild Indian mutch [sic] moor [sic] a Laterday [sic] Saint.

—Lieutenant James Pace,
E Company, Mormon Battalion,
March 25, 1847

Pueblo de Los Angeles, California, May 10, 1847
"Here puppy, here puppy, puppy," Gabriel Hanks called.

"Try Spanish," Orson Everett said. "They won't know English."

They walked an unpaved street in the Pueblo de Los Angeles with their muskets loaded. Gabriel stopped and rolled up a pant leg. "Don't know Spanish, but this oughta work." He rolled up the other pant leg.

Orson lifted his eyebrows.

"Bait," Gabriel said. "If they're gonna bite, here's their chance."

"Miss your shot, and you'll end up like the Maryland baker, God rest his soul," Orson said.

Over the tops of the one-story adobe homes the countryside rolled with vineyards and orchards of fig and apple trees, vegetable gardens, and cattle grazing green fields.

"Travel clear across the continent, Maryland to California to set up a bake shop, and what'd he get? Bit by a rabid dog. Where's the Lord in that, Brother Orson?"

All lay as still as the short shadows of midday. Orson cradled his musket in the fork of his left arm, pushed his hat up with his right hand, and wiped sweat from his forehead. "He crossed the Lord somewhere," Orson said.

The space between adobes on the street they patrolled varied from right next door to within shouting distance of each other. Streets divided the Pueblo in squares, more like a city of gridded barnyards than building-filled blocks.

"Hear yet from the brethren in San Diego?" Gabriel asked. "Word or whisper, either one?"

"Not yet."

They walked by a whitewashed wall, shoulder high. A rainbow of azaleas, peonies, and roses bloomed in pots spaced along its top.

"They weren't supposed to divide us, but they up and done it again. Repeat of the sick people, if you know what I mean, them they packed off to Pueblo. Now it's K Company left in San Diego, the sick ones left in San Luis Rey, and us other ones marched up here. To them officer bosses, it don't matter a hen's peck what Brother Brigham and Colonel Allen said would be."

Orson said, "We've learned the army adjusts to circumstances.

If it weren't for the Frémont trouble, we might have remained in San Diego."

A handful of sheep clustered under a lean-to's thatched roof at the back of an adobe home, heads hung as if they hid from heat. Strips of meat hung from the rafters above them.

"What are we supposed to do? Frémont and his men to one side of town, Cooke and us to the other. Both scared to kick the dog, if you know what I mean. Can't settle who's the farmer and who's the hog."

On its east side, the Pueblo de Los Angeles lay tight to the hills where the hills met the valley. On its other sides, it abutted fields and orchards and hedgerows and pastures, and beyond those, west of the Rio de Porciuncula, an uncut forest stood. Beyond that, further yet to the west, the ocean lay still and endless.

"Like they was eyeballin' each other to fight over a sweetheart."

"What would you know about that?"

"Nothin'. Heard it told is all."

Orson estimated the Pueblo at twenty-five blocks, some with a few adobes and some with a dozen or more, all with flat or low-sloped tarred roofs. This did not count the city center with its larger, odd-shaped blocks and plaza, Catholic Church, and city structures.

"Buildings and people. What do you figure, Brother Orson?"

Orson figured several hundred houses and a thousand people, maybe more.

"Spaniards and Mexicans and Indians and such, and foreigners throwed in to stir the stew a little," Gabriel said. He whistled a few bars from "Come, Come Ye Saints." "San Diego we could handle, but this here."

"I didn't know you could whistle."

"Couldn't in the desert. Too parched."

"You might whistle to call a dog in."

They crossed an irrigation ditch that ran a full head of water. Up ahead, a donkey, tended by a herder on foot, pulled a cart across the packed-sand street.

"Good time of day to hunt them dogs. Might catch 'em nappin'," Gabriel said.

"The word is *siesta*, and, if you see a dog, use judgment. We are ordered to shoot the strays, not someone's pet sleeping on a front step."

"Powder in the pan and a ball in the barrel. I'm the reaper hisself, stalkin' on them bitin' dogs." Gabriel hunched over to mimic stalking a deer. He hugged close to an adobe at the corner of First and Spring Streets and stuck his bare calf out from the corner of the structure, shook it, and whistled. A dog snarled.

Gabriel jumped back. "A damn dog's there!"

Orson wagged a finger at Gabriel.

Gabriel stepped around the corner of the adobe. A dog stood in the center of Spring Street at fifteen paces, teeth bared and snarling. Two other dogs stood with him, ears perked. Gabriel cocked his musket, shouldered it, pointed it at the dog's teeth, and pulled the trigger. Fire and smoke rose from the flash pan, and the musket boomed. Through the smoke at the muzzle Gabriel saw a water bucket at the side of an adobe on the other side of Spring Street splinter, and he saw the three dogs run into the home. A man stepped from the adobe, looked at the damp sand where his bucket had been, picked up the splinters, and yelled at Gabriel in Spanish.

"Must not have been a stray," Gabriel said. He turned and walked down First Street, where Mexicans stepped out to see what the fuss was.

"Don't swear, Gabriel."

They smiled as they walked by the Mexicans, and Gabriel

said to them, "Spiced up your day a little." The sun caught his teeth. Some watched with sullen eyes. Others smiled and jabbered in Spanish.

"Scared me and the swear words jumped out. That don't happen much." Gabriel smiled and nodded to the handful of people they passed.

Orson said, "That's what concerns me about you joining General Kearny's escort."

Two blocks away Orson motioned to a wicker bench woven from paloverde that sat on a veranda of an adobe home. "Surely the resident won't mind if we beg a seat for a bit." He patted his musket and smiled, then leaned his firearm against the wall of the adobe and sat down. A hind quarter of a goat, skinned with chunks carved off, hung under the veranda with a boning knife stuck in it.

"Three dogs," Gabriel said. "I'd have cut his feed bill by a third. He shoulda thanked me for tryin' and cussed me for missin'."

Gabriel stood his musket on its butt, pulled a paper cartridge from the cartridge box on his belt, bit the ball off, and poured the powder down the barrel. "That there was a dog man," he said. "Prob'ly his supper I shot at." He took the ball from his mouth with thumb and forefinger and placed it on the bore of the musket.

"Gabriel, have you ridden before?"

"Rode the milk cow once, but she wouldn't go nowhere." Gabriel pulled the ramrod from its keeper and rammed the charge into the base of the barrel. "Rode the neighbor's plow horse when I was ten, but he quit me halfway from the house to the barn." He returned the ramrod to its keeper in the stock at the bottom of the barrel.

"That's it?"

Gabriel looked at Orson with wide eyes. "Ain't that enough?"

He leveled the musket and pulled the hammer to half-cock, flipped the frizzen forward, poured powder in the flash pan from his powder flask, and snapped the frizzen over the pan to close the primer in place. He leaned his musket against the wall of the adobe and sat down, then broke into a laugh and slapped his knee.

"Leadin' you on a little, Brother Orson. Actually, I'd ride the nigh mule to and from the field, and I'd ride the off mule when we cut wood and hauled wool. Don't know why I done it that way. Just did."

"So you have ridden."

"Some, but not far and fancy, and never on a bona fide ridin' horse."

A Mexican woman stepped from the home, looked at them and their muskets, and went back inside.

"*Buenos dias, señora,*" Gabriel said, and tipped his hat to the empty doorway.

"Ever sat a saddle before?"

"Never knew anyone who owned one."

"And now you'll mount an animal you've never ridden, on a saddle you've never sat, and ride from here to Fort Leavenworth. Are you sure you want to do that?"

Gabriel smiled. "Never walked that far neither, same as you. Now look where we're sittin'."

The woman returned with an earthenware pitcher and cups. She jabbered in Spanish, poured each a cup of water, and set the pitcher on a turned-over vase at the end of the bench.

"*Muchas gracias, señora,*" Orson said and tipped his hat.

She smiled, went back in the adobe, and pulled the door closed. They heard the latch fall.

"Let me put it this way," Gabriel said. "The Lord lit the general's lantern a little, made him to see he wanted Saints in his escort." His smile widened. "What's there to think about?"

"You'll be with gentiles, Gabriel. Fifteen Saints in an escort of seventy men, or something close to that number. You fifteen will need to abide by each other to keep your faith."

"Raised a Saint and schooled by you. Don't know any other way."

"You learned to swear somewhere."

Across the hard-sand street a woman tossed a rug over a clothesline and beat it with a broom.

"Better off there than here, Brother Orson, with the bad-man liquor and the she-devil females that populate this pueblo. I know as well as you do some of the brethren up and tumbled in it."

They watched the woman across the way beat the rug.

"Won't find neither one of them on the trail, even if a man wanted to. We seen that on the march out here. So there's another reason to mount up and ride, lay down the miles between me and it, while the Lord give me the chance to."

The woman pulled the rug down and carried it back inside.

"That rug will be you if you stray from the Saints. Only the thumps you take will be much harder."

Methodical falls of an axe carried from the woodpile behind the adobe at their backs.

"The way I see it, the road forks three ways here." Gabriel gripped his left index finger with his right hand. "I can join the escort and ride back to where we come from, or close to it." He added the middle finger to his grip. "I can stay here until our enlistment is up in two months." He added his ring finger to the grip of his right hand. "Or I can re-enlist like some of them others."

"For heaven's sake, no! To re-enlist would not serve the church, and it would not serve our families."

Behind the adobe, metal struck metal.

"Must a' got her axe stuck," Gabriel said. Metal struck metal twice more. "Sledge on an axe head. Like splittin' stove wood back home." Gabriel turned his head to look down the street. When he spoke, his voice came softer. "We been gone a long time, Brother Orson. That's another reason to ride in the escort. I want to get home."

"We all do," Orson said. "Anymore, we do not know where home is, other than somewhere between here and the Missouri River."

Gabriel sipped from his cup. "All the more reason to start lookin'. That's where the escort comes in. Let the mule do the walkin'."

A Rosecomb hen chased a grasshopper in the street, caught it, tipped its head back, and swallowed.

"You've never sat in a saddle, and you're starting with two thousand miles."

"Then I oughta know how to set one when I get there. Plop your hind end in a saddle seat, set all the way to Fort Leavenworth, enjoy the scenery, and draw soldier's pay to do it. It don't get no better."

The chicken scratched in the street and darted where ants ran.

"Provided you keep the faith. Lose that and you lose your way, even if your personal yearnings are satisfied, and perhaps especially so."

"The sooner I leave and the faster I travel, the sooner I get to Latter-day Saint land, wherever that'll be. So I see it as a going to, more than a running from, if you see what I mean."

"If that is your goal and you keep your focus . . ." Orson's voice trailed off.

"I'll get there when your enlistment runs out here." Gabriel tapped his temple with an index finger. "Thunk it out a little in the head bone."

Orson nodded.

Behind the adobe, the axe split wood again. Orson stood and picked up his musket.

"Better set a little yet," Gabriel said. He remained seated. "A man'll need his rest." He looked over the adobes to the fields and the hills and pictured the eastward reach. "Got a lotta country comin' at us."

CHAPTER 35

This place, whether the "Paris of California" or not, is a hot bed of sedition, and originates all the rebellions or revolutions; and women, they say, play an influential part.

—Lieutenant Colonel Philip St. George Cooke,
Pueblo de Los Angeles,
March 27, 1847

Pueblo de Los Angeles, California, May 10, 1847—later in the day
"If it ain't Mormons with guns," a man called from the shade of the veranda. Beer spilled when he indicated Orson and Gabriel with a wave of his mug. "Shit," he said and licked beer from the back of his hand. A patch covered one of his eyes.

Orson and Gabriel had crossed the pueblo square on a diagonal footpath. A dirt street, broad as a plaza building, encompassed the square. The footpath passed the plaza's Catholic church and ended at the street in front of a low adobe building that boasted a grog shop that hummed with customers with Frémont's California battalion camped nearby.

They stopped when a big man stepped out to stand in front of them. Stout as a beer barrel, his eyelids drooped over bloodshot eyes. He studied them.

A girl led a milch cow across the plaza. The bell on the cow's collar called.

"They's shit all right," the big man said.

A laugh sounded from the parlor porch. Four men sat in

296

chairs, two on each side of a door that opened to the grog shop.

The man with the eye patch left his chair to stand with the big man. He shut his good eye and lifted his patch to reveal an empty eye socket with sunken eyelids long since sutured closed. He replaced the patch and opened his good eye.

"Land-grabbin' Mormons. A blind man could see that."

The big man laughed.

"Far be it from us to trouble Frémont's soldiers," Orson said.

"Like hell," the man with the eye patch said. He pointed to a hill where the Mormons were constructing a fort that overlooked the Pueblo de Los Angeles. "You're buildin' that fort to watch us, afraid we'll burn you out like in Daviess County." He smiled and nodded his head. "Imagine that. To think we won't be neighborly." He made a *tsk*ing sound with his tongue and shook his head.

"Don't sleep too tight," a voice said from the veranda. "Patch Eye gave you the evil eye." The voice laughed.

Another called out, "Your so-called fort won't stop us."

"Fort," the big man said. "Shit."

A bell at the plaza Catholic church tolled four times to sound the change of the hour.

"I hate church bells," the big man said.

"Brings out the fight in him," Patch Eye said.

"We're on the same side here," Orson said. He looked at the two in front of them. "If you'll excuse us, we're due at garrison and will get out of your day." He moved, and the big man moved to block him.

"What'll you do?" Patch Eye said. "Ride our coattails? Steal California after we captured it? Grab it off us, like you done in Missouri?"

The patrons of the grog shop, soldiers mostly, with women dressed for the evening, collected on the veranda. Moses Cole stood among them.

"Country thievin' shit bags," the big man said. He blinked and spoke slowly.

"Till we run your pot-licker asses out," Patch Eye said. He tilted his mug and drank. The eye patch moved when he gulped his beer. He lowered his mug and adjusted the patch. "Oughta hang you, so you don't follow us no more. I'm tired of this Mormon shit."

"School them two," the big man said. He swayed slightly, raised his fists and moved them in slow, tight circles, one foot ahead of the other in a boxer's stance.

Moses stepped off the porch.

"Big Man's mean when he's drunk. Loves to hurt people." Patch Eye laughed and sipped his beer.

Moses walked up and stood in front of the big man. Smithwick and Donovan waited at the parlor steps.

"This don't concern you," Patch Eye said.

"These Mormons are all right," Moses said. "Odd religion, is all."

"Back in '31," Patch Eye said, "Ole Joe Smith come out to Missouri, had him a look, and claimed it was the Garden of Eden of the Bible, right there in Jackson County. Said Christ himself would show there for the second go-round. Put the call out to build their City of Zion and here they come. Ends up we give a whole county, Caldwell County made special for them." He lifted the eye patch and rubbed the empty eye socket. "They kept a comin', and they filled her up, and they wanted another one, and maybe one more just to be sure, and the pot she boiled over." He reset the eye patch. "The burnin' and the shootin' quit when they left Missouri for Illinois, to build their City of Nauvoo." His eye slid from Moses to Orson to Gabriel and back to Moses. "More proper, it quit in Missouri. Started again in Illinois when they learned what we learned." His beer mug moved when he laughed and settled when he stopped. "You watch. They'll steal the land you stand on."

"Beat the piss outta them two," Big Man said with slow words. He lowered his head and widened his stance. He looked at Moses over his fists. "You, too, shithead."

"You can try," Moses said. "I'm not bound up by God like they are."

The big man stepped forward and swung a fist, slowed by his time in the saloon. Moses ducked and kicked the man's shin hard enough to break a board in a barn wall. The big man cried out and grabbed his shin. Moses kicked him in the other shin, and the big man fell to his knees. Moses stepped behind him, jammed a knee in his back, and shoved him to the ground, face down. He grabbed the big man's hair and pulled his head back, put the point of his sheath knife under the big man's jaw, and spoke into his ear.

"Leave these men alone." He pushed the knife until blood trickled down the blade.

The big man squirmed, and Moses turned the knife. The blood ran faster.

"Do you understand me?" Moses said.

Patch Eye stepped toward Moses and raised his beer mug as he would a hammer but stopped, lowered his arm, and stepped back when Gabriel pointed his musket at him, cocked it, and said, "It's loaded, from huntin' them redeye slobber dogs that caught the rabies."

The big man's arms jumped to grab Moses, but, with his belly on the ground and a man on his back, his movement suggested fins on a fish. Moses turned the knife a tick. The blood trickled faster.

"You son of a bitch!" Big Man said.

A soldier of Frémont's California battalion picked up a chair on the veranda.

Smithwick held a hand up to indicate "stop," stepped toward

Moses, and said to the soldier, "I'll take care of it."

Donovan put a hand on the horse pistol in his belt and said, "That means he'll settle our man Moses down while you set still and be comfortable."

The man put the chair down.

"As a rule, I don't lug this thing"—Donovan tapped the pistol—"but rabid dogs are about."

Moses pulled the big man's head back until his chin jutted up with his mouth open. The knife tip stuck in a half inch towards his tongue.

Smithwick approached and placed a hand on Moses's wrist to stay the knife blade. "Easy, Moses," he said. "Push that knife anymore and you'll split his tongue."

"Do you understand me?" Moses said in the big man's ear, louder this time.

"Go to hell," the Big Man said.

Moses turned the knife anther tick.

"Fine, son of a bitch," Big Man said.

Moses pulled the knife and stood up. The big man rose to his hands and knees and watched his blood drip on the plaza's dirt street. He stood up, wiped under his chin, and looked at the blood smeared on his hand. His eyelids no longer drooped.

"Mind your own goddamn business," Patch Eye said to Moses. "And you two"—he pointed at Orson and Gabriel— "get the hell out. This land is too good for you."

"You're dead," Big Man said to Moses. "Watch your backside." He turned and walked away, pressing his hand against the underside of his chin.

"This place ain't fit for a Latter-day Saint," Gabriel said. He lowered his musket and eased the hammer to half cock. "Them Missouri liquor sippers are right at home, though."

Moses watched Patch Eye and Big Man walk into the grog shop.

Gabriel said to Orson, "What's it been?" He counted on his fingers. "Three months since we seen him?" He looked at Moses, turned back to Orson. "Unless I'm mistook, that's the dragoon Moses Cole under that moustache."

"No mistakin' it," Moses said. "That's the Mormon Gabriel behind them teeth, and the man who quit the Bear Grease, Orson Everett, under those eyebrows."

Orson said, "You are an angel of the Lord, Moses."

"No," Moses said. He picked a handful of dirt from the plaza street and rubbed his hands with it, brushed the bloodied dirt off, and wiped his hands on his pants. "Devil maybe."

"Our man Moses," Smithwick said, "he's as kind as you'd want a man to be, but put him in a fight"—he shook his head—"the lid blows off, and an animal pops out, and then it gets ugly, doesn't it, Moses?"

Orson said, "Angels bear many guises, Moses. You are a Danite at heart."

"There you go, talkin' Mormon on me," Moses said.

"Takes a while to get him bottled up again, but he settled down quick here," Donovan said. "Must be,"—he thought a moment—"maturity."

"To tell it straight, Orson, your religion is a strange one, but I'll say it again, you showed something when you crossed that desert."

Orson said, "The strength of the Lord carried us. Shall I preach to you the tenets of our faith so you may know the strength of the Lord as well?"

"Don't need it, don't want it. Not now, not never. It don't suit me."

"Be that as it may," Orson said. "You risked a lot to help us. Thank you."

Gabriel leaned forward to peer at the moustache. "Hides your scar though. Takes the mean off a little. Won't scare folks no more. Not as bad anyway."

Moses smiled.

"Until you do that. Shows a hole where a tooth used to be. One of them pointy ones." Gabriel studied the moustache. "Shave them lip whiskers, you won't need a knife and a square-toed shoe to handle a big man. Sideways glance oughta do it."

"I hope you didn't break a toe," Orson said.

"Felt like it for a minute there," Moses said.

"Don't need a toe. Got him a mule," Gabriel said.

A laugh came from inside the grog shop.

"Moses Cole, them two are gonna hunt you," Gabriel said.

When they parted at the edge of the plaza, the dragoons and the Mormons each to their own camps, Gabriel said, "If the Lord made a country that a man ought to have, this could be it." He waved to the hills and the orchards and fields of cultivated green. He breathed in to smell the bloom of spring. "But then he put Missourians in it, like he built a beautiful princess, then up and stuck warts on her nose."

A dog trotted by, swaybacked with swinging teats, patched with bare skin where mites worked, trailed by a litter of pups.

"How come we never get shut of Missourians, Brother Orson?"

They walked by adobe homes where women swept walkways, tended flower pots, and smiled.

Orson stopped, set his musket butt on the ground and rested his hands on the bore, one on top of the other, and looked over the sparsely-filled city blocks that abutted the central structures.

"Unlike San Diego, where there were no Missourians"—Orson looked down and paused—"save one"—he paused again and looked back up—"grog shops and brothels and gambling establishments form the social fiber of this city. 'For wheresoever

302

the carcass is, there will the eagles be gathered together,' saith the Lord."

"Vultures, I'd say. Them ugly ones with the red, old-man-bald heads. Bare skin on a bird, right there for the sun to shine on, like turkeys. Somethin' wrong with that."

Orson pursed his lips and exhaled. He gripped the barrel and twisted the butt on the ground as if grinding grist. He said, "To answer your question, I suppose the Lord has a lesson we haven't learned yet, so he keeps sending it."

"Don't make no sense, a lesson ricocheted off Missourians to hit us."

"A lot of things don't make sense. It's for the Lord to know and for us to seek." Orson cradled his musket in the crook of his arm. "My concern for you is that you won't know what to seek, and, if you do know, you won't know where to seek it."

"The what and where is simple enough, Brother Orson. *What* is a four-legged mule? Horse if I'm lucky. *Where*"—Gabriel smiled—"is the general's escort."

Orson shook his head and said, "I'll miss those teeth."

Gabriel looked back toward the plaza. "I got a worry on me though, Brother Orson. Them two liquor sinners. I'm afeard the end's not come yet."

CHAPTER 36

All hail the brave Battalion!
The noble, valiant band,
That went and served our country
With willing heart and hand.
Altho' we're called disloyal
By many a tongue and pen,
Our nation boasts no soldiers
So true as "Mormon" men.

—*Private Thomas Morris,*
B Company, Mormon Battalion

All persons at San Diego are anxious that the Mormons should
remain there, they have by a correct course of conduct become
very popular with the people . . . and if they are continued they
will be of more value in reconciling the people to the change of
government than a host of Bayonets; they have made Bricks,
dug and bricked up eight or ten wells and furnished a town
heretofore almost without water at certain seasons of the year
with an abundant supply. They are about to build a brick Court
house . . . in short when within 80 miles of the place the inhab-
itants of every ranch asked permission for some of the good
Mormons to come and work for them . . .

—*Colonel Jonathan D. Stevenson,*
1ˢᵗ New York Volunteer Infantry Regiment,
to Colonel Richard B. Mason, Commander,
10ᵗʰ Military Department, June 28, 1847

Mormon Battalion, Pueblo de Los Angeles, California, May 13, 1847

The battalion stood at attention, muskets at order arms at the soldier's right side. Lieutenant Colonel Cooke stood before them on a podium of boards tacked on ammunition crates. An officer unknown to them stood by the makeshift platform. Cooke surveyed the troops, their rank and file precise as squares on a chess board, the ragged hats, patched and tattered clothing, sun-worn faces, once-white baldrics faded gray, a common hue of weathered earth.

Cooke said, "At ease" in a voice that carried through the ranks with the clarity of a mission bell. The men relaxed but stayed in place.

Cooke motioned to the officer by the podium. "Colonel Stevenson recently arrived with his First New York Volunteer Infantry Regiment after a five-month sail from New York City. The First New York will reinforce the Army of the West." A breeze crossed the fields between the pueblo and the troops, carried the faint bang of hammer on anvil, a faded call of a cow for its calf, a touch of budding flowers. Some of the troops looked at Cooke, others at Colonel Stevenson.

"I depart tomorrow with General Kearny for Fort Leavenworth. Colonel Stevenson is your new commanding officer."

Cooke sensed more than heard it, as if three hundred men sucked in breath. All eyes locked on his.

"Before I leave you, I want to remind you of your accomplishment." He lifted a paper to within reading distance, steadied it with both hands, and read.

"History may be searched in vain for an equal march of infantry. Half of it has been through a wilderness where nothing but savages and wild beasts are found, or deserts where, for want of water, there is no living creature. There, with almost hopeless labor we have dug deep wells, which the future traveler will enjoy. Without a guide who had traversed them, we have ventured into trackless tablelands where water was not found for several marches."

Although at ease, the troops stood still as pillars.

"With crowbar and pick and axe in hand, we have worked our way over mountains, which seemed to defy aught save the wild goat, and hewed a passage through a chasm of living rock more narrow than our wagons. To bring these first wagons to the Pacific, we have preserved the strength of our mules by herding them over large tracts, which you have laboriously guarded without loss."

Cooke glanced up. Their attention remained with him. Some nodded.

"The garrison of four presidios of Sonora concentrated within the walls of Tucson gave us no pause. We drove them out, with their artillery, but our intercourse with the citizens was unmarked by a single act of injustice. Thus, marching half-naked and half-fed, and living upon wild animals, we have discovered and made a road of great value to our country."

The bell from the Catholic mission tolled, soft in the distance.

"Arrived at the first settlement of California, after a single day's rest, you cheerfully turned off from the route to this point of promised repose, to enter upon a campaign, and meet, as we supposed, the approach of the enemy; and this too, without even salt to season your sole subsistence of fresh meat."

Cooke lowered the paper and looked over the troops.

"Thus, volunteers, you have exhibited some high and essential qualities of veterans. But much remains undone."

Some heads turned away. Some looked down.

"It has been my honor to serve as your commander. I now relinquish that command to Colonel Stevenson."

Cooke saluted Colonel Stevenson and stepped from the podium. Stevenson returned the salute and stepped up to address the troops.

"Lieutenant Colonel Cooke has demonstrated exemplary leadership in the command of this battalion. His tireless efforts, his commitment to his soldiers, his selfless sense of duty, and his firm yet fair hand have marked a very high standard. Under his command you have acquired the discipline and toughness of veteran soldiers. I will give every effort to prove equal to the task and worthy of the command. I am honored to lead you."

Gabriel thought, *Ain't 'a gonna lead me, not far anyway.*

"As Lieutenant Colonel Cooke mentioned, much remains to be done. Your enlistments will expire in one month, yet we are still at war with Mexico. We need seasoned troops to secure the conquest we have made. This battalion is critical to that effort. Your continued service is vital if we are to sustain that which you worked so selflessly and diligently to achieve. I give you my hearty encouragement to reenlist."

Easier to burn a lake than get me to give another go-round. Orson Everett, too.

"You've obeyed your officers. You've demonstrated your patriotism and acquitted yourselves well as soldiers. Your countrymen, however, have not witnessed your noble efforts. One more year of service would do much to dispel what prejudice they hold against you and raise you to a stature equal to theirs."

Some smiled, a few sniggered, most stood stoic. Orson Everett's jaw dropped.

"Thank you for your service. I am eager to lead you through another term of enlistment."

Snowman's chance in the fires of Hades, Gabriel thought.

Bullneck Ruben handed the mule's lead rope to Gabriel. "They'll equip us in Monterey, they say, but this here will get you there," Ruben said.

Gabriel studied the mule. "Kinda short, ain't he?" His withers stood breast high to Gabriel.

"Half horse, half donkey, tough as an iron tire," Ruben said.

"Mostly donkey," Gabriel said.

"More iron than tire," Ruben said.

Gabriel's smile lit up his face, and he bobbed on his toes and petted his mule. "I can't hold it no more. I don't care if he's two foot tall. He's a mule, and he's mine to ride." He turned under the lead rope as if it were the hand of a dance partner and danced a jig. The mule stepped back, pulled the slack from the lead rope, and looked at Gabriel, ears perked.

"Ruben, keep an eye on Gabriel for the Lord and for me. The Lord will appreciate it, and so will I," Orson said.

"I'll do my best, Brother Orson, but it might take a passel of sheep dogs to keep him gathered up." Ruben smiled. "Are you sure we shouldn't reenlist him in the infantry?"

"Not for that new colonel," Gabriel said.

"It's Colonel Stevenson," Orson said. "Lieutenant Colonel Cooke's replacement. You need to know his name."

"Hawk Nose 'a goin' and Stevenson 'a comin'," Gabriel said. "Cooke says how good we are. Glows about it, like they don't come no better than Mormon soldiers. Then Stevenson pipes in. Ranks us with Irish and Indians, one step off the bottom rung. Sign up for another go he says, and the American gentiles will think us Saints are a square deal a little." He petted the mule's face. "Couple of barnyard cows. One gives a pail of milk, and the other kicks it over."

"None of us owe this army more than one enlistment," Orson said. "We've done what we said we would do."

The fifteen brethren who would accompany General Kearny and Lieutenant Colonel Cooke to Fort Leavenworth gathered to Orson Everett. They stood in a circle, close to Brother Orson, who stood at the center.

Orson said, "You will travel with gentiles, some of whom will be profane and motivated by baser instincts. Do not succumb to their influence. Stick by each other. Support each other. Be your brother's keeper."

Orson turned to look at each as he spoke.

"Remember, always, what Brother Brigham instructed us to do. Avoid swearing and gambling. Do not play cards, and do not mingle with Missourians. Do not take any medicine other than herbal remedies or concoctions that you yourselves make. You have the power within you to heal with the laying on of hands. Use it. I will pray daily for your safe journey, and that we will reunite under a banner of peace with Brother Brigham in our new Zion."

Orson laid his hands on each, blessed each in turn by name. Only then did Gabriel see what a father Orson had been to him, the father he'd never known, taken by pneumonia before he could walk, too young to know him, too young to make a memory. He felt then that Orson had treated him like the son he'd lost at Haun's Mill, felt he'd fallen short of the man Orson wished his son to be. Gabriel choked back a sob when Brother Orson laid his hands on and said, "May God be with you, Brother Gabriel, and guide and strengthen you always. I will pray for you as one of my own blood."

CHAPTER 37

A pious man *is not to be seen in the country. Occasionally you hear of a woman who may have been under the influence of religion.*

—*Captain Henry Smith Turner,*
First Dragoons, Monterey, California,
April 8, 1847

Moses Cole, Courier to Monterey, California, May 13, 1847
In his dream the white boy with the Apaches spoke Apache and traded blankets for tunic buttons. A headdress of white feathers bloomed above the boy. Spirits danced on the tips of the feathers and left when the feathers reddened. An Apache brave hoisted a lance and chanted. Scalps hung from the lance with ghosts braided in the scalp hair. Abner Black blinked behind blood-specked lenses, then held his eyes open and gestured, tried to speak with frenzy in his face.

In his dream, blood ran up the blade of the knife Moses held in his hand, ran up his arm and under his tunic to wrap around his torso and squeeze till his breath tightened. The lancer at the San Gabriel became the greatcoat and floated. In his dream, Patch Eye laughed. His good eye showed snake fangs where the pupil should be. Patch Eye lifted his eye patch where the rattlesnake denned, and its rattle buzzed in the empty eye socket. Moses swam in a desert spring, and a ten-pound catfish butted his ribs. In his dream, Big Man lumbered toward him with the lancer's head in his hand, forehead smashed from the rock at San Pasqual. Big Man held the head up and said, "You're dead." He threw it, and it hit him in the side.

Moses woke. Big Man stood over him. "You take kickin' to wake up. Sweet dreams?"

Moses sat upright.

"You're dead," Big Man said.

Patch Eye laughed. "Where your friends now?" Patch Eye's musket lay in the crook of his arm.

The firelight from his campfire had dimmed to coals. A three-quarter moon in a sky lighted with stars gave faces to the shapes. Moses sat in his blankets, en route to Monterey as a courier for General Kearny. He heard his mule's jaws work as he grazed at the end of his picket rope.

Moses nodded toward his mule. "Some watch dog he is."

Patch Eye said, "Big Man likes to victimize people he don't like, and he don't like you."

"Told you to watch your backside," Big Man said. "Shoulda done it."

A wind brushed a nearby tree. "Shoulda stayed on the grog shop veranda," Moses said. An owl hooted in the dark. "Shoulda done a buncha things different."

"Get up," Big Man said. "We got business to finish." He grabbed Moses by the tunic collar and neck scarf and pulled him from his blankets, then screamed and dropped him when he felt the knife in his thigh.

Moses jumped up, bloody knife in one hand and dragoon's horse pistol in the other, pointed at Patch Eye. He thumbed the hammer back.

"Lay it down, nice and easy," Moses said.

Patch Eye laid the musket down.

"You son of a bitch!" Big Man said. He sat down and looked where blood oozed from his thigh. "Chicken little shit. Stick a knife in a bare-knuckle man."

"Got a temper on me. You seen it but couldn't leave it lay."

"Should have shot you in your sleep," Patch Eye said.

"Should have," Moses said, "but Big Man wanted his fun." He smiled. "Them should-haves."

"Shit bag," Big Man said. He sat on the ground and held his hands on his thigh. "You're worse than a Mormon."

"Be thankful," Moses said. "Could've stuck ya in the guts."

"You always sleep with a pommel pistol?" Patch Eye said. "Diddle the bore in the bed covers?"

"Only in Missouri." Moses smiled, spit through the hole where his incisor had been. "Never know when a snake might come to cuddle."

"You're a rough one," Patch Eye said.

"Had a good teacher."

Big Man sat on the ground, held his thigh, watched blood seep between his fingers.

"You better get him doctored on." Moses tossed a handkerchief to Big Man. "It's cleaner on the inside."

Big Man refolded the handkerchief, inside to the outside, and stuck it through the cut in his pants and pressed it to stem the bleeding. Moses untied the neck scarf, balled it, and tossed it to Big Man. "Tie that around it." Big Man tied the scarf around his thigh to pressure the handkerchief bandage.

Moses said, "Don't say I never done nothin' for you." *Learned that from Abner.*

"This ain't settled yet," Big Man said.

"It's settled," Moses said. "Mount up and leave now, and you'll get to garrison before gangrene sets in. You don't want that. It don't smell good."

"Shit bag," Big Man said.

"Don't know where you left your horses, but you didn't get here afoot."

"They're safe," Patch Eye said.

"Slide that musket over," Moses said. "Gentle like."

"You wouldn't leave a man out here without a gun, would you? Indians and Mexicans and God knows what crawlin' about?"

"Looks like I would, but I won't keep it." Moses gestured with his pistol. "Slide it over."

Patch Eye pushed it with a foot. Moses picked up the musket and threw wood on the fire.

"I'll give it to somebody headed this way, which there oughta be in a day or two. I'll tell him, get it to the man with the eye patch in Frémont's camp, and he'll pay you for your trouble. Either that or keep it. Up to him."

"You're a renegade," Patch Eye said. "Should have joined Frémont. Would have fit you better than befriending Mormons."

Moses said, "Stay put, right there in the fire light, while I hunt someone to return your gun." He rolled up his blankets, saddled his mule, mounted, and said, "I'll look for somebody honest."

He turned the mule and rode north toward Monterey, pistol in the pommel holster, carbine strapped to his saddle, Patch Eye's musket across his lap.

The dream agitated Moses as he rode. Had Abner come to warn him? Push him from his bedroll with the alarm he brought? He'd not responded soon enough, had sensed the warning but didn't act. He remembered something Abner had taught him—listen to the little things in hidden places. They speak a language from a strange land but one as real as our own, one to which, perhaps, the lives we inhabit are but appendages. *Be mindful, my young private. What we perceive is not all that is. Listen to the language without sound.*

Moses had told him, "There you went again, talking that way

that makes no sense." Trying to bend his mind, he'd told Abner, was like a blacksmith bending iron without a forge. "It don't go too good," he'd told Abner.

His dream was more than a dream—a warning sent by Abner Black, a command to action, Abner would say, that ferried a larger lesson, like much that Abner had told him so often did. He could hear Abner now. *Look beyond sight, my young private. That's where the meaning will be.*

Be mindful. He'd done that. He needed to hone his senses to messages from other places.

He remained unsettled from the dream as he rode. He saw the Big Man at San Diego with the knife in his chin and bleeding and, way back, the boy he beat with the oak axe handle. He saw the *Californio* whose skull he'd crushed to avenge Abner Black. He saw the *Californio* he'd shot with calculated aim at San Gabriel, and the lung blood that bubbled from the bullet he'd placed there. He pictured the skin broken on the horseman's throat from the blade he'd honed with a whetstone. He would have cut to the bone had it not been for Abner's words, "the stain of regret."

He said out loud, "I got a temper on me. The hardest thing I done is rein it in, but I only done it once." He looked inward, found no remorse for the brutality he'd shown. It erupted to protect or avenge those he held close.

You're to be commended, my young private, he heard Abner say, *for thick walls to a soft heart.* He could see Abner remove his spectacles, examine and clean the glass in the wire rims, and he could hear him say, *Life may be easier should you leave in place the walls you've raised*—he would hook the wires around his ears before he'd resume the sentence—*but it won't be as rich.* He would focus on Moses through the lenses and he would say, *The time may come for those walls to fall, coincident with closing the distance you've travelled from that which you hold most dear.*

That which you hold most dear. My mentor and friend who's dead, and Ma, dead on account of my doin'. The farm and Miss Isabella. A place and its people. What folks call home. What I had before the drowning. What'd the preacher say at the grave, with Ma and the baby brother in it? Blame not, but have mercy and forgive. He looked at Pa when he said it, but Pa never seen him. Then he looked at me and said it straight. Forgive each other and forgive yourselves. Set it right with Pa was what he meant.

I never forgive nobody. Not that boy, brassy to Isabella. Not Pa or me either for the weasel and the river ice. Not the Big Man for roughin' up on the Mormons, or was gonna anyway. Not that lancer who lanced Abner or the one who dug him up. One quick cut and I'd have killed him twice, once for Abner and once for me, but I weakened. Could've drove it through his heart with a rock for a hammer. Thank Abner or cuss him for stayin' my hand, don't know which. Some worm he set to work in me. Somethin' my body knows but my mind don't. Them heart walls he talked about. Startin' to soften. Abner's worm eat a hole through there. Don't know from what or wherefore. That smashed-in head maybe. That brain stain.

Moses thought he might be turning Indian, hearing spirits, haunted by the presence of the dead, aware that he remained unaware of too much, like lessons Abner and the preacher and his parents planted that hadn't blossomed yet.

He trusted the mule's night vision, his sure-footed hooves, his animal instinct. "Need me some of that," he said to the mule. *That instinct that stands up neck hairs, brings on a feeling that says, "whoa up," see what sets beyond the senses and the thinkin'. Use that thing Indians have, but how does a white man do that?*

He rode on, riding for daylight.

CHAPTER 38

*The party . . . made twenty miles the first day and encamped
by two springs, which were about six feet apart, one of which
was hot and the other cold . . . On the 18th [day], they ascended
a mountain through a rain cloud to fair weather above.*

—*Sergeant Daniel Tyler, Mormon Battalion,
regarding the Mormon escorts' journey from
San Diego to Monterey,
May, 1847*

*General Kearny's Escort, Pueblo de Los Angeles to
Monterey, California, May 13–30, 1847*

The battalion escort left the Pueblo de Los Angeles on May 13
to ride El Camino Real, the coastal trail the Spanish missionaries marked in the 1770s to link missions one to another,
sprinkling mustard seeds along the way to brighten the trail of
the church. Twelve of the fifteen escorts from the Mormon Battalion rode mules and drove pack mules ahead of them, commanded by a regular army lieutenant. The other three escorts
would travel by ship to Monterey with General Kearny and
Lieutenant Colonel Cooke.

On the second day of the ride, en route to the mission at
Santa Barbara, Gabriel Hanks said, "They didn't tell me about
saddle sores."

"Welcome to the horse soldiers," Ruben said.

They rode up the coastal plain, often with the sea close by

and islands in sight.

"You're no horse soldier, and neither am I," Amos Binley said. "You're a Saint on a saddle mule, floppin' in the saddle like a fish on a crick bank."

They trailed the pack mules that followed the lieutenant. Sea lions barked from an outcrop offshore.

"Look at them things," Amos said. "Big as slop-fed hogs."

Amos wondered how they'd taste. Ruben reckoned like dead fish with stink on it. Gabriel ventured pig meat and possum with seaweed throwed in.

Bullneck Ruben said, "Horse soldier now, Brother Amos, by the Book of Ruben anyway."

A sea lion waddled across the outcrop and slid in the water.

Gabriel pulled a foot from the stirrup, held his leg out and rubbed the inside of his knee, and said, "Maybe it's the saddle."

"Couldn't be," Ruben said. "Had the rough spots wore off when you was a pup."

"Back when," Amos said, "if someone said tits you thought of a cow."

Gabriel blushed.

Rocks as big as barns jutted from the surf with seabirds perched on top.

"Look at those stirrup straps." Amos pointed to the straps that linked the stirrups to the saddle-tree, on the outside of the saddle skirt, where the rider's knee rubbed them. "When that saddle was new, those straps were square as a door edge. Now look at them. Sharp enough to shave paper. Edges beveled by a trooper's knees."

They rode by beaches with foam lines, kelp and driftwood, the smell of rotting fish where the tide retreated.

"Don't you never ride you a new saddle, Brother Gabriel. Squeak 'til your ears ring," Ruben said.

"Squeak like a whiny wife," Amos said.

"Nothing like that one there." Ruben smoothed a hand through the air. "Glide along quiet as an owl hunts mice."

Seabirds chirped on a rock outcrop.

"You might fix that seat," Ruben said. "By the looks of it, your sit bones will pinch live mule hide pretty quick. That little mule will throw you to yonder bird perch, your sit bones pinch him like that."

"Raid a nest of its eggs while you're up there," Amos said.

"The Lord's own word if he won't," Ruben said. "Throw you clear to the ocean. You'll need fish fins to get back."

Gabriel stood in his stirrups and touched the holes in the saddle seat. The quilted, sheep-leather seat had worn through to the saddle tree. He felt canvas, screw heads, iron, and the stretched rawhide that covered the hickory tree. He sat back down, slipped a hand between his leg and the stirrup strap to rub the inside of his knee. "Start with a new one, and it'd wear in to me," he said, "instead of to a trooper with gravel in his pants."

With the rainy season behind them they camped in open air, lulled by the surf that battered rocks. Further up the trail they camped at Mission Santa Barbara and rode north from there, still on El Camino Real, a long, thin strand speckled yellow in places. They rode by brown hills studded with valley oak, majestic and broad-branched, each to its own as if sentinels to homesteads. They rode to the Mission San Luis Obispo and woke to coastal fog. They rode in the fog, unsure of their bearings, unnerved by ancient oaks, lonely as ghosts that loomed and melted away. They rode inland, then north near the Salinas River, a valley uncluttered with brush and free of forests and open to the sun, as if God had cleared it, Amos said, uncovered it for the plow. All along the way, the mules had grass to graze and more to lie on. A freight ox, Amos said, would double his weight in this country. Near Monterey, they rode through giant redwoods that made them feel no bigger than midgets.

On the thirteenth day they reached Monterey Bay, two days ahead of General Kearny and Lieutenant Colonel Cooke and the three other members of the Mormon Battalion who sailed up the coast aboard the USS *Lexington*. They would meet here, join the rest of the escort, and ride to Fort Leavenworth, from the coast of the Pacific Ocean to the west bank of the Missouri River. In addition to the escort of fifteen Mormons, the party would include citizens returning east, guides, and dragoons.

Moses Cole set the horse's hoof down, straightened to stretch his back and watch the Mormon escorts herd their pack mules to the horse corral. He picked the hoof back up, nailed in the final three nails, rasped the hoof even with the shoe, blocked and crimped the nails, and set the hoof back down. He straightened and saw Gabriel Hanks standing in front of him with his mule at his side.

Gabriel moved his head forward. "The dragoon Moses Cole. That still you under that moustache?"

"Mostly," Moses said.

Amos led his mule up.

"Can't get used to it," Gabriel said. "Looks like you tore the eyebrows off Brother Orson Everett and sewed 'em on there."

Amos chuckled.

"That's the dragoon Moses Cole I told you about," Gabriel said. "See that moustache spread a little? Means he's smilin'."

Moses said, "Heard you was in that escort." He noticed Gabriel's saddle and said, "Must have bounced your way here, by the wear on that thing. I'll bet the poor brute pissed blood."

"Some pointy-bone dragoon done that."

"Better fix it," Moses said, "before we get to where there's nothing to fix it with." He untied the lead strap of the horse he'd shod and handed it to Gabriel. "You'll need another mount to get from here to clear back there. This ole boy steers like a freight wagon and stops like a ship, but he's all horse from the ground up."

Gabriel gaped at the horse, a tall bay gelding with a warm eye and black hooves and white hair on his withers.

Moses covered his eyes with his arm and said, "Too many teeth to see, all at one time, with that yap hangin' open."

"He's mine to ride?"

"Between him and that mule," Moses said, "maybe they'll get you there."

"Got me a horse and mule both," Gabriel said. "Mostly horse." His smile widened. "Who woulda knowed?"

"I won't tote you, so they better get you there. Got enough to pack on my saddle."

Gabriel looked at him.

"I'm goin' too. Army's orders."

"Bona fide horsehide and the dragoon Moses Cole to ride alongside of. Don't know whether to shout or sing or go to my knees and thank the Lord for his many blessings."

"Fix that saddle is what we'll do," Moses said.

They went in a shed that served for a leather and wood repair shop. The doors, wide enough to admit a one-horse buggy, swung open to sunlight. The sheepskin seat, woolless and pliable and suited for padded saddle seats, was not as hardy as cowhide. This one wore through, Moses reckoned, clean to the screws and the rawhide somewhere east of the Rio Colorado. Either it fit its former rider like a broke-in boot or he'd taken to laziness and applied no repair or, more likely the case, had nothing to repair it with. "Just like the army," Moses said, "expects you to get what it don't have."

The skirts were cracked from desert air and horse sweat. They worked them with kidney fat, rubbing the leather in the sun with the fat in their hands. The seat was padded with corrugated rows thick as workmen's fingers, quilted with hair from horse manes and tails that the saddle maker curled when he inserted it. The two holes from the pelvic points of previous riders suggested empty eye sockets. Gabriel pulled hair from horse tails, stuffed the holes, and Moses sewed on cowhide patches. Gabriel examined the patches, a browner hue than the Ringgold saddle leather and evenly spaced one to a side. He thought of an owl and the symmetrical feathering of its face, the well-defined eye sets, remembered what Ruben said about the saddle, quiet as an owl's glide.

Gabriel said, "This saddle is Owl Eyes."

"What?" Moses asked.

"Look at them patched over sit-bone holes. Like eyes on an owl. So that's its name, right there. Owl Eyes."

"Never known anyone to name a saddle."

"That big bay you give me, his name's Jonah. Come on me just now, heaven sent workin' this saddle leather. For I feel I've been spit from the belly of a whale and saved from the life of a foot soldier. Mule-back rider betwixt the two, how-some-ever, like purgatory to a padre."

"The Mormon Gabriel in a saddle named Owl Eyes on a horse named Jonah," Moses said. "What'll the dragoons do with you?" He thought, *Abner would fun around with that,* and he heard Abner's voice, soundless and real as a shadow brushing a wall. *I taught you many things, some of which you do not yet know. Among them is how to teach. Look to Gabriel.*

"Mister Moses," Gabriel said, "thank you, for the horse and the saddle help and all."

Moses shot him a look.

"Didn't throw nothin'," Gabriel said. "Just thank you, is all."

Moses looked off. "That Abner," he said.

"Didn't know how to turn a wore out saddle into Owl Eyes, but you showed me, so I'll say it again, provided it don't fright you too bad. Get braced up on account of here it comes. Thank you, Mister Moses."

Moses wondered when he'd last heard those words. Orson Everett when he waylaid the big man. Miss Isabella for the letter Abner sent. His mother before that. He smiled and said, "Mormons and women, the most thankin' people I ever seen."

CHAPTER 39

June 4.—Move 20 miles to the banks of the San Joachim, find it out of its banks & covering the plain to a considerable extent. Encamped near the river and pass a restless night in consequence of mosquitoes.

June 6.—During the day, a large elk was lassoed by Lt. Butron (Californian) brought into camp and presented to the General.

—Captain Henry Smith Turner
with General Kearny, 1847

General Kearny's Escort, Monterey to Cannibal Camp, California, late May through late June 1847

General Kearny's escort, sixty-four men and enough horses and mules to outnumber them by three to one, left Monterey on the last day of May. They traveled in a ribbon of riders on horse- and mule-back, pack mules, and a remuda of remounts. They rode on a trail at the edge of a lake where reflections mirrored their movement, a line of single-file riders that stretched the length of the shoreline.

They rode through the Salinas Valley and over Pacheco Pass, crossed the Diablo Range, and rode to the San Joaquin Valley, where they found the ford of the Stanislaus River swollen with snowmelt. They made a boat of hides, ferried the river a few men at a time, followed by the supplies emptied from the pack-mule panniers.

Gabriel Hanks volunteered to herd the horses across the current. He nudged his horse, Jonah, into the river. Jonah snorted as if he smelled bear, resisted going deeper than his knees. Gabriel urged him forward with his heels thumping the horse in the ribs. "Just walk on out there, Jonah, hind end after front end, and churn them feet like paddle wheels." Gabriel had never swum a horse. Jonah stepped one step more, then another, and then the bottom fell away. Gabriel sucked in his breath when the water reached his waist. When he recovered, he shouted, "Flowed off the north pole!" Jonah plowed ahead with Gabriel astride and drifted downstream as he swam in the mountain runoff among tree trunks and branches and a drowned cow.

A pack mule drifted by with a broken tree snagged in a pannier on its pack saddle. Either the mule carried the tree or the tree the mule until an end of the trunk struck a boulder in the current and spun, and the mule spun with it, full circle, legs churning under the surface looking for purchase. The pannier tore away from the pack saddle, and the mule swam free while the pannier sank with Lieutenant Colonel Cooke's rations and journal and one hundred dollars of his salary, in gold.

On the other side of the Stanislaus they repacked the mules while an Indian guide retrieved the journal that floated in an eddy. They remounted and rode to Sutter's Fort, where they stayed two days to resupply. From there they rode to Johnson's Ranch on Bear Creek, then on through Bear Valley, Steep Hollow, and Mule Springs. They rode through big pine and scrub oak and passed a solitary grave. They rode through Emigrant Gap and to the Yuba River, rode through the high Sierras with snow as deep as twelve feet, rode by Crystal Lake and Pyramid Peak. On the east side of the Sierra Nevada they rode to Truckee Lake and camped on June 21.

Amos Binley's horse had thrown his right-hind shoe and showed a tender-footed limp. Amos fetched a horseshoe, a rasp, hammer, and a handful of horseshoe nails from a pannier. He'd not handled his horse's feet before. He had no need to since the horse had been shod when issued to him. Amos stroked the horse's rump, ran his hand down to the hock and down the cannon bone, and when he reached the fetlock his horse kicked his hand away. On the third attempt Amos grabbed the ankle and held while the horse attempted to kick, the force dampened by the hands that clenched the horse's ankle. Amos held until the horse jerked free and kicked Amos square in the ribcage, snapping two ribs where they met the backbone. Color drained from Ruben's face when he heard the bones break.

Amos did not think he'd breathe again, but after a bit he gasped. Ruben wrapped Amos's torso with his own spare shirt. He cut the sleeves off, tied one to the other on the hemless ends, and pulled it snug around the broken ribs and tied the cuff ends together. He did the same with the body of the shirt—cut it into hand-width strips, tied the strips end to end, placed them around the ribs as if a ladder of bandages, pulled them snug, and tied them. This would keep the ribs from moving as much when Amos walked or rode, Ruben told him. They helped Amos mount his horse, and they rode on.

Amos could not sleep that night. The next day, with no wagon to ride and a destination to reach, they got him on his horse with the right hind shoe replaced after Ruben and Gabriel and Moses Cole employed ropes for the purpose. Amos gripped his saddle while they rode.

"Should have left him barefoot," Amos whispered between short breaths. "Wear that hoof to the hairline. See how he likes being crippled up."

They rode down the lake and found the cabins they were told they would find. Kearny's escort was the first to see the site since snowmelt. Stumps twelve feet tall indicated the snow level that trapped the Donner party there.

Bodies, or the remnants of bodies, lay scattered about in the manner of a desecrated cemetery or a place where bears tore carcasses apart and birds roosted on the bones they'd left. Bones nicked by a knife's edge and the bite of saw teeth. Bones sawn through and bones broken as butchers break beef shanks. Bones cleaned of marrow and breastbones wedged open. A skull lay separate from its skeleton, its top sawn off forehead to crown. Another held its hair, shoulder-length patches either side of a gash that would fit an axe blade. Another stared with empty eye sockets, teeth gleaming from mummified gums.

Gabriel pondered, leaned over, and retched.

Household and emigrant items lay strewn about—books with mildewed pages; calico cloth in rag-like pieces; a wooden doll with black beads for eyes; a leather pouch, its clasp crafted from a tip of deer antler; a porcelain cup and pewter spoon; a lantern empty of lamp oil with its wick untrimmed; a wagon, free of its wheels, collapsed from the weight of snow; a saw by the remains of a body with a thigh removed.

They named this place Cannibal Camp.

Moses stared at feathers scattered from a feather bed, thought of feathers plucked from stewing hens. A feather lifted, and Moses wondered, why only one? A breeze would lift it but a breeze would lift the lot of them, and he felt no breeze. He remembered the dream, the spirits that danced on the tips of the white feathered headdress, wondered if the ghost of a child carried the feather away, to use its scent, perhaps, to track its mother.

Eat or be ate, Moses thought. *Not mean, just savage. It was them who weren't dead or it was the birds and the worms that was gonna eat. Either which way, they're ate.*

No birds chirped. The horses and mules stood mute. No one spoke.

What did Abner say? Desperation breeds desperate acts. We're more animal than man when it's act or die.

Remember the tale of the whaleship *Essex,* Abner could say, told to regale you during the monotony of the march, to teach you of what one is capable when survival is at stake. What one may give so another may live.

Not me, Master Private. Would not have done that.

But you have done that which, had you considered it, you would have said you would never do. The moral pose is easy to assume when one is not faced with the immediacy or heat of the moment.

Here I am, talking to a dead man. This place has got to me.

This place of the tethered dead, my young dragoon, spirits fettered to the savage act. Unlike mine, anchorless and wayward and free to visit upon you.

Moses shook his head like a dog shakes water away. He looked about. A handful of cabins stood here. Most showed the crude work of rushed construction and roofs of canvas and brush to slow the penetration of snow. One resembled a shell above a den, more cellar than cabin with a fire pit in the floor. Bones and tufts of human hair, some coarse as wire, some pliable and full of color as if snipped for remembrance from the heads of children, lay about the fire pit.

They gathered bones, and the bones clattered when dropped in the den to bury them.

The mean in me. Ma would wonder where it come from. That savage, too. Didn't know I had it that bad.

He imagined Abner: Bind it or be bound by it, Abner would say. Bury it with the bones you're here to bury.

The quiet broke open when the bugler fumbled his pistol and shot himself below the collarbone. Moses jumped at the gun shot as if the pelvis and leg bones he carried jerked on their own accord. The bugler clutched his shoulder and sat down.

Moses dropped the bones, ran to the bugler, and examined the wound. Moses told him the ball passed clear through and stuck in the tree behind him, poked a hole but didn't mash the bone. "I could fish with a finger in there and not find nothin' hard and sharp and jagged. The good of it is, it'll heal without no trouble but discomfort." *Don't lie too bad,* Moses thought. "I know. Had me a tore-open shoulder, parts of a lance shaft in it. Worser than yours, and it healed up good."

Gabriel lifted his hands to heaven, and he prayed out loud. "Oh, God Almighty, watch over us in this place of evil. You took the devil off us in the desert, Lord, but it looks like he lit here. Pull him off us, Lord, I beseech of you. The devil's had his feed on these people a little, Lord, and he's lookin' for more in Amos and the bugler there. Don't let him to have them or any other, Lord, but let him to starve and burn in his own fires of hell. Help us bury these folks and to get clean away from here, I pray of you, Lord." Gabriel lowered his hands and bowed with the other Saints that gathered around him. "Hosanna and Amen," Gabriel said.

"Amen," the others said.

When they had gathered the bones to the burial den they collapsed the roof and the walls and covered it with dirt and rocks. They burned the other structures and mounted and rode away and found the scene repeated further on. General Kearny remained silent, and they left the bones as they lay and rode by, unwilling to look and powerless not to. They camped a mile away. Few spoke in camp that night but stared into cook fires to watch flames at play.

The next day they rode east through Dog Valley and down the Truckee with Amos and the bugler clutching their saddles, jaws clenched to hold in their moans.

CHAPTER 40

No wood and but very little grass. The water is salty and bitter. It seems as though the curse of God rested upon this country. It is all a barren unfruitful waste.

—Nathaniel V. Jones,
Mormon Battalion & Gen. Kearny's escort,
June 27, 1847

General Kearny's Escort, East of the Sierra Nevada [Nevada],
c. July 1, 1847

General Kearny's adjutant rode his horse to the edge of the water and stopped. His horse lowered his head and drank.

"Captain, sir?" Gabriel said. "My orders are to let no horse or mule drink before the men is all watered up, sir."

Moses Cole, a guide, and a handful of regular army soldiers drank and filled canteens at the water hole. They stopped. A sagebrush basin stretched around them.

The adjutant smiled while his horse drank.

"Sir? The Lord knows it's the general's order, and they put me here to make sure it's followed, sir."

The men at the water hole sat on their haunches and watched the captain's horse drink.

"We got sixty-four men, Captain, and not all has had a chance to drink, sir."

"Stand down, Private." The captain's horse stepped forward, placed a hoof in the water, and continued to drink.

"Captain, sir. I'm here to enforce the general's order a little."

Kearny's adjutant chuckled. Gabriel shouldered his musket. The captain pulled his horse's head up.

Low-elevation mountain ranges stood off, some further away than others and each to its own, like bands of different animals that kept to themselves.

The adjutant glared at Gabriel. "Lower your musket at once, Private."

"Captain sir, the sooner you leave the sooner the soldier men get their fill and the sooner your horse can water, like the order says, sir."

"Do you understand that you threaten a superior officer, Private?"

"Lieutenant Colonel Cooke taught an order's an order, sir, and they give me my order." Gabriel kept his musket at his shoulder. "Remove your horse, sir."

"You may want to think about the ramifications of your actions, Private."

"Doin' what was told us, sir. No four-leggeds to water until the two-leggeds is done, since we come on the desert country, sir."

Grass stood between the sagebrush, too sparse to hide a jackrabbit.

"Lower your musket, Private."

Gabriel cocked it.

"You're done now, sir, until all these men is watered up. Just back your horse up and set a little, nice and easy like, so I don't twitch on the trigger, sir."

"What's your name, Private?"

"Gabriel Hanks, sir." Gabriel's trigger finger rested on the trigger guard. The muzzle of his Mississippi rifle moved in figure eights centered on the captain's chest twenty feet away. "Mormon Battalion, sir."

"That explains it." The captain's eyes moved with the bore of the musket. Sun glinted from the brass tip of the ramrod sheathed under the barrel. "You will hear about this, Private Hanks." He backed away from the water hole and rode off.

Gabriel eased the hammer down and cradled the musket in the crook of his arm.

"What birth date do you want on your headstone?" Moses asked.

"He won't get him a headstone," a soldier said. "He'll get him a board off a cracker box that says, 'This here's what comes to the private soldier that defies the general's staff officer and follows orders.' " He snickered. "That adjutant will make him carve that before we shoot him."

"He can't write," the guide said. "He's Mormon."

"Their own order," Moses said. "He ought to follow it." He placed the stopper back in his canteen and stood up. "Is that musket loaded?"

"Powder, patch, and ball," Gabriel said. "The pan is primed, and the flint will spark."

"Private Gabriel Hanks," Moses said. "You got balls big enough for church bells and a skull empty of sense."

"Ain't shot nothin' since dog man's water pail."

Moses pondered, worked his moustache with his lower lip.

"Dog man won't be usin' that pail no more, except for kindlin' wood." Gabriel smiled.

"Gabriel, if there's a thread to your logic, it broke somewhere," Moses said.

"My 'feat of arms,' Brother Orson called it. This here's another one. Didn't burn no powder though."

"Never mind him," the guide said. "Could not follow reason if it left tracks in the mud on a walled-in road."

"If I took the time to tell it, you'd quit your so-called reason and follow the faith, but I ain't here to explain or preach a little."

"See them officers gathered up like that?" Moses said, indicating a cluster of officers with his nose. "That is never a good thing."

"What'll they do to me, Moses?" Gabriel set the butt of his musket on the ground.

"They won't hang you, and they won't shoot you, but they'll make you wish you wouldn't have run off the general's adjutant with a loaded rifle."

"It don't look good, the general's staff man defyin' his boss's order, right there in front of the men," Gabriel said. "Don't he got eyes in his head?"

"Sure he does," Moses said. "They just see different than yours do."

"If it 'a been him and me, maybe I'd 'a had to tie my shoe. Maybe I'd 'a blurred up from sand in them eyes of mine. Maybe I'd 'a whittled a canteen stopper and not seen him, but that ain't how it went. He rode his horse in the water with soldier men gurglin' canteens."

"They'll make an example of you." Moses mouthed his moustache. "Little dog run off a big dog. Big dogs don't like that."

"Got an idea what they'll do," a soldier said. "But I won't spoil the surprise."

"One will give out—legs or thumbs—don't know which," Amos said. His phrases came between shallow breaths.

They would have used a tree if one grew there. Without one they constructed a frame from muskets—two muskets to a side, muzzle to muzzle joined by pegs in the bores, with Gabriel's musket lashed across the top for a crossbar. The muskets at the base of the frame were set in the ground, butts dug and tamped as gate posts. The end result resembled an empty door frame large enough to ride a horse through. Gabriel's arms stretched overhead, held by rawhide strips that linked his thumbs to the crossbar. He stood on the balls of his feet, heels off the ground, to keep his thumbs from bearing the weight of his body.

"There's more to them legs than looks let on," Ruben said. "Packed him from the Missouri River to the Pacific Ocean."

Amos held his ribs. "Those are not—the thumbs—of a clerk." He paused to breathe. "Whether to grip a shovel—or a tow rope—on a wagon stuck in sand." He took several breaths. "Those thumbs are more—than callous and thumbnail."

"I'll bet a biscuit his legs give," Moses said.

The three stood away from Gabriel, uncertain if army protocol allowed them to approach close enough to speak with him.

"I'll cut him down first," Bullneck Ruben said.

"Walkin's one thing. Standin' on tippy toes is plumb another," Moses said. "I'll bet when they let him down them thumbs will stay there, swingin' from them rawhide nooses. Gabriel's gonna wonder how to button his britches with four fingers to a hand."

"Even if they shoot me for it. I'll cut him down first, by God I will," Ruben said.

"I'd take a thumb stretch—over broken ribs. You ever rode—with broken ribs, Moses?" Amos took a few breaths. "Hurt all day—hurt all night—it does not quit." He paused to breathe. "But Gabriel—what will he get?" Amos smiled. "Long thumbs." He started to chuckle but gasped and held his ribs.

"They'll cut him down soon," Moses said. "We've got a long way to go, and the general don't need another man crippled up."

Gabriel called out. "Moses? How's my ridin' been?"

Moses approached the musket frame that stretched Gabriel

like wet rawhide weighted with rocks and hung from a rafter. Amos and Ruben followed.

"I'm wonderin' if you'll keep your thumbs, and you're worried about how you ride." Moses shook his head. "The guide's right. The mind of a Mormon is a hard thing to follow. Like trackin' a fish in a lake."

"Takes my mind off my predicament a little." Gabriel winced and danced on his toes.

"You ride like a sack of shit, only not as smooth."

"This hangin' frame don't feel too smooth neither."

"Think about what I'm telling you. You know how you bounce at a trot?"

"Jonah bounces, so I bounce right along with him."

"Don't bounce. Post. But if you're gonna sit there, sit there. Bouncing's as hard on your horse as it is on you. Try moving your hips and stomach in and out, not up and down."

"In and out, not up and down," Gabriel said. He gritted his teeth, lifted a foot and flexed his ankle up, held the flex, set it down, and did the same with the other ankle.

"Like you was in a weddin' bed, makin' a baby Mormon."

Gabriel's smile spread over his teeth.

"You still ain't growed to them teeth."

"How long they gonna stretch me, Moses?"

"Another thing, don't use the cantle for a back rest. You're not ridin' a rockin' chair. Sit up straight like you're proud to be there."

"I am proud to be there."

"Then show it. Don't ride with the stirrup shoved to your arch. Heel below the toe. Say it."

"Heel below the toe."

"And the other."

"How long, Moses?"

"The other, what's the other?"

334

"Stirrup to the ball of the foot."

"And that other thing I told you."

"Cantle's not a chair back."

Moses listened for an order to cut Gabriel down and heard a gust in the sagebrush.

"Keep your weight on the balls of your hip bones, not the fat of your butt, if you had any. Balls of the feet, balls of the hips, straight up the backbone to the shoulder blades. Not slumped like you're asleep and dreamin' of biscuits and syrup."

Gabriel winced and moved his feet.

"Straight as a bridge plank, but limber."

"That's contrary," Gabriel said. He moved on his toes. "Like stayin' in place and movin' to another, both at once."

"Straight, not stiff."

"How long's this stretchin' gonna take?"

" 'Til you're straightened out." Moses looked for an officer but did not see one move or look their way. "Not long."

"This is a little tough."

"You got it tough?" Ruben said. "Them at Cannibal Camp had it tough."

"Don't make me retch a little. I can't bend over at the moment." Sweat beaded on Gabriel's forehead. "Moses? What'll you do with your discharge papers?"

"Reassigned, not discharged." Moses stroked his moustache. "Look up that pretty little Isabella, if she ain't took by now, if I get that far."

"If you're worried about her bein' took, why'd you leave her in the first place?" Gabriel asked.

"Figured there was more to travel than walkin' in circles with the ass end of a plow mule for a view. Even then I'd have stayed on account of Isabella, 'cept Pa took the shovel to me for the plow I broke turnin' field stones big as billy goats."

Gabriel rested his right heel on his left big toe. "Then what?"

"Pa gets mean when he sips liquor, and he sips it a lot, ever since Mother died. Decided then and there I wouldn't take it no more. Up and left. No food, no gun, no bedroll. Just turned and walked off. Clear to Carlisle Barracks, Pennsylvania."

Gabriel turned his head to stretch his neck muscles.

"My hand's on my knife handle," Ruben said. "You say the word, you're comin' down."

Gabriel said, "Keep on talkin', moustache man."

Moses kept talking. "Belly got the best of me. Turns out there's a cavalry school there. Hot food, a bed and a roof and full set of clothes, flat cap to ankle boots. Might not fit, but they was new. Wrote my name on the paper they give me. Ended up in the First Dragoons, and here I am."

"You rode all that country so you could turn around and do it all over again, clear back to what you run from?" Ruben said. "And you think a Saint makes no sense."

"Makes sense to me a little," Gabriel said. "That's a lotta country in a saddle seat."

"Seen enough to know there ain't nothin' like Virginia, and that Isabella," Moses said.

Ruben asked, "What if she's married off?"

"Then I should've stayed and courted her to give myself a chance, but I didn't." Moses fingered his moustache. "If she's married up, I'll stay or go, one or the other." Moses thought a moment. "Shoot him, most likely. Make a widow out of her."

Gabriel shifted feet to rest his left heel on his right big toe. "How long they gonna leave me here, Moses?"

"Not long enough," Moses said. He smiled. "Keep your humor, Gabriel. It won't be long. We have a march yet today."

CHAPTER 41

*He [Gen. Kearny] is a great soldier, one who knows no fear,
and minds not fatigue.*

—*A newspaper report at the time, quoted in*
Army of Israel—Mormon Battalion Narratives,
Bagley & Bigler, p. 248

*We . . . ate the last bit of provision we had, even a pair of
rawhide saddle bags which I had brought from California on a
wild mule.*

—*Edward Bunker,*
Mormon Battalion,
on the return to Council Bluffs, 1847

General Kearny's Escort, Oregon and Nebraska Territories
[Idaho and Wyoming], July and August 1847

General Kearny's escort met the first settlers of the season
headed west near the Snake River, emigrants bound for the Wil-
lamette Valley on the Oregon Trail. The wagon trains spread
from the Snake to the Platte River, the emigrants said. They
supposed that if one flew like an eagle they would see thousands
of wagons and tens of thousands of livestock spotted from South
Pass to Chimney Rock, grazing the prairie bare for miles either
side of the Oregon Trail. They supposed it would look like the
navies of the world, grouped one behind the other with a period
of days between each navy, sails unfurled to assault a continent.

Kearny's escort rode on, east on the Oregon Trail counter to the current of the time, as if to plumb the source of a great river. They rode the usual thirty to thirty-five miles a day, nooning where grass was plentiful to restore their animals before grass grew sparse.

They crossed the Green River and crossed over South Pass and rode up the Sweetwater and climbed Independence Rock, a promontory that offered two things scarce on the prairie—a vantage point and free-flowing water with the Sweetwater at its foot. Domed and bare in the plains around it, as if God placed it there for a prairie cathedral, Amos said, smoothed it for the faithful to climb to pray and inscribe a name as a gift to the Lord. From here they saw where Devil's Gate swallowed the Sweetwater to the southwest. They rode northeast to the North Platte, where they met a party of Latter-day Saints, hunters sent ahead to lay in buffalo meat for the company of Saints further downriver.

From the hunters, the escort learned of the Saints' migration to the Great Salt Lake. They learned the brethren and sistren and their wives and children wintered west of the Missouri River at a place named Winter Quarters where disease claimed many and food was scarce. They learned that, second to their religion, hardship was their common bond. They learned they'd find companies of Saints between here and Winter Quarters and that some remained in Council Bluffs to plow and plant the tallgrass prairie to supply Latter-day Saints on their way to the Great Basin.

Amos Binley's ribs had not healed. The officers agreed his ribs would knit if he remained with the hunters and their wagon and their slower pace.

"Goodbye, Amos," Gabriel said. He felt as if a turnip had lodged in his throat. He wanted to embrace this brother of the foot and horse soldiers, but the wrapped ribs held him back. Gabriel took the hand Amos extended, felt a piece of him rip away, felt his eyes well, turned, and left as if he'd been called to an urgent errand.

They rode on and met the next company of Saints on the North Platte River, a half-day ride east of Fort Laramie. Ruben received a letter from his wife, who remained at Council Bluffs, the first he'd seen since they'd left Fort Leavenworth one year ago. The letter reported the death of their daughter. Constriction by pneumonia, the letter said. They'd buried her on a bluff overlooking the Missouri River, where she'd find peace in the vista of a new land and the endless current of the Missouri.

Gabriel heard the air leave Bullneck Ruben, as if an invisible fist had punched him in the gut. He watched Ruben unsaddle and picket his horse, watched him go through the motions of eating supper while voices spoke of hunger and cold and disease and headstones in Winter Quarters and the power of the Lord to carry them through it all. He watched Ruben unroll his bedroll and turn his back to the gathered brethren who talked at campfires.

A few days later, further east on the North Platte, Gabriel met his mother in the next company of Saints. They hugged and laughed, and Mrs. Hanks implored General Kearny to release her son from his enlistment since their one-year term had expired, and she was a poor widow woman and needed a man in the family to help with the two younger children and the wagon and the stock. Besides that, she told the general, it would save Gabriel a turn-around trip once he reached Fort Leavenworth. The obvious, sensible, expedient, and just thing, she argued, was for General Kearny to relieve Private Gabriel Hanks from his service in the Mormon Battalion, a battalion that would be released upon arrival at Fort Leavenworth anyway in a mere few weeks. Clearly, he had latitude as general to grant this, and in service to the civilian population and to the settlement of this country, his conscience would be well served in doing so. What's more, she said, she needed her boy back before the army starved him to death.

General Kearny bowed, kissed the hand of the Widow Hanks, remarked that she would make a splendid aide-de-camp, and consented. Gabriel did not know whether to laugh or protest, to thank the general or beg him to reconsider. The general told Gabriel that the Mississippi rifle and twenty-one cartridges were his to keep, but the horse and tack would remain with the escort as government property.

Gabriel unbridled Jonah, left the halter on, and tied the bridle to the saddle. He unbuckled his bedroll from the pommel and removed his woolen underwear from the cantle valise. He emptied his saddlebags of hard bread and dried venison. He patted Owl Eyes, his saddle, and wrapped his arms around Jonah's neck. He wanted to tell Jonah what he meant to him but felt as if a cow's cud plugged his throat. His eyes burned, and he felt his face fall away. He wanted to tell him that he was more than a horse, that a horse carried a spirit that was better than that of a man, strong and quiet, one that gave and kept on giving, one that asked for respect and the rudiments of care, for a rider with a fair and certain hand, who would deliver the horse from danger, who valued the horse's movements.

"Abner told me long ago," Moses said. "Don't fall in love with your horse."

Gabriel loosened the cinch but left it snug enough to hold the saddle in place.

"Each one you do is a broken heart."

Gabriel rested his forehead on Jonah's neck.

"You'll have another one someday. Probably better," Moses said. He took the lead rope to lead Jonah away. "I'll look after him. He'll be all right."

Moses extended his hand, and Gabriel took it in both of his.

"If you get bored of bein' Mormon, or want to change your

whereabouts and trade your wearables," Moses said, "get yourself to Carlisle Barracks. I'll recommend you to the lieutenant for a dragoon recruit."

Gabriel held onto Moses's hand. "Goodbye to you and Jonah both." Gabriel started to say more, stuttered, shook his head.

"You done me good," Moses said. "My turn to say thank you." He slapped Gabriel on the back and mounted with the lead rope in hand. "You and I done some growin' up together." Moses felt his throat tighten. He looked away, gave himself a moment, and turned back to Gabriel. "Take care of yourself, Horse Teeth." He smiled, turned his horse to join the escort, and rode east leading Jonah. Dust bloomed behind them.

Gabriel watched his brothers-in-arms ride off with Jonah and Owl Eyes and the dragoon Moses Cole, and he felt his world melt. These men had been stronger than family, but the center of his being, the fuel in his fire, had been Jonah. This horse confirmed his calling. This horse had been his ballast, the hub of his heart, the reason he'd enlisted, as if Jonah had been calling him all along.

He looked at his mother, her hollow cheeks, weather-worn face, hair tinged with gray, tear streaks down her cheeks. He felt her hands brush his tears away. The two young ones hugged his legs, and he found, for the first time he could remember, that he had nothing to say.

CHAPTER 42

Moses Cole, Bridgewater, Virginia,
the Second Sunday of October 1847

The parishioners lingered, exchanged pleasantries before they rode in buggies or on horses or mules or walked home after church. He'd come hoping to see her, and there she was, in a blue print dress with lace on the cuffs and collar, the fair complexion of a shop girl, a red ribbon tied in her hair for accent.

Moses looked at Isabella, and she looked right back. He thought he saw her start, a flash of impact, a quick catch of the breath. He blushed, smiled. Isabella dropped her eyes. Must be the hole in my top teeth row, he thought.

"It's Moses Cole!" Isabella's aunt strolled up to him. "I did not recognize you at first! Moustaches will do that, you know. What a pleasant surprise to see you here! Why, just look at you!"

She placed a hand on each of his arms as if to frame him and moved her eyes to take in everything in his face.

"That's quite a moustache, young man, and it does become you, but it will take getting used to. Oh, and you've lost a tooth!" She lowered her voice and leaned closer. "We all do, you know." She laughed and stepped back to look him over. "You look so well, young man, and I understand you've been off to the war in Mexico? How noble of you! When did you return? We'd heard you were back, but no one had seen you! How good of you to come to church. It's been years since I've seen you! And still I miss your mother so. Such a tragic thing." She caught herself and put a hand over her mouth.

"We all do, ma'am."

"I'm so sorry. Oh, Isabella! You know Moses Cole, don't you?"

Isabella approached. Moses's heart jumped into his throat.

"Why, Moses Cole," Isabella said.

"Oh, dear me." Isabella's aunt placed a hand on her chest. "There's that poor Mrs. Mayfield who just lost her husband. I must speak to her. How good to see you, Moses. I beg your pardon." She flitted off to comfort Mrs. Mayfield.

"You've changed," Isabella said.

"You have, too, Miss Isabella."

To Moses Cole the blue of her eyes let heaven swell his heart.

"I can't imagine how far you've gone and what you've seen."

"There's a lot of miles out there. Seen more than I wanted to."

"How does it feel to be home?"

"I'm not sure. Right now, pretty good." He smiled and thought he saw her blush.

"You've been gone a long time," Isabella said. "A lot can happen in three years."

"Yes, ma'am. Then again, some things stay the same, seems like."

Her smile faded. "I must say, Moses, how awkward of you to have left without a word to anyone. No one knew what became of you for the longest while. You might have drowned crossing a river for all anyone knew."

"I didn't think anyone cared."

"People cared. Your pa cared."

"He had an odd way of showin' it."

"I know. But he did."

"Did he tell you?"

Isabella paused. "He said as much."

Moses didn't know what to say, so he nodded his head.

"And you've been off to the war. Probably the only boy in the county who did so. Next thing you know they'll want to make you mayor."

She smiled, and Moses thought of rain in the desert.

"Isabella! Come along now!" her mother called.

"I'll come visit," Moses said.

"So nice to have you back, Moses." She turned away and went to her parents, looked over her shoulder, and smiled. Moses felt like he was riding a rainbow.

Her father looked at Moses, placed Isabella's arm over his forearm, and walked with his daughter and wife to their home on the backside of the dry-goods store.

Isabella walked like a young woman walks coming into her prime. Moses felt the pull in his chest, as if tethered to her with a picket pin through his heart. He watched her for what he realized was a bit long for polite behavior, turned his head away to see the minister approach.

"Hello, Moses. Remember me?"

Moses considered him. "Last I seen you was on the other end of an axe handle."

"Let's say that started my turn-around."

"You got brassy on Miss Isabella. I didn't take to that."

"You were an agent of the Lord's retribution. I should thank you."

"Was glad to give the Lord a hand."

The pastor nodded. "Are you home to stay?"

"Hard to tell. Got army time left."

"I understand you've been to California with the Mormons."

"There were Saints there."

"One of their missionaries will pass through on occasion.

Odd religion. Blasphemous, truth be told. How did you find them?"

"Tough."

The pastor waited for more.

"Most the time, same as anyone else."

"Were you in the war out there?"

"Some. Enough." Moses looked at people as they mingled.

"How's your pa getting on? I see him come to town on occasion, cleaned up like he's headed for church, but he won't stop here."

"Maybe he's changed," Moses said. "Used to be, he'd about starve out before he'd come to town."

The pastor nodded.

"Still got that axe handle," Moses said.

The pastor laughed.

Moses felt like he was floating as he walked home. He had missed the beauty of Virginia—the turning leaves, the gentle hills, the tended fields, the forests and abundant forage. After the expanse of the landscape he'd crossed, the desert and prairie that held no end, he saw how a man could feel confined by trees and farmsteads and snake-rail fences, but he'd longed for the luxuriant closeness of it and the life it breathed. And the colors, the leaves of autumn—how he'd yearned for that. Their beauty seemed deeper, richer, than he remembered.

And the way she moved. Good Lord.

He walked the four miles home to find his father rocking in the porch rocker.

"How'd you find the church house this mornin'?" George Cole said. "Sing about heaven and thunder about hell, did they?"

"So, you have been to church."

His father studied him. "There's a girl about. Seen her there, didn't you?"

Moses didn't answer.

"You're walkin' four foot off the ground." George Cole chuckled. "The power of budding femaledom. The only reason I can see for a man to attend such a place." He got up from the hand-crafted rocking chair. "Coffee's hot."

Moses followed him into the cabin.

His father pulled a tin coffee cup from a shelf and set it on the table. He grabbed the coffee pot's handle, lifted the pot from the wood stove, and carried it to the table. "I've had it in for you ever since your mama died." He filled the plain tin cup that sat in front of his chair. He filled the cup he'd set for Moses, seated at the square pine table in the center of the cabin, returned the pot to the stove, and sat down at the table. The chair scraped the floor when he scooted it forward. His pipe and tobacco pouch lay next to his dented cup.

"You know it as well as I do," George Cole said.

Moses held the cup by the handle and blew to cool it.

"If you'd 'a shut the damn gate it wouldn't have happened."

"I was a boy, chasing a weasel from the hen house."

"That don't change it."

"He ran me half a mile, and by then it was over."

His father watched steam rise from his coffee.

"Since you marched off to conquer Mexico, wherever the hell that is, the work's got harder and the day's got longer and the mule's got meaner." George Cole exhaled smoke through his nose. "Why you thought Mexico mattered I do not know."

"I left here to leave you. It was that or kill you."

"Wouldn't have blamed you if you did, and left me dead for the chickens and the hogs and the bugs that was hungry."

"I might yet. I'm trying to decide if I'm over it, George."

"I noticed that, along with the whiskers on your lip and the hole in your smile," his father said. "You used to call me Pa."

"It's George now. You quit bein' Pa a long time ago."

George Cole opened his tobacco pouch and removed a pinch.

"That girl you seen in church." He placed and packed the tobacco in his pipe bowl with a whittled wing bone carved for the purpose. "I quit my courtin' her."

Coffee spilled when Moses's cup thumped the table.

"Don't give me that look. You ain't been here."

Moses swept the spilled coffee to the floor with his hand. "You courted Isabella?"

"In case you misperceived, I ain't that old. When we had you, we was younger than the man sittin' across the table cleanin' up his mess."

"Thought I'd seen everything," Moses said.

"She's at that age, son. Needs a man, whether she knows it or not, and she knows it."

"But you? George Cole?"

"Her daddy seen me for a prospect. A man of property. A provider. Farm to my name, crop land good as any in the county."

"George Cole, courting Miss Isabella." Moses shook his head.

"Don't amount to a thing. Put on my Sundays when I go to get my goods is all, which I shoulda done anyway. I keep hopin' that clean-up will worm its way inside of me, but that don't happen." George stepped to the stove. "Shouldn't have told it. Honest is all." He bent down and rummaged through the kindling box and pulled out a thin stick. "Nothin' come of it." He rose and paused like his back spasmed, stalled halfway to standing straight with a hand on a chair back. "It's water under ice, flowed to the ocean they say is out there, that place where everything goes." He stood up and looked at Moses. "You know what I mean."

Moses looked where his coffee had spilled.

George removed a stove lid. "Never did like lies." He held the stick in the fire. "Slim pickins' here for a girl like her." He pulled the lit stick from the stove. "There's the preacher."

"The preacher," Moses said.

George held the lit stick to his pipe bowl. "She don't take to him, but he don't see it." He puffed until the smoke came. "You might point him to the light of the Lord, help him see where he stands in the matter. She told me you done it once." He replaced the lid and returned to his chair. "Her daddy wants her married to a man of means. Her mama now, if I traded there more than I needed to, and spent more time doin' it, she'd see the lecher I want to be. Wants her back to Richmond, or married to the preacher with the scrubbed-off heart."

"Should've stole my pistol and brung it loaded," Moses said. "That or stayed away."

"Ease up, boy. Nobody's done nothin'."

"When you quit courting her?"

"Day you got back." George smoked. "Day after maybe." He smiled, drew smoke, and blew smoke rings. "Plain as the day is bright you took a shine to her this mornin'. Got reacquainted maybe. Coulda had a puppy crush when you was a kid. How was I to know? You ain't been here. Not word one from you on your whereabouts. You know letters enough to write, 'Here I come,' or, 'Won't see me no more.' Maybe they don't have a pen in the army. Maybe you forgot the address. George Cole, Bridgewater, Virginia."

"Should've took you to Santa Fe and left you there," Moses said.

"Never heard of it."

"Fits you like fangs on a snake."

"The way you talk you'd think I sullied her, but I ain't done nothin' but put on my Sundays and be sociable." George smoked. "That preacher now, I can't speak for him." He chuckled.

Moses tightened his grip on the cup. "That's not a laughin' matter."

George puffed his pipe. "Her daddy seen there was more to me than what I'd become. Told me his daughter needed marryin'. Asked what I was waitin' for. Cracked my cocoon a little bit. Crawled out of the hole I fell into to peek at daylight. Eased up on bein' bitter."

George Cole blew a smoke ring and stabbed it with the pipe stem. "Here's what I'll do. Planned it out since you got back"—he looked at his son— "and I seen the man where the boy used to be."

His father chewed on his pipe stem. "After you left I seen what hog slop I fell into." He drew smoke and pointed the pipe stem at Moses. "What happens when you clean a hog?" He waved the pipe. "Right back in the slop and lay in it, and I'm no different." Smoke floated each word. "The problem is, a hog likes slop." He chuckled, then pulled a letter from the drawer in the table and slid it to Moses. "Read this, if you remember how."

Moses studied the envelope. "You haven't sweetened up any. Kinda like burdock wine." He pulled out the letter. "With horse piss in it." He lifted his eyes from the letter and looked at his father. "You just get more bitter."

"Crusty mean old son of a bitch and I like it that way, or at least I did. Keeps them church people off me, come tellin' it all fit God's plan, like the Old Man above was fixin' on takin' your mama all along, and they praise Him for it." He poked his pipe stem at Moses. Smoke curled from the bowl and the tip of the stem. "A man develops a taste for bitter after a bit. It tastes like," he paused, "sunshine." He chuckled and put the pipe stem between his teeth.

Moses shook his head, read the letter, put it back in the envelope, and slid it back across the table.

"Things are upside down here, and you want me to worry about that," Moses said.

"You can see she's in a fix. She can't run that place with her husband sick. Hell, he's probably dead by now."

The clock ticked on the mantel.

"Bitter, is what it's come to," George said. He thought a moment and looked at the floor. "I hear a wee little voice your mama sends, tellin' what I've become should scare me. She was a good woman, Moses. I've never quite been upright without her."

A fly bumped against the window glass.

"Them voices," Moses said.

"She give you the goodness you have, but thank me for your mean streak." He chuckled. "Takes both to get along in this world."

A bell from a nanny goat traced her trot toward the shelter shed.

"One to enjoy it and the other to survive it," his father said.

"I'm not acquainted with my goodness."

"It's there." George gave three quick puffs to bring glow back in the pipe bowl, took a deep breath, and exhaled the smoke slowly. "Sister's in a hell of a bind. Needs a man about."

"I got two years of army left. Instructor for dragoon recruits at Carlisle Barracks, Pennsylvania."

"That ain't my problem," George said. "Sister Agnes is." He stood up, walked to the corner by the stove, lifted a floor board, and pulled two deerskin pouches, one smaller than a fist and one larger, from under the floor. They clinked when he placed them on the table. A string of tanned deer hide tied the top of each pouch closed. He sat back down.

"The only way to get out of the hog slop is to stop bein' a hog. Thought that girl would do it, but that ain't right, not with you back. So then, to stop bein' a hog you got to stick the hog, if you follow me." He touched the smaller of the two pouches with the stem of his pipe. "That's my adventure stake. I'll use that to commit sin."

"You don't make sense."

"Makes better sense to use the big pouch." He chuckled. "Push me and I might."

"You've went around the bend, George. Took a turn I can't follow."

"I got to slaughter the hog, and I do not intend to swallow a horse pistol to do it." He drew a breath of smoke. "I'll go to the city where no one knows me. Richmond. Buy a bowler hat and a bow tie and brand new shiny shoes." Smoke meandered from his nose. "See what the other side of life is like. The one the Bible says, 'Thou shalt not commit.' Befriend a night woman. Sip on liquor from a bottle with a label on it. Throw dice on a table with a green felt cover." He rubbed his nose. "If there weren't nothin' to it, the preacher wouldn't thunder about it."

"I do not know what to make of you."

"Never had an adventure. Never been but twenty miles from here. Done nothin' but work and scrape all my life. Unlike you, off God knows where, doin' God knows what." He nodded at the smaller pouch. "I'll use that to bleed the hog, if you follow me, before I end up like Sister's husband, wonderin' what it was I missed in life when it's too late to look for it." He poked the pouch with his pipe stem. "When that one's gone, I'm done adventurin'. The hog is stuck and scalded and scraped and ate, if you follow me. Then I'll go to Sister Agnes and do what needs doin', until her husband recovers or she marries again, neither of which is apt to happen."

"What about the farm?"

His father chuckled. Smoke puffed with each chuckle.

"Here's me, bored with chore work and wore out from makin' a livin' off dirt. Curious about the world that starts where the farm ends, and here's you. A runnin' young stud huntin' somethin' to shove his dick in." He waved his pipe in the direction of the church. "Get that sweet young thing and breed her. Put a ring on her finger if she needs one." He drew a breath through the pipe and blew smoke rings.

Moses leaned back in his chair. "This don't sound like father-son talk," he said.

"I ain't your pa no more, remember? I'm George Cole, the mean old widower man, tellin' the best he knows to a young feller who needs tellin'. Only thing I done right was make a life with your mama." He tamped the pipe bowl with the whittled bird bone and puffed to rekindle it. "What about the farm, you say?" He drew a few whiffs of smoke before turning the pipe upside down and tapping the bowl empty on a tin plate that served for an ash tray. He looked at Moses. "You can have the son of a bitch. Bring it to life. Make this cabin squeal again. Hatch out a young 'un. Raise up a boy to pack a pail and hoe a garden row and gather the hen house eggs."

"You'd up and give it to me?"

"Just done it. It don't hold my heart no more. Not since your mama died."

"You give me the farm." Moses sat stone still. "That is not the George I know."

"It's a good farm, but it needs a woman about."

"I got the army yet."

George shrugged. "Rent it to the neighbor. Court her on leave. Bring a pistol when you do. Chase off the sniffers at the dry-goods store, but get her. Your life won't mean much until you do."

George picked up the bigger pouch. "She'd ask after you whenever I went there to trade." He untied the deerskin string, dumped the pouch of assorted coins on the table, and counted them out into two piles of equal value.

"You're a man of property now. War hero for all we know. Her daddy will see that you bring more to the table than the preacher does. Her mama now, you gotta work on her. Likes the Bible too well."

George put one of the piles back in the pouch, tied it closed, and set it next to the full pouch. He pointed to the pile on the table.

"That stays here. Seed and mule shoes and such. This other," he lifted the half pouch, "goes to Sister Agnes."

George drank off the cup of coffee and slid his chair back from the table. Moses watched him walk to the bedroom, heard him open and close a drawer, watched him walk back and set his mother's wedding ring on the table.

"You know where that come from," George said. "You know where it oughta go."

The tarnished silver of the wedding band looked blued by fire.

"See my grip?" He motioned to the canvas bag with a handle and buckled leather straps just inside the door. "Packed it this mornin', when you was off to see what town had to offer."

George picked up the cup, pouches, pipe, and tobacco and packed them in his grip. He said, "Send me a letter when I got a grandkid." He laughed, pulled his coat and hat from a wall hook, walked outside with his grip in hand, and shut the door.

ACKNOWLEDGMENTS

To my fellow writers who helped me develop and refine this manuscript, and to friends and family who asked along the way, thank you. You gave me more than you know.

In gratitude for Richard Hugo and Bill Kittredge, who kindled an itch that wouldn't die.

HISTORICAL CHARACTERS

Brief biographies appear below for nonfiction characters presented in the manuscript.

James Allen, Jr.

Born in Ohio in 1806, James Allen moved to Indiana and then to Kentucky with his parents, first-generation Scots-Irish. He returned to Indiana as a young man and won an appointment to the U.S. military academy and attended with classmates and future Confederate generals Robert E. Lee and Joseph E. Johnston. Other cadets during his tenure at West Point would also rise to prominence in the Mexican-American War and the Civil War, including Jefferson Davis, Albert Sidney Johnston and Leonidas Polk (Confederacy), and Philip St. George Cooke (Union).

Allen served in the infantry after graduation and mapped the Northwest Territory (Minnesota) while part of an expedition that looked for the source of the Mississippi River. Allen transferred to the Regiment of Dragoons, later to become the First Dragoons, when it was formed in 1833 and was promoted to first lieutenant in 1835 and captain in 1837. Fort Des Moines, constructed under Allen's command, would later become Des Moines, the capital of Iowa. While in the dragoons, Allen served in frontier posts in what are now Kansas, Arkansas, Iowa, Illinois, and Michigan and participated in a march into what is now South Dakota.

After recruiting the Mormon Battalion, Captain Allen became ill while it was camped at Fort Leavenworth, and he ordered the battalion to march west without him. He died shortly after (August 23, 1846) and was the first officer buried in what would become the Fort Leavenworth National Military Cemetery.

Maria Gertrudis Barceló (aka Madame La Tules)

Not much is known or agreed upon about Barceló's life, but it is likely that she was born in the state of Sonora, Mexico, in or about 1800. In the early 1820s her family moved to the Mexican territory of New Mexico. She was married in 1823 and is reputed to have been four years older than her husband and four or five months pregnant at her wedding. Barceló was known by her maiden name and retained her property throughout her marriage.

In 1825, she was fined for running a gambling establishment in a mining camp in the Ortiz Mountains. By 1835 she relocated to Santa Fe and established a saloon and gambling house, which prospered from traffic from the Santa Fe Trail. She was known for her skill in the card game monte, at which she was reputed to have won large sums of gold—evidently enough to loan funds to the U.S. Army in 1846.

Barceló died in Santa Fe in 1852 with a fortune of ten thousand dollars and deeds to several houses.

Edward Fitzgerald Beale

Edward (Ned) Beale was born in Washington, D.C, in 1822. He attended Georgetown University before being appointed to the Naval School in Philadelphia, from which he graduated as a midshipman in 1842. In 1845, he served under Captain Robert Stockton and sailed with Stockton's squadron to Texas, California, and Oregon. He was promoted to Stockton's private secretary and sailed to England to acquire information about the British disposition toward Oregon. Beale returned to

Washington in 1846 to brief President Polk on Britain's senti-ments, then sailed to join Stockton and the USS *Congress* in Peru, from whence they sailed to California via Honolulu.

In San Diego, Beale was dispatched with marines to reinforce General Kearny's forces, arriving shortly before the battle at San Pasqual. After the Battle of San Pasqual, Beale returned, by stealth, to San Diego with a Delaware Indian and Kit Carson to request reinforcements. While still in ill health from the trek from San Pasqual to San Diego, Beale returned to Washington with dispatches from Stockton. That fall he appeared as a defense witness in the court martial of John C. Frémont.

Beale resigned from the Navy in 1851. In 1853, he was ap-pointed superintendent of Indian affairs for California and Nevada by President Fillmore. En route to California, with a small survey party he surveyed a route for a transcontinental railroad across Colorado and Utah to Los Angeles. In 1856, he was appointed brigadier general in the California state militia by Governor John Bigler. In 1857, Beale was appointed by President Buchanan to survey and construct a wagon road from New Mexico to the Colorado River, which is now generally fol-lowed by Route 22 and I-40. In 1861, he was appointed surveyor general of California and Nevada by President Lin-coln.

In 1865 and 1866, Beale purchased what is now the Tejon Ranch Company, the largest private land ownership in Califor-nia. He entertained guests on a regular basis and was known as a delightful host. Beale served as ambassador to Austria-Hungary in 1876 and 1877 under appointment by President Grant, after which he returned to Washington and made annual trips to the Tejon Ranch. In 1877 Beale purchased and renovated a historic home opposite the White House. He owned a horse farm near Washington, where he entertained Presidents

Grant and Cleveland, and Buffalo Bill Cody. Beale died in Washington, D.C., in 1893.

Zemira Brown

Zemira Brown was born in 1835 and was fourteen when he served as an orderly to Captain James Allen. When Lieutenant Smith served as acting commander following Captain Allen's death, Zemira may have served as an orderly to Lieutenant Smith.

Zemira completed the journey to San Diego with the Mormon Battalion and his parents. His father, Ebenezer Brown, was a sergeant in the Mormon Battalion. His mother, Phebe Brown, was a laundress and cook. Sergeant Brown re-enlisted in San Diego and remained in the army until 1848, after which the family moved to Sutter's Fort where Ebenezer worked until they left for Utah in 1849.

Christopher Houston (Kit) Carson

Christopher Houston (Kit) Carson was born in Kentucky in 1809 and was reared in Missouri. At age sixteen he ran away from an apprenticeship to a saddler and went west on the Santa Fe Trail with a party of trappers. He settled in Taos, in present day New Mexico, where he learned Spanish and some of the language of different tribes, and how to trap. From 1829 to 1840 he explored much of the West from Arizona to Montana with well-known mountain men of the time, attended mountain men rendezvous, and had some hostile engagements with natives of various tribes.

In 1841, at the end of the mountain man era, Carson worked for a time as a hunter for Bent's Fort in present day Colorado. Carson guided expeditions for John C. Frémont in 1842, 1843, and 1845 that explored parts of present day Wyoming, Oregon, Utah, Nevada, and California. In 1846, during the third expedition, Carson participated in the massacre of a Klamath Indian village in Oregon and the execution of three Mexican sympathizers at the outset of the Mexican-American war.

Also in 1846, while en route from Los Angeles to Washington City to deliver military dispatches to President Polk, Carson met General Stephen Watts Kearny on the Rio Grande in present day New Mexico and was ordered to return to California as a guide to Kearny and his one hundred dragoons. On this return trip Carson participated in the Battle of San Pasqual and led a dramatic escape with two other messengers to secure reinforcements from San Diego.

Beginning in 1849, Carson's reputation was mythologized in dime novels, the pulp fiction of the day.

From the late 1840s to the early 1850s Carson ranched east of Taos (New Mexico). In 1853, he purchased some six thousand sheep in New Mexico, drove them to northern California, and sold them to gold miners for a handsome profit. In the 1850s Carson was appointed Indian agent to the Ute tribe and used his Taos home as the office for the agency. Carson and his wife, Josefa Jaramillo, the daughter of a prominent Taos family, had four children by this time and would eventually have eight. Carson also had two daughters from a former marriage to an Arapaho.

In the 1860s Carson served in the Union Army as a colonel of the First New Mexico Volunteers. After participating in engagements with Confederate forces, which forced the Confederates to return to Texas, Colonel Carson led U.S. troops on campaigns against the Mescalero Apache and the Navajo, and in the Texas panhandle against the Comanche and Kiowa.

In 1865 Carson was given the honorary appointment of brevet brigadier general of volunteers by President Lincoln. Although in ill health, in 1868 Carson traveled to Washington to lobby for a permanent reservation for the Ute tribe. Carson died in Colorado in 1868.

Jean Baptiste Charbonneau

Born in 1805 to Sacagawea and Toussaint Charbonneau, Jean Baptiste accompanied his parents as an infant on their journey with Lewis and Clark, for whom Toussaint Charbonneau served as an interpreter, as did Sacagawea with the Shoshones. As a boy, Jean Baptiste lived with William Clark in St. Louis and attended St. Louis Academy at Captain Clark's expense. At age eighteen Charbonneau traveled to Europe with Duke Friedrich Paul Wilhelm of Württemberg and lived at his palace until 1829 where he learned German and Spanish and became more fluent in French and English. He accompanied the Duke in his travels in Europe and North Africa. Charbonneau returned to St. Louis in 1829 and was hired by Joseph Robideaux as a fur trapper for the American Fur Company. In 1843, he guided a Scottish baronet, Sir William Drummond Stewart, on a hunting trip in the West. In 1844, he worked as a hunter for Bent's Fort (Colorado) and trader until he began serving as a scout and interpreter for Lieutenant Colonel Cooke and the Mormon Battalion.

In 1847 Charbonneau was appointed as *alcalde* at Mission San Luis Rey de Francia by Colonel Stevenson and served in that capacity until 1848 when he left to pan for gold in northern California. In the early 1860s Charbonneau left for points north, presumably to mine for gold in Montana. He contracted pneumonia en route and died in 1866.

Philip St. George Cooke

Philip St. George Cooke was born in Virginia in 1810 and graduated from the U.S. Military Academy at West Point in 1827. He served in the Black Hawk War and in 1833 was appointed first lieutenant in the First Dragoons. He was admitted to the Virginia Bar and served for a time as a recruiting officer for the dragoons. In 1845, he was selected by Colonel Stephen Watts Kearny to accompany him and a troop of dragoons on a march from Fort Leavenworth to South Pass (in what is now Wyoming), then south to the Santa Fe Trail and east back to Fort Leavenworth.

After commanding the Mormon Battalion, Cooke returned to Fort Leavenworth with General Kearny and was commissioned as a major in the Second Dragoons and dispatched to Mexico in 1848 but arrived after the war had ended, having been delayed as a witness in the court martial of John C. Frémont. From 1848 to 1851 he served as post commander for Carlisle Barracks. After serving as post commander Cooke was dispatched to Texas to pursue Apaches and in 1853 was promoted to lieutenant colonel of the Second Dragoons. His service included a march in severe winter weather with Kit Carson as guide in pursuit of Jicarilla Apaches.

In 1855, Cooke was appointed commander of Fort Riley, a new cavalry post in eastern Kansas. In 1857, Cooke led six companies of the Second Dragoons in a winter march to reinforce the Army of Utah in the Utah War, making it as far as Fort Bridger (in current day Wyoming) that winter. Cooke proceeded to Salt Lake City in June 1848 and established Camp Floyd some 40 miles away.

Cooke was promoted colonel in the Second Dragoons and left Camp Floyd in 1858 to travel to Europe to study cavalry tactics. Cooke wrote a manual, "Cavalry Tactics," based on what he'd learned on that trip, which became the training manual for Union cavalry in the Civil War.

Cooke returned to Camp Floyd (in what is now Utah) in 1860. At the outbreak of the Civil War the camp, now called Fort Crittenden, was closed, and Cooke returned east to join the Union army. Cooke was appointed brigadier general of volunteers and commanded five regiments of regular cavalry. After the Civil War, Cooke was assigned to the Department of the Platte. In 1870, he was appointed to the Department of

Lakes and retired in 1873. Cooke died at home in Detroit in 1895.

Cooke and his wife, Rachael, had two daughters and a son. His older daughter, Flora, married J. E. B. Stuart, who served with distinction as a general in the Confederate cavalry. His son, John, became a general in the Confederate army and was wounded at Gettysburg. His younger daughter, Julia, married Jacob Sharpe, who became a general in the Union Army.

John C. Frémont

John C. Frémont was born in Savannah, Georgia, in 1813 and attended the College of Charleston. He was appointed a second lieutenant in the Corps of Topographical Engineers in 1838 and assisted in exploring lands between the Mississippi and Missouri rivers. In 1841 he married Jessie Benton, daughter of Senator Thomas Hart Benton of Missouri.

During the period of 1842 to 1854 Frémont led five expeditions to explore western territories, which took him through many of the present-day western states, including Oregon, California, Nevada, and Colorado. Kit Carson guided three of the five expeditions.

During the Mexican-American War, Frémont was appointed commander of the California Battalion, made up in part by Frémont's survey party and volunteers. Frémont captured Santa Barbara and accepted the surrender of Mexican forces to end the war in California.

In 1847, Frémont was court martialed in Washington, D.C., on charges brought by General Kearny and was found guilty of mutiny, disobedience to a superior officer, and military misconduct. President Polk commuted Frémont's sentence, and Frémont resigned his commission. He returned to California and purchased a ranch near Yosemite, where miners he employed discovered gold. Frémont moved to Monterey and used his new wealth to purchase significant landholdings in San Francisco.

Frémont served for six months as U.S. senator from California (1850–1851). In 1856, he ran for president as the candidate of the newly founded Republican Party but lost to James Buchanan.

Frémont was commissioned as a major general for the Union Army in the Civil War and was appointed commander of the Department of the West, charged with expelling Confederate forces from Missouri. After four months he was dismissed by President Lincoln for insubordination.

After the Civil War John and Jesse Frémont lived in Hudson Valley, New York. Frémont purchased the Pacific Railroad, which proved an unsuccessful business venture. Frémont was appointed governor of the Arizona Territory in 1878 but spent little time there and resigned after several years. Frémont died at home in New York City in 1890.

Lafayette Frost
Corporal Lafayette Frost shot and killed a charging bull a few feet before it would have struck him as he stood near Lieutenant Colonel Philip St. George Cooke at the Battle of the Bulls on the San Pedro River in what is now Arizona. He was promoted to sergeant and reenlisted with the Mormon Volunteers in San Diego for an additional six months. He died in September, 1847, during his second enlistment and is buried near San Diego.

Jefferson Hunt
Appointed captain of Company A, Hunt served as acting commander of the Mormon Battalion when Captain Allen remained at Fort Leavenworth to convalesce, and before First Lieutenant A. J. Smith arrived to replace Hunt as acting commander. Jefferson's wife, Celia, and their seven children accompanied

Jefferson and the Mormon Battalion until being sent to Pueblo with the Higgins Detachment (first sick detachment) from the juncture of the Arkansas River and the Cimarron Cutoff. Jefferson's plural (second) wife, Matilda, also accompanied Jefferson and the battalion but was discharged to Pueblo with the Brown Detachment (second sick detachment) from Santa Fe. Jefferson remained with the battalion and continued to California. Captain Hunt again served as acting commander of the Mormon Battalion under Colonel Stevenson, Commander of the Southern Military District, from May 13, 1847, to July 16, 1847, when enlistment expired.

Hunt returned to the Salt Lake Valley after discharge and made several trips to California, eventually helping to establish a Mormon settlement in San Bernardino in 1851. He served as a member of the California State Assembly from 1853 to 1857 and introduced legislation to create San Bernardino County. Hunt served in the California State Militia and was appointed a brigadier general of that militia in 1857.

Hunt returned to Utah and represented Weber County in the Utah Territorial Legislature in 1863. He established a ranch near Oxford, Idaho, and spent much of his time there. He died in Oxford in 1879.

Diego Hunter
Although Diego's parents are fictional in this story, Diego's parents went to San Diego with the Mormon Battalion. Born April 20, 1847, in San Diego, Diego was the first child born to American parents in California and was named after his place of birth. Diego's mother, Lydia, served as a laundress in the Mormon Battalion and died shortly after giving birth to Diego. Jesse D. Hunter, Diego's father, served as a captain in the Mormon Battalion and practiced polygamy. Jesse's first wife (Lydia was his second wife) and their five children had remained at Council Bluffs but joined Jesse in California in 1848 or 1849.

The family remained in California at least through 1850.

Diego was raised by Juanita Machado Wrightington, remained in Los Angeles, became a cattle herder, and died in 1877.

Stephen Watts Kearny

Born in New Jersey in 1794 to a prominent family, Stephen Watts Kearny attended public schools before attending Columbia University for two years. He left school in 1812 and joined the New York Militia and was a first lieutenant in the War of 1812, where he engaged in several battles, was wounded, and was honored for bravery. He remained in the army and was posted to the western frontier, which took him to what is now Nebraska and, in 1825, to the mouth of the Yellowstone River. In 1826, he was appointed commander of Jefferson Barracks south of St. Louis. In St. Louis, he was entertained by William Clark of the Lewis and Clark expedition and married Clark's stepdaughter, Mary Radford, with whom he had five children who survived childhood.

In 1833, Kearny was appointed lieutenant colonel in the First Dragoons in Fort Leavenworth (Kansas) and in 1836 was promoted colonel and groomed it into an elite regiment, later to become the First U.S. Cavalry in 1861, for which Kearny was dubbed the "Father of the United States Cavalry." Kearny was also appointed commander of the Third Military District, charged with keeping peace with the Native Americans on the Great Plains. During the early 1840s Kearny's troops frequently escorted emigrants on the Oregon Trail to prevent attacks from the natives.

In 1845, Kearny led several regiments of the First Dragoons from Fort Leavenworth to South Pass (Wyoming) via the Platte and North Platte Rivers. From South Pass they turned south to Bent's Fort (Colorado) and returned to Fort Leavenworth via the Santa Fe Trail, covering about 2,200 miles in three months.

In 1846, Kearny commanded the Army of the West, a force

of about 2,500 soldiers including volunteers, dragoons, and the Mormon Battalion. Kearny was promoted to brigadier general in 1846. After taking control of New Mexico, a northern territory of Mexico, Kearny split his force and sent part to Mexico to join the war effort there, part to remain in Santa Fe to maintain order in New Mexico, and part to proceed to California. Kearny accompanied one hundred dragoons to California and was wounded, though not seriously, in the Battle of San Pasqual.

In 1847, Kearny's forces, including dragoons, marines, sailors, and two companies of John C. Frémont's California Battalion, won the battles of San Gabriel and La Mesa and took control of Los Angeles. Kearny served as military governor of California, albeit after some uncertainty as to who the commanding officer was—Brigadier General Kearny or Navy Commander Stockton—until August, 1847, when he returned east. Arriving in Fort Leavenworth Kearny had Frémont court-martialed for insubordination.

Kearny returned to war duties when he went to Veracruz and then to Mexico City to serve as military governor in the final months of the Mexican-American War. Kearny contracted yellow fever while there, returned to St. Louis, and died in 1848.

Antoine Robideaux

Antoine Robideaux was born in St. Louis in 1794. His brother, Joseph Robideaux, founded St. Joseph, Missouri. His brothers, François and Louis, were well-known fur traders in the Northwest and Southwest. Antoine guided with Kit Carson for John C. Frémont, and he had a trading post in Taos (New Mexico) in the 1820s. Robideaux built a fort in Colorado in the late 1830s and one in Utah, which was in use in the 1840s. He died in St. Joseph, Missouri, in 1860.

Andrew Jackson (A.J.) Smith

Born in Pennsylvania in 1815, Andrew Jackson (A.J.) Smith graduated from West Point in 1838. As a first lieutenant, he served as acting commander of the Mormon Battalion for a short time and continued with the battalion into California. He was promoted to captain in 1847 and participated in engagements against Native Americans in Oregon and Washington territories.

Smith was appointed colonel in the Second California Volunteer Cavalry at the outset of the Civil War. He led Union troops during engagements in Missouri, Mississippi, Tennessee, and Alabama. During the Civil War, he commanded infantry as well as cavalry, and brigades, divisions, and finally a corps under General Sherman and General Grant. In 1864 Smith was appointed lieutenant colonel in the Union Army and major general of volunteers.

After the Civil War, Smith returned to the West as colonel of the Seventh Cavalry, with Lieutenant George Armstrong Custer as Lieutenant Colonel. He retired from the U.S. Army in 1869 and was head postmaster in St. Louis. He died in St. Louis in 1897.

George Stoneman, Jr.

George Stoneman was born on a farm in New York in 1822. He attended Jamestown Academy and graduated from the U.S. Military Academy at West Point in 1846 where he roomed with Thomas "Stonewall" Jackson. He was assigned to the First Dragoons as a second lieutenant and served as assistant quartermaster for the Mormon Battalion. He served in the West, primarily in Texas, until the Civil War.

In the Civil War, Stoneman rose to command the Cavalry Corps of the Army of the Potomac and was appointed brigadier general in 1861. Stoneman became a corps commander of infantry and was promoted to major general of volunteers in

1862. In 1863, he returned to cavalry service as commander of the Cavalry Corps of the Army of the Potomac. After disappointing service in the Chancellorsville campaign, Stoneman was assigned to desk duty in Washington. In 1864, he commanded the Cavalry Corps of the Army of the Ohio. In 1865, he was appointed commander of the Department of Tennessee.

After the Civil War, Stoneman was appointed commander of the Department of Arizona but was relieved of command in 1871 due to controversy over how he handled Indian uprisings.

Stoneman returned to California and served as a state railroad commissioner before being elected governor of California, serving from 1883 to 1887. He returned to New York for medical treatment and died in Buffalo in 1894.

Brigham Young

Brigham Young was born in 1801 in Vermont. He worked as a traveling tradesman with skills that included blacksmithing and carpentry. Young left Methodism to join the Mormon Church in 1832. He served as a Mormon missionary in Canada and helped establish a Mormon community in Kirtland, Ohio. He became a member of the church's governing council, the Quorum of the Twelve Apostles, in 1835. He served on a Mormon mission in the United Kingdom and organized a move of church members from Missouri to Illinois in 1838.

After the death of Joseph Smith in 1844, president and founder of the Mormon Church, Young organized the relocation of the Latter-day Saints from Nauvoo, Illinois, to the Salt Lake Valley from 1846 to 1847. He became the second president of The Church of Jesus Christ of Latter-day Saints in 1847. Consistent with doctrine of the Mormon Church of that time he practiced polygamy and had numerous wives.

Under Young's leadership Salt Lake City was founded and became the hub of the Latter-day Saint community with satellite settlements in other parts of Utah and in what are now the states of Idaho, Nevada, California, Arizona, and Colorado. He was appointed governor of Utah Territory and superintendent of American Indian Affairs by President Fillmore. Young was instrumental in founding the University of Deseret in 1850, later to become the University of Utah, and Brigham Young University in 1875.

After the Utah War of 1857–1858, Young was replaced as territorial governor by a non-Mormon, Alfred Cumming. Young continued to wield much influence in Utah Territory and was instrumental in developing a vibrant Mormon community in the Great Basin. He died in Salt Lake City in 1877.

ABOUT THE AUTHOR

Scott G. Hibbard is a fourth generation Montanan where his family has owned and operated a cattle and sheep ranch for over one hundred years. Scott attended public school in Helena and received a B.A. in English Literature from Williams College and two graduate degrees, an M.F.A in Creative Writing and an M.B.A., from the University of Montana. Scott worked for the family ranch for a number of years, and while continuing his involvement with the ranch, he started and continues to operate a ranch management enterprise that provides management and consulting services to other ranches. He lives near Helena, Montana.

The employees of Five Star Publishing hope you have enjoyed this book.

Our Five Star novels explore little-known chapters from America's history, stories told from unique perspectives that will entertain a broad range of readers.

Other Five Star books are available at your local library, bookstore, all major book distributors, and directly from Five Star/Gale.

Connect with Five Star Publishing

Visit us on Facebook:
  https://www.facebook.com/FiveStarCengage

Email:
  FiveStar@cengage.com

For information about titles and placing orders:
  (800) 223-1244
  gale.orders@cengage.com

To share your comments, write to us:
  Five Star Publishing
  Attn: Publisher
  10 Water St., Suite 310
  Waterville, ME 04901